MW00426858

IRON SPIRES
OVER THE WHITE CITY

JOSEPH ROLLINS

To Jalie
Enjoy!

Black Rose Writing | Texas

[signature]

©2020 by Joseph Rollins
All rights reserved. No part of this book may be reproduced, stored in a
retrieval system or transmitted in any form or by any means without the
prior written permission of the publishers, except by a reviewer who may
quote brief passages in a review to be printed in a newspaper, magazine or
journal.

The author grants the final approval for this literary material.

First printing

This is a work of fiction. Names, characters, businesses, places, events, and
incidents are either the products of the author's imagination or used in a
fictitious manner. Any resemblance to actual persons, living or dead, or
actual events is purely coincidental.

ISBN: 978-1-68433-554-1
PUBLISHED BY BLACK ROSE WRITING
www.blackrosewriting.com

Printed in the United States of America
Suggested Retail Price (SRP) $20.95

Iron Spires Over the White City is printed in Georgia

*As a planet-friendly publisher, Black Rose Writing does its best to eliminate
unnecessary waste to reduce paper usage and energy costs, while never compromising
the reading experience. As a result, the final word count vs. page count may not meet
common expectations.

For all my family and friends who
made this possible

IRON SPIRES
OVER THE WHITE CITY

CHAPTER 1

London

Douglas Tank was born in the county of Cumberland in northern England, in the Year of Our Lord, 1731. His father, grandfathers, uncles, and brothers all worked deep below the earth as coal miners, feeding Great Britain's booming industrialization.

Douglas graduated from primary school at age eleven with the highest marks in his class. His mother made him an apple pie for his grades, and a second pie for the letter of praise sent by the schoolmaster. Douglas spent the next three days fishing and gallivanting about with his former classmates. On the fourth day, his father took him down into the black mines beneath Cumberland.

Douglas's introduction to life below ground was harsh. He spent his days squeezing in and out of nooks and crannies, shredding his clothing and slicing his skin on sharp rocks. Every night the boy went home blackened with coal dust and dejected beyond reason.

Six months after Douglas started his life underground, the foreman pulled him aside. "I talked with your father yesterday. He said you are a clever lad." Douglas's boss turned his head and spit on the ground. "More clever than the rest of these sots."

"Suppose," muttered Douglas, scratching a layer of grime off the back of his neck.

"You heard about Wilkes?"

"Sir, they say he broke his hand working the pump."

"Right, he's hurt, and the engineer needs a helper to keep the steam engines running. Mine number four flooded yesterday. The water rose faster than the old man could pump it out."

"All right."

"Good lad. Report to the engineer; you work for him."

Douglas excelled in his new role, absorbing the knowledge of the head engineer. He spent his days building and rebuilding the single piston steam engines that pumped water from the mines. Douglas loved his new job, preferring oil to coal dust entrenched under his fingernails.

When Douglas was seventeen, tragedy struck the Tank family when Douglas's father contracted the dreaded black lung. The family nursed the sick man for a year, the wives of Douglas's older brothers responsible for the brunt of the sick man's care. Death claimed the soul of Douglas's father in 1749. The young man wept over the coffin for days, stopping only after the undertaker sunk the plain pine box in the earth. For a week after his father's burial, Douglas did not speak a word. He broke his silence on a Sunday, at the dinner table with the entire family.

"I'm leaving for London in the morning," muttered Douglas.

Douglas's mother was the first to reply: "Don't be ridiculous. I will not allow it."

"I am sorry," said Douglas, "but my mind is made up."

"What'll you do in London?" asked one of his brothers.

"It does not matter," said Douglas, eyes on his bread and bacon. "I will never go down in the mines again."

"Why would you ever dream of doing such a foolish thing?" asked his mother.

"People that work down there die. Father died."

"Everybody dies someday. The mines always provided for this family. London streets will not be so kind."

"I do not care," muttered Douglas, pushing the food around his plate. "I'm leaving in the morning."

"You are a damn ungrateful twit, Douglas Tank," said his mum. She slammed her palms on the table and left the room.

The eldest Tank boy broke the uncomfortable silence, "Good luck to you, brother."

"Mum's really upset," said Douglas.

"She'll be all right," said another brother.

"We've all been talking about the death that follows us down in the mines."

"We understand; go make your fortune in London."

"And if you ever need to come home, you are always welcome."

"Thank you," said Douglas, struggling to get the words out and keep tears from falling on his bacon.

•   •   •   •   •

The northern shoreline of New Granada meandered along the Caribbean, coves and narrow beaches wedged between the salt water and jungle. Anne Goulden strolled along a rocky alcove on a warm, late summer evening in 1888. She squinted at the brilliant reds and oranges as the sun dipped beneath the horizon line where the sky kissed the jungle. The pebbles strewn across the beach glistened like gray marbles trapping the sunlight.

Damp salt hung in the air, heavy and sticky, clinging to Anne's skin and tickling her nose. The evening breeze was still. Squawking gulls fought in twos and threes along the beach over scuttling crabs and rotting pieces of fish. During high tide, waves pushed to the jungle's tree line. For now, the ocean had retreated, providing a narrow beach for her to walk.

This was Anne's secret place.

A narrow path cut through the jungle from her home to the shoreline. Somewhere beyond the Goulden estate lay Cartagena, the capital of Queen Victoria's New Granada colony.

The teenager sat on the rocky sand and sucked sea air between her teeth. She exhaled and reclined back on her elbows, then sat back up to tuck her trousers into her leather boots. Anne's eyes flickered left and right across the horizon, spotting a zeppelin plodding its way west.

After the sun set, Anne searched a place to bunk down for the night, close to the tree line and away from the rising tide. She tripped over a broken branch from an avocado tree and stumbled to one knee. A tarantula the size of her palm dropped from somewhere over her head and landed on her arm.

Anne leapt up and sent the spider tumbling onto the sand. Acting on instinct, Anne stomped on the tarantula. She heard hard fibers cracking, grinding the life out of the spider.

Anne lifted her foot and bent over to examine the creature. Black fluid leaked from the spider's torso. A coiled spring unwound from the center of body, splitting the shell in half. Miniature clockwork gears and springs revealed themselves as the creature's insides slid out onto gray stones.

Anne stood up and swept her eyes up and down the beach. The only other creature visible were the sea gulls, pacing the sand and yelling at each other. Anne turned her eyes towards the jungle a few meters in front of her.

A black jaguar twice Anne's size perched near the top of a short, broad tree. She stepped back, slipping on slick stones and landing on her backside. The jaguar leapt from the tree, covering the distance between him and his prey in one jump. Anne shrieked as the cat unhinged its metallic jaws and swallowed her whole.

CHAPTER 2

No one ever described London as hot and humid until Victoria took the reigns. The air was thick and sticky as Margaret Goulden walked the brick road past the river docks along the Thames. Smoke from the factories along the northern shoreline scratched at Margaret's throat as she quickened her pace. The river to her left twinkled with a black, oily sheen. Six months ago, a lit wad of tobacco ignited the surface. After three days, the industrial waste burned off and city officials declared the water clean.

After years at Oxford University suppressing her grating Scottish tongue, Margaret appreciated any opportunity to trade crass gibes. Striding along the waterfront, she watched and waited for the dock hands to call out.

"Oye, bonnie luv. You and me later ta-nite. We'll go out and get pissed."

"What about your sweet little trouble and strife waiting up for you at home?" Margaret called back. "Won't she be angry when you stumble in, skint left from a week's pay?"

"She's not my bloody guv. What do you say, luv? Want to see what I have hidden in me strides?"

Margaret let him have it: "I've seen plenty of little hampton wicks before. You can take it to rub a dub dub without me and wank it yourself."

The dock hand's neck turned crimson and he ducked his head, pretending to focus on his work while his coworkers laughed. He wandered away, punching buttons and pulling levers mounted to a flat iron bar on his belt. The small control panel operated a set of four mechanical arms strapped to the dock worker's back. As the contraption hiccupped to life, it vibrated and belched black soot. The steel arms jerked in awkward, unnatural motions as they loaded cargo crates onto a barge.

Margaret kept walking, threading the complicated London docks. After passing Battersea Park, she noticed the black smoke belching from a cigar-shaped vessel, slung low in the Thames with most of the ship beneath the waterline. Margaret slowed her pace and squinted at the iron hull plowing upriver. Two mechanics stood on deck wearing thick leather jumpsuits and goggles with layers of flip-down lenses. Sewn into the jumpsuits were dozens of canvas pockets stuffed with pliers and scissors, switches and coils, hammers and screw drivers and springs. They worked together, welding damaged sheets of metal along the hull.

Margaret tripped over a child standing still at her feet while staring at the war ship. Along the docks and in the south of London, a child never stood still unless they were hiding. Young and old kept the kilns burning day and night in the brick and mortar factories stacked on top of each other. Most factory workers in this part of town were foreign born. A dozen languages filled the stale, smoky air, blending into a single indecipherable montage. European languages like French, Spanish, German, Gaelic, and Russian clashed with tongues from the far corners of the globe: Mandarin, Vietnamese, Korean, African dialects, Arabic, and Persian.

Margaret danced around the people blocking her path. As the military vessel steamed past, the air along the shoreline became charged with an electric fury, venomous hatred leashed and tethered. Most people living in the south of London had seen an armada of ships similar to this one storm the beaches of their homeland. As governments fell, the displaced and hungry immigrated to the British Isles in droves.

Passing through the crowd, Margaret shook her head to dislodge the anger, smiling to herself and picking up the pace. The Vauxhall Bridge spanned the river up ahead; she had a date with her husband's young cousin Constance.

•   •   •   •   •

Constance Ventor stood on the north side of Vauxhall Bridge facing the street. She spun a small toy away from her, tossing it down until it reached the end of its string before tugging on the string looped around her finger. The toy shot back up before it hit the ground. Constance gripped it tight and tossed it back towards the ground. This time, as it reached the end of the string, the gadget spun like a weathervane in a storm and threw off yellow and green sparks. A moment later the toy settled back into her hand.

The young woman noticed a boy staring at her and smiled. She brushed her mousy-brown hair away from her eyes and tossed the toy down again. A new barrage of red and blue and green sparks threw themselves from the toy as the boy's caretaker appeared behind him. He tugged on the clean sleeves of her dress, prompting her to lean over as he whispered in her ear.

She straightened up and approached Constance. "My charge is very much taken by your toy."

"Thank you," said Constance, bowing her head while smirking at the child. She lifted the lid of the wooden box at her feet. A dozen toys twinkled in the hazy afternoon sun, winking and promising a good time. The nanny looked back at the boy, then turned again to address the young woman in the threadbare white dress and worn leather corset.

"I assume that you are selling these toys?"

"Yes, ma'am," replied Constance.

"How much?"

"Three shillings. Chose whichever you like."

The woman nodded, motioning to the boy to pick out his new treasure. She opened her handbag and dug around the bottom for three coins. The boy knelt on the paved bricks and picked up the gadgets one at a time. He weighed each one, turning them over and over in his pudgy hands.

"If you want to try, slip your ring finger through the loop like this," said Constance, slipping the string of her own toy on the boy's finger. "Toss it down to the ground." He let go and a pinwheel of sparks leapt off the toy before it climbed back up the string.

The boy smiled, but remained silent. He returned Constance's toy, then tried out each of the five finalists. Twice.

His nanny smiled, "These are clever toys. Where did you get them?"

"I made them myself."

"Where did you learn such a skill?"

"My father was a tinkerer. I spent half my childhood in his workshop while he built toys and gadgets like these."

The woman tugged her thick frock coat closed. "I hope he was not one of those scoundrels responsible for so much discord and terrorism in the Empire."

"No, ma'am. He was a loyal Queen's man. Taught me the same."

The woman offered Constance a weak smile. The boy returned to the wooden box, double-checking the toy he picked against the others, lest he regret his decision later.

"Do you do anything else with your skills other than make toys and trinkets?"

Constance returned the woman's weak smile. "I am a student at Oxford University. Tuition is expensive, so I make toys and trinkets for sale."

"Oh." The woman's voice rose three octaves. "I did not know Oxford admitted women."

"Yes ma'am."

The woman gave Constance no visible reaction. She turned her attention back to her ward, who was admiring his shiny new prize.

"Thank you," said Constance as they turned to leave. "Have fun." The boy looked back over his shoulder and smiled at the lanky woman with the plain brown hair.

Constance flipped the lid of her box closed with the toe of her boot. She checked the time on her pocket watch, the square and compass of the Freemasons glinting from the backside. Margaret was late.

• • • • •

Margaret approached Vauxhall Bridge and spotted Constance on the other side beside her box of tricks. The young woman looked thin and awkward, spinning her toy on her finger. Margaret watched Constance crouch down and tie her boot lace, the soft brown leather reaching to her knee. Constance stood up and spotted Margaret. She stashed her spinning toys and waved a hand full of cracked nails with grease pressed beneath them. The stale smell of engine oil and tanned leather lingered underneath Constance's perfume. Constance picked up her wooden box and the ladies walked north together, away from the river and towards Hyde Park.

Constance chatted without paying attention to her friend. "I have had trouble building an automaton arachnid for a professor. I turned in a functioning model and received low marks. Are you even listening to me, Margaret?"

Margaret turned her head to look at Constance. "Sorry, luv. But something doesn't feel right." She scanned the crowds on the street in front of them.

"You are acting paranoid again."

"These days the Resistance operates across the Isles without fear of reprisal," said Margaret, not bothering to hide her Scottish twang. "I'm afraid that bill will come due soon."

"I take it back. You are not paranoid, you're a bloody loon." Constance bit her lip and sighed. "I am uncertain why I agreed to attend this rally with you."

"Because you want to open up your mind to other possibilities besides Victoria's."

"I agreed to go with you because it was so important to you." replied Constance. "And to get you to stop hassling me about my love for Queen and Country."

"If you already know, then why did you ask?"

"Because," Constance said with another sigh, "I am uncertain why I caved. If I am arrested at an anti-government rally, I might lose my scholarship."

"They would never take away your scholarship," said Margaret. "You're too bloody brilliant."

"But what if I get arrested?"

"There hasn't been a single arrest at a rally in months." Margaret bit her lower lip as she walked. "It's a bad sign. The Brits are planning something big for the Resistance on the Isles after the holidays."

"Some would call it a good thing that no one has been arrested in months," said Constance.

"It is only a matter of time. I cannot believe you forgot what happened in Liverpool last year."

Constance furrowed her eyebrows. "If the Resistance would stick to distributing pamphlets, people would not die."

The conversation slowed as the women hurried down the busy street towards Hyde Park. Navigating the roads in the heart of London required concentration to dodge the droves of pedestrians, peddlers with pushcarts, and the occasional team of horses. Steam-driven carriages and taxis were a unique hazard. They plowed through the narrow cobblestone roads at higher speeds, trailing soot and smoke that obscured the vision of everyone in their wake.

"How are the new boots?" asked Constance.

"I haven't had much of a chance to see what they can do." Margaret's boots were well-worn brown leather, laced halfway up her shins.

"I added a dozen hidden bells and whistles: collapsible blades, spikes on the bottom for traction, skeleton keys, smoke bombs."

"Did you add the tiny pistol I gave you?"

"Yes, but I fail to see why you need a firearm with you at all times," replied Constance. "I see you have gone back to trousers."

"I always feel more comfortable in trousers; easier to move. Ever try to chase somebody through crowded streets in a petticoat?"

"Is that a rhetorical question?"

"Of course not."

They walked by Buckingham Palace, Constance staring at the red and blue banners imprinted with the Union Jack, hung from the highest eaves and the lowest iron fences for Douglas Tank Day. Hundreds of guards surrounded the palace in the neat and trim uniforms of the British army. Each one shouldered a steel rifle with a wooden stock.

Some soldiers stood at attention, the rest at ease. All watched and waited; a visible force deterring any foolish notions of aggression against the Crown.

"I learned at university they have an entire garrison of a thousand soldiers stationed beneath the palace. Same underneath Parliament."

"I remember hearing that," muttered Margaret.

"The upper ramparts have steam-driven mechanisms that fire iron spears taller than me. They can throw the spears a full kilometer."

"I cringe thinking about that amount of firepower hanging over our heads," said Margaret.

"This is our nation, and that is our firepower."

Margaret sighed but bit her tongue. A minute later she came to stop surveyed the scene at Hyde Park. They had arrived.

•   •   •   •   •

Margaret and Constance stood on the edge of the crowd in Hyde Park. The speaker had worked the young men and women packed in front of the stage into a self-righteous rage. A larger group of curious onlookers and passersby hung around the edges of the congregation.

Margaret leaned over and to talk to Constance: "That's Mattie. She's head of the London Resistance."

Margaret and Constance stood on the side of the wooden platform on high stilts. Mattie stood in the middle of the stage holding a cone-shaped devise that projected her voice across the park.

"Do not let yourselves be fooled," Mattie said, her voice intense and angry. "The British Empire does more than fight wars to ensure our protection. The British Empire does more than colonize sparsely populated corners of the globe." Mattie's voice danced with the engaging, up-and-down pitch of a practiced orator.

"What have we done with the technology that Douglas Tank gifted this nation? Was he sent from heaven to bless us all? Or was he a false prophet, sent by the devil?

"For decades, Victoria's soldiers slaughtered innocent people across the world. They subjugate villages and towns, cities and nations. British soldiers force the relocation of countless natives. You see the proof all around you; displaced people from around the world toil in factories across the Isles."

A pair of young men hanging on the outside of the crowd pulled the tarp off their stockpile of rotten vegetables. They let loose a volley of tomatoes and cabbages, shouting taunts and laughing. Most of the rotten produce hit people pressed against the stage. A group of men in plain clothes hustled the troublemakers across the park, knocked them to the ground, and pelted them with their own rotten vegetables.

"I appreciate you accompanying me here." Margaret spoke to Constance without looking at her. "I know that Mattie's beliefs are different from your own."

Mattie's voice boomed across the park, filling the air once again with a measurable electrical charge. "Our isles have not been invaded by a foreign power in hundreds of years, yet we wage constant wars. The only course of action for Great Britain, if we are a peace-loving nation, is to end all foreign conflicts."

"I am a supporter of peace," muttered Constance. "But her logic is questionable."

"It's the logic used by the British Empire that's flawed," replied Margaret. "Mattie's message is simple: if we want peace, stop invading other nations."

"That's not what she said," said Constance.

"That's essentially what she said."

"What about how Britain provides aid to primitive civilizations around the world? Without us they would have no medicines, no roads, no schools," said Constance.

"That's the flawed logic I mentioned."

Mattie's voice grew with intensity: "Toppling an independent state only improves the lives of the conqueror. Subjugated people are no better off exchanging modern conveniences for the exploitation of their homeland." Mattie paused, then raised her voice for the final sentence, driving her point home. "Colonization is not our God-given right."

"The rights of a backward people to govern themselves is a controversial idea," said Constance. "But it is one that has gained a considerable amount of traction in the past few years."

"I bet the controversial theory becomes accepted fact in the coming years." Margaret perked up her head and scanned the edges of the crowd. "I see someone I know," she said. "I will be right back."

Margaret slunk down behind the onlookers flanking the stage and disappeared towards the back of the crowd.

• • • • •

Mattie kept preaching, working herself into an angry fury on the wooden platform. Suddenly she stopped mid-sentence and stared over the heads of the crowd.

A half dozen iron plated, steam-driven tanks bore down on the crowd, emerging from the tree line on the far side of the grassy park. They looked clumsy, heavy and unbalanced, spilling ash and oil on the manicured lawn. Despite their awkward appearance, the tanks had a wicked reputation. The gun turrets perched on top fired cannon balls with enough force to collapse a building. The flanks were battle-beaten metal, emblazoned with the Union Jack.

Onlookers watching from the rear fringes of the crowd saw the tanks first and started screaming. They ran from the park and scattered in every direction. Individuals in the center of the crowd were not as lucky, trampling each other trying to escape.

A minute later, the tanks plowed through the heart of the crowd. People threw themselves left and right, avoiding the tanks' paths. Several individuals were not fast enough and fell under the heavy treads.

With harsh persuasion, Margaret bullied rallygoers away from the wooden stage. She swept them left and right in groups of two and three, clearing the edges of the crowd before working her way inward.

The tanks maintained their line, all six lurching forward, side by side, cutting a path thirty meters wide. Rallygoers still in the park began stuffing rags in bottles of alcohol and tossing them at the tanks. The armored vehicles held their course as they headed for the rickety wooden stage.

Bottles broke on the iron plates and lit small fires, but did no damage. The bullets fired from an unseen gunman bounced off the tanks like birds flying into glass windows.

"Get off the stage, Mattie," shouted Margaret. "I will stop them."

"You are insane," shouted Mattie from above her. "You cannot stop them. Just get everyone out of here."

Margaret turned and ran towards the armored vehicles. She shouted at every individual standing their ground with a lit bottle of booze or service revolver.

"Flank them," she yelled. "Line up alongside and trap them in the middle. Light the grass and trees around the tanks."

Constance grabbed hold of Margaret's wrist and spun her. "People are dying," shouted Constance. "They are trampling each other. Come back and help me clear the park." Margaret pulled free of Constance's grip and disappeared into the smoke and haze.

Mattie stood on the stage giving orders to the crowd through her voice amplifier. No one was listening.

"Get off the stage and run," shouted Constance, on the grass below Mattie's feet. "The tanks are lining up to fire."

Mattie looked at the stranger standing below her. Her eyes swept left and right, digesting the horrors around her. A few followers stood their ground in front of the stage, shouting insults at the tanks and throwing rocks and empty bottles.

The tanks ground to a halt, belching smoke and soot, appearing to laugh at the stones and bullets and bottles that bouncing off their plates. The guns mounted on the top of the armored cars raised up and took aim at the stage.

"Run," yelled Constance, shoving a pair of stone throwers clear of the stage before diving for cover.

The six tanks fired as one. Cannon balls tore through the wooden platform like hurricane winds through a thatch roof. The tanks rolled back from the recoil of the guns. They shifted gears and plowed forward, crushing the splintered debris and any trapped souls. The tanks kept rolling forward and out of Hyde Park, forming a single file line and driving down the middle of Vauxhall Road until they were out of sight.

CHAPTER 3

Margaret sat opposite her husband on the drawing room sofa, retelling her adventures in Hyde Park for the fourth time. Constance stood in front of the fireplace, turning over a trinket from the mantle, disengaged from the conversation.

"Aye, husband, the tanks appeared without warning. No notice to clear the park, no declaration of an illegal gathering from a magistrate. Not even a bloody bobby nailing a sign to a tree."

"I simply find it hard to believe is all," said Edward. "There must have been some provocation for Her Majesty to roll tanks through a peaceful demonstration."

"Honestly, cousin," said Constance. "Just because it is improbable does not mean it did not happen."

Edward sat in quiet contemplation. "How many dead and wounded?"

"Four dead. Another nineteen carted off on stretchers to St. Mary's." Constance turned her attention back to the fireplace mantel.

Margaret turned to face her husband. "You should have seen Constance in action. After the tanks left, everyone ran. Only us and two others stayed to help the wounded."

"What did you do?" asked Edward.

"We applied first aid to everyone we could. Constance tore her petticoat to shreds making tourniquets."

Edward stared at the back of his cousin. "I never realized you are such a calm person under pressure."

Constance pulled down a clock from the mantel, unaware that she was the topic of conversation. The clock was short and squat, shaped like a crouching frog and twice the size of Constance's hand. The etched crystal inlaid in the onyx frame captured the room's ambient light and split it into a rainbow that floated across the clock's movement. It was a centuries-old family heirloom that had not worked since Edward's grandmother gifted it to him.

"We could have saved more lives." Constance set the clock back on the mantel while keeping her back to the others.

"How was that?" asked Edward in a weary voice.

"Margaret was the first person to see the tanks coming. She cleared people out of the park before the tanks got close. She could have saved more, but she got carried away trying to stop the tanks."

"How?" asked Edward, exhaling.

"By throwing rocks and bottles at the tanks."

"I am right here," said Margaret. "If you have a problem with what I did, I would appreciate it if you talked to me."

"You could have saved more lives if you had stayed focused on helping people." Constance paused, "You could have saved Mattie."

"Mattie Pennington of the London Resistance?" asked Edward.

"Yes, dear," said Margaret, "try to keep up. And as for your take on the events, Constance, I made a tactical decision. If I had stopped those tanks, no one would have died."

"You lost your grip."

"That's your opinion," said Margaret. "I did not see you pulling people out of the line of fire."

"That's true," muttered Constance. "But I lack your skills."

"This is pointless," said Edward. "What is relevant is why you still insist on risking your life?"

"Oye, luv," said Margaret. "What else was I to do? Watch people die in front of me?"

"That's not what I meant," said Edward. "Why were you at the rally at all?"

Margaret glared at her husband. "The military has not been deployed at a rally since Liverpool. And I have not been involved with Resistance operations since I left Glasgow."

"I just worry about your safety is all."

The conversation pivoted again as Edward and Margaret compared notes about the London Resistance and who might have been the primary targets.

Constance picked up the antique clock and turned it over three times, deducing the probable cause of every scratch and blemish. She knelt down to pull a small tool kit from a hidden pocket in her boot, unrolling the thin leather bundle across the mantel.

Constance turned and interrupted Edward and Margaret. "Margaret, why did you get involved with the London Resistance?"

"You know that I was in the Glasgow Resistance years ago. It seemed natural when Edward and I moved here after Oxford." Margaret paused and bit her lip. "Truthfully, I'm not nearly as involved here as I was in Glasgow. I do not take part in operations." Margaret sighed, "Propaganda and speeches bore me."

"Why did you become involved with the Glasgow Resistance?"

"Because her father died in a Glasgow weapons factory," said Edward.

Margaret leaned back and locked eyes with her husband. "His death is not the reason I work against the British Empire."

"Sorry, dear," mumbled Edward.

"No need to apologize, luv. Just don't speak for me."

"Of course, dear."

"The British Empire has taken countless lives."

"Yes, of course, dear."

"Then why did you get involved with the Glasgow Resistance?" asked Constance again.

Margaret sat quietly, staring at the wall. "My older brother was in the Resistance. I got my hands on information about weapons factories in Glasgow for him. Easy for a young girl."

"Your brother got involved when your father died working in the weapons factory," said Edward. "Four workers died in that accident because the plant was designed to be productive but not safe."

"Edward," said Margaret.

"Yes, dear."

"Do shut up."

"Yes, dear."

Constance tuned out the others. Her hands moved without thought over the clock's case and removed the onyx and crystal shell. She identified the culprit on first inspection: a tiny, worn spring north of the pendulum. It looked the same as a dozen other springs in the clock, but Constance knew it lacked elasticity. The clock ran when wound, but did not keep accurate time. Constance tuned back into the conversation across the room.

"Tell me, luv," said Margaret, "how did your father's death change your perspective of the British Empire?"

Constance ignored them and scanned the room. She spotted a pendulum trinket sold on street corners for a shilling; she had the parts strewn across the mantel in under a minute. Constance plucked a tiny, taut spring from the wreckage and reassembled the pendulum trinket in a different configuration. It still ticked, but kept a different rhythm.

Margaret and Edward's conversation returned to the Hyde Park raid: "There are rallies in Hyde Park every week. Why would the military strike this one?" asked Edward.

"I do not know," replied Margaret.

"Only the London police and the Queen's Guard are in the city. The closest armored tanks are stationed several kilometers north of London." Edward's words trailed off in thought.

"That's what I thought," said Margaret. "I hoped your contacts in the London bureaucracy would have some information."

"Perhaps, but the orders to bring the tanks into the city bypassed me."

"Do you think your superiors know of my ties to the Resistance?"

"I doubt it," Edward mumbled.

Constance inserted the new spring into the body of the crystal clock with the skill of a surgeon. She reassembled the clock, wound it, and nudged the pendulum. The clock began ticking.

A slender, middle-aged woman in a black and white servant's uniform entered the room. "Supper is served, luvs," she said. Her voice sounded bored and far away. "Game hens and boiled potatoes. Squash fresh from the market. Delicious tonight."

"Thank you, Gertrude. We will be in momentarily."

• • • • •

After dinner, the trio adjourned back to the drawing room, patting their bellies after the filling meal.

"Gertrude really is a cheeky one," said Constance.

"Why do you keep her around?" asked Margaret. Both women looked at Edward.

"Mum said if I moved into this house, I had to have at least one servant."

"Seems a bit silly; you are doing your mother a favor keeping this house occupied."

"She was concerned the family home would fall into disrepair if I did not hire someone to maintain it." Edward avoided Margaret's glare, "Besides, someone has to cook our meals."

"I have more important things to do," replied Margaret.

"Of course, dear."

"It is not even that big of a house," muttered Constance. "Just a few bedrooms.

"Whether or not you need hired help isn't my point," said Margaret. "Why do you keep Gertrude on when she is talks to you the way she does?"

Edward shrugged, "She does not bother me." He wandered over to the mantel and picked up the polished black onyx and crystal clock.

"What's wrong?" asked Margaret, looking at her husband's stunned expression.

"This clock has not kept time for years. The last time it worked I was a small boy."

"I apologize," said Constance, blushing. "Sometimes I look for something to tinker with when I have a problem to solve. I hope I did not overstep my bounds."

"My grandmother gave me this clock. I remember, she used to wind it every morning." Edward turned it over in his hands, examining every detail with his fingertips. He held it up to his ear and grinned at Constance. "You are truly amazing, cousin. I took it to the best clockmakers in town; no one could fix it."

Gertrude interrupted the conversation, marching into the room and planting herself in the middle of the floor: "You've visitors, guv. I informed them it's past a descent time to call on a gentleman and his wife, but they say it's important." Gertrude raised her hand to the side of her mouth. "They're from Her Majesty's mil'tary," she whispered in a voice as loud as her regular speaking voice.

"By all means," said Edward, setting the clock on the mantle. "Show them in." Gertrude spun on her flats and left.

"If they meant to arrest you for the events of this afternoon, they would not knock on the front door and ask the maid to speak with us." Edward's tone was not as confident as his words. "Political arrests happen swiftly and without warning; individuals plucked off the street or taken from their beds while they sleep."

Gertrude's heavy shoes were audible on the wood floors before she reached the drawing room. She marched onto the oriental rug in the middle of the room, cleared her throat and arched her neck.

"Master Goulden, Misses Goulden, Miss Ventor. This is Lieutenant Geoffrey Balsak from Her Majesty's mil'tary. And his privates."

The lieutenant stepped forward, cheeks flushed. "Basalt, ma'am. I am Lieutenant Geoffrey Basalt." Following him into the room were a pair of young men wearing formal uniforms and blank expressions.

The lieutenant turned to address Edward: "Master Goulden, I am afraid it is my great displeasure this evening to be the bearer of unwelcome news."

"My, aren't those regal words for a soldier," interjected Gertrude.

Constance glared at Gertrude. Margaret looked like a caged lion tethered to the ground, ready to slice through her bindings and incapacitate any perceived threat.

"Please continue, lieutenant," said Edward, stiff and formal. "What is the reason for your visit at this late hour?"

"It's your sister, sir," replied Lieutenant Basalt. "Anne Goulden disappeared from your family's estate in New Granada thirteen days ago."

Margaret relaxed her stance; Edward stopped breathing.

"There were several other kidnappings in Cartagena in the last two years. All were perpetrated by the New Granada Resistance." The lieutenant paused, staring straight ahead and avoiding the gaze of the family members. He cleared his throat before continuing. "At this time, the British government believes Anne Goulden was likely executed."

"When did the New Granada Resistance become such a militant organization?" asked Constance.

"New Granada is currently classified as a 'colony under extreme duress' due to the exceptionally large and aggressive local Resistance. Her Majesty's Armed Forces here in London are coordinating their response with the governor of Cartagena. Military intervention is probable."

Margaret took the lead when Edward's face lost all color. "What other information can you give us?"

The lieutenant nodded at a subordinate; the soldier stepped forward and handed a thick folder to his commander.

"Details are in here. Statements from the local regency, investigation reports, things of that nature." Lieutenant Basalt paused, waiting for a response. Receiving none, the soldier handed the stack of papers to a stunned Edward.

"I do not have to tell you that this is more information than most grieving families are privilege to. Your government position allows you access to otherwise confidential information." Lieutenant Basalt cleared his throat one last time. "Also included are a number of communications from your mother in Cartagena. They were withheld during the early stages of the investigation."

Silence shrouded the room. The soldiers maintained their stiff postures; these were men who delivered bad news for a living.

After a minute, Edward composed himself enough to break the silence. "Thank you, Lieutenant Balsak. Gertrude, please see these men out."

"The name is Basalt, sir," said the officer. Gertrude peeled herself out of the corner where the wallpaper camouflaged her and led the soldiers out.

• • • • •

Silence followed the soldiers' retreat from the house. Edward opened the roll top desk and put down the thick stack of papers. He flipped through the pages to find the letters penned in his mother's immaculate script. He dropped into the desk chair and started reading.

"Why would any Resistance movement kidnap Anne? What do they hope to gain?" whispered Constance.

"Anne is a British colonist," said Margaret, pacing the length the of the room. "She comes from a family with money and a history of service to the Crown. That makes her a valuable bargaining chip."

Constance picked another trinket up from an end table and started taking it apart. "Edward told me Anne shares his desire to end the British wars of conquest. It makes little sense for a political movement to take someone prisoner with similar ideals."

"Again, Anne is a British colonist," said Margaret, adding a sigh for effect. "To natives wanting to drive out Victoria's armies, she is the enemy."

"The New Granada Resistance must be bloodthirsty savages," said Constance.

"The New Granada Resistance are working for the greater good," replied Margaret.

"Mother appears to have given up hope," Edward interrupted. "She has resigned herself to my sister's death. She barely mentions any efforts to bring Anne home safe, although she does devote an incredible amount of ink to cursing the savage natives and the Resistance."

Edward put one letter down and picked up another. "She wants me to use my influence with Parliament. She wants them to send an army to dismantle the Resistance."

"Dismantling any colonial Resistance is a violent, messy affair," said Margaret.

"Anyone who could kidnap Anne must be violent savages," said Constance.

Margaret visibly shuttered as her efforts to sway Constance against the British Empire's war machine unraveled. "Please, stop," she said, holding up her.

Constance lay the disassembled parts on a table. "I hope Her Majesty's Forces wipe them off the planet."

"This kidnapping is just the reason Victoria needs to wage all-out war," muttered Margaret.

Edward lifted his head from the disheveled pile of papers, ran his fingers through his hair, and spoke to the wall. "Her Majesty's Forces have never needed a kidnapping to justify rooting out a violent Resistance group." Edward rifled through the paperwork again, holding up a single page for inspection. He rotated his body in the chair to face the others. "The local military commanders in Cartagena discounted the possibility of Anne being alive from the beginning. The governor was willing to sign her death certificate after only ten days."

"That seems odd," said Constance.

"But without a body the law requires thirty days before she can be declared dead," said Edward.

Margaret stepped over to her husband's chair and knelt in front of him, taking both his hands in her own. "Edward, we do not have to give up until we are certain Anne is really gone. We both have ways of getting things done. You can lobby inside the government and get the search reopened. I can talk to my contacts in Glasgow and get the real story on the New Granada Resistance."

Edward swallowed and nodded his head, "First thing tomorrow I will have words with the Lord that oversees New Granada. And I can contact General Brash. He is second in command in South America and in London for another few days. I aided him by gathering documents about the western coastline of South America for a new offensive. He gave me a meaningful commitment to divert resources to improve the lives of thousands in the Sao Paulo ghetto. The general understands that his career trajectory would suffer without my assistance.

"I apologize; I am rambling," Edward said, pausing to take a deep breath. "You are right, dear. Anne is not lost to us yet."

CHAPTER 4

Edward walked at a brisk clip through the catacombs below Parliament; a labyrinth of plain hallways lined with heavy oak doors. Dim light radiated from the gaslight sconces lining the walls, the smell of burnt kerosene tickling his nose. The people working here facilitated the needs of Parliament and the military brass. Edward paused in front of the unmarked door of his direct superior. He took a deep breath, straightened his jacket and tie, and rapped on the door.

"Enter."

Simple, matching filing cabinets lined all four walls of the office. Edward knew his supervisor locked every drawer and cross-referenced every slip of paper. Not a single personal item adorned the walls or cabinet tops.

Mr. Jonathan White sat behind a desk the size of a rowboat in the middle of the room. The desk appeared to be from the same oak tree as the door and the cabinets, the top decorated with neat stacks of paper. The sole personal effect in the room, Mr. White's prized pen set, rested between the stacks.

"You wished to speak to me?" said Edward.

"I heard that the research on Australian prison project stalled. As we discussed last week, I need a rough estimate of infrastructure costs and local resource acquisition. I am scheduled to present your figures to a Parliamentary sub-committee Monday."

"I assure you, sir, that everything will be in your hands before then," said Edward.

Mr. White took off his reading glasses and set them on his desk. "Mr. Goulden, you are perhaps one of the most gifted civil servants ever to grace these catacombs. In exchange for your brilliant contributions to Great Britain, you have an unprecedented amount of leverage in public policy decisions."

"Thank you, sir. I am grateful for that freedom."

"Personally, I would not do what you do as it is outside of my job description. However, I see the value in your efforts. You extend a humanitarian touch, true Christian values, if you will, to the far corners of the Empire."

"Thank you, sir. Your compliment means a lot to me."

Mr. White sat back in his chair and studied the young man standing in front of him.

"You have been gathering a significant amount of information on Cartagena and the New Granada colony over the last two days. You have also been using agency resources to dig into the investigation of your sister's disappearance." Mr. White leaned his tired frame forward, resting his elbows on his desk. "Mr. Goulden, I assure you that all relevant documents were handed to you when the military delivered the news to your home. I saw to it personally."

"I did not realize that was the case," said Edward. "Almost everything I procured in the last two days I already had. I apologize for wasting resources on this matter." Edward paused, debating how much to disclose to Mr. White. "I believe my sister may still be alive, sir."

"I have read the files, Mr. Goulden. Those leading the investigation have little hope of finding her alive."

"There is no proof that she is dead, only speculation."

"That is true," said Mr. White.

"Then you agree with me that she might still be alive."

"I am a bureaucrat. I save my speculating for the downs." Both men paused and sat in uncomfortable silence.

"I am not yet sure what I can do, but I must do something," said Edward.

Mr. White sighed and pushed himself away from the desk. "I assumed as much. I also assume you will not complete any work while your family is dealing with such a tragedy. Therefore, I am placing you on administrative leave, effective immediately."

Edward's face darkened; he mounted a weak protest that Mr. White silenced: "You will remain on payroll for up to eight weeks. Contact me when you are ready to return," said Mr. White. "I wish you nothing but the best."

•　　•　　•　　•　　•

After lunch at his desk, Edward left the catacombs and walked across the street to St. James Park. His digging had turned up the name of a young soldier who returned three days ago from a post in Cartagena. Private Nutten agreed to meet and give his account of the investigation into Anne's disappearance. Edward sat on a bench beside the pond in St. James Park. He checked the time; he was early.

A group of boys in white linen shirts and velvet breeches cutoff at the knees were launching mechanical boats out on the water. Each boat was the length of their child operator; each had a steam engine and a hopper large enough to hold a few pieces of coal. Edward watched as the children prepped the boats and set a course using tiny levers mounted on the stern. The switches were so small the children had to pinch the ends to move them.

The boats traveled out to the middle of the pond, skirting the shoreline and the tall reeds in a wide circle. They ran out of fuel before returning to shore if the course was incorrectly laid in.

The children danced each time someone launched another boat. They ran through the soggy grass along the shoreline, keeping themselves as close as possible to their boat. They brushed past Edward where he sat, unaware of his presence.

A ship ran out of steam in the middle of the pond. After checking for loitering bobbies, the owner kicked off his shoes and waded in the water.

Edward pulled out his watch and checked the time. Private Nutten was fifteen minutes late. He sighed and dropped his watch back in his pocket. Edward sat for another thirty minutes watching the boats propel themselves awkwardly across the water, pitching and rolling and exhaling puffs of soot and steam. The bureaucrat checked his watch one last time before returning to Parliament.

• • • • •

Constance entered the student laboratory at Oxford University carrying an overstuffed book bag that dwarfed her small frame. She banged her bag on the door frame, then tripped over a wooden stool crossing the room. Constance perched on a tall stool and dropped her bag. She knocked over an assortment of beakers and glassware on the table in front of her, then lay her head down on the wooden surface.

Professor Lecturn entered the lab and navigated the maze of sinks and tables with much less commotion. He pulled out a stool and sat next to the young woman. Harold Lecturn was a large man, taller and bigger around than most. Despite his size, he did not present as an imposing figure. He habitually wore mismatched socks and a disheveled dress shirt. A mop of tangled hair that looked like a wig, even though it was not, sat perched on top of his head. Dr. Harold Lecturn, Oxford professor, looked like someone who needed assistance finding the cafeteria, not a brilliant engineer and physicist.

"What are you working on this morning?" asked the professor.

"Struggling through an assignment for Professor McIntyre," replied Constance.

"What's the assignment?"

"Build a mechanical arachnid. Eight legs, minimum two pairs of eyes, maximum seven centimeters across the abdomen."

"Does not sound like that would be a problem for you," said Lecturn in a garbled British accent. "What exactly are you struggling with?"

"The engineering specs are simple enough. I put together a functioning automaton using pocket watch gears and thin sheet metal," said Constance. "But Professor McIntyre said I would receive low marks if I submitted the device I built. He wants me to breathe life into the machine. Plus, he said it should have a secondary function; something useful to the owner."

Professor Lecturn took his time responding to his protege, "The British Empire produces war machines on an enormous scale. A single design change for a tank is duplicated in thousands of machines, which in turn impacts warfare across the globe."

"I know that."

"Professor McIntyre understands that the homogeneous nature of the British war machine is its weakness."

"I fail to understand what you are getting at," said Constance.

"The British Empire produced a class of tanks about ten years ago with a single design flaw. After six months in service, nearly every tank developed an identical oil leak in the internal engine. Repairs were not feasible, so a replacement was designed. Engineers simply added more oil to the leaking tanks, then abandoned them in the field wherever they stopped running."

"I know the history of the Empire's machines. And I understand that diversity in design limits reproducing mistakes. What is your point, sir?"

"To be a successful engineer, you must design and build a wide variety of machines that are so perfect they are lifelike. A machine you breathe life in to will tell you its flaws before it becomes utterly worthless."

"I heard a lecture to that effect last month when I swore my oath," said Constance.

"What oath?"

"I joined the Freemasons as an Apprentice."

"I assume that you joined the York Rite," said Lecturn.

"Yes, of course."

Harold Lecturn dug into the pocket of his plaid jacket. He removed a half-eaten sandwich and laid it on the table, then returned to the pocket and produced a pocket watch. Inscribed on its face was the square and compass symbol of the Freemasons. Lecturn pressed the nob on top, opening the cover to reveal the watch face. Etched into the brass opposite the face the phrase *14° Grand Elect Mason*.

Constance furrowed her eyebrows and stared at the pocket watch: "Are you a member of the York Rite as well, sir?"

Lecturn turned over the pocket watch. On the back was a two-headed eagle etched in the brass. "Actually, I am a member of the Scottish Rite, otherwise known as the Rose Croix."

Constance leaned back, "The Rose Croix is devoted to dismantling of the British Empire. They are outlawed as a tool of the Resistance."

"You are aware that I spent a number of years working abroad with various Resistance groups."

"I thought that life was behind you."

"I am no longer an active member of any Resistance group, but my beliefs have not changed. The moral code of a Mason is the most important tool in his kit." Lecturn snapped closed his pocket watch and dropped it back in his pocket.

"Years ago, Professor McIntyre was a member of the Resistance," said Lecturn. "Mass production is not an option for Resistance engineers; we can only build a single weapon at a time. Therefore, each is carefully crafted to meet specific needs."

"I heard about a Resistance movement in the jungles of India that built a mechanical elephant ten meters tall that carried soldiers in a basket atop the beast's back. It was used to spearhead an open rebellion. British forces sent an entire brigade into the jungle after the elephant. The creature destroyed a dozen tanks and river transports before being brought down."

"I remember that story," said Professor Lecturn, eyes cast down on the table. "The mechanical elephant had the advantage of being a large, formidable weapon that could traverse jungle thickets and rivers like a living elephant."

"Valiant effort, I suppose," said Constance. "But they lost just the same."

"The Russians have a proverb I believe applies in this situation: *Quantity has a quality all its own.* The volume of weapons the British Empire produces overwhelm the most brilliant creatures built by the Rose Croix."

"Professor McIntyre is teaching necessary engineering skills by insisting I add more depth to my arachnid."

"I believe so," replied Lectern. "Resistance engineers must do things others cannot."

Constance took a deep breath, "I plan on applying for an internship at Her Majesty's Department of Engineering and Advanced Design. Professor Mayflower said she will write me a letter of recommendation. I decided that I do not want to build weapons for either side. I have been working on several new bridge designs that can be constructed in remote corners of the globe with limited resources."

"Most engineers in Her Majesty's D.E.A.D. create weapons of war. They design the entire production process, including manufacturing plants and requisitions." Lecturn sighed, "I appreciate your desire to design machines that benefit everyone. However, if you take employment with the D.E.A.D., you will inevitably build war machines for the British Empire."

"The Empire does a lot of good around the world, sir," said Constance. "We bring roads and hospitals and schools to uncivilized places around the globe. That is the type of work I want to do. I showed my designs for a new kind of water reclamation facility to Professor Mayflower and she said it was brilliant."

"I am sure it is brilliant," said Lecturn. "But working for the Department of Engineering and Advanced Design will not go as you think."

"You know I respect your opinion, professor, but I believe you are wrong in this case."

"I doubt we can accomplish much by continuing this debate," said Lecturn. "I have something I would like to show you."

Professor Lecturn navigated his way across the room. He pulled an antique set of keys from the same pocket holding the sandwich. He picked his way through the ring and unlocked one of the walnut cabinets lining the back wall. The professor removed a small wooden box from the top shelf and wound his way back to Constance.

"When I was a member of the Ohio Valley Resistance in North America, I built small automaton animals." Lecturn lifted the lid of the box. "This was one of my finest."

Lecturn reached inside with both hands and cupped the object in the box. Carefully he lifted out a perfect mechanical squirrel. Shades of brown fur covered the strong hind legs, shorter front legs, and a narrow torso. Other than the sharp incisors and dirt caked in the fur, the squirrel resembled a cuddly stuffed animal a child could love.

"The key to making a believable automaton is getting every detail perfect. Or, perhaps more appropriately, getting every detail imperfect." Lecturn held up the squirrel and ran his finger along the bottom of its body. "Matted fur on the underbelly, bone ridges visible along the length of the spine."

Professor Lecturn set the squirrel on the table between them. Constance leaned over and examined the squirrel without touching it.

"Granted it looks very much like a live squirrel," said Constance. "But what does it do? Walk up to a British tank and explode?"

"Nothing as crude as that." Lecturn picked up his gadget and turned it over in his hands, examining his own craftsmanship. "It is common for Resistance engineers to build tiny creatures, sometimes even swimming fish, birds that fly, even insects."

"Building a flying mechanical bird would be an incredible project," said Constance, suddenly far away and dreaming.

"I have heard within the Rose Croix that some members have gotten close to perfecting large birds of prey that can carry passengers." Professor Lecturn turned his attention back to his squirrel. "Small critters such as these typically spy on the enemy and gather information."

"Is that what your squirrel does?"

"It tracks and follows whomever I assign it to track, transcribing every conversation around it. If possible, it returns to me every three days so I may remove the rolled tape inside its belly. The best part is it can live and function on its own indefinitely. It refuels on organic matter it scrounges, then burns it to generate power."

Constance snorted: "It eats like a real squirrel."

"Yes," said Lecturn, smiling like a proud father. "I programmed it to seek out acorns and nuts and even small pieces of wood and tree bark."

"How does it work?"

"The glass eyes have photo-like lenses inside. I face it towards its target and lift the third toe, left rear paw."

Professor Lecturn turned the animal towards Constance and lifted the third toe on the left rear paw. Clicking and spinning sounds came from the squirrel and a spark of life shuddered through the rodent. It darted across the room and climbed to the top of the walnut cabinets, never taking its eyes off Constance.

"It will maintain a visual lock on you until its toe is reset. In the meantime, it is transcribing every word it hears. Unfortunately, the rolls of paper have to be translated with a transmographier machine before they can be read."

"I believe the British military uses a similar spy technology."

"Yes, but nothing as elaborate or capable as my squirrel," replied the professor. "They tend to hide devices that transcribe conversations in fixed locations."

Constance walked over to the walnut cabinets and opened a student locker. She retrieved the scorpion she built from sheet metal and watch gears.

"Professor Lecturn, would you please assist me in breathing life into my scorpion?"

"I would be delighted."

Within an hour, two of the greatest engineering minds in the United Kingdom had a lifelike scorpion scurrying back and forth across the table. They equipped it with a timer and an empty hypodermic needle in its tail; there was no need to arm their assassin with a poison dart inside the walls of Oxford University. After locking the scorpion away in the walnut cabinet, Constance thanked her mentor and left. The squirrel clicked and whirled followed her out the door.

●　　●　　●　　●　　●

Edward rapped on the chamber door of Lord Samuel Bullington, a member of Parliament's House of Lords and minister of the colonial governors in South America.

A stiff British accent answered Edward from the other side of the mahogany slab: "Enter."

Edward opened the door and stepped inside the office. He closed the door behind him and gave a shallow, polite bow.

"My Lord, it is kind of you to see me on short notice."

"Yes, yes, of course," said Lord Bullington. "You have been of great assistance to me in the past and I felt I could not turn down your request. You will forgive the lack of help. I sent my office staff home. Getting late, you know."

"I will make my request brief, sir," said Edward.

Lord Bullington responded by bowing his head from his seat behind his ornate maple desk. "Thank you in advance for your brevity. Please, proceed."

"My family holds significant land and title in the New Granada colony. My father relocated the family when I was a small child, carving a plantation out of the jungle and amassing a sizable fortune. He served as an officer in Her Majesty's Armed Forces as a young man; then lost his life when called back into service for the Brazilian campaign nine years ago. My mother and sister still make their home in Cartagena."

The expression on Bullington's face betrayed his surprise that a bureaucrat came from a family of means.

"Fifteen days ago, my sister Anne disappeared three kilometers from the family estate. The local military commander declared it a kidnapping by the New Granada Resistance. However, after an investigation lasting only a few days, the governor conceded defeat and declared my sister deceased."

Lord Bullington cleared his throat and coughed like a man who enjoyed too many cigars. He pulled himself upright in his overstuffed leather desk chair.

"Am I to assume that this meeting is a call to action," said Bullington. "Since the governor of Cartagena falls under my jurisdiction, you would like me to order him to reopen the investigation?"

"My Lord," replied Edward, pausing to select his words. "I do not believe the local authorities adequately pursued the possibility that Anne may still be alive."

Bullington's stare lingered on the hand-carved decorative border of his maple desktop. When he spoke, his eyes remained fixed downward.

"Master Goulden, I have been in direct contact with Governor Pratt since the kidnapping. For years we have had an exceedingly difficult time securing the safety of the colony while locking down access to inland resources. Exports of agricultural and forest products are at a crawl. Mining operations are nonexistent. It has become such a problem that Her Majesty personally called upon me last month, and, shall we say, strongly encouraged me to take action to rectify the problem."

"I am I do not follow, sir," said Edward. "I only wish for you to insist the local authorities reopen the investigation."

"Anne Goulden's kidnapping is one of many blatant acts of terrorism in New Granada in recent months," said Bullington. "When Governor Pratt wired me about the disappearance, I instructed him to cease the search and rescue operation and devote every resource to dismantling the New Granada Resistance."

Bullington pause and lifted his eyes to meet Edward's, "I am terribly sorry. We have lost many colonial citizens to this Resistance group. I believe the best way to ensure the stability of the colony is to concentrate our efforts on weeding out the savages that kidnapped your sister."

"You do not understand, sir," said Edward. "I am only asking for a small amount of resources dedicated to bringing my sister home safely. I fully support a military operation to uproot this particular Resistance group."

"Many fine men and women lose their lives in the service of Queen and Country every day." Lord Bullington sighed and made eye contact with Edward. "I am sure your sister was among the finest. But diverting military resources to seek out your sister, if she is even still alive, would hinder the operation and risk more lives."

Edward shuddered, "Of course, My Lord. Her Majesty would undoubtedly replace both you and Governor Pratt if banana exports fall below quota. That would be a tragedy."

Lord Bullington rose from his leather chair. "Master Goulden, I know the sight and sound of a man who is broken inside so I will ignore that last statement. However, I believe it would be wise for you to let this matter drop. Tomorrow our professional relationship may return to what it was before this conversation began."

Edward took a moment to compose himself before replying. "My Lord, I understand you are unable to assist me. I will take no more of your time tonight. However, I no longer count you as a man worthy of maintaining a professional relationship with."

Having burned his first bridge ever, Edward Goulden spun around and marched out the office.

CHAPTER 5

Edward paced the floor of the drawing room in his London home. Every couple of minutes he checked the time on his grandmother's clock above the fireplace.

Gertrude marched into the room at eight o'clock sharp: "Your cousin's here now, guv."

Edward nodded a thank you and stopped pacing. When Constance entered the room, Edward did not waste time with polite greetings.

"Did you discover any information?"

"Yes, I did," replied Constance. "Although no one at Oxford knows anything about Anne."

"What do you mean?"

"The weapons and resources at the New Granada Resistance's disposal are extensive. They employ two high-ranking Freemasons of the Scottish Rite, both engineers of exceptionally high caliber."

"Leading to the conclusion that if the Resistance did abduct my sister, and every piece of evidence indicts they did, they would have ample means to elude the authorities." Edward's voice trailed off as he lost himself in thought. "Did you discover anything else useful?"

"The active Resistance members number in the thousands, mostly Natives and Spaniards. They are well organized, dedicated, and claim several victories over British forces in recent years."

"That is all consistent with what I learned," mumbled Edward.

"What else have you learned?" asked Constance.

"Nothing good, I assure you. The British Empire has thus far failed to contain the New Granada Resistance. Queen Victoria herself has apparently gotten involved, initiating a change in priorities. Dismantling the Resistance is more important than individual lives."

"That seems unbalanced to me," said Constance. "Why would so much emphasis be placed on dismantling one group?"

"This particular Resistance group has disrupted resource acquisition across the entire region. Agricultural surpluses, lumber and rubber, mineral extraction; all reduced to nearly nothing."

"Because the colony has so much potential, the Queen personally weighed in with a policy decision." Constance paused and bit her lower lip. "Both sides seem willing to let an innocent young woman die."

Edward leaned back and blinked at his cousin. "That's very perceptive of you."

"You seemed surprised. I am capable of thinking deeply on subjects other than gadgets and the like."

"Yes, of course. I apologize," said Edward in a quiet, hurried tone.

"Knowing where Queen Victoria stands, I assume you were unable to convince anyone in Parliament or the military to throw their weight behind reopening the search."

"It's worse than that. People are afraid to talk at all. I had one officer tell me I should accept the honors associated with my sister's martyrdom," said Edward before falling silent while pacing the drawing room.

Constance allowed Edward's information to soak in while disassembling a broken thermometer and pressure gauge she brought with her.

"The two Freemasons working with the New Granada Resistance each carry a degree higher than twenty," said Constance. "They must be brilliant engineers. Actually, they are a married couple."

Edward jerked his head up and slowed his pacing. "A married couple working as Resistance engineers, both ranking members of the Rose Croix. That is unusual."

"The wife was born Ezmeralda DeCampino. Her family immigrated from Spain to Mexico a century ago, before the British seized control of Mexico. She grew up on a hacienda outside Puebla."

"What of the husband?" asked Edward.

"Francis Lefount. His father was an assessor for the French government. The family traveled throughout Mexico after the French and the Catholic Church expelled the British. The Lefounts became trapped in Mexico when the British inspired their own uprising and reclaimed the country."

"Sounds like the backstory for a ten-cent romance novel," said Edward.

"I suppose it does," said Constance, smirking. "They are both brilliant engineers and fell in love over their shared passion. They joined the Mexican Resistance together under Benito Juarez."

"Where did you learn all this?"

"A student in my cohort spent time in the Orient. At that time, the Lefounts had fled Mexico and were working for the Hong Kong Resistance. Apparently both the colonials and native population told wildly inventive stories about them."

Gertrude interrupted the conversation, plodding into the room and announcing the return of the lady of the house. Margaret entered wearing her heavy brown leather traveling corset. Her green and brown dress billowed behind her, despite Margaret's disdain for fluffy clothing. Gertrude gave an exasperated sigh and exited the room.

Edward met Margaret half way across the room and embraced his wife, then pushed back to talk to her: "What news from the Glasgow Resistance?"

Margaret caught his gaze for a moment, then turned away. "News was scarce and sobering."

"Please do not make us wait," said Constance.

"My sources say the New Granada Resistance is one of the most militant groups in the Empire," said Margaret. "Thousands of active soldiers. They are well supplied and regularly raid British outposts. Plus, they have at least one high-ranking Freemason working for them. They may've two; I'm uncertain."

"Our investigations produced similar information," said Constance. "Did you learn anything else?"

"My contacts believe Anne was taken for political leverage. She's a bargaining chip with little other value to the Resistance. They believe Anne might be released if the colonial government does not get in the way."

"That is absolute rubbish," said Constance.

Margaret ignored Constance and turned back to Edward. "Will any of your contacts pressure the Cartagena governor to find a diplomatic solution?"

Edward's face grew long and somber: "Working with Parliament and military officials was less than productive."

"I am so sorry," whispered Margaret, taking her husband's hand in both of hers.

"The New Granada Resistance was so successful at disrupting Her Majesty's plans for the region that the sole focus is now on dismantling them. Anyone caught in the crossfire, including Anne, are little more than martyrs for the cause." Edward trailed off as the mood of the room darkened.

"At this point I am convinced of two facts," said Constance, leaning her narrow frame against the wall. "The first is that Anne is likely alive and in the custody of the New Granada Resistance. The second is that the government will not rescue her."

Edward sighed and walked over to the roll top desk. He slid open a drawer and removed a piece of paper.

"This arrived today from my mother," he said, handing the piece of paper to his wife. "She has agreed to sign my sister's death certificate. There is a memorial service in Cartagena in two weeks. Mother wants me there to pay my respects."

A fire lit in Margaret's eyes: "We should all travel to Cartagena. Officially for the funeral, but really to find Anne and bring her home safely."

Edward lifted his head and looked at his wife. There was no spark in his eyes.

"Why not?" said Constance. Margaret smiled at the young woman. "Travel arrangements will not be difficult. Once there, we can contact the local government and plead our case. If that fails, perhaps Margaret's Resistance contacts in Glasgow or London can arrange for us negotiate directly with the New Granada Resistance."

Edward lifted his eyes and met his wife's gaze. He looked at Constance and saw hope plainly written on her face.

"Very well," he said, "we will travel to Cartagena to bring Anne home ourselves."

•   •   •   •   •

Constance returned to Oxford early the next morning. She wore the same brown leather corset, and tall, well-worn boots, her mousy-brown hair pulled tight behind her head. Soon the sun would rise high enough to project its heat through the tall windows and the bodies of students would warm the rooms. At this moment, though, the marble floors and hardwood wall panels sapped the warmth from Constance's body.

Constance walked at a brisk pace through the halls, the steel inside her boots echoing down the hallways, announcing her arrival to the empty building. She entered the lab shared with her cohort and Professor Lecturn, passing the tall stools and workstations and making her way to the walnut cabinets along the far wall. She jammed a small utility knife into the cabinet lock, twisted and pried up at an awkward angle, then wrenched it a quarter-turn counter-clockwise. The cabinet lock snapped open.

Constance pulled on the strap of a large leather bag hanging off a high shelf. It fell to the floor at her feet, hitting the ground with a heavy thud. She pulled the front flap open and examined the collection of tools. Satisfied, Constance closed the leather flap and cinched it tight with a strap and brass buckle.

The bag weighed almost as much as Constance. She took a deep breath and hoisted it on her shoulder, her skinny frame swaying under the weight like a drunken sailor. Remembering another item she wanted, Constance dropped the bag. This time it hit the hard floor with a dull clank that echoed to the lab door and back to her.

Constance leaned into a cubby inside the walnut cabinet and removed a rough-sawn wooden box. She lifted the lid, keeping one hand underneath to relieve the strain on the tiny hinges. Inside, resting on the threadbare velvet lining, lay the scorpion she and Professor Lecturn built together. Constance closed the lid and tucked the wooden box into the leather tool bag.

After re-locking the cabinet, Constance heaved the tool bag back over her shoulder and stumbled a half-step forward. She braced her narrow frame against the cabinet before proceeding, picking her way around the stools and tables. Constance halted a few steps from the lab door. Professor Lecturn stood in the doorway, blocking Constance's path forward.

"Miss Ventor," the professor said. "You look like a child caught with her hand in a cookie jar."

Constance paused to size up her mentor, "Good to see you, professor. I was just leaving."

"Ah. And may I ask where you are going with a set of the university's tools?"

"I have to borrow them for two or three weeks. My cousins need me, and I need the tools to help them."

Professor Lecturn relaxed his stance and stepped inside the door. He reached his right arm behind his head and scratched the back of his neck. The professor pulled out his pocket watch etched with the two-headed eagle of the Rose Croix. He checked the time, staring at the inside of the watch for a long minute.

"I am unaware of the problems your family is experiencing," said Lecturn, breaking his silence. "Therefore, I will not minimize the urgency of the situation. Having said that, the university views the removal of expensive tools for any reason as theft. Students have been expelled for less."

Constance dropped the bag to the floor and collapsed onto the closest stool, throwing her head down on the table and covering it with her arms. Professor Lecturn sighed and stepped over to her, reaching out a hand and patting her on the shoulder. Her narrow shoulders shuddered twice. Lecturn yanked back his hand when Constance jerked up and met her teacher's gaze. The elder searched the eyes of his young protege, noting her damp cheeks and splotchy skin.

Her mentor's compassion caused Constance's demeanor to soften. She told him the tragic tale of Anne's disappearance, words pouring from her and onto the table in a deluge. Lecturn listened without saying a word. When Constance finished, the professor picked up her ill-gotten tool bag and handed it to her.

"Go, and I will invent a story to explain the missing tool bag," said the professor. "Promise me you will be careful. Remember the lessons I taught you and remain confident in your abilities."

Professor Lecturn paused before adding: "Remember, the third toe on the left, rear paw. Good luck." He bent over and gave Constance a kiss on her forehead.

After she disappeared, Lecturn dropped down on a stool. A furry squirrel leapt up on the table and sat in front of him. Lecturn flipped open a concealed trapdoor on the critter's underbelly and removed a tiny roll of paper.

"It was clever of you to seek me out and inform me she was here," said the professor to his furry friend. He reloaded a new spool of paper and snapped the trap door closed. Harold Lecturn released an exhausted sigh into the chilly morning air and nudged the squirrel on its way.

•   •   •   •   •

Constance arrived at the Back Again Pub across from Heathrow Airfield at the designated time. The Back Again was not a seedy tavern full of sad, belligerent drunks at eleven in the morning. Instead Constance found the building packed wall-to-wall with families on holiday. Children ran wild, fueled by the excitement of their coming adventures and bribes of sweet treats. Mothers and nannies chased the youngsters, grabbing them by the collars and forcing them into straight-backed chairs whenever they could. Fathers sat hunched over their pints, pretending they were somewhere quiet.

Traveling merchants spoke in a variety of languages, flailing their arms and hands to accentuate a variety of dialects. Some merchants did not even notice the children plowing into their chairs. Others scolded and scowled, stopping conversations to track down errant parents.

After scanning the room, Constance spotted Edward and Margaret huddled in a dark corner in the rear of the establishment. Skulking in the shadows made the couple appear sinister, like amateur thieves doing a poor job of hiding in plain sight. Constance sighed and heaved the enormous tool bag onto her shoulder.

"Constance, what a relief to see you," said Margaret.

"Why do you say that?" asked Constance. She dropped her bag and it hit the ground hard.

"No reason," replied Margaret. "Edward booked us all passage on an airship to Cartagena."

"We depart on an airship called the *African Queen*," said Edward in a high pitched, excited voice. "We will be airborne for a day, then stay in Morocco overnight while the zeppelin refuels. Then we cross the Atlantic and land in Cartagena a week later."

Margaret stared at her husband. "You are supposed to be the calm, rational one. Get a hold of yourself." An awkward silence hung over their small corner table in the Back Again Pub.

"Is there something you two aren't telling me?" asked Constance.

"We sent word to Edward's mother that we were traveling to Cartagena for the funeral," said Margaret. "This morning, a colleague told Edward that the message set everyone in government pissing and moaning."

"What does that mean?" asked Constance.

"My mother informed Governor Pratt of our travel plans," said Edward. "Apparently, word reached him of my attempt to get Anne's investigation reopened. He contacted members of Parliament, setting off a string of memorandums throughout the London bureaucracy. Governor Pratt believes we will instigate trouble by rallying the colonials to search for Anne."

"We figured it was smart to get airborne before the authorities held us for questioning," said Margaret. "We were worried you would not make it in time after Edward wired you about the earlier flight."

Constance sat quietly for a minute, digesting the new information. "Whatever the situation, I will be happy to be airborne," she said. "When do we board?"

"Now," said Edward, checking his brass pocket watch.

• • • • •

Outside of the Back Again Pub Edward negotiated with a young taxi driver to take them to the *African Queen*. The scrawny boy loaded the bags into his steam-powered cab, tossing Constance's unwieldy leather bag onto the trolley like it was a sack of flour.

The airfield stretched before them as the taxi zigzagged towards their waiting dirigible at a dangerous speed. Row after row of black iron spires resembling Paris's Eiffel Tower dotted the green field like occupied squares of a chess board. A ten-minute walk separated any two towers on the grid.

"Why do you suppose the government is so concerned about us looking for Anne?" asked Constance. She grabbed hold of an aluminum bar running along the inside of the cab's door. The vehicle made a sharp left and the passengers tilted in their seats.

"Bloody wankers probably kidnapped her themselves," muttered Margaret.

"Why in the world would they do that?"

"No idea," said Margaret. Sitting behind Constance, she grabbed the same aluminum bar as the cab cut sharply to the left. "But I will find out."

"That idea is ridiculous," said Constance. "Everyone but you believe the New Granada Resistance is responsible for the kidnapping." Margaret did not reply, leaving Constance to listen to the cab driver's tour.

"The London bureaucracy oversaw the building of the Great Western Aerodrome," said the skinny cabbie. "Heathrow was a brilliant choice, being twenty-kilometers out of London."

The driver rambled on, since part of his job description was to fill the silence with bits and pieces of information about his airfield. Constance looked back and found Margaret rubbing the back of an ill-looking Edward. Every time the driver dodged and darted and skidded to a stop, Edward turned a shade greener.

"There are a hundred large spires for docking commercial airships. Twice as many smaller spires for private dirigibles and military transports. The designers of this place were bloody brilliant. You know this was the first aerodrome with iron spires modeled after the Eiffel Tower? Now they are across the globe." As the cabbie rattled on, only Constance bothered to feign interest.

The motor cart spewed steam and soot, leaving a smoky trail of breadcrumbs. The driver whipped around airfield employees loading coal and peat onto airships. He maneuvered through lines of passengers trudging across fields in straggling lines. The taxi passed a large motorized carriage hauling passenger luggage to the Back Again Pub.

"Bloody hell, I hate those blokes," said the driver. "Think they run the place."

"Are we almost there?" asked Margaret, watching her husband's face change shades with every swerve.

"Yes ma'am, we are getting close. The airfield covers over twenty square kilometers of earth, you know. You can see the iron spires form a neat grid when you take off."

The cabbie continued rambling on for another ten minutes, dodging and swerving around obstacles, tearing new wheel-ruts in the grassy Heathrow fields.

"We are here," said the cab driver, slamming the brakes and grinding the vehicle's wheels into the damp dirt. Edward fell out of the door and landed on his hands and knees, losing his lunch on the wet grass. The driver unloaded their luggage beside the lift running up the length of the iron spire.

Edward stood up and composed himself, taking careful inventory of each one of his body parts. "Thank you," he said in a hoarse whisper, handing the boy eightpence.

The trio stood on the ground staring up at the airship. A modest one hundred meters long with light-weight aluminum girders crisscrossing the giant black balloon. The undercarriage looked small from the ground, covered in glass windows and hanging off the balloon. Painted in giant letters was the name *African Queen* beside the logo of the East India Company, the letters *E.I.C.* inside three intersecting crosses.

Without a final look back, Edward, Margaret and Constance walked to the lift that climbed up the iron spire to the zeppelin with a quick pace and heavy foot.

CHAPTER 6

Edward and Margaret sat at a round table in the zeppelin's dining room with a deck of cards. The couple played card games or trivia games or games of chance nearly every evening. A long trip in an airship presented an excellent opportunity to catch up after a busy week apart.

"How long until we arrive in Cartagena?" asked Margaret.

"We land in Tangier first. Day after tomorrow." Edward shuffled the deck. "Rummy?"

"Rummy is fine. Why are we landing in Tangier?"

"Routine stop to refuel."

"Arse," said Margaret, looking at her cards. The people at the next table sipping tea and nibbling sandwiches looked at her. Edward noticed; Margaret did not.

"The trip across the ocean is bloody long enough. Why are we stopping to refuel?"

"Because it is a long bloody trip and we need lots of bloody fuel." Edward picked up a card and played a trio of eights on the table. Margaret swore again. "You are rusty, dear." The subtle insult earned Edward a glare from Margaret. Her gaze wandered away from Edward and out the window behind him. The window was a wall of glass stretching floor to ceiling for the entire length of the room, aluminum girders spaced every ten meters.

"How many hours are we in Tangier?" Margaret set three cards of her own on the table.

"Overnight," answered Edward, playing a single card off Margaret's set.

"Arse." Margaret picked up the entire discard pile, adding another six cards to her hand. Edward smirked to himself, careful to keep a straight face.

"When I began my studies at Oxford, I traveled to London, stopping overnight in Tangier," said Edward. "It was years ago. I followed the recommendations of a nice couple I met regarding what sights to see and where to spend the night. Had a lovely time."

Margaret nodded, studying the cards in her hand and the ones on the table. Edward's hand was down to three while she held ten.

"I'm sure we will have a lovely time. Bit of a holiday, I suppose." She laid down a set of four cards. "I'm just eager to begin searching for Anne."

"I am eager as well, dear." Edward picked up another face-down card from the deck and discarded it immediately.

"How long until we arrive in Cartagena once we are back in the air?" Margaret picked up a card and played a pair in her hand off Edward's set. "I trust we are not stopping in Cuba to restock the kitchens."

Edward squirmed in his seat; Margaret was turning around the game.

"Four days." Edward picked up another card and set it on the discard pile.

"Bloody arse," said Margaret.

"Please, dear, language," said Edward, nodding towards the table beside their own.

Margaret glanced around her and tugged on her trademark brown leather corset to reveal more of her chest. Edward failed to suppress a smile at the incorrigible woman seated across from him.

Margaret picked up the next card in the deck and dropped the facade. She smiled and reveled in her victory, setting down the five remaining cards in her hand.

"I believe the hand is mine, dear." Edward swept up the cards to shuffle again.

•   •   •   •   •

Constance Ventor prowled the catwalks and engine rooms of the airship. Her inquisitive self would allow for nothing less. Coming around from behind a grouping of boilers, Constance bumped into a man twice her size.

"Bloody hell, watch yo'self," the giant bellowed. Constance tucked her chin in her chest and muttered an apology. She tried to squeeze past him without further conversation.

"You ain't one o' mine crew, is you?"

Constance froze, her feet locked in place on the metal grating. She muttered another apology and forced herself to keep walking.

"What? No, miss, stop right there."

Constance froze again. The airman walked around Constance to face her. He stood still, blocking her path and studying her face.

"What're you doin' here?"

"I am interested in engines," replied Constance. "I wanted to explore the ship."

"This ain't a place fo' a young woman unescorted. Some of these mechanisms get very hot. Burn you if'in you don't know what you're doin'."

"I know what I am doing," replied Constance.

The airman grunted. "Johnson," he yelled over Constance's shoulder. "Escort this young lady back to the promenade."

"I know what I'm doing," repeated Constance. "I am an engineering student at Oxford."

The airman grunted again, then stared at the young interloper. "I heard that they's accepting female students. Is you an Apprentice?"

Constance pulled her pocket watch from a pocket in her corset. She flashed a symbol of the Freemason's York Rite on the back of the watch, popping it open to display her status as Apprentice.

"What d'you wanna know?" asked the airman.

Constance smiled at the magic key in her hand before stashing it back in her pocket. She looked up at her fellow mechanic and Mason: "Everything."

• • • • •

Edward led the small parade through the streets of Tangier, pointing out the sights and sounds to his wife and his cousin: "The old city is to the north. That's the direction we are headed. Truly a sight worth seeing."

"I noticed it when we flew over," said Constance. "It looked intriguing."

Conversation became impossible as the trio worked their way through downtown. Sounds of Arabic vendors were all around, hawking their wares to tourists and locals. Spanish dialects diffused from clusters of Jewish and Catholic merchants.

"What beautiful wives," shouted an old man. "Buy them something pretty."

"I am not his wife," Constance yelled back.

"Oh," said the old merchant, drawing out the sound. "Good for you. Do not marry them if you do not have to."

"Let's go," muttered Edward, head down and face flushed red.

"The mosques are absolutely brilliant," said Margaret, stopping to stare at an ornate piece of architecture. Edward continued narrating the tour over the din of the city streets, focusing on the gilded religious buildings.

"Why has the Queen not mandated more colonies accept Christianity?" asked Constance.

"People fight harder to protect their faith than anything else," said Margaret.

"Instead the Anglican Church sends evangelicals to every corner of the Empire," said Edward.

"Bloody bores," muttered Margaret. "I cannot believe they ever actually convert anyone."

"Spiritual conquest through subtle undermining," said Constance. "How very British."

They continued their tour of the city, traversing narrow and winding streets paved with flat stones the color of mud; they climbed up and down hillsides lined with squat stone structures and waist-high, beige stone walls. After an hour, they found their way to the shoreline where

British citizens on holiday lay in droves, soaking up the Mediterranean sun. Local vendors patrolled stone walkways wearing steam-powered contraptions built from scraps. The tin suits did most of the heavy lifting, allowing the vendors to carry huge displays of trinkets and gizmos on their backs.

Smells of charred meats mixed with the salty air. Boisterous chefs pushed wooden carts with meats roasting over portable stovetops. They called out to tourists, English masked behind thick Arabic accents, claiming their kabobs were the best on the beach. Smoke and steam each hid each vendor behind a dense white cloud. Only the smells and sounds breached the clouds.

Margaret and Constance picked a cart and braved the wall of smoke. Edward hung back, shaking his head and mumbling how his stomach rarely tolerated foreign foods.

They sat in the sun on a low stone wall facing the sandy beach and ate. The conversation was light and airy, matching the warm Mediterranean breeze. The women picked at their goat and chicken kabobs, discussing grand adventures in foreign lands. They finished their supper as the sky changed colors over the Atlantic in anticipation of the autumn sunset.

A dark-skinned man draped in expensive red and brown fabrics presented himself. His traditional Moroccan Berber attire resembled a robe beneath an overcoat, with a belt cinched loosely around his waist.

The stranger spoke in perfect Queen's English behind black eyes: "Good afternoon Master Goulden, Mistress Goulden, Miss Ventor. Please allow me to introduce myself. I am Ahmed, a humble servant of Her Majesty." He bent at the waist in a deep bow, his eyes fixed on Edward.

Constance slipped backwards from her seat on the stone wall. Her knees still slung over the wall, she planted her hands on the ground and pushed herself back up on the wall.

"How do you know our names?"

"I know a great many things. I assure you that my intentions are honorable."

"It is a pleasure to meet you, sir," said Edward, bowing his head without standing.

"Who in the bloody hell are you?" asked Margaret. She rose to her feet and disposed of her kabob so smoothly no one noticed.

"I humbly beg your pardon, I did not wish to alarm you," replied the Arab.

"What is it that we can do for you?" asked Edward.

An evening wind whipped across the beach, tugging Ahmed's robes. He paused in the conversation long enough to straighten his clothing.

"I am but a humble messenger of the Queen. She wishes to confirm your intentions regarding your holiday in New Granada."

Edward furrowed his brow, studying the Arab as he struggled to adjust his billowing robes. "The three of us are traveling to Cartagena to attend my sister's funeral."

"That is good," replied Ahmed. "If I may be so bold as to inquire further, do you intend on renewing the search for your sister? I was informed she was executed by the local Resistance."

"We only plan to attend Anne's funeral," said Margaret, hips squared, hands hanging loose at her sides. Ahmed disregarded her and looked to Edward for confirmation. The wind blew hard once more, revealing a long, curved sword tucked between the layers of his robes.

"I assure you, we plan only to attend the funeral and see to the affairs of my family," said Edward.

"Ah, you have other family business in Cartagena," said Ahmed.

"My mother is now the sole surviving member of the family colonial estate."

Ahmed checked the time, flashing the pocket watch of a Freemason Apprentice. Constance was unable to spot either the symbol for the York Rite or the Rose Croix etched on the back. She did notice a half-dozen unusual gadgets concealed under Ahmed's billowing robes, beside the grotesque curved sword.

"On behalf of myself and the British Empire, I offer my sincerest condolences for your loss. I wish you safe travels on your most regrettable holiday." Ahmed bowed his head, more shallow this time, eyes up. Without dramatics, he turned and walked away towards downtown Tangier.

•   •   •   •   •

Constance made her way to the bottom floor of the hotel early the next day. The morning rush of guests checking out filled the voluminous stone room with a background din, broken by the occasional bellhop hollering for assistance. From the base of the stone staircase, Constance spotted Edward leaning over the front counter speaking with the hotel manager.

Every hotel employee wore a fez for the benefit of their patrons, the hotel manager's slipping forward several times while conversing with Edward. The manager was good at his job, answering Edward's questions while fielding problems from his employees.

Constance surveyed the room, noting each individual and group, the layout of the furniture, and every exit just as Margaret taught her. Spotting her friend standing beside a stone pillar near the main door, Constance heaved her bag of mechanic's tools on her shoulder and worked her way across the room.

"Edward's trying to get information from the hotel manager about our friend Ahmed. I spotted him this morning on the balcony below ours, working on some sort of gadget," said Margaret.

"Good morning to you, too," said Constance. "I slept great, thanks for asking. Must be the warm Mediterranean air."

Margaret's eyes shifted from the chaos at the front desk to Constance. "He is going to be a problem."

Constance sighed and dropped her bags. They hit the stone floor hard, the heavy clank drawing the attention of nearby guests.

"Why do you assume everyone who works for the British government is a bloody problem?"

Margaret held Constance's gaze, then averted her eyes back to Edward. He left the front desk and made his way across the room, trying to dodge bellhops and guests with little success.

"The manager claims to know nothing about our friend," said Edward. "He confirmed Ahmed checked in for one night. That's all the information he would share." Edward lifted a pair of suitcases at Margaret's feet. "Shall we go?"

· · · · ·

Edward, Margaret, and Constance took a steam-powered rickshaw from the hotel back to the Tangier airfield. The driver acted and drove remarkably similar to the young man that taxied them across the Heathrow Airfield two days earlier. Edward kept his breakfast down this time, spending the entire ride preaching about the health benefits of daily walks.

The rickshaw dropped them beside the iron spire docking the *African Queen*. They checked in with the zeppelin's ticket taker and carried their luggage onto the lift of the Eiffel Tower clone. When the lift reached the top, an eerie thump echoed from above, followed by the sound of metal scratching metal.

"That came from the top of the lift," Margaret whispered. "Someone is up there."

The lift door opened, revealing a steel cable bridge leading to the passenger entrance of the *African Queen*. The thumping above continued, rattling their cage.

"Both of you get off the lift and walk towards the ship. Chat, act natural."

"Margaret, dear," said Edward, "I do not like this situation. All three of us should board the ship and report this to the crew."

Margaret leveled her gaze at her husband: "Get out. Now."

Edward sighed, took Constance's arm, and walked out on the bridge. Margaret stood on her luggage and reached up to the trap door repairmen use. She turned the latch and let the door swing free, leaping off her bag and out onto the bridge. She crouched in an attack position and drew a pistol from somewhere on her person.

Another dull thump followed by a scratching sound echoed through the lift shaft, louder than last time. The cage rattled back and forth. Margaret climbed back on top of her bag and waved at the others to stay back. She jumped up and caught hold of the trapdoor frame, pulled herself up, and disappeared through the hatch.

Edward stared up through the hole in the ceiling, "Margaret, what's happening. Are you hurt?"

Margaret dangled her head down through the trapdoor. "Constance, I need you up here with me. Stand on the bag and I will give you a hand."

Constance followed Margaret's lead and climbed up into the elevator shaft. Her jaw dropped when she saw the squirrel tangled in the cables, flopping its body over and scratching at the lift's steel roof. The fur on the animal's hindquarters was torn from its body, revealing its thin metal skin.

Constance remembered Professor Lectern's unusual parting words. She found the third toe on the left rear paw, pushing it down until it gave a quiet click. Constance unwound the injured critter from its steel cable cage and passed it through the trapdoor to her cousin.

•   •   •   •   •

Her haul bursting with fuel pellets, the *African Queen* began its trek across the Atlantic Ocean. Lifting off from the iron spire took half the morning, the airship's ascent coordinated by the airfield's flight control tower. They picked up speed and headed out to sea once clear of the city.

Edward, Margaret, and Constance spent the afternoon in the zeppelin's main sitting room. The large glass walls provided passengers with panoramic landscape views. The trio stood and stared at the sights of the ancient city, the African coastline, and the Atlantic Ocean.

Opulent Louis XIV furniture littered the sitting room; passengers scattered about, whittling away hours lounging on sofas and chairs. A round-the-clock barkeep stood between a solid oak bar and glass shelves lined with crystal bottles. Travelers hung around the bar with a glass of wine or bourbon before the ship was even airborne.

"Once we are on the ground in Cartagena, we can take a cab to the family estate." Edward sat on a short French sofa with sculpted armrests. "The trip across the city is not far."

"Who lives at the estate now?" asked Margaret, sitting in the chair across from her cousin.

"My mother and my sister." Edward paused to reflect on those words. "Plus, any number of servants and caretakers. Mother always had a high turnover rate, so it is impossible to guess how many are currently employed."

"What are our plans after we have exchanged pleasantries with Lorraine?" Constance's head swiveled back to Margaret, like a spectator at a tennis match.

"Mother had extensive conversations with the local government and military commanders concerning Anne. I plan to use those contacts as a springboard into launching our investigation."

"I hope there is more to your plan than pressing individuals who have thus far failed to produce results," said Margaret.

"Yes, as a matter of fact, there is," said Edward. "But since you seem to know better than I, please tell us your plan."

"I apologize, Edward," said Margaret, sighing. "I'm not trying to tie your drawers in a knot. The prospect of dealing with bloated, self-righteous government officials is unappealing."

"Apology accepted," muttered Edward, as Constance's head swiveled back to him. "I plan to pursue the investigation that the military investigators failed to adequately conduct. And I intend to requisition government assistance whenever possible."

"I doubt working from the inside will yield any results," said Margaret.

"Because those on the inside have already conceded defeat?"

"Because I believe that the colonial government is at least partially responsible for Anne's disappearance," replied Margaret.

"That's absurd," chimed in Constance.

"Why is it absurd?"

"The New Granada Resistance claimed responsibility," replied Constance. "They sent a ransom note and everything."

"You believe that's the entire story?" asked Margaret.

"Why on God's green Earth would the British government kidnap its own colonist?"

"I am not saying that the British government kidnapped one of their own. I am only implying that everything is not as it appears."

"Bloody hell, Margaret," said Constance. "Why must every situation involve some sort of conspiracy on the part of the British government?"

"Because the British government does dastardly things, then lies about them."

"Please," said Edward, interrupting the discord. "I plan on exploring every avenue possible. I also want to say that starting the investigation with preconceived ideas may hinder our search."

The conversation came to an awkward pause as both Margaret and Constance reflected on Edward's statement.

"I intend to contact the New Granada Resistance," said Margaret.

"Brilliant idea," replied Edward.

"I never met Aunt Lorraine," said Constance, changing the subject.

"It's been years since I have seen mother," said Edward. "She wrote me that Governor Pratt has been accommodating throughout this entire affair. Apparently, they have become quite close."

Constance snickered: "His name is Governor Pratt? I can hardly wait."

"What do you mean *they have become quite close*?" asked Margaret, ignoring Constance.

"I do not know, exactly. Manfred Pratt was given charge of Cartagena years ago when it was little more than a trading outpost. I remember father disliked dealing with him." Edward paused, lost for a moment in memories. "Regardless, mother believes Pratt is a good man and an asset to the colony."

"Really, his name is Pratt?"

"Constance, please. I hear the humor in his name, but it is not like the man is an over-grown, spoiled child."

"Of course not."

●   ●   ●   ●   ●

Constance sat in her stateroom, hunched over the small desk in the corner, her giant leather satchel of mechanic's tools strewn across the bed. There was nowhere else to spread them out in the cramped quarters.

"Professor Lecturn really is a strange fellow," said Constance. Like all good engineers, she talked to her projects as if they were alive and capable of conversing back. "Why would he send you after me? He knew

I was leaving England. What good is a spy devise that cannot report back to its owner?"

Constance's hands flew across the furry machine, her fingers and tools moving so fast they were hard to see. She fetched a new tool from her narrow bed.

"Even if he is an old sot, he is bloody brilliant." Constance pushed on a tin leg, mangled by the lift cables. Giving up on bending the distorted metal neatly back in place, she unscrewed a series of retaining bolts and removed the leg altogether.

"Design concept is straightforward. Simplistic even." Constance's hands picked up speed as she talked to her project. "A single camera lenses in your eye locks onto your target." With the leg repaired, Constance reattached it. "Dictating every word said on this." She opened the squirrel's underbelly and held up a tiny roll of paper to the light. "You sneaky little bastard," she said to the lifeless ball of fur. "A half-dozen extra rolls of paper stashed inside for extended time in the field."

With a twist and a snap and a quick exchange of tools, Constance moved up to the squirrel's metallic brain cavity. "Of course the old man put all decision-making functions in your head." A generous array of gears and springs and tiny copper circuitry packed the inside of the squirrel's head. "I have an idea, if you would not mind humoring me just a bit. Promise this will not hurt." Constance's hands moved deftly over the machine's brain. "I am adding a new function to your programming."

Constance closed up surgery. "Now when I raise this toe, you will come to life, same as before." She flipped over the squirrel and picked a toe on the front foot, separate from the toe Lecturn programmed to start up the critter. "But instead of following around one person, you will roam about looking for interesting conversations."

Constance finished work on the squirrel and raised the front toe. The critter came to life, scanning its surroundings before leaping off the desk.

"I think I will call you Walden," said Constance, smiling at her own cleverness and the irony of Christening a tiny fur ball Walden. She rubbed her eyes and checked her pocket watch for the first time in hours. Constance cracked her stateroom door and Walden scampered out into the dim yellow light of the hall.

CHAPTER 7

Edward and Margaret sat over a cup of tea and a deck of cards in the zeppelin's dining room. Margaret won the last two hands, running up her win total for the trip.

Edward sipped on his tea. "It's getting late, dear. One more hand before I turn in for the evening."

Margaret kept shuffling without breaking eye contact with her husband. "Are you going to bed because I am winning?"

"No, of course not," said Edward. "It is late, the sun has set, and I am tired." Margaret held her tongue and began dealing.

Without warning, Constance materialized in the empty seat to Edward's left. Her eyes darted around the room, refusing to settle on any one thing.

"Hello, cousin," said Edward, picking up his cards one at a time and arranging his hand. "Where have you been hiding yourself?"

"I spent the day in the engine room with the head engineer," said Constance. "He's a Mason and a very agreeable fellow. I learned quite a lot about practical engineering."

"What's wrong?" asked Margaret. Cards dealt, she picked up her own hand and rearranged the cards.

Constance's eyes continued darting around the room, like a fly uncertain where to land. She placed her hands flat on the table, then lifted them up and twisted her fingers together.

"He is on board and he is planning something dastardly," said Constance.

"What in the world are you talking about?"

"Ahmed, the man from Tangier." Edward and Margaret sat up straight at the mention of the swordsman's name. "He is on board this airship and is planning something."

"How do you know this?"

"Walden."

"I am sorry," said Edward, "but you will have to give us a bit more than that."

"Walden found him."

"Who is Walden?" asked Margaret, her tone flat.

"Walden is the squirrel we found on top of the lift."

"Your professor's mechanical spy?"

"Yes," said Constance. "I repaired him and reprogrammed him to creep about the ship and search for interesting conversations to record."

"Please tell me you did not turn it loose on our fellow passengers," said Edward.

Constance ignored her cousin, "I repaired Walden last night, then I spent today in the forward engine rooms. When I retired to my cabin a half-hour ago, Walden was there waiting for me. I pulled his tape and deciphered all the conversations he recorder. Then I came straight here."

"I believe you skipped a step, cousin," said Edward in a dry voice.

Margaret sat up straight, revolver drawn and resting unseen in her lap: "What did the tape say?"

"Walden wandered about and transcribed dozens of conversations." Constance leaned forward and whispered: "Guess who's having an adulterous affair with a handsome cabin boy?"

"Constance, please," snapped Edward, drawing judgmental stares from his fellow passengers. He lowered his voice, "Get on with the story about Ahmed."

"About two hours ago, Walden heard a man using our names. He was apparently speaking into a photophone, talking about us to someone not on board this ship."

"How is that possible?" asked Edward.

"A photophone allows two people to talk over long distances without the use of wires. A recent invention from a group of entrepreneurial engineers in the North American colonies."

"That must have been what I saw Ahmed putting together at the hotel," said Margaret.

"Perhaps," replied Constance.

"Do you know who Ahmed was talking with?" asked Margaret.

"Unfortunately, no," said Constance. "Photophone users wear a headset over their ears and speak into a devise that fits in the palm of their hand. Walden only recorded what Ahmed said, not what the person on the other side said."

"What did Ahmed say?"

"He believes we plan on searching for Anne in Cartagena. He said if we find her, it would spoil everything."

"Spoil what, I wonder," said Margaret.

"With the investigation called off, the New Granada Resistance could extort whatever price they want from my mother," said Edward, staring down at the table.

"I thought Ahmed worked for Queen Victoria," said Margaret.

"If he works for the Queen, then the government is responsible for Anne's kidnapping," replied Edward in a droll voice.

"That is more than a little unlikely," said Constance.

"Why is it unlikely that the government did something terrible?" asked Margaret.

"Seriously, dear," said Edward, sighing. "The Resistance kidnapped my sister." Margaret huffed and crossed her arms but did not argue.

"Ahmed said he plans to neutralize us," interrupted Constance. "He's plans to drug us and put us on an airship back to London."

After a couple of minutes Constance disrupted the silence she triggered. "What are we going to do?"

"Do you know which room Ahmed is staying in?" asked Margaret.

"Yes."

"Good." Margaret's eyes swept from her husband to her best friend. "We will sit here and play cards for the next several hours. We won't separate and we will stay in full view of the crew and passengers."

Edward and Constance nodded and acknowledged Margaret's authority in the moment of crisis.

"Late tonight, we'll break into Ahmed's room and incapacitate him with a blow to the head. We'll make it look like he tripped and fell. By the time he recovers, we'll be in Cartagena."

"I may have an easier way," said Constance. "I brought something with me, a gadget I built in school. It is a gear-driven assassin that looks like a scorpion. It injects its victim with whatever poison is loaded in its tail."

"Brilliant," said Edward. "But we do not want to kill him."

"I agree," said Margaret. "Can you load the stinger with a non-lethal poison?"

"Yes, of course," replied Constance.

"Good."

•　　•　　•　　•　　•

Edward, Margaret, and Constance played rummy in the dining room until the early morning hours. Thanks to a run of good luck and a sequence of astute plays, Constance took half the hands, easily beating the other two. At the agreed time, Margaret and Constance rose from the table.

"Do you really think it is a good idea for me to stay behind?" asked Edward.

"Yes, I do," replied Margaret. "Constance and I will return in thirty minutes, as we discussed."

Edward steadied himself and nodded. "All right, then, better get on with it."

Constance and Margaret made their way through the halls of the airship's sleeping quarters. At Constance's room, Margaret stayed in the hallway to stand watch. In under a minute, Constance returned and nodded to her accomplice. Without a word, Margaret led them through the halls to Ahmed's room.

Constance crouched in front of the cabin door and pulled a black scorpion from a matchbox hidden inside her corset. Margaret's breath stuck in her throat when she saw the grotesque automaton; the arachnid's features triggered the same flight or fight response as its biological cousin. Constance rotated the scorpion's head. It clicked and whirled and spun to life. She slipped it under the gap at the base of the door and the assassin vanished.

"If the scorpion has not completed its task in three minutes, it will shut itself off."

Margaret pulled out a pocket watch, moving her lips as she counted down the seconds. She snapped the watch shut and tucked it away: "That's three minutes."

Constance nodded and pulled a pair of pins from her hair to pick the door's lock. Margaret entered first with a two-shot pistol in her hand. A narrow bed stood in the center of the room, sheets pulled taut and neatly tucked under the mattress. An oak wardrobe shared the wall with the door; a simple desk and wooden chair occupied the far wall. There was just enough space between the pieces of furniture for a single person to navigate.

The scorpion lay on the bed's pillow, stinger full of venom and hanging like a metallic question mark over its back. Constance scooped it up and tucked the scorpion back in the matchbox. She turned back towards the door and ran into Margaret, knocking them both to the floor.

Before they could untangle themselves, the door slammed shut and a heavy mechanical sound filled the room. Metal parts ground against each other, punctuated by a hiss of steam.

A muffled, familiar Arabic accent called out from the hallway: "Goodbye, ladies."

•　　•　　•　　•　　•

Edward sat alone at the table in the dining room staring into his cup of icy tea. His only companions this late at night were two drunken men across the room. He dragged a silver tea egg through the cup of bitter brown water, eyes following the clock pendulum mounted beside the door.

After thirty minutes, Edward rose from his chair. Before he could leave the table, Ahmed appeared in the high-back chair to Edward's left.

"Good evening, Master Goulden. Please, sit."

Ahmed met Edward's shocked look with a smile and a rehearsed speech, delivered in immaculate Queen's English: "I am incredibly pleased to find you here. I would care to say we have much to discuss, as a conversation with you would undoubtedly prove fascinating. But alas, I am afraid we were done conversing before we began. You are resolute in your quest to find your dear sister, and I cannot allow that to happen."

Ahmed paused, his smile and polished vernacular never wavering. "Once again, Master Goulden, please do as you are told and sit down," said Ahmed. Edward sat.

"Right now, a weapon is aimed at you under the table. When I tell you, rise and walk through the exit on the far end of the room. If you yell for help, run, speak, or resist in any way, you will quickly find yourself dead."

Numb and unable to produce a single coherent thought, Edward nodded at his captor. When Ahmed told him to, Edward stood and walked from the room, followed by the Arab in the elegant robes.

•   •   •   •   •

Margaret kicked the knob off the stateroom door with her boot heel. She beat on the door with a brass lamp from on top of the wardrobe. Breathing hard and glistening with sweat, she struck the wooden door over and over with the heavy piece of metal, but it did not budge.

"What's wrong with this bloody door?" yelled Margaret.

"Ahmed attached a mechanical barricade to the other side," said Constance, examining the items on the bedside table. "We need half a million joules of energy to blast through."

"What does that mean?"

"We need half a stick of dynamite to blow out the lock. There's no other way to open it from this side." Constance dropped to her knees and peered underneath the bed.

"You would be surprised what you can put your boot through," replied Margaret. "Come over here and help me."

Constance ignored Margaret, instead dragging a woman's hatbox out from beneath the bed. "I think I know how to get through the door."

Margaret stopped banging on the door, "What are you talking about?"

"Ahmed left a bomb in this hatbox."

Margaret goose-stepped over to Constance and peered into the round box. Inside was an assortment of glass vials and copper wires, bolted together in a helter-skelter configuration.

"Can you disarm it?" asked Margaret.

"Possibly, but it would be dangerous. If I brush my hand against one of those copper spools, it might vibrate rapidly enough to detonate." Constance looked at the sealed door, then at her friend. "This bomb has more than enough blasting force to tear down the mechanical barricade. Move so I can drag it over to the door."

Constance wiped the sweat off her forehead after moving the hatbox up against the door. "We need a blast shield, or the bomb will tear us apart, too."

"Bullocks, Constance," said Margaret, as the hatbox began to rattle and shake on the floor. "Why didn't you start with that?"

"We need that blast shield right now," Constance shouted as the rattling grew louder.

Margaret crossed the room in three steps and shoved open the cabin's washroom door: "What about that?"

"There's no washroom in my cabin," said Constance. "I have to use the facilities down the hall. Do you and Edward have your own private washroom?"

Margaret stood over a cast iron bathtub resting on four squat legs in the middle of the room. "Help me tip this over."

"I have to share a washroom with ten other rooms. Some of them are the dirtiest young men I have ever met." Constance joined Margaret and the two of them began rocking the tub back and forth. "Worse than the dormitories at Oxford."

"Shut up and focus on the problem," said Margaret. "Drive your shoulder into it."

Together they heaved their collective weight against the tub, rocking its feet higher and higher off the floor. The tub's iron feet cracked and splintered the brittle ceramic tile every time it landed. With a final shove, the bathtub's plumbing ripped from the floor and it stood on its side. The girls scrabbled under the metal basin and pulled it down on top of them moments before the bomb detonated.

•   •   •   •   •

A tangled series of catwalks separated the *African Queen's* passenger compartments from the engines. Crew members crossed the outdoor iron grating on their way from their cabins to the engines they maintained. Apart from young lovers looking for a secluded haven, passengers rarely ventured out on the rickety bridges.

When Ahmed marched Edward out onto the catwalk, they found a couple experiencing a windy, wonderful world all to themselves. The Arab in billowing Kaftan robes led Edward to the lovers and picked the young man up by the back of his hair. Ahmed turned the dangling rogue to look him in the face and smiled a wicked smile. Ahmed dropped the young man and he scrambled towards the passenger compartment door. The young lover's companion bowed her head and hurried past the brutish Arab.

"Now, sir," said Ahmed, drawing a long, curved sword from somewhere under his robes. "It is time for us to conclude our business together." Edward backed up, eyes fixed on the dark sword, glimpsing brilliant silver as Ahmed moved through the moonlight. "How do you wish to proceed?"

Edward looked from the sword to the face above the billowing robes. "What do you mean?"

"Personally, I would prefer a man such as yourself to die with honor. If you have the courage, defend yourself by attacking my person. If you cannot summon the courage to do so, fling yourself over the railing and plummet to the sea."

Edward fixed his feet in place and locked eyes with his captor: "I choose neither option, sir."

Ahmed's smile sent shivers down Edward's spine. "Then I will mortally wound you before throwing your body over the railing. I assure you that is the worst option available to you."

In the face of certain death, Edward's train of thought finally remounted the rails. He remembered every lesson his wife gave him on facing down mortal danger. He had to stall.

"I wish to throw myself from the railing," said Edward in a steady voice.

Ahmed's smile fell and he sighed. "Very well. Please, proceed." He waved his sword towards the railing behind Edward.

"Before I do, I have questions. Surely it is of no consequence to humor a dying man?"

"Very well, sir. What do you wish to know?" replied Ahmed.

"What of my wife and cousin?"

"I regret to inform you they have already met their demise." Edward's knees failed him and he collapsed to the metal grate.

"While I sympathize with the plight of your family, this behavior is unbecoming of a gentleman. I insist you rise and make haste in joining the members of your family." Ahmed pointed his sword a breath away from Edward's throat.

Edward did not move except to lift his face towards the assassin. "Why, sir? Who ordered the deaths of my family? You claim to serve Her Majesty, but I fail to see what the British government hopes to achieve with our deaths."

"My orders were never to kill you. Rather, I was to divert you from arriving at your destination. When I discovered your cousin's treachery, I was forced to take more extreme actions."

"Who ordered you to stop us from arriving in Cartagena?" asked Edward. "What do they hope to gain?"

"That, sir, is a conversation for another day."

"Why will you not disclose the details of your assignment? I make this request at the hour of my death and I demand that you honor it, sir." The force with which Edward delivered his words caused Ahmed to take a step back and lower his sword.

"Finally, a bit of fighting spirit. Very well, I will answer your questions."

• • • • •

At that moment, the doorway from the passenger section of the zeppelin burst open, splintering the wood around the door latch. Margaret flew onto the catwalk, clutching a floor lamp from the dining room. The lamp was as tall as she and a formidable weapon.

Margaret wielded it like a martial arts master, closing the gap between herself and the stunned Ahmed in the blink of an eye. Stumbling backward, Ahmed caught Margaret's initial overhead thrust with his sword.

The duel ended there as Margaret swung the bottom of the lamp up, catching Ahmed behind his right knee. His feet flew up in the air and he fell backwards over the catwalk railing. Ahmed plummeted from the zeppelin and into the dense clouds below, his billowing Kaftan robes flapping all around him like a parachute tangled around itself.

Margaret leaned over and took her husband's hand, helping him up from the floor, escorting him in silence back inside the zeppelin.

CHAPTER 8

Cartagena

Eighteenth century London was not the glittering vision of riches immigrants imagine. Most came to London out of necessity. They did not have enough to eat, could not keep their families warm. Others came seeking a better life. London offered an opportunity for diligent workers and sharp minds to reach their potential. What they found was something vastly different. Crushing poverty forced most immigrants into a life of filth and obscurity, drunken opium stupors and prostitution, unchecked disease, and untimely death.

This was the London Douglas Tank found in the summer of 1749. Despite rejecting the vices of the big city, he burned through his pittance of coins in a shockingly short amount of time. After that, circumstances compelled Douglas to sleep in the gutters and beg for scraps while searching for work. He might have returned to his family and a truncated existence beneath the ground in Cumberland if he had a pound sterling for a seat on a stagecoach leaving town.

When the night seemed darkest, Douglas found gainful employment on the docks of the Thames. The work was laborious. Douglas toiled twelve hours a day, six days a week, lifting and hauling, loading and unloading cargo crates. Inspiration struck him one day while toiling away beside the Thames. From that moment on, the idea consumed his thoughts like dry lightning sparking a grass fire.

Douglas mastered the mechanics of the single-piston steam engine while pumping water out of mine shafts. He went to work designing a coal-burning, steam-powered, multi-piston engine, complete with the world's first crankshaft. He built models and prototypes from spare parts and scraps of metal scavenged from shipyards. He worked on his engine at night and in his precious free time. After fourteen months, countless setbacks, redrafted design flaws, and six prototypes destroyed by fire or explosion, Douglas succeeded.

Next Douglas assembled a robust, four-wheeled carriage, sturdy and slung low to the ground. He built a platform and a lifting mechanism on the front of the carriage using a complicated system of pulleys and levers. Last, he mounted the engine in the rear of the carriage and connected it to the axles and lift pulleys.

Douglas debuted his mechanized cargo loader one morning, driving it from an abandoned corner of a shipyard to his place of work on the docks. That day he completed the work of ten men, while his gawking and rubbernecking coworkers completed little themselves. Douglas went home that night with energy to spare and a spring in his step. The second morning Douglas drove his loading machine to the docks, he found a group of children with dirty faces and blackened fingernails waiting.

"Oye, mister," shouted a boy over the roar of the engine. "What is that thing?"

"Douglas Tank's Mechanical Loading Machine."

"Who's this here Douglas Tank?" asked a second boy.

"I am."

A brief murmur swept through the gaggle of children: "Can we drive on it?"

"This is a serious tool, built to do serious work."

"Does that mean no then?" Douglas looked at the pile of cargo crates waiting for him; the other dockworkers had graciously left the biggest and heaviest items for him to load.

"Wait 'til my shift is over," Douglas said to the children.

"Then you'll let us drive it?"

"No, but I will let you ride on the platform up front while I drive." The children responded with a murmur of approval before getting comfortable to wait patiently for the end of the day. Douglas kept his word after the sun set over London. He drove the children in groups of twos and threes along the docks of the Thames, letting them pull the levers to raise and lower the lift.

"It's really loud," said a little girl, palms clamped over her ears and scraggly pigtails as Douglas lifted her back down to the ground. "And it stinks."

"Can we ride again tomorrow?" asked an older boy.

"After work, same as today," replied Douglas. "That's it for now. Go home to your mums and dads."

A pair of shipping magnates waited and watched all evening while Douglas gave rides to the children, leaving their posh offices to see the miracle machine for themselves. After the last child left, Douglas sauntered over to talk to them.

"Quite a machine you have there," said one gentleman, nodding towards Douglas's carriage.

"Thank you, sir."

"Build that all by yourself, did you?"

"Yes, sir. I ran the water pumps in the Cumberland coal mines."

"I am sure that's relevant in some way, but for the life of me I cannot imagine how."

"Suppose you will expect a raise in pay now," said the second gentleman.

"Not necessarily, sir. But since the machine allows me to get more work done, I believe you should supply the coal it burns."

"Reasonable demand, I suppose."

"I would appreciate a place to leave the machine at night, and a chain and lock to secure it."

"Cheapside is not the neighborhood it used to be, eh?"

"No, sir, it's not," replied Douglas. "And finance repairs and improvements."

"You're pressing your luck, boy."

"Yes, sir."

Douglas left his now infamous Tank's Machine on the docks that night, secured to an iron girder with chains and a heavy lock. He took the security of his loader a step further and removed a small part from the engine so the machine would not run.

When a pair of thieves failed to steal Douglas's marvel a week later, they resorted to smashing the buggy's wooden planks and beating on the engine with iron bars. Douglas spent two weeks repairing his machine, sleeping underneath the buggy with a pair of pistols.

To deter future vandals, Douglas scrounged an assortment of discarded iron plates and bolted them to the outside of the carriage. Feeling whimsical, he mounted several non-functioning musket barrels. Douglas Tank's Mechanical Loading Machine resembled a futuristic weapon of war.

•   •   •   •   •

A deep red hue overshadowed the orange and yellow flames burning in the brick fireplace. The coals buried down low with tiny flames licking the air smoldered for days. The rain outside was no longer the deluge it was an hour earlier. By the standards of the South American jungle, it was a light rain.

Two dozen faces flickered in the dying light. Persons of different sizes and ages. Dark skin, pale, and mixed heritage. Most spoke Spanish, some with a German accent. A few spoke English, some with a French accent. Distinct indigenous dialects rounded out the din.

They were a group on the cusp of making an important decision. One side of the room came to a consensus amongst themselves and focused their attention on the group across from them.

A man with the dark skin of an African and facial features of a Native tribesman stood apart from the others. Everyone in the room was aware of his presence and watched him from the corner of their eyes. The room fell silent as Jose Tairona Marquez spoke.

"You have all heard that Governor Pratt rejected our ransom demands." Marquez's English was good despite the accent; his Spanish had the impeccable qualities of a man born in the northwest corner of South America. "*Mi compañeros*, there are two problems before this council. We will discuss both tonight."

Jose Marquez paused, drawing the last inattentive eyes and ears to him. "First is what to do with the young English woman. *Haciendas* around Cali are paying well for conscripted labor." He looked around the room at his brothers-in-arms, "Many of you believe this is what we should do."

A man with pale skin and fair hair spoke: "This is the best solution. Our only other options are to kill the girl or return her to Cartagena. I do not want to shed the blood of an innocent girl, but returning her would make us appear weak in the eyes of the British."

A Frenchman standing in the corner shifted positions against the wall. "Kidnapping the colonial girl means the British will come and try to burn our villages and homes. Her fate no longer matters."

"That is why we should sell her as an *Entienda*. She will be treated fairly as a plantation worker. And then she is away from here if the British come."

"The British will come, *monsieur*, I promise you," said the Frenchman. "They planned a day of reckoning for years. And without Ezmeralda, we stand a worse chance of defeating the *fis a putain*."

"If we treat her fairly, I am sure the British will be lenient if their soldiers find us."

"It does not matter," interrupted the Frenchman. "Once you stand apart from Queen Victoria, your homes, villages, families, everything you have is forfeit in their eyes."

"*Por favor*, Francis," said Jose Marquez. "There is no need to be so dramatic. Taking the young woman hostage made sense. We have exchanged prisoners with Manfred Pratt before. But keeping her here no longer makes sense. We must decide what to do with her now."

A rumble of approval rose from the congregation in the cramped and humid room.

"What if I return Anne Goulden to Cartagena instead of selling her as a laborer on an *Encomienda*?" General Marquez stood in the center of the room as a wave of anger swept away the dull din of approval.

"We will appear weak in the eyes of our enemy."

"The British will never again negotiate."

Marquez raised a hand and the room fell silent. "The second problem before this council concerns the British military. Our spies in Cartagena informed me that the military plans to enter the highlands and wipe us from the jungle."

"We have heard that for years," said another officer, "but the British never sent an army this far into the jungle. They have never found our base."

"Our spies in Cartagena warn that this time may be different," said Marquez.

The council again erupted from both sides of the fire. The small man with dark skin in the middle of the room grew silent as the arguments and anger flickered at the air like the dying fire.

CHAPTER 9

Edward and Margaret waited their turn in the queue to ride the lift down the iron spire. The *African Queen* docked in Cartagena two hours prior without incident. Constance appeared and cut in line behind Edward.

"Where were you hiding yourself for the last two days?" asked Margaret.

"Primary engine room, with my new engineering friend," replied Constance.

"What were you doing with this new friend?"

"He tutored me in commercial airship mechanics. Propulsion, navigation, steering, lift, all the inner workings of the steam engines." The queue moved as another group boarded the lift. "He's an excellent instructor."

"He's the head engineer, right?" asked Margaret.

"For the primary engine room. He works directly under the head engineer for the entire ship."

"Out of curiosity, what's his educational background?"

"No formal education. He joined a zeppelin crew when he was twelve shoveling coal into a hopper. He learned on the job and worked his way up. Quite a clever man, actually."

"Did you teach him anything new?" said Margaret with a snicker. "You are the most brilliant engineer I know."

"I helped him construct a workstation so he can repair broken parts in half the time." Constance paused and bit her lower lip. "The design of these ships is a bit inefficient. I hypothesized an engine overhaul process that would boost average speed by ten kilometers an hour while reducing fuel consumption by fifteen percent."

"Only you would propose redesigning a zeppelin that has served the East India Company well for decades."

"He plans to sit down with superiors tonight while the zeppelin is in dock. The proposed overhaul can be done before they leave as a sort of unofficial trial." Constance spoke straight-faced and matter of fact. She looked up at the others and the surprised expressions on their faces.

"Why are you both looking at me like that?"

"No reason," said Margaret.

"Most likely, you just earned your new friend a promotion," said Edward. "And perhaps changed the trajectory of commercial air travel."

"Bah, you two have no idea what you're talking about. All I did was collaborate with a fellow tinkerer. We spent time together doing what we love."

Constance stepped on the empty lift. Edward, Margaret, their luggage, and Constance's enormous tool bag left no room for any other passengers.

"What about you two?" asked Constance as the lift lurched downward. "What have you been doing since our encounter with you-know-who?"

Edward's face turned a pale gray. As the lift dropped, he almost left his lunch on top of the spire.

"We've hardly left our stateroom," said Margaret. "Edward's felt ill since the incident on the catwalk."

"I am sure I caught a minor virus of some sort while I was out on that catwalk," Edward muttered. Margaret and Constance said nothing.

"Like I said," said Margaret, "we stayed in our room." Margaret was quiet for a moment. "There is another thing Edward and I wanted to talk about."

Constance raised her eyebrows, "What's that?"

"The three of us have conflicting ideas about what happened to Anne, who is to blame, and how we should proceed."

"We certainly do," replied Constance. "First, you believe Ahmed worked for the Queen, which is an absolutely ridiculous idea."

"It's not ridiculous. Ahmed said he worked for the bloody British government."

"That makes no sense unless the British government is behind the kidnapping," said Constance. "Why would they do that?"

"I haven't the faintest idea why they would do that," replied Margaret. "But I'm sure Ahmed wasn't part of any Resistance."

"How can you possibly know that?"

"I just do," replied Margaret. "Ahmed was all wrong for the Resistance. His tactics were spot on for an agent of the Crown."

"You are a fool," said Constance. "Edward agrees with me."

"Please exclude me from your squabble," said Edward. "I agree with Constance that Ahmed was working with the Resistance, but I will never agree that Margaret is a fool."

"We're not achieving anything having this discussion again."

"I agree."

Margaret exhaled and continued, "We can all agree that we are walking into a dangerous situation. Anne is missing. Someone tried to kill us. If we hope to find Anne, we have to work together."

"I agree," muttered Constance.

"Then I propose we all approach this situation with an open mind," said Edward. "Our objective is the safe return of my sister, not to assign blame. We will conduct this investigation without bias or agenda."

"Agreed," said Margaret and Constance together as the lift came to a halt.

The doors opened and they stepped out to a floor of hard-packed mud and ground-down grasses that refused to die under the constant traffic. Constance was still inside the elevator, struggling to lift her giant bag onto her adolescent-sized shoulder. She stumbled out the lift and into the sun. Margaret caught her and braced her before she fell.

•   •   •   •   •

The colony of New Granada had a land mass half the size of Europe; Cartagena was home to its primary commercial airfield. The entire airfield had six iron spires, isolated along the Caribbean coastline northeast of the city. A small brick building with a corrugated iron roof sold tickets and handed out flight schedules.

A row of steam-powered taxis lined the dirt road in front of the building. Some transports-for-hire had two wheels, most had four. They all showed extensive repairs and retrofits with poorly fitting salvaged materials, hanging off the carriages in awkward ways.

"It reminds me of the airfield in Tangier," said Margaret. "But not as dry." She squinted at the dense, broad-leaf jungle plants encroaching on the patch of ground cleared for the airfield.

Edward led them to a waiting taxi with four oversized wheels and negotiated a fee for a ride. The driver took his time tying their bags to the steel platform lashed on the rear while the passengers took their seats.

The lethargic driver sprang to life after sitting behind the wheel, flipping switches and firing up the steam engine. He spoke broken English and loved to practice on his fares.

"I can drive thirty kilometers in one hour even though the roads are not so good. Mud and big holes is no problem." The driver smiled and looked at his fares; only Constance was listening. "She has a flint-firing steam engine," he said, patting the steering wheel like it was his child.

"Remarkable," muttered Constance, "the latest technology all the way out here."

As the vehicle plunged forward, Edward's stomach lurched with it. His face paled and Margaret rubbed his back.

"Where am I taking you?" asked the driver. His vehicle hit a weather-worn hole in the packed-earth road and launched a meter in the air.

"West of the Walled City, along the coast," replied Margaret. "The Goulden Family Estate."

"The Goulden family. Is that the family with the missing girl?"

Margaret confirmed the driver's suspicions; Constance gazed out of the open vehicle, soaking in the jungle scenery. Dense foliage lined the south side of the road with pockets cleared for small homesteads farms. Enormous ferns of endless varieties filled the gaps between trees and cast shadows over the grasses.

The driver continued rambling on about his vehicle's mechanics. Constance soon lost interest: he was often incorrect.

"I have often seen bamboo in books," said Constance as they sped past bamboo thickets towering ten meters over the road. "But they always show it growing in the Orient."

"I heard that from other Europeans," said the driver. "Bamboo is everywhere here. We use it for many things."

"What are they growing on those farms we just passed?"

"Plantains," replied the driver.

"What are plantains?" asked Constance.

"They are like bananas, only different."

"I had a banana once."

"Those are mango trees," said the driver, taking his eyes off the road. He pointed to the left and the cab swerved in that direction. "They are another fruit. Very sweet, very delicious." The driver corrected the swerve without returning his eyes to the road.

The taxi bounced over another hole in the pressed-mud earth. Edward gulped down air from the back seat.

Without warning, the taxi emerged from the jungle to the outskirts of Cartagena; the farms and jungle thickets replaced by city streets lined with houses and shops. Each structure connected to the next like European row houses. The plaster walls painted bright colors and roofs were covered with orange Spanish tiles.

"The Walled City is across the water," said the driver, pointing right and swerving left.

"Never thought I would see a purple house with yellow trim," muttered Constance.

The narrow road intersected with another and transitioned from dirt to paving bricks, momentarily easing the ride for Edward. Other mechanical vehicles sped past, swerving around the taxi as the driver dodged to the left and right in a helter-skelter, high-speed mess.

"Which side of the road do vehicles drive on here," asked Constance. "Left or right?"

"Yes," replied the driver, drawing uneasy stares from all three passengers.

Cafes and coffee shops lined the streets, outdoor tables and chairs sitting between the road and the restaurants. Half the homes had outdoor living space visible from the street. Some spaces hid themselves behind iron gates, others had only a roof and two walls. Shops displayed colorful clothing on shelves along the street, vendors with push carts sold fresh juice and fried meat concoctions.

As quickly as the cab entered Cartagena, it exited out the other side. The ocean was again visible to the right, the jungle springing up on the left.

The steam engine propelled the passengers for another twenty minutes, weaving back and forth across a road that itself weaved between bamboo thickets and sand bars. They passed colonial plantations as the engine began hissing and bucking. Each estate had a large, redbrick house, surrounded by broad expanses of fruit trees and lush cultivated fields the inhabitants could hardly contain.

Edward leaned forward and put his head between his knees. Margaret patted her husband's back, graceless in her role as caretaker.

The taxi came to an abrupt halt in front of wrought iron gates flanked by white stucco walls two meters tall. Iron rods jutted up from the top of the wall. Short trees with broad leaves, shiny and smooth like silk plants, poked out between the black rods. Stomped-down grass grew underneath the gate and between the flagstones on the road visible behind the gates, slowly prying the stones apart.

Edward stumbled out of the vehicle and hurried to a cluster of ferns at the base of the wall and vomited. Steam and black smoke and soot sputtered from the engine's overworked exhaust system. Margaret and Constance stepped from the cab to look through the bars. Edward regained his composure and returned to the group, handing the driver a couple of coins.

"We will walk up to the front door. Please meet us there with our luggage." Edward unlatched the black gates and swung both sides inward, letting the cabbie pass before closing them again.

"Why is the estate surrounded by tall walls with metal bars?" asked Constance.

"Theft," replied Edward. "The gates are locked at sundown." The group walked in silence up the flagstone driveway towards the manor.

"It looks the same as I remember it," said Margaret.

"I did not realize you had been here before," said Constance.

"Once, shortly before Edward and I wed in London."

"I attended your wedding in Glasgow," said Constance. "I do not remember Aunt Lorraine being there."

"She was unable to attend due to pressing business concerns," said Edward. Margaret mumbled something inaudible under her breath.

Constance changed the subject: "I visited here once as well. I attended Uncle William's funeral with my mother and father when I was young."

"I remember you coming," said Edward. "My mother begged your parents to accept the Queen's offer and move to Cartagena as colonials. She needed a lot of help after father died."

"I do not remember that, but I was very young," said Constance.

"Your parents refused. They were happy in Liverpool and saw no reason to change."

"I remember becoming fast friends with Anne on that trip."

"I know you two corresponded for several years," replied Edward. "When was the last time you wrote?"

"Not since I left home for Oxford," said Constance.

The group walked in silence for another minute, Edward breathing deeply and after the torturous ride. The thick, clean air weighed heavy with humidity under the midday sun. Despite their clothing clinging to their bodies, the group felt refreshed walking through the lush surroundings after so much time spent in cramped quarters on the zeppelin.

"How many acres were gifted to your family when they agreed to become colonials?" Constance asked.

"Five-hundred acres, plus capital for supplies and expenses," said Edward. "My father built our house, adding on more every year as we prospered."

"I only have a vague idea of how well your family fared," said Constance. "My mother told me it was from agriculture."

"That's only part of the story," said Margaret. "Displaced natives work the plantation for low wages. The family negotiates prices with exporters."

"What Margaret says is true, except that the natives do not have to work the plantations," said Edward. "They are free to stake out their own land and farm for themselves."

"Then why do they work for you?"

"Some farm for themselves. However, we pay our laborers more than most could earn on their own."

"Natives are forbidden from negotiating directly with exporters," said Margaret. "By law, contract negotiations must be done by a British citizen."

"Independent, native farmers typically sell their goods in Cartagena and feed the local population," said Edward. "Plantation produce is exported."

They emerged from the canopied road onto a wide clearing, paved with flagstones and accentuated by a small white fountain in the center. Beyond that was a wide, tiled staircase leading up to the main entrance of the manor. The tall double doors were wide open in the hot afternoon sun so the ocean wind could flush the stale heat from the corners of the house.

$$\bullet \quad \bullet \quad \bullet \quad \bullet \quad \bullet$$

Edward, Margaret, and Constance entered the house through the big double doors and startled a young woman cleaning the floors. She jumped to her feet before disappearing through another doorway to her right. Moments later, a dark-skinned man dressed in meticulous black tie and tails greeted them.

"Good afternoon, sir," he said to Edward. His thick Spanish accent made the words ring like a line from a song. "May I help you?"

"I am Edward Goulden. Please inform the lady of the manor that her son has arrived."

"Yes, sir," replied the steward with a shallow bow. "Allow me a moment to do so." He disappeared down the hallway towards the rear of the manor.

Edward turned towards Margaret. "He's new; mother never could keep help around for long."

They stood in the front entranceway, discussing everything they saw: the crystal chandelier, dark wood tables lining the hallway walls, tiled floors clean enough to eat off of.

"The gilded wallpaper is the same as the wallpaper in the hallway of your London house," said Constance.

"Mother likes to import goods from the Isles," said Edward. "Father always insisted on purchasing as much locally as possible."

Lorraine Goulden swept into the room, followed by the steward in black tie and tails. She was an attractive older woman, wearing an elegant if impractical black velvet dress with gold trim that reached her ankles. Her brown hair, streaked with thick strands of gray, was twisted and pinned on top of her head.

"Edward, my dear boy. I am so happy you came." Lorraine rushed forward and embraced her son. "I have not known what to do with myself these weeks after those savages murdered your dear little sister."

Lorraine released Edward from her suffocating hug and turned to Constance. "And Constance, my dear, I am so pleased you came to pay your respects to your dear departed cousin. She always thought so highly of you." Lorraine broke from Victorian protocol and wrapped up her niece in her arms. Releasing her, she stepped back, still holding Constance's hands. "Tell me, dear, how are your parents? I received a letter of condolence from your mother just two days ago."

"Both my mother and father are well. They asked me to offer their deepest sympathies."

"How considerate of them," said Lorraine. "Anne's death is truly a loss for the entire family. She was so young. A young man of proper family here in Cartagena recently professed his intentions."

Edward began coughing, struggling to regain his composure: "I am sorry; I choked on my breath."

"I told her it was for the best," continued Lorraine. "She should settle down and stop her ridiculous excursions across this godless countryside."

"What was Anne's opinion of the proposal?" asked Edward.

"You know your sister. She was always resistant to the things that were in her best interests. Still, I believe she was beginning to come around.

"And Margaret, so good to see you. How have you been?" Lorraine's greeting was cordial but lacking in warmth.

"As well as one can be in these trying times." Margaret's uncharacteristic display of Victorian politeness triggered a cough in Constance she struggled to control.

"Sorry," muttered Constance. "Something stuck in throat." Margaret glared at her.

"Please come inside. You can rest and refresh yourself while we converse." Lorraine turned to her steward. "We will take tea and biscuits in the drawing room. Direct the staff to prepare three bedrooms for our guests."

"Yes, madam."

"Edward and I are married now. We share a bed," said Margaret.

"Three bedrooms," repeated Lorraine to her steward. She hooked her son's elbow and led him down the hallway towards the rear of the house. "Manuel has been a welcome addition to the otherwise incompetent staff. His parents were born into slavery here in New Granada before Her Majesty outlawed the practice. Manuel's parents still live outside the city, though. It's as if they are afraid to join civilized society."

•   •   •   •   •

Edward and Lorraine sat next to each other on a sofa in the drawing room, engrossed in conversation. Margaret and Constance sipped tea across the room in a pair of high-back, uncomfortable chairs, discussing lighter affairs.

"I will never understand why you insist on a menial service position within Her Majesty's government," said Lorraine. She sat facing her son, holding his hands in her own. "You are so much better than that." She paused and looked down. "Although it does sound as if you have gained influence over some powerful individuals. Perhaps I should not be so quick to judge the decisions of my only son."

As the conversation turned towards Anne, Lorraine broke down and wept in her son's arms. He held her and said nothing as her tears flowed for a quarter-hour. Constance and Margaret remained engaged in quiet conversation, averting their eyes from the couple across the room.

"Eventually, the savages admitted they took my Anne. They sent a ransom letter demanding the immediate expulsion of British citizens from New Granada," said Lorraine. "Governor Pratt is certain the bloodthirsty bastards executed my daughter when he refused."

"Why is the governor so certain Anne was executed?" asked Edward.

Lorraine ignored the question, shifting the conversation. "The governor confided in me that six other young colonial women have been kidnapped from the Caribbean coastline in the past year. Each time they were ransomed for some small concession; most often the release of a member of the Resistance held in jail. The governor believes the mindless beasts grew bolder with each successful ransom." Lorraine sniffled and began to cry again.

"When the governor rejected the ransom, what was the response from the Resistance?" interrupted Margaret from across the room.

Lorraine glared at Margaret, "The Resistance never sent a formal response. Governor Pratt told me Queen Victoria herself weighed in. She relayed her condolences through the governor and demanded military intervention to end these acts of terror. The military is planning an offensive into the jungle. The commander of the Cartagena garrison is determined to stop Anne's fate from befalling another young woman."

Edward sighed and looked across the room without letting go of his mother's hands. "We are here to support you, mother. And to say goodbye to Anne as best we can."

The two conversations continued in quiet tones on opposite sides of the room. Edward and Lorraine locked in a long exchange involving lots of tears; Constance and Margaret engrossed in their own conversation over tea and biscuits.

"Aunt Lorraine seems upset at you. What did you do?"

"I married her son," replied Margaret, face stoic and voice flat. She nibbled on a biscuit.

"She really believes her daughter is dead," said Constance.

Margaret snorted as she sipped her tea, "Lorraine's role in life is to play the victim. This situation suits her."

"Seems a bit harsh; her heart is broken."

"Again, she is a willing victim of circumstance," replied Margaret. "Lorraine is at her finest when she can point a finger at those who hurt her."

Constance paused for a moment to reflect on Margaret's words. "It seems to me that you lie in judgment of Aunt Lorraine as well."

Margaret choked on her tea and glared at Constance, then softened her face. "Perhaps I should rethink my opinion of Lorraine."

"I believe you should."

"Always pushing me to be better than I am, aren't you," said Margaret. "To change the subject, now that I have heard Lorraine's story, I am more certain than ever that Anne is still alive."

"Why do you say that?"

"No Resistance movement anywhere would believe that the British would abandon an entire colony in exchange for a single kidnapped citizen. If there really is a ransom letter, I want to see it."

"I don't know," replied Constance. "The London Times ran several pieces last year highlighting foolish things various Resistance groups have done."

"Bullocks, Constance, don't sell me that dog."

"A month ago, the Times said a Resistance group destroyed a convoy carrying food and medicine to a village in Africa. Was that a lie?"

"No, not exactly," replied Margaret. "But I was led to believe the local Resistance commander was fed false information."

"But Resistance groups do make serious mistakes sometimes."

"Mistakes are made by both sides in any conflict," replied Margaret. "But kidnapping and killing a colonial is nothing but a waste of resources that pushes us farther away from our goal."

"We know that the New Granada Resistance did kidnap Anne."

"We do not know that for certain," snapped Margaret.

"Yes, we do. What we don't know is if Anne is still alive. By kidnapping a harmless teenage girl, the Resistance showed themselves to be savages and pirates. Their actions are not rational, and their goals are highly questionable." Margaret held Constance's stare, but did not respond to her words.

CHAPTER 10

Constance rose from bed early the next morning. She washed, dressed, and arrived downstairs ready to start the day. Margaret and Edward were already in the drawing room and greeted her when she entered.

The head steward, Manuel, entered the room wearing the same black tails he wore the previous day. "Breakfast is served on the outdoor patio."

"This is one of the most picturesque living spaces I have ever seen," said Constance as they stepped out on the patio.

Terra-cotta tiles blanketed a huge patch of earth. Clay pots full of black soil housed an herb garden that any European restaurateur would envy. Just beyond the tiled patio, dense rows of fruit trees stood low to the ground: wide leaf bananas and plantains, mangoes, and citrus. Towering avocado trees bearing fruit the size of melons towered over the fruit trees. Tropical flowers and bamboo groves decorated every nook and cranny visible.

Sitting in the center of the patio like a queen on her throne was Mistress Goulden. She sat alone at a wrought iron table with a milky glass top big enough to accommodate a dozen diners. Lorraine had a lite breakfast spread out in front of her: juice and tea and crumbly white pastries. A pair of servants stood at attention behind their employer.

"Good morning Edward, Constance, Margaret. Please forgive the casual setting, but I love to sit amongst the trees and flowers in the morning sun," Lorraine said.

Lorraine waved at the servants and they disappeared into the house. They reappeared a minute later carrying two pitchers of fruit juice, a plate of white crumbly cheese, baked breads, a pile of fried plantains, and a steaming pot of tea. The sweet smells of the fried foods pulled the travelers far from England and the boiled, heavy foods they were accustomed.

A young woman leaned over the table to address Constance, "*Chocolate con queso?*"

Constance looked to Edward, "I know what *chocolate* is, but what is she asking?"

"*Tres, por favor,*" Edward said to the kitchen maid.

"You speak Spanish?" asked Constance.

"Yes, although I am a bit rusty having lived on the Isles for so many years. I learned after our family emigrated when I was young."

"You don't sound rusty to me," said Margaret.

"Locals are incredibly prideful about their language," said Lorraine. "Pronounce a word incorrectly and they claim your Spanish hurts their ears."

"Most Britons can hardly speak English," said Margaret. "They get by."

"Mother is correct," said Edward. "I speak the language as little as possible while I am here because my accent is an embarrassment."

The servant returned with a tray carrying three steaming ceramic mugs. She set one down in front of each guest.

"Smells good," said Margaret, leaning over her mug.

"It's hot chocolate," said an excited Constance.

"It tastes different than usual."

"Local cocoa," said Edward into his mug. "*Con queso.*"

"Do not tease them, Edward," said Lorraine. She pointed at the tray of white crumbly cheese. "It is hot chocolate with cheese."

Margaret stared into her mug trying to see the bottom, while Constance stuck her finger in her cocoa. They each sipped the *chocolate con queso* again before nodding their approval and draining their mugs.

"Governor Pratt asked me to join him in Cartagena this morning to discuss the plans for Anne's funeral service," said Lorraine, nibbling on a round piece of bread that vaguely resembled a bagel. "The service will be a public affair. So many people in the city have expressed their condolences. If it is a public event, everyone in the city can pay their respects for a child who sacrificed her life for the cause."

"What cause is that?" asked Margaret. Edward broke into a coughing fit while sipping his juice. Constance reached over and smacked her cousin on the back to clear his throat.

"Really, Edward," said Lorraine, before turning her attention back to Margaret. "The cause, my dear, is bringing civilization to the barbaric corners of the world."

Manuel interrupted the conversation: "Madam, you wished to be informed when the nine o'clock hour approaches."

"Are the horses and carriage ready?" asked Lorraine without turning her head.

"Yes, madam."

"Very good." Lorraine turned towards her son. "I have to prepare myself for our trip into Cartagena. Please be prepared to leave at half past. After we meet with the governor, I have to stop by the office of Master Johannes."

"Master Johannes manages the estate's financial affairs since father passed," Edward said to Margaret and Constance. A reproachful look from his mother cut off his explanation. Lorraine stood and left without another word. The others stayed and enjoyed their meal.

• • • • •

"My William was shot and killed by savages in a foreign land. His amphibious craft failed during a beach assault. I was told the engine just stopped working from an unknown mechanical issue. He abandoned the vessel with his platoon thirty meters from shore. He never set foot on to the beach. Murdered by uncivilized, bloodthirsty Natives led by a group of Portuguese. Can you believe that? Portuguese."

Edward held his mother's hands as they bounced down the road towards Cartagena. "Father's death was a horrible event."

"And now, bloodthirsty savages have taken my Anne from me."

Margaret and Constance sighed at the same time. They were sitting next to each other, across from Edward and Lorraine. They each looked out separate windows at the crowded, colorful row houses of Cartagena. The road was so narrow that second-story balconies hung over the middle of the street.

"This is the first time in years I have ridden in a horse-drawn carriage," said Constance.

Lorraine did not pay any attention to her niece. "You simply cannot imagine how hard it has been, Edward. Losing Anne just a few short years after I lost William. How much more must our family give to the Empire? When will the uncivilized barbarians in this world understand we only mean to help them?"

Lorraine let out a dull wail. The other women in the carriage were noticeably uncomfortable at the emotional outpour, fidgeting in their seats, checking the time, and trying to focus on anything of interest outside the windows.

"All these buildings are either government administration or offices of British companies," said Constance, nodding towards the three-story buildings lining both sides of the street.

"How can you tell?" asked Margaret.

"Every building is painted a shade of brown."

"At least they are not all the same shade," replied Margaret.

"Too true."

"We've nearly arrived, madam," called the driver from the top of the carriage.

Lorraine straightened up in her seat, sniffed twice, and produced a small silk scarf hidden somewhere on her person. It took a mere minute for her to compose herself, dry her tears, and cover up the redness in her cheeks and swollen eyes.

The carriage turned left at a narrow intersection onto a road wide enough for one-way traffic only. They passed between tall, tan stucco buildings with wide windows and narrow wooden balconies overhead. The alley ended at a set of wrought iron gates, watched over by a pair of British soldiers standing at attention.

The carriage came to a stop and Mistress Goulden identified herself to the guards. Constance gave a slow whistle as the horses pulled their passengers down a gray-brick driveway, the square stones laid in a montage of spiral designs. Exotic trees and shrubs with blooming flowers as large as tea kettles lined the drive. The flora extended deep off both sides of the road, with small brick foot-paths disappearing into the foliage. The carriage pulled up to the driveway's final loop and the front doors of the three-story mansion. Centered in the loop was a stone fountain with a gray cherub spewing water.

A footman opened the carriage door and greeted them: "Mistress Goulden, a pleasure to see you again. The governor is expecting you. This must be your son, Master Goulden."

"Yes, thank you Sebastian. This is my son, Edward. His wife, Margaret, and my niece, Constance."

The footman greeted each member of the Goulden family as he helped them from the carriage. Sebastian led the party inside the mansion before turning them over to Private Doughty, the governor's personal guard and messenger.

Constance leaned over to Margaret and whispered, "How did my aunt commence with the weeping and gnashing of teeth, then pull herself together so quickly?"

"Practice."

● ● ● ● ●

Doughty led the small party through the mansion halls, narrating the tour through steep stairwells and long hallways with small doors packed close together. The paintings on the walls and rugs covering the tile floors reminded the travelers of home.

The private brought them to a set of propped-open mahogany doors on the third floor. Two members of Her Majesty's Armed Forces sat with their backs to the door. No one noticed the small party standing in the hall until Private Doughty rapped his knuckles on the wood. A man sitting behind a heavy desk motioned for the Gouldens to enter.

"Governor Pratt, sir," said the skinny young man. "Mistress Goulden is here, plus her son Edward and his wife Margaret. And Mistress Goulden's niece, Constance Ventor."

The two military men rose to their feet, standing tall, hands clasped behind their back. A lanky man stood and stepped out from behind the enormous mahogany desk. Despite his balding head and sweaty demeanor, he had an air of authority around him. Governor Pratt extended his right hand to Lorraine as he approached her.

"My dear Mistress Goulden," said Governor Pratt, taking Lorraine's hand in his own and bringing it to his lips. "I see you have brought your infamous son to us today."

Edward shook hands with the governor, "A pleasure to meet you, sir."

"Ah, and this must be young Constance," said Pratt, stopping in front of Margaret. He pulled her hand to his mouth while Margaret stood still, jaw hanging open. Constance snickered.

"My Lord, this is my niece Constance," interrupted Lorraine. She pulled Constance in front of the governor.

"My apologies," said the governor as Margaret yanked her hand back.

"Edward, Margaret, and Constance traveled here from London to pay their final respects to our dear, departed Anne," said Lorraine, seizing control of the pleasantries.

Margaret and Constance dispensed with any more hand kissing by giving a minimal, polite curtsy in their leather bodices and calf-length dresses. The governor devoured both with his eyes before turning back to Lorraine.

"Please allow me to introduce the commanders of the local regiment, Major Robert Ulperlip and Staff Lieutenant Lucius Vickers." Both men dipped their heads in a modest bow.

Major Ulperlip sounded a basic greeting, "Sir, ladies, a pleasure to meet you. My deepest condolences for your loss."

"Thank you. Your sympathies mean a great deal." Edward stepped forward and shook hands with the two military men. "We greatly appreciate your efforts to return my sister to us. If I correctly remember the reports I received in London, you were the lead investigator on the case."

"Yes, I was," replied Major Ulperlip in a voice solemn.

"My Lord," said Mistress Goulden, addressing the governor. "How are the plans for the memorial service progressing?"

"My lady, last time we met I mentioned many members of the community, both British and native, have expressed a desire to offer their condolences for your loss. After all, we are all citizens of the Empire. Whenever one suffers, we all feel the loss."

Lorraine interrupted the governor: "Oh, that is wonderful, my Lord. Cartagena was the only home Anne knew. I want everyone to show how much she was loved and how much she will be missed."

"The mood of the citizenry has seen a significant shift in recent weeks," said Major Ulperlip. "All the people, regardless of their ancestry, are frightened and calling for the monsters responsible to be brought to justice. We hope this memorial service will bring a measurable amount of calm to the city."

"We have organized a proper military escort to show respect as well as ensure the safety of all involved," said Lieutenant Vickers, twirling his mustache.

"Brilliant," said Pratt. "Before we further discuss the plans for the memorial service, would anyone care for a cup of tea? I just received a new automatic tea kettle, shipped from the motherland."

Pratt walked back behind his desk. He flipped a single switch on a flat copper plate wrapped in wires with a tiny fuel hopper bolted to the side. Latched to the top was a custom fitted teapot. After a minute, the kettle lid began rattling back and forth, shaking the desk and knocking pens and trinkets on the floor. Black oil pooled underneath the copper plate.

"Bloody hell, I forgot to add the water again," Pratt muttered.

"Sir, language," said Lorraine.

"That contraption does not even use oil. Where did the leak come from?" said Constance.

Major Ulperlip cleared his throat and spoke in a loud voice: "Sir, I really must excuse myself. Duty calls, you know. Lieutenant Vickers, you're with me."

"Yes, yes, of course," replied the governor, still distracted by his teapot. "I will be in touch about that other item I mentioned."

"Very good, sir."

The officers stood to leave; Margaret sidestepped in front of Ulperlip and blocked their path. "Edward and I would like a bit of your time to discuss the investigation into Anne's disappearance. When can we meet to review the case?"

If looks could kill, the daggers Lorraine shot at her daughter-in-law would have taken Margaret to the afterlife and back again. "Governor Pratt and Major Ulperlip spared no expense attempting to find my dear Anne. I wish you would trust them in their ability to do the job they are employed to do."

Margaret ignored the reprimand, "Sir, it is my understanding that you abandoned the search after just a week without any evidence of Anne's death."

"My dear," replied the major, "while I am happy to answer all of your questions, if you believe there is hope of finding Anne still alive, I am afraid there is none. Although I do not disparage you for your faith."

Edward spoke up before Margaret could reply: "Regardless, reviewing the case files would allow us to put Anne's memory properly to rest."

"Very well; most days I am on the regiment's primary base east of the city. Come by and I will open the case files to you."

"Thank you, sir. We will take you up on your offer very soon."

The major acknowledged Edward with a shallow bow before turning on his heels and leaving. Lieutenant Vickers followed. Governor Pratt sputtered for a moment, uncertain where to guide the conversation.

Lorraine seized the moment: "Edward, would you, Margaret, and Constance mind excusing yourselves? The grounds are open for citizens to explore during daylight hours. I would like to finalize the plans for Anne's services alone with the governor."

Edward looked down at his feet and mumbled, "Yes, of course, mother." Margaret and Constance followed Edward out of the office, down the stairs and through the French doors leading out to the courtyard.

•   •   •   •   •

Edward, Constance, and Margaret walked the grounds behind the governor's mansion, strolling with their chins down, lost in thought. Brightly colored birds squawked in the canopy overhead. The interwoven brick pathways led them through a display of dense native foliage with broad leaves and flat flowers.

Constance pulled a tarnished brass pocket watch she acquired on the *African Queen* from her pocket. She popped it open and examined the corroded hands, frozen in space and time. She put her left boot up on a bench and extracted a pair of screwdrivers the size of iron nails.

"What beautiful native birds," said Margaret.

"They are found in the wild jungles to the south. All these birds have had their wings clipped," Constance replied, the pocket watch already in a half dozen pieces.

"It has been years since I last met Governor Pratt," said Edward. "I must admit that I have little confidence in his handling of this situation."

"I agree," said Margaret. "The man is a buffoon. What do you propose we do first?"

"I want to start with Major Ulperlip at the garrison," said Edward. "He seems like a reasonable fellow, even if he is a bit too pragmatic. I want to fact-check his assumptions."

"All right," replied Margaret. "When should we go to the garrison?"

"No time like the present. I will leave a message for my mother that we left in a taxi. She would prefer to visit Master Johannes's office in private anyway."

Constance clasped the brass casing back on the watch and inserted a set of tiny screws to hold it together. She checked the time on the watch she strapped to her wrist with a short length of leather, set the time on the old pocket watch, and smiled as it started ticking.

Edward and Constance turned around and headed back towards the mansion.

"You two go hear what the major has to say," said Constance. "I have a couple ideas I want to investigate on my own. I will meet back at the family estate."

"Very well. Please be careful." Edward and Margaret headed up the brick path towards the mansion. Once they were out of sight, Constance dropped to one knee to feed a squirrel.

CHAPTER 11

The taxicab bobbed and weaved down the packed mud road, belching smoke and ash into the noonday air. The cab brushed the jungle thicket running along the left of the road. Brown banana leaves twice the size of dinner plates slapped the passengers in the face. The driver veered right, and the vehicle rubbed against a wall of bamboo.

The garrison was east of Cartagena, wedged between the Caribbean and the coastal road. A living wall of bamboo rising twenty meters in the air wrapped around three sides of the base. Soldiers with rifles slung across their backs manned the brick watchtowers, spaced at uneven intervals along the bamboo barrier.

When the taxi reached its destination five kilometers east of Cartagena, the driver slammed the brake pedal with both feet and cranked the steering rod left. The cab skidded to a stop, splattering mud across the road.

A rear door opened and Edward tumbled from the carriage. His face was the same gray-green hue as the moss-covered mud banks lining the road. Edward hiccupped and belched, taking deep breaths through his mouth like a drunk trying to keep down the pickled eggs eaten at the pub. He succeeded.

Margaret stepped out from the other side of the taxi, straightened her green skirt, and tugged her corset into place. She handed the driver a pair of coins.

"Please wait here for us," said Margaret. The driver agreed and she walked around the cab to check on her husband. Margaret hooked her elbow under his and helped him to his feet.

"Thank you," muttered Edward, swaying and burping. He took one final deep breath before walking with Margaret up to the main entrance of the garrison.

•　　•　　•　　•　　•

Edward and Margaret presented their identification papers to the guards: "We met with Major Ulperlip earlier today and he invited us to come by at our convenience."

"Yes, sir." The guard disappeared into the base with the paperwork, reappearing several minutes later. "Major Ulperlip will be here to meet you shortly. He requested that you wait."

"Do we have a choice?" asked Margaret.

"Yes, ma'am. Master Goulden's position in the British government allows him unescorted access to the base."

"Then we wish to enter the base unescorted," said Margaret.

The soldier turned to Edward: "Sir? Do you want to enter the base now or wait for the major?"

"We would like to enter the base now, private."

"Yes, sir. Please remain in the common areas. Do not cross any signposts into restricted areas. Major Ulperlip's office is in the northeast quadrant of the base. If you need assistance, ask someone in uniform."

Edward thanked the young soldier and entered the base with Margaret. To their left and right, soldiers in faded work attire hacked at the inside of the living bamboo wall with machetes.

"Brilliant fortifications," said Margaret. "It must be ten meters thick."

"I remember how much work it was to keep the jungle from encroaching on the house and fields at home. Father used to hire a team of locals twice a year to cut it back."

The couple strolled through the garrison, past platoons of soldiers marching and drilling in the midday sun. The hardened mud streets formed a neat checkerboard pattern of roads, each square occupied by a sizable brick building with a corrugated iron roof. Soldiers hustled in and out of doors labeled *Kitchen* or *Barracks or Mechanical.*

"I would have assumed that the military studied the architecture of the locals and built their living quarters in the same manner," said Margaret, squinting up at the sun. "It must be sweltering inside these buildings."

"I am surprised as well. We British are known for our flexibility and ability to adapt."

"You're usually not so cheeky," replied Margaret, glancing sideways at her husband.

Edward grunted as the couple continued to wind their way between brick buildings and hustling soldiers towards the shoreline. Twenty yards from the sand bar, the couple ran into a series of *Restricted Area* signs nailed to a row of palm trees. Edward stopped, but Margaret's eyes focused on the scene along the shore. A pair of soldiers standing guard tensed as Edward reached out and grabbed Margaret's shoulder to stop her from walking forward.

Towering over the beachhead were three massive pieces of artillery. Built from steel and brass, each gun barrel reached thirty meters into the air. Two of the guns stood at attention on iron turrets, pointing out at the horizon. The third gun tipped down, its barrel just north of parallel with the sand. On the sand and centered between the three spinning turrets was a brick watch tower taller than the guns themselves. Convoluted bundles of copper wire collected at the base of each gun and ran up the sides of the brick tower.

Margaret stood and stared at the heavy weaponry. After a minute of study, she seized the opportunity to educate an apathetic Edward.

"The guns fire a lead shell a full meter long. They are accurate up to five kilometers, particularly if the soldiers in the targeting towers have a clean line of sight. Therefore, they are most effective along a coastline such as this. These three cannons could repel an attack from an entire fleet of ships on the water or in the air."

"That is correct," said Major Ulperlip. He strode up to the couple, hands behind his back, each step covering a remarkable amount of distance. In a moment he stood in front of the *Restricted Area* signs, between Margaret and the guns.

"As you know, this is the primary garrison for Cartagena," said the major. "However, we have another six guns just like these, plus two watchtowers and a small barracks, positioned on Isla Tierrabomba, a sandbar offshore from the Walled City. Those guns guard the port and the city itself from foreign attack."

"How many men to operate one gun?" asked Margaret.

"Four on the ground, loading and prepping the cannon between rounds. All aiming and firing is done by a two-man team in the towers."

"What happens if the tower is destroyed?" asked Edward.

"The ground teams can aim and fire the cannons. Unfortunately, they are essentially firing blind. We have had limited success sinking flotillas at short range during drills aiming from the ground. But from the towers we are remarkably accurate; as you stated, up to five kilometers."

The group stood in silence as a soldier prepared to scale the cannon lying parallel with the ground. He wore the leather jumpsuit of a military mechanic. Dozens of canvas pockets were triple stitched into the leather, full of neatly organized metal tools that twinkled in the sun. Other pockets concealed an array of common trade materials, including lengths of copper wire, steel screws, adhesives, and bits of rubber tubing.

Margaret broke the silence, "Why not build redundant towers?"

"That idea occurred to us as well," said Major Ulperlip redirecting his gaze at Edward. "I submitted a requisition request to London six months ago for the materials. I have yet to receive a reply."

"I am sorry, sir," said Edward, "but that is not my department. We have a bureaucrat responsible for military requisitions from the South American colonies."

"Of course. However, my personal experiences with bureaucracies leads to me to believe that it could be your responsibility if you wanted it."

"Again, I am sorry," said Edward, enunciating every word. "But I cannot solve this problem for you." Margaret looked at her husband, amused at what an accomplished diplomat and liar he had become.

Major Ulperlip turned his attention back to the guns. The mechanic strapped on a backpack with four mechanical limbs protruding from its sides. The augmented arms scaled the gun barrel, reaching forward and grasping like the legs of a spider, dangling the mechanic's body beneath the weapon. The backpack was a bird's nest of plumbing and wiring; a compact steam engine powering the hydraulic arms. The mechanic stopped halfway up at a square steel box, a meter long and wrapped around the gun barrel.

"This morning during firing drills we noticed an anomaly in the recoil," said Major Ulperlip. "Accuracy suffered. That box houses a series of springs that function as shock absorbers designed to dull Loretta's kickback."

"Who is Loretta?" asked Edward.

"I apologize," said the major, chuckling. "The men often name the larger weapons and vehicles, same as the navy names its ships." He paused to gaze out at the cannons. "We name anything intricate enough to have operational quirks and therefore a personality."

"Major, would it be possible to sit down with you and review Anne's investigation at this time?" said Margaret. "My husband and I are anxious to find some answers."

"Yes, of course." Major Ulperlip squinted towards the ocean, scrutinizing the horizon. "The rain appears to still be hours away. Shall we retire to my office and out of this blasted sun?"

Margaret and Edward followed Major Ulperlip across the military compound, walking around several squads drilling in the humid afternoon sun. The major narrated the tour as they passed mess barracks and storage sheds.

"Up ahead is the tank depot. We house twenty-three steel plated tanks, although they are an outdated model. I am led to believe that a new model of armored vehicles recently went into production that excels in jungle combat." Major Ulperlip looked at Edward like a child at Christmas, wondering if his eccentric uncle brought him anything worthwhile.

"Are you implying that your tanks are not of much use in the New Granada jungles?" asked Margaret.

"Unfortunately, they are not. They would be indispensable on the streets of Cartagena. But in the jungles, at a certain density of trees and plant life, they become useless." Edward made a mental note that the

Cartagena garrison was incorrectly equipped; the compound should have less, not more.

"Behind the barracks on your left are our mechanics' workrooms, plus storage for tools and materials. Primary fuel dump is behind that, occupying a large section of the base. Most is ground and pressed wood pellets, harvested from the jungle and processed in Cartagena."

The major stopped in front of a brick building with a metal roof, identical on the outside to every other building. "I am accustomed to giving tours to government dignitaries, military brass, and that sort. My office takes up this entire building. I am the only one with a set of keys."

"Do you not trust your officers?" asked Edward.

"It is not a matter of trust. Most items in my office are inconsequential; however, there are sensitive materials in here that my officers have neither the need nor the security clearance to view."

"What about your second in command, Lieutenant Vickers?"

"Lieutenant Vickers purchased his commission some years ago, whereas I earned mine," said Ulperlip. "His transfer orders to this garrison were signed by Queen Victoria. Apparently, they are old chums."

"You're bloody joking," said Margaret. "Pull a few strings to turn his military career into a Caribbean holiday?" The major did not reply, instead picking through a heavy ring of brass keys.

"I have a second, locked room accessible only from the inside. That is where I keep all the garrison's files: Resistance activity, personnel reports, requisitions, and the like. I have an aide who assists with clerical duties twice a week." The major turned the lock and led them through the door. "It is one of the most secure rooms on this base."

Edward's reply stuck in his throat; Major Ulperlip valued paperwork.

•　　•　　•　　•　　•

The bare-bones office inside spoke to Major Ulperlip's personality. A functional desk with a square meter of surface area occupied the rear corner of the room. Built of native wood, the desk was simple yet well-built, the ends and drawers fit neatly together with small iron nails. On top sat tidy stacks of requisition forms, personnel requests, and communiqués.

To the right was a large wooden conference table. Margaret walked past the table to the steel and glass gun cabinet on the far wall. Inside, a shiny row of long-barreled rifles stood at attention. On a shelf above the rifles was an assortment of pistols, brass scopes, and cleaning tools. Margaret squared her shoulders in front of the case and exhaled a low whistle.

"Is that an XB-1000 oscillating targeting scope mounted on the Winchester?" asked Margaret.

Major Ulperlip smiled, "Your knowledge of firearms is commendable. I have an affinity for the latest in personal firearms technology. My particular passion is firing accuracy. I love the American guns, especially the Winchester. Simple, accurate, and never fail in the field."

Edward eyes fell on a large, detailed map of New Granada covering the brick wall beside the desk. He drifted towards it, stopping at a meter-wide Union Jack tacked to the wall. Underneath it was a collection of medals and accommodations, including the Victorian Cross and a handful of Distinguished Service Orders.

"You have had a remarkably distinguished career in Her Majesty's Armed Forces," said Edward.

"Thank you," replied Ulperlip, breaking from his conversation with Margaret.

"I see you were in the campaign to retake the Brazilian colony nine years ago," said Edward, studying a piece of parchment covered in sprawling calligraphy.

"Yes, I was. That campaign led to my post here in Cartagena." The major paused, "I was ordered to retake a strategic hill overlooking the ocean. I led my squad up that hill thirteen times before we succeeded."

"I lost my father in that campaign," said Edward. "My family was living in Cartagena and my father a decade retired from military service. When the Portuguese and Natives banded together and retook Brazil, Her Majesty's Forces were engaged in Southeast Asia. Thousands of South American colonials were conscripted."

Major Ulperlip's eyes glazed over and he stared through the visitors in his office. When he spoke, his voice came from far away; a whisper of a violent din from a storm on the horizon.

"We lost a lot of good men in that campaign. The charge up that hill cost the lives of over half my men."

"You seem like an honest man, major," said Margaret. "A soldier with integrity who always follows orders. I know that can be a rare thing in Her Majesty's Armed Forces."

Major Ulperlip's face hardened: "What is your point, ma'am?"

"You were given a respectable position here in Cartagena in accordance with your service record. A position where a man like yourself can be useful without being a liability."

"Bah," said the major, unhappy that the conversation turned so personal. "If they wanted to hide me away, why would they give me the command of a colonial garrison?" He sighed and the room transitioned into an awkward silence.

Major Ulperlip cleared his throat: "I believe you wanted to review the investigation into Anne's disappearance."

"Yes, sir."

The major unlocked the door behind his desk and stepped into a cavernous file room. He returned a minute later, locked the file room door, and dropped a thick folder on the conference table. Ulperlip sat at the head of the table and motioned for Edward and Margaret to join him. He started his story from the beginning, spreading out supporting documentation as he went.

The garrison was on high alert for several days prior to Anne's disappearance. Known Resistance members were spotted, armed and in conspicuous locations around Cartagena. On the fifth day, a message from the constable's office: a young colonial woman from was missing.

A hysterical Lorraine Goulden divulged that Anne often trekked through the jungle to a secluded beach front. She went there alone, often not returning till the next day.

"I did not realize your sister was so adventurous," said Margaret, interrupting the major's story.

"Lady Goulden did not know the exact location of Anne's beach, but described it in detail as Anne described it to her," said Ulperlip, ignoring the interruption. "We immediately sent a small team to find the beach, suspecting she may still be there, possibly injured and in need of assistance."

"That was sensible," said Edward.

"My team was unable to find the route through the jungle Anne took. However, they did locate the beach by taking a small boat along the coastline." The major flipped through the pages in front of him, pulling up the mission report from that venture. "On the beach, they found a pair of shoes that Lauren Goulden later identified as Anne's."

Major Ulperlip stopped his monolog and retrieved a wooden cigar box from the top drawer. The wilting paper label, embossed with a gold stamp and peeling off the box, said *Cubanos*.

"Cuban cigars? Fringe benefit of your post?" asked Margaret.

Major Ulperlip walked back to the table and set down the box. "I do keep several boxes of Cubans on hand; and yes, they are a benefit of my post." He unclasped the simple brass latch and lifted the lid. "But this box does not contain cigars."

Edward and Margaret leaned over the table to peer into the box.

"It looks like a squashed tarantula," said Margaret, squinting her eyes.

"Are those tiny copper gears I see inside the slit in its abdomen?" asked Edward.

"Yes, they are," replied Ulperlip. "This came back from the beach. The thing was coated in a sheer layer of oil. The soldier in charge had no idea what it was, so he dropped it off with one of the engineers here on base. He cleaned it up and studied it for hours, finally reporting that it was an unidentifiable spy contraption. Obviously not standard issue for Her Majesty's Armed Forces."

"That cannot be right," said Margaret.

"What do you mean?"

"It must have been a British spy contraption. That's the only story that makes sense."

"Actually, that story make no sense," said Ulperlip.

"Not if one of your own was behind the kidnapping," replied Margaret.

"Let's not engage in speculative arguments, dear," said Edward. "We are here to collect facts."

"Right," said the major, continuing his narrative. "We believe the devise was stalking Anne. She squished it, stepped on it, swatted it. Whatever she did, she disabled the devise. We found it on a log beside her shoes. There were signs of a struggle on that same spot. Broken branches, trampled plants, that sort of thing."

The major snapped the lid closed and moved to put the cigar box back in his drawer.

"Sir," said Edward. "Would you object if I took the tarantula and had my cousin examine it? She is quite an accomplished engineer and I would appreciate her opinion. Anything we discover we would share with you, of course."

The officer sat still for a moment considering the request. "I dislike the idea of handing over a unique piece of evidence to non-military personnel."

"I am a member of Her Majesty's government with a security clearance higher than your own."

"I may be inclined to part with this contraption if I was assured that future requisition requests I send to London are answered in the affirmative."

Edward did not hesitate: "I assure you that all reasonable requests will be fulfilled."

Major Ulperlip slid the cigar box across the table to Edward; it vanished into a fold in his clothing.

The major continued to tell his story. After the beach discoveries the investigation hit one dead end after another. A week later, the ransom note arrived.

"The letter demanded all British leave New Granada immediately or Anne Goulden would be killed," said Ulperlip.

"Absolute rubbish," muttered Margaret. Her husband silenced her with a hard glare.

"Where is the letter now?" asked Edward.

"Governor Pratt sent it to his superiors in London."

"You must have seen the letter before it was sent to London. What was your impression?" asked Margaret.

"I never eyes laid on it," replied Ulperlip.

"You oversaw the entire investigation. How is that possible?" asked Edward.

Ulperlip shrugged his shoulders, "A high-ranking London official demanded it sent immediately. The governor dispatched the letter within hours. I was not particularly concerned; our eyes and ears here in Cartagena confirmed that the Resistance sent the ransom letter."

"Why make such a ridiculous demand?" asked Margaret. "They must have known the British would not abandon New Granada to save the life of a single colonial."

Major Ulperlip shook his head, "I cannot answer that. To tell you the truth, the ransom demand made no sense to me neither."

"What happened next?" asked Edward in a hushed voice. He struggled to continue breathing while listening to the story.

"Three days later, I received orders from London to stop the investigation."

"That's it?" asked Margaret. "Was there an explanation?"

"I was to devote garrison resources towards dismantling the New Granada Resistance."

"Who signed the orders?" asked Edward.

"Some bloody bureaucrat in the London offices," replied Ulperlip. He walked back to his desk and dropped down into his chair, rooting around in the top drawer. He pulled out a thin, inexpensive cigar and lit it with a match before rejoining Edward and Margaret at the table.

"Not a lot I could do after receiving orders. Bloody hell, we knew the Resistance was responsible from the beginning. They have kidnapped colonials before, then offered them in exchange for their own captured members. But this was different; the demands were different. I had little recourse, having hit a dead end in the search."

"Are you certain she is dead?"

Major Ulperlip sighed and laid both hands on the table, interlacing his fingers and leaning forward. "Yes, unfortunately, I am," he said, keeping his eyes on the polished wood table. "I have years of experience dealing with the New Granada Resistance. Once we rejected the ransom, she would have become too substantial a liability to keep alive."

"Why not just release her?"

"Many Resistance movements in the outer colonies are extremely militant. They disrupt supply routes, ambush soldiers in the jungle, and seize raw materials marked for export."

"I fail to understand how that leads to the assumption that Anne was executed," said Edward, his voice an octave higher.

Major Ulperlip lifted his eyes from the table and stared at Edward. "Master Goulden, the New Granada Resistance is a violent, militant organization with a stated set of objectives. Releasing a hostage after a ransom demand is rejected results in a significant loss of credibility."

"The next time the Resistance make a demand based on a threat, it will be ignored," said Margaret. "But I believe the Resistance had more options than executing Anne or releasing her back to her family."

"It is true that there are other possibilities," replied Ulperlip. "The next most likely scenario is that Anne was sent to Popayán or Cali."

"Popayán?" asked Edward.

The major grunted, "I would have thought a man with your bureaucratic clearance level would know about the White City." Major Ulperlip walked over to the map of South America and the Caribbean covering the wall beside his desk.

"Here, in the mountains to the southwest, a thousand kilometers from Cartagena." The major pointed to a black dot on the map. "Three hundred years ago, the Spanish found a village of savages living around a ruined pyramid. They built a colonial town on the spot, inland from the Pacific coastline. It served as a trading hub and regional capital. The city became a religious center with white-washed cathedrals, statues of saints; Catholic propaganda used to convert Natives."

"Why would the Resistance send Anne there?"

"We believe that as many as 100,000 people live in Popayán. Women, children, families, elderly. People from Native tribes, freed African slaves, exiled Europeans. They live in poverty, farming the surrounding lands to survive."

"You still have not answered my question, sir. Why would the New Granada Resistance send Anne to Popayán?"

"Anne would be a forced laborer, most likely put to work on a plantation," replied Ulperlip. "Popayán declared itself a free city, operating inside New Granada, independent of British rule. Queen

Victoria has made no move towards integrating the city into the commonwealth because of their strategic location and defensive fortifications."

"Why not attempt to rescue Anne from Popayán?" asked Edward.

"It would be suicide for the military to try such a feat, assuming Anne was taken there and not executed. We would lose too many men. The only way into the city is by air. We would have to disable their anti-aircraft defenses, then put soldiers on the ground."

"Assuming Anne was not executed, why not attempt a rescue before they take her to Popayán?" asked Margaret.

"Again, it would be a suicide mission. Air assault, troops landing. But the biggest problem with that idea is that we do not know where the New Granada Resistance's primary base is."

Major Ulperlip sighed again, eyes dropping back down to the tabletop. "A half-dozen mid-sized assault zeppelins are en route to Cartagena as we speak, equipped with tracking and sensory equipment. These will accompany the zeppelins already here at the garrison in a search-and-destroy mission over the jungles to the south. Our goal is to ensure that Anne's fate does not befall another colonial by finding and neutralizing the New Granada Resistance's primary base. But a ground rescue is impossible. We could lose entire airships and their crews if we attempted landing to retrieve a person from the ground."

"Why are you telling us of your invasion plans?" asked Margaret. She glared at the major, a touch of annoyance in her voice.

"The air assault is public knowledge. The outcry after Anne's disappearance required Governor Pratt to announce Her Majesty's plans."

•　　•　　•　　•　　•

A deafening explosion rocked the walls of Major Ulperlip's office. Edward stood up and fell back over his chair. Margaret and the major shoved each other out the door and into the blinding afternoon sun. They spun around in circles in the street, searching for the source of the blast. A second explosion shook the ground, the blast's echo rattling their teeth.

Margaret sprinted away, followed closely by the major. Edward stood still, watching them turn a corner and disappear.

"Let the soldiers do their job," he muttered to himself. "Stay here. Stay safe." Looking around, Edward found himself alone as another explosion shook the ground. "If someone is attacking the garrison, being by myself is most definitely not safe," he said, scampering off in the direction his wife ran.

•　　•　　•　　•　　•

Edward caught up with Margaret and Major Ulperlip in a concealed alcove on the eastern edge of the base. In front of him was a sea of mangled, twisted iron spires. Black smoke burned the inside of his nose; fire crews raced about helter-skelter. Another explosion decimated a structure twenty meters from Edward and Margaret. The heat from the flames forced them to step back; the explosion's echo reverberated in their ear drums, drowning out everything else.

"Loretta," screamed the major. "Someone's firing her at us." He grabbed a sergeant by the collar, frozen with shock. "Get to the beach and stop the attack," he yelled, his face an inch from the officer's. Conditioned to respond, the soldier turned and signaled others to follow.

It was an airfield still under construction; a collection of completed iron towers stretching skyward, half-finished spires, stacks of iron, and dormant construction equipment. The airfield took eleven more direct shells from the enormous cannon on the beach. The shelling stopped as Ulperlip formed a second, haphazard group of soldiers into an assault squad.

Firemen extinguished the blazes one by one and the blistering heat dissipated. A young soldier reported back to Ulperlip: they secured all three cannons on the beach, but the attackers killed two soldiers before fleeing.

"Shut down the base. No one in or out without my explicit permission." Major Ulperlip hailed his chief engineer, who promptly marched over and saluted. "Damage assessment," he barked.

"My men are still suiting up, sir," replied the chief, nodding at a group of technicians donning full-body canvas jumpsuits, hydraulic spider legs, and face masks.

Margaret stood gazing out over the seven-acre airfield. Edward stood beside her, wrinkling his nose. The chemicals used to douse the flames made the airfield reek like a wet dog. The half-finished grid of iron spires reached a hundred meters into the sky; eight spires ran north and south, another eight east and west. An airfield of sixty-four spires under construction, half of the iron towers now bent and smoldering.

Margaret turned to Major Ulperlip: "Six new iron spires, major?"

Ulperlip pivoted, already red-faced, to confront the unwanted interlopers. He found the closest soldier and grabbed his arm, spinning the soldier until he faced the major.

"Private, escort these two off the base. See that they get into a taxi headed back to Cartagena."

"Yes, sir," replied the private with a sharp salute.

Margaret bowed her head to the major and fell in line behind the private. Edward stood, feet nailed to ground, ears ringing, eyes fixated on the scene of burning, mangled towers in front of him. The frustrated private almost knocked Edward to the ground trying to move him forward.

CHAPTER 12

Constance wandered the grounds of the governor's mansion to clear her head. She paced the brick pathways crisscrossing the manicured jungle, reveling in the salty smells of the ocean just a couple blocks away. As Constance rounded the mansion and headed towards the front gates, she spotted Lieutenant Vickers bounding down the front steps of the manor. He waved off the waiting carriages and military transports and left on foot through the estate's iron gates.

"Curious," muttered Constance. "I saw you leave an hour ago with Major Ulperlip." She followed the lieutenant's path down the drive and through the gates.

Vickers crisscrossed the streets of the Walled City, walking along the battlements in view of the ocean before turning south. He moved as if he were the only person on the busy streets. Vendors pushing carts hustled out of his path. Street dancers paused their performances; old men flattened their backs against brightly painted plaster walls.

Constance followed from a half a block away. She had more problems navigating the disorderly streets than her quarry. The thick dialects of the Caribbean mixed with crisp Castilian Spanish in the salty air. Vendors waved long toothpicks with slices of colorful fruit and glasses of salted juices at her. Steam-driven carriages barreled through the streets. Constance picked her way through, shaking her head at everyone that spoke to her.

Lieutenant Vickers worked his way through the streets, strolling across plazas and grassy parks in the middle of intersections, down wide boulevards and narrow alleys. He marched like a man with a purpose, head high and chest extended.

"How far is he going?" muttered Constance, stumbling as a child playing in the street barreled into her.

Vickers kept moving, winding past kids playing soccer on the paved stone streets and the overgrown trees of the Plaza de Fernandez Madrid. He stopped at a tiny cafe along the edge of the plaza and bought an espresso in a petite ceramic mug. The lieutenant pulled up a chair at a small table on the side of the street and sipped his coffee.

Constance sat on a park bench facing Vickers's back, panting and trying to catch her breath. "Bloody waste of time, that's what this is," she told the pigeons picking at the dirt around her feet.

Vickers finished his coffee and stood to leave. A burly native with sun-darkened skin and a woven palm-frond hat stumbled over an errant stone and fell over the table opposite the lieutenant. He shoved the table into the rising lieutenant, striking him in the thigh and sending Vickers tumbling to the ground. A pair of thick envelopes and several slips of paper fell from inside Vickers's shirt.

"*Mi siento, señor,*" said the clumsy native. "I am sorry." He hurried around the table to help the lieutenant to his feet and help gather the papers.

"You imbecile," bellowed Vickers slapping the short man across his unshaven face with a white glove. The lieutenant grabbed the crumpled pages from the man's hands while locals shuffled away.

Vickers stuffed the papers and envelopes back in his shirt and marched down the street. Curiosity renewed, Constance renewed her pursuit, following Vickers for another twenty minutes before he slipped into an alley between a pair of homes. One house was green and the other painted a bright, sunshine yellow. The alley was narrow enough for Constance to touch both walls at once. She ducked her head under the low terra-cotta eaves and picked her way over small piles of household trash. A brick wall blocked the end of the alley, three meters high and layered with crumbling stucco.

"Bloody brilliant, Constance," she mumbled to herself.

Constance turned on her heels and found herself looking down the barrel of a revolver. Lieutenant Vickers smirking at his trapped prey.

"If I may be so bold, Miss Ventor, what are you doing following me through the streets of Cartagena?"

Constance froze, feet glued to the ground, breath caught in her chest. "I was hoping to catch up with you and accompany you back to the garrison," said Constance, pushing through the shock to clear her head. "My cousin and his wife are probably already there."

Lieutenant Vickers stared at her for a long minute, considering her explanation. Deciding to play along, he lowered his gun and returned it to the holster.

"Of course. You will have to pardon me for being so jumpy." The lieutenant tugged on the ends of his uniform shirt. "Unfortunately, I am not going to the garrison at the moment. I have business inside the walled armaments that encircle the city." He nodded towards the old Spanish fortifications lining the beach front, over his shoulder and looming above the row houses across the road.

"Well, sir, then I thank you for your time. I will be on my way." Constance gulped a breath of air walked towards Vickers and the mouth of the alley.

The lieutenant grabbed her arm as she passed by him. "Cartagena is a dangerous city, Miss Ventor. Please find your way back home and stay there. I would hate to see tragedy befall a young lady as pretty as yourself."

Constance yanked her arm free and broke into a run. Back on the main street, she found the closest crowd and melted into it.

•　　•　　•　　•　　•

Constance wandered the top of the wall running along the waterfront. The walls ran for miles, rising several meters over the beach with stone bastions at every jetty. The fortifications protected Spain's original settlement from marauding pirates sailing the Caribbean. Constance paused and stared out over the ocean, noting the six massive cannons mounted on the stone battlements of Isla Tierrabomba.

A street vendor with a throng of small children took pity on the confused-looking white woman and shoved a pair of fruit skewers into her hand. The fruit was so sweet Constance puckered her lips with her first bite. She muttered her gratitude and descended the ancient stone stairs to wander the streets without a destination in mind.

A few blocks later, paranoia crept over Constance; something was not right. She paused and leaned against a gas lamppost to survey the surrounding scene. Her mind worked at lightning pace, capturing an image of every face on the street. Constance pushed herself off the lamppost and walked on, stopping another block away to document every face on the street. A handful of individuals remained that were present two blocks earlier. She repeated the process, finding only a single man still walking with her. Just to be certain, Constance repeated the steps twice more; he was always half a block behind her.

Constance's stalker wore white linen pants and a button-down white shirt, dyed different shades by dried sweat. He was unshaven and short. He stared into a storefront, making conversation with the proprietor. Although his attire and demeanor were that of a European gentleman on holiday, his complexion gave away his Native heritage.

Constance stood still, watching the mystery man reflection's in a glass window of a row house. When his head turned away from her, Constance disappeared into an alley next to the house. She zig-zagged out the alley, across the street, and through another alley before sliding into the backseat of an idling taxi.

"The colonial estates west of the city," she said to the driver. "And please be quick about it."

The driver stayed mute as the carriage tore through the city streets, leaving a black cloud in its wake. The city seemed to spit the cab out across its own western border, the stone roads transforming to packed mud flanked by the encroaching jungle. After depositing his fare in front of the Goulden manor's iron gates, the cabbie fired up his carriage and spun it around, rocketing back the way he came.

Constance stood in front of the gates for a long time, wondering what her next move should be. "My investigation has not gone as expected," she said to herself, nibbling on her lower lip. "I need to take a different approach."

Constance dropped to one knee and unlatched a steel rod from the side of her boot. She gripped the top of the small bar and began twisting from the bottom. With each turn the bar grew, a razor-sharp blade rising from its interior, like a snake charmer drawing a viper from its basket. After a dozen twists, Constance locked the machete in place with the click of a button and held the blade up to study it in the sunlight.

"If I take this up to the house, I could strap a small engine to it and add a set of teeth that run along the edge," she mumbled. "A saw that cuts with a sharpened chain." Constance shook her head to dismiss the idea. "Perhaps I should stop dreaming up new inventions and focus on the investigation."

The reports given to Edward in London marked the coordinates of the beach where Anne vanished. Constance walked west, away from the black gates and away from Cartagena. She studied the foliage alongside the road as she walked, stopping to explore broken branches and flattened ferns, hacking at the jungle growth with her machete. Each time the trail went cold a few meters from the road. Two kilometers from the Goulden estate, Constance got lucky. Anne's trailhead was well concealed. Once Constance slashed through a cluster of ferns taller than herself, the path became clear. She rarely needed her machete after that.

Emerging from the jungle an hour later, Constance stumbled onto a barren strip of sand and stones that separated the rain forest from the ocean. She threw her hand over her eyes as the darkness of the jungle gave way to the brilliant late afternoon sun.

As Constance explored the private shoreline, the tide completed its daily ritual, recycling the sand and silt on the beach. The coastline was under a hundred meters long, with steep rocky cliffs bookending the alcove. Constance searched for clues to Anne's fate, scouring the sand, the smooth black stones, and decomposing vegetation left behind by the tides. Eventually she stopped and built a simple shelter from bamboo stalks and fallen palm fronds. She started a fire before the sun set.

•　　•　　•　　•　　•

The streets of Cartagena were quiet the night Constance slept on Anne's private beach. Locals stayed indoors rather than congregating under the city's gas lamps to dance and eat and celebrate the day.

The first raindrops fell an hour after sundown, bouncing off terra-cotta roof tiles and paving bricks in the roads. Broad leaves filled with water like cupped palms held under a slow faucet. Minutes after it started, the sky opened and a deluge of cool water poured down along the northern coastline. Rivulets of water cut grooves in jungle floors and sandy beaches; narrow streams formed in the streets, racing downhill and dragging the city's grime out to sea.

Edward stood behind a second-story bedroom window in his mother's house. He watched as trenches lined with stone that crisscrossed the estate overflowed with rainwater while moving silt away from the manor and to the fruiting trees. Margaret walked up behind her husband and embraced him; Edward barely noticed her.

On a beach not far away, the wind and rain and ocean waves created a constant din. It was too loud for Constance to hear herself speak, yet too monotonous to notice without concentrating. She could only see a short distance past the end of her lean-to shelter. Accustomed to the cold, foggy rains of England, Constance found the shelter surprisingly warm. The deluge of rain trapped the heavy air inside; it was so dense it was hard to breathe. Damp but comfortable, she fed another piece of wood to her small fire.

Hours after Constance fell as asleep, Margaret rose. The air in the bedroom she shared with Edward was damp and heavy. The rain had stopped, but water hung in the air, making her skin glisten and her hair curl into tiny twists.

Margaret carried her luggage out of the bedroom without a sound, slipping into the empty room next door. She bathed in a sink of cool water, brushing and dressing in a loose white shirt and well-worn brown leather corset. It was Margaret's corset for serious business; it had a dozen hidden pockets she loaded with thin knife blades and survival gear. After pulling on a pair of lightweight male breeches, she strapped an arsenal of small munitions to her legs.

Margaret sat down at the writing desk in the cold, hollow bedroom. She dug through empty drawers until she found paper, pen, and ink. After composing a note to Edward, Margaret folded the pages and sealed the letter with wax from the candle burning beside her. She dragged her fingernail through the soft, red wax to make the letter *M* and smirked at the dramatic touch.

Margaret crept downstairs and out to the stables, saddled the fastest horse in the barn and disappeared into the predawn glow of the jungle.

•   •   •   •   •

Constance returned to the Goulden estate late the following morning. Edward met her inside the front door, marching up the hall and waving a wrinkled sheet of paper over his head.

"She's gone," said Edward.

"Good morning to you too, cousin," said Constance, removing her coat and hanging it in the hallway.

"I swear, this time she will not get out alive."

"Slow down. Who are you talking about?"

"Who do you think?" Edward stood and stared at Constance, expecting her to understand.

"Just explain what happened," said Constance, punctuating the statement with a sigh. "From the beginning."

Edward shoved the page he held at his cousin. He spun around and marched back down the hall, calling for a servant to heat a tea kettle.

Constance sat down in a stiff Georgian chair by the front door and flattened the piece of paper against the wooden arm of the chair.

Dearest Edward,

I write this letter as I have decided to take another step towards our goal of returning Anne home safe. This journey is one I take on my own; and knowing how you are certain to disapprove and would attempt to stop me from going altogether, I will have already left by the time you read this letter.

My contacts in Glasgow secured a meeting with General Jose Marquez, the leader of the New Granada Resistance. I intend to travel into the jungles with members of their militia and plead with him for Anne's safe return. Despite what the colonial government claims, my sources say General Marquez is an honorable leader and a reasonable man.

I depart tonight as I intend to be back in Cartagena before the coming British air invasion. If all goes according to plan, I will return to Cartagena with Anne in ten days.

Yours truly,

Margaret

Constance folded the letter and creased it along its original lines. She closed her eyes, leaning her head against the back of the chair. In her mind she was back at Anne's beach, unraveling a complicated mystery while a warm fire evaporated the raindrops before they could touch her.

•   •   •   •   •

Constance found Edward pacing the gardens behind the house. "Margaret is the strongest person I have ever met," she said. "I truly believe she will return safe." Edward ignored her until she blocked his path and forced him to stop walking.

"I know." Edward sighed and dropped down on a stone bench. He stared at a gap between two trees for a minute before speaking again. "It was that strength that I fell in love with. She is so fierce and independent." He sighed again and looked up at the birds. "But she is also stubborn and foolish. Worst of all, she can be dangerously reckless. She views conflict with a devil-may-care attitude that scares me."

Constance sat beside Edward, "If you believe she is so strong, then you should trust her now."

"Perhaps," Edward said in a hushed voice. "But I have seen her rush in without thinking a situation through and people have gotten hurt. I also know that if Margaret told me before she left, I never would have let her go."

Constance leaned back and paused, searching for the right words for her next question: "Did you tell your mother about this?"

Edward's chin fell and he kicked a pebble at his feet. "I was so distraught when I first read the letter, and mother was right there asking what was wrong. What was I to do?" Constance nodded but said nothing further on the subject.

"Do you truly believe Margaret can find her way to the New Granada Resistance camp?" asked Edward. "The whole of the British Empire has failed to locate their base in the jungles."

"Margaret was once an important member of the Glasgow Resistance. If she says they found a way in, I do not doubt her."

"The Glasgow Resistance is little more than a propaganda machine; the New Granada Resistance is a genuine military operation."

"Regardless, if Margaret successfully contacts them, she might have an opportunity to plead for Anne's life."

"Are you suggesting that this was the correct course of action?"

"I am uncertain; but I do not think it's a horrible plan." They sat in silence for a minute until Constance asked: "What did you discover at the garrison?"

"Nothing, although I believe Margaret was finally convinced it was the Resistance that kidnapped Anne. Everything else we learned only complicated matters." Edward recounted his trip to visit Major Ulperlip, ending with the attack on the garrison's new airfield. "I returned with the mechanical tarantula they found on the beach for you to examine."

Edward produced the wooden cigar box and handed it to Constance. She lifted the lid and poked at the ball of thin, twisted metal, stained with oil, faded to the color of mud. "I assume it is a listening devise, similar to the squirrel Professor Lecturn sent after me."

"What else can you tell?"

Constance shrugged, "It's smashed rather well. I will disassemble it and see if I can discover anything useful." Constance put the box down and stood to stretch her legs.

"I am confused regarding Major Ulperlip," said Constance. "He appears to have made progress searching for Anne until they ordered him to stop. Furthermore, he allowed you to take a key piece of evidence to examine yourself. Yet he lied about the number of iron spires under construction. Do you believe Ulperlip was truthful with the facts of Anne's case, or was he deceitful in that area as well?"

"That's a great question," replied Edward.

•　　•　　•　　•　　•

Edward sat alone in the drawing room, staring out the window at the sweeping gardens on display behind his family's estate. Constance walked into the room and sat, thrusting several sheets of papers at her cousin. Edward looked down at her hands without taking the pages.

"What is that?" he asked, his voice far away.

"I dissected the tarantula you brought back from Major Ulperlip's office."

"And?"

"It's a spy devise like Ulperlip's engineers said. I believe it was linked to another devise, likely acting as its eyes and ears."

Edward looked away from the papers Constance still clutched. "I wonder if it will rain again tonight," he mumbled. After the previous night's storm, the humidity in the air was almost thick enough to see.

Margaret opened the cigar box and flipped the spider onto its back. With the legs disconnected and abdomen splayed open, it looked like a mischievous young boy had dissected a living spider.

"See here," said Constance, using a pair of tweezers to point at a tiny roll of stained paper in its belly. "An audio input recorder, next to a wireless communication node. The roll of paper records what it hears in the field. I cannot decipher it because it was soaked through with oil when the spider was crushed."

"I believe I'll get a cup of tea. Do you want one?"

"Edward," snapped Constance, raising her voice. "Pay attention. I was able to decipher the information held in the tarantula's input devise. The device's operator programmed it with this." She waved the sheets of paper at her cousin.

Edward took the pages from Constance and began reading. After the first page, he leafed through the final three handwritten sheets and looked back at Constance.

"I do not understand," he said. "It's just a list of names and places."

"Exactly," said Constance. "Pratt, Ulperlip, Vickers, plus a dozen other military officers here in Cartagena. After that, the rest of the names are wealthy British colonials, including your sister."

Edward looked back at the list and reread every name. "It's a list of potential targets."

"That's what I believe," said Constance. "Except for the first name on the list: Ezmeralda Lefount. She is one of the two Freemasons who are members of the New Granada Resistance."

"The rest of the names are obviously of the New Granada Resistance. Do you think Lefount fell out of favor with the Resistance leadership?"

"Perhaps," said Constance, biting her lower lip. "I think it is safe to conclude that everyone on this list may be in danger."

Edward rose and resumed staring out the window.

"It truly is a remarkable piece of engineering," said Constance. She closed the cigar box lid and set it on a table. "I have never seen so much functionality squeezed into so small a devise."

"I cannot bear sitting in this house and making no progress towards finding Anne," said Edward. He dropped back down on the couch, ran his fingers through his hair and slouched in his rumpled white shirt.

"Have you washed or changed your clothes since yesterday, cousin?"

Edward sighed: "I am far too worried that Margaret's full-frontal assault will result in her death."

"We already discussed this," replied Constance. "I trust Margaret to handle herself in any situation."

"I cannot lose both my sister and my wife."

"You will not lose them both."

"You did not see the preparations at the garrison yesterday. The military is organizing for a major operation; they plan to purge the Resistance from the colony. Even if Margaret navigates through the Resistance, she will likely be caught in the crossfire when the shooting starts."

"The odds are certainly not in her favor," Constance replied in a quiet voice.

Edward sat up on the uncomfortable couch: "You never told me how your investigation went yesterday."

"I spent the night on Anne's private beach."

"You mentioned that over lunch. What did you find there?"

"A few clues," said Constance with a sigh. "Probably nothing that will bring us closer to locating Anne."

"That's too bad." They sat in silence until Edward asked: "What else happened yesterday?"

Constance blinked both eyes and stared at Edward; in all the excitement she forgot to mention her encounter with Lieutenant Vickers.

"He pulled a revolver on you?" asked Edward, his jaw hanging open five minutes later.

"Yes, he did. And he warned me to be careful and stay at home. He said the city is not safe."

"He could have killed you."

"I doubt it. He obviously spotted me following him and wanted to scare me off."

"It sounds like much more than that."

"I am trained to solve problems relying on empirical evidence," said Constance, nibbling on her lower lip. "At this point, there is no evidence against Lieutenant Vickers. But there is something about him I find unsettling."

"What happened after you left Vickers?"

Constance returned to her tale, telling Edward about wandering Cartagena, taking the taxi, then finding Anne's hidden beach.

"What clues did you find there?" asked Edward.

"Several smudges of oil and grease on rocks and tree trunks. There's an area of heavily trodden vegetation, as if there had been a struggle."

Constance dug into a waist pocket of her corset. "And this." She held up a spindly mechanical contraption in her open palm, caked in mud and broken off something larger. "I was uncertain what it was, but now I am certain it broke off of the automated tarantula Ulperlip gave you."

"What else did you find on the beach?" Edward said, poking at the contents of his cousin's hand.

Constance sighed and dropped the hairy leg into the cigar box: "Claw marks in several trees. Unnaturally large and deep in the wood."

"Is it possible Anne was attacked by an animal?"

"I am not certain what to think. I flipped through reference materials in the upstairs library before lunch. The markings resemble those of a jaguar, but they are far too large and deep. What I found were not made by any known animal."

CHAPTER 13

Lorraine Goulden entered the drawing room of her own home like a bull through a gate: head down, fists balled, eyes locked on her son. A pair of servants followed in her wake.

"I sent a message to Governor Pratt earlier informing him of your wife's actions. He requested that we all come to his mansion this afternoon. I fear things with the governor are not as well as they once were."

Edward stared at his mother and her unimpressive rage. "I do not agree with Margaret's actions, but she is only trying to help Anne."

"Your sister is gone, taken from me by the same barbarians that took your father. Now your wife has gone off to make friends with those same murderers. Margaret dying at their hands may be our best option, lest she disrupt Her Majesty's plans to end the threat those savages pose."

"Really, Aunt Lorraine," said Constance, rising from her chair in the corner. "You go too far."

Lorraine dropped her head and took a slow breath. "I am so very sorry for you. But how many times, Edward? How many times did I warn you about that girl? I encouraged you to seek other options before marrying her. I have always feared Margaret will lead this family to ruin."

"Margaret is the only person on this entire continent acting on the facts," said Constance. "There is ample proof the Resistance kidnapped my cousin, and we know they attempted to ransom her. But that is where the facts stop. There is no proof she was executed, only assumptions and speculation. Right now, Margaret is attempting to parlay with the Resistance to spare Anne's life."

Lorraine squared her shoulders at Constance. "My dear, I expect that sort of attitude from Margaret, but not from my own blood. I will hear no more."

"Mother, please."

"Edward, your sister is dead, and her funeral is tomorrow," interrupted Lorraine. "Now please prepare yourself. We leave for Cartagena within the hour."

·   ·   ·   ·   ·

Edward and Constance arrived at the governor's mansion with Lorraine as the sun set. A groom took the horse and buggy around to the stables while a second servant ushered the Goulden family to Governor Pratt's office.

"Mistress Goulden," said the governor, rising from his chair. "It is always a pleasure to see you, even if our meetings continue to revolve around such dire circumstances." He stumbled around his desk, nearly knocking a short jumble of papers on the floor.

"Miss Ventor, a pleasure to see you as well." Constance cringed at the sound of Lieutenant Vickers's voice. "I hope you don't mind my being here. Since I am tasked with coordinating the upcoming military excursion over the jungle, Governor Pratt requested my presence." He smiled a thin, charming smile and twisted the end of his mustache.

"Lieutenant Vickers," said Lorraine, stepping to the trim military man in the immaculate uniform. "Did you know my young niece is a promising student at Oxford University? Can you believe she is still unattached?"

"Mother," exclaimed Edward.

"Quiet, dear," said Lorraine. "The fine lieutenant has obviously conversed with our young Constance on his own already."

Governor Pratt interrupted the exchange: "If you do not mind, I am very busy. I want to discuss the matter at hand."

"Yes, of course," replied Lorraine. "Please proceed."

"If I understand the message you sent this morning, Margaret Goulden disappeared from your estate sometime last night. The note she left indicated that she intends to contact the local Resistance in the hope of gaining passage to their primary camp. Is that correct?"

"Yes."

"Margaret also indicated in her letter that she believes Anne is still alive and being held by the Resistance at this camp. She intends to plead for Anne's safe return."

"How on Earth can someone rescue a dead woman?" Vickers interrupted.

"Lieutenant, please refrain from any further crass comments regarding my sister." The room fell silent as all eyes turned to the timid Edward.

Lorraine broke the silence: "Edward, mind your manners. The lieutenant is merely stating fact."

Governor Pratt cleared his throat, drawing the eyes of the room back to him. "Yes, well, while the lieutenant's choice of words may have left something to be desired, the unfortunate fact is that Anne Goulden is deceased."

"Sir," said Constance, taking her turn addressing the room, "I know Margaret's tactics leave much to be desired. However, I have great faith in her abilities. If, by some miracle, Anne is alive, Margaret will find her. If Anne is no longer among the living, then Margaret's actions may bring a certain measure of closure to this affair for Edward, Margaret, and myself."

"I think I finally understand the miscommunication between the governor's office and your family," said Lieutenant Vickers. "The New Granada Resistance have no similarities with Resistance movements on the British Isles. The Resistance here do not waste time holding public rallies. They do not distribute propaganda or give speeches on street corners. What they do, madam, is kill British citizens."

"I fail to see what the Resistance stands to gain by executing Anne," replied Constance.

"It is true that Anne is an innocent young girl," said Vickers. "Yet to the Resistance, she is the face of the enemy; a symbol of British superiority that does not deserve to live."

"Your entire argument relies on the notion that these people are animals, incapable of higher thought or basic human compassion."

"Constance, hold your tongue," said Lorraine. "This sort of debate is not suitable for a young woman."

Pratt sighed, "We have exchanged prisoners with the New Granada Resistance in the past. If they released Anne after we rejected their demands, they would look weak and lose a considerable amount of leverage in future negotiations."

The room fell silent once more as the gravity and truth of the governor's words weighed down on them. Edward sat in a chair across from Pratt's desk and rubbed his eyes with his palm.

"If you exchanged prisoners with the Resistance in the past, why would they change their ransom demands this time?" asked Constance. "They must have known the British would never abandon New Granada for the life of a single colonial girl."

"That puzzled us as well," said Lieutenant Vickers. "Our only explanations are conjecture."

"Such as?"

"Constance, that is enough," said Lorraine, grabbing hold of her niece's arm.

"Whether or not you or Edward or Margaret accept Anne's death is not the point of this meeting," said the governor. "In two days, Her Majesty's fleet of airships will arrive."

"We will begin our offensive three days from today," interrupted Vickers. "Our goal is to find the primary Resistance camp somewhere in the jungles to the south. We will attack with enough firepower to cripple their war machine."

Governor Pratt cleared his throat and sat down at his desk. "I asked you here today to inform you that if Margaret Goulden is at the enemy's base, she will be regarded as a hostile combatant and may die in the crossfire."

"You have my blessing to proceed, sir," whispered Lorraine, breaking the silence that followed Pratt's statement.

Edward lifted his head, his face a familiar shade of pale green. He swallowed twice and opened his mouth to speak but nothing came out.

• • • • •

In front of the governor's mansion, Edward turned to his mother. "Take the horse and carriage back home without us. Constance and I wish to walk around the city."

"Edward, wait," said Lorraine. Edward and Constance ignored her and walked down the front steps.

"I still cannot believe his name is Pratt," said Constance.

Edward looked at his cousin and snickered. "He really does fit his name."

The red flagstone drive ended at the iron gates. A vendor had wandered down the narrow road to sell fried treats to the guards. A small ball of fur popped out of the ferns beside the drive. It whirled and clicked before sitting motionless at Constance's feet. Edward shielded her from the guards as she knelt to scoop it up, tucking it under her arm before passing through the iron barriers and into the city.

• • • • •

Edward and Constance wandered the streets of Cartagena for hours. They ate dinner from street vendors: chicken soup with vegetables served in a paper cup, bread, and fried plantains with cheese. After eating, they walked the several kilometers back to the Goulden estate. Edward picked an overripe mango hanging low on a tree, peeling and eating as they walked down the dirt road in the dark.

"The soup is called *sancocho de gallina*," said Constance.

"Correct."

"The bread was *pandebono* and the bananas with cheese was *aborrajados*."

"Correct, except they were not bananas, they were plantains," replied Edward.

A young parlor maid met them just inside the front door. "Mistress Goulden requested that you wait in the drawing room when you arrive. She will join you shortly."

"No," replied Edward.

"*Perdóname*?" the maid replied.

"*Lo siento*," said Edward. "Please inform Mistress Goulden that myself and Miss Ventor will retire to our bedrooms for the evening. We do not wish to be disturbed." The young woman nodded, understanding his words but confused; no one denied a request from the lady of the house.

Edward and Constance proceeded up the stairs to Constance's bedroom, Edward locking the door as Constance set Professor Lecturn's furry contraption on the desk.

"Explain to me again what the squirrel does?" asked Edward.

"Walden is a spy devise," said Constance. She walked to the wardrobe and pulled her giant leather tool bag down from a shelf. Constance took a deep breath and heaved it up on her shoulder, then staggered across the room to the desk.

"I understand that. I am asking how it spies on people."

"Sounds waves change the air pressure as they travel," replied Constance, unlatching the heavy leather straps wrapped around her bag. "There is a membrane in Walden's torso sensitive enough to move with the changing air pressure. A pin attached to the membrane scratches the sound waves on waxed paper."

"I see," said Edward. "You realize that makes no sense at all."

"It really is not all that complicated," replied Constance. She sat at the desk with a tiny screwdriver, pulled back a small piece of fur, and began removing the cover from the squirrel's belly.

Edward walked over to the fireplace and stacked wood and kindling inside the cold brick cavity. He struck the flint resting on the mantle and nursed the flames with a gentle breath. Constance pulled a flexible tin cone from her bag of tricks. She plugged a copper wire into the squirrel's belly and the other end to the cone. She put her ear to the other end of the cone and concentrated on what she heard, scribbling every variation in her notebook.

After a half-hour, Constance put down the cone and looked at her cousin. "You need to read this."

Edward turned away from the fire and took the notebook, reading the pages by the flickering light while Constance repacked her leather tool bag. When he finished, Edward walked over to the desk and laid the pile of pages in a neat stack.

"Governor Pratt and Lieutenant Vickers do not know if Anne is alive."

"And they do not care," said Constance. "They seem preoccupied with the upcoming military offensive."

"Right," said Edward, slowly pacing back and forth from the desk to the fireplace. "What was most disturbing was the conversation regarding the funeral. They are planning something, but they did not say what."

"I can only assume by their implications that it is something awful."

"Even if Governor Pratt is an idiot," said Edward, "I thought I could trust him to do no deliberate harm." He turned back to stare into the twinkling flames in the brick fireplace.

The conversation paused, each lost in their own thoughts. "What do you make of this?" asked Constance, flipping to the last transcribed page. "Vickers said he has soldiers secretly following us."

"I do not know," said Edward.

"Do you think it will be a problem for Margaret?"

"Only for the poor soldier following her," replied Edward. "He never had a chance."

•　　•　　•　　•　　•

The funeral procession wound its way through the somber streets of Cartagena. Roads were slick with the previous night's rain; the moisture in the air left a visible haze hanging over the city. Some streets were barely wide enough for the military carriages to pass, while others circled grassy parks or broad cobblestone plazas decorated with stone statues of conquistadors. Natives and colonials lined the streets dressed in their finest black attire. They stood in front of shops and restaurants and homes, dark clothes accentuated against walls painted in greens and blues and oranges.

At Lorraine Goulden's insistence, each vehicle in the procession was a horse-drawn carriage, painted black and emblazoned with the royal family's coat of arms. Lorraine and Governor Pratt rode atop the first carriage. The governor smiled and waved to the crowd like this was a victory parade.

Edward and Constance sat inside the second carriage. Following them was a flat lorry, drawn by a team of six young horses, black haunches glinting in the wet morning air. Resting on the flatbed carriage was an elegant coffin of black wood, assembled with rows of shiny brass pins. A stylized, golden letter 'G' decorated the casket's top and sides. A half dozen colonial Scotsmen in traditional dress followed the lorry, playing bagpipes and marching in loose formation. Behind the pipers came row after row of marching soldiers and officers on horseback. The procession crawled through every street in the city, stopping traffic and halting the perpetual hum of the colony.

"Stay alert," said Edward in a hoarse whisper. "We do not know what the governor planned."

"Relax, cousin," replied Constance, staring out the carriage window. "No need to whisper in here."

Edward fidgeted with his hands while looking out the windows. "I only wish we knew more. If we had more time, we could plant that squirrel of yours right outside Vickers office."

"Walden," muttered Constance as she continued to gaze out the window. The carriage hit a water-filled pothole, the tall, spindly wheel dropping down and back up again. Muck splashed up and painted the surrounding stones brown.

"Blasted horse-drawn contraption. It's as if we still live in the days of the Neanderthals."

"What?" asked Edward.

"Neanderthals were primitive peoples who populated the Earth thousands of years of ago."

"I don't care about the bloody Neanderthals," said Edward. He sighed and changed the subject as the carriage clunked through another hidden hole full of brown water. "Why did you name Lecturn's gadget Walden?"

"I thought it an appropriate name. You have to admit; he has a rather cheeky personality." Bagpipe music drifted on the wind, around a corner and into the carriage.

"We are here," said Constance. She took a deep breath, inhaling the smells of the cut cemetery grass.

The horses came to a stop a minute later and a soldier in full dress uniform opened the carriage doors. Constance stopped halfway out to watch as eight soldiers hoisted the black wood coffin in the air and marched in a neat line across the grassy graveyard.

"An empty bloody coffin," she muttered, turning her head to look at Edward. "That fancy box costs more than a semester tuition at Oxford. Probably costs more than my father earns in a year as a courier running about Liverpool."

Edward nudged Constance forward. "There are hundreds of eyes on us." Opposite the carriages and beyond the initial layer of trees and ferns and stone crucifixes were rows of mourners standing in the morning sun.

"It appears that every single British colonial is here," said Edward.

"Ulperlip made attendance mandatory for all off-duty military personnel," said Constance, as they trudged across the lawn. "I did not expect so many natives to attend."

A pair of soldiers in dress uniforms ushered them to a pair of seats in the front row beside Lorraine and the governor. Other soldiers placed the ornate box representing Anne's mortal remains beside a pulpit of bamboo planks. A minister in black robes and a bright purple stole took his position and cleared his throat.

"Please bow your heads and join me in prayer to Almighty God." Hundreds of heads dipped as the priest prayed over the coffin. He delivered a brief, somber sermon, focusing on God's love for his children, His divine will, and the flawed choices of men.

"Without a doubt, Anne is basking in His warmth and His love, even as we mourn," said the priest, wrapping up his address. "Ashes to ashes, dust to dust." He stepped around to the front of the coffin and bowed his head to the governor. "Now, I believe Governor Pratt would like to say a few words."

The governor popped out of his seat and sauntered up to the podium, turning to dip his head towards the minister. "Thank you for the poignant words, vicar."

The priest muttered his thanks before scurrying off to a nearby empty chair. Manfred Pratt stood with his forearms resting on the podium, fingers gripping the front of the wooden frame, surveying the crowd.

"I met young Anne Goulden only once, at a gala event two years ago. That single introduction was enough to imprint on me what a beautiful, vibrant young woman Anne was. Lively, intelligent, inquisitive, and gracious in manner; I will never forget her face.

"Young and full of life, Anne Goulden trekked to a secluded beach near her family's estate to enjoy the beauty of this colony we call home. She went alone and without protection. Anne did not fear the evil that lurks in our jungles. Perhaps she did not believe it even existed."

Governor Pratt leaned over the pulpit and raised his voice. "But that evil is real. It attacks our soldiers and burns our farms. It haunts New Granada, crippling our colony and forcing us all to live in a state fear.

"Colonies around the world have Resistance movements. These people forfeit peace and prosperity for a misguided belief that self-rule is the path to happiness.

"These groups martyr themselves by forgoing benefits of living within the British Empire. Even though they all go without an education or medical care or basic amenities, most do not rob us of our daughters and sisters and mothers. They do not make a habit of kidnapping and murdering innocent young women who never committed a transgression against them. But the New Granada Resistance does."

Governor Pratt raised a fist in the air and brought it down hard on the podium. "But we will not abide," he shouted. "We will not sit idly by and watch as murderers and rapists and thieves ravage our homes and our families, laying waste to our peaceful, prosperous lives. The people responsible for Anne Goulden's death are unworthy of the air they breathe. They are not worthy of forgiveness, nor are they worthy of the grace of Our Lord."

Governor Pratt paused, scanned the crowd of mourners, and took a deep breath. "Our mothers and daughters, sisters and friends will continue to disappear until we strike back. In a few days I am sending an armada of airships from Her Majesty's Armed Forces into the jungle to seek the villainy that has plagued our colony. This armada will hunt down the evil men who took Anne Goulden from us, one at a time if necessary, and bring them to justice. Our soldiers will tear away the darkness these men hide in and bring them out into God's light where He may judge them. We will ensure that the people of New Granada can visit a beautiful beach without fear of losing their lives."

Governor Pratt finished his speech with a flourish, his hair falling over his flushed face, one fist raised back in the air. The crowd sat in stunned silence as the governor stepped out from behind the pulpit and took his seat.

The vicar stood to address the congregation in a practiced, somber tone. "Anne's brother, Edward, would like to say a few words about his sister." Edward walked up to the pulpit as the priest sat.

"Thank you," said Edward, glancing over the congregated mourners. "I thought about preparing a written eulogy for today, but opted instead to speak from the heart when the moment came." Edward paused again to clear his throat and stare down at his hands.

"If my sister Anne were here today, she would be delighted to see all of you here today. My sister was a loving person with a gentle soul. To see so many gathered for her would touch her heart. If my sister Anne were today, she would not want anyone to seek vengeance on her behalf. She would not want bloodshed in her name."

Edward stopped talking and stared as Constance leapt from her seat in the front row and raced past the empty coffin like her shoes were on fire. Edward spun around to watch his cousin dash towards a solitary figure on the far side of the cemetery, leaning against a tree and smoking a cigarette.

The man Constance charged was a burly native in need of a shave. He wore light colored clothing and a small sombrero of woven palm fibers. He eyed the skinny girl racing towards him with raised eyebrows and his cigarette clenched between his teeth. Her plain brown hair trailed loose behind her as she dodged tombstones and leapt over gnarled tree roots. At the last moment his smile faded to panic and he turned to run.

He took a few steps before Constance brought him to ground with an expert rugby tackle, forcing the air from his lungs and grinding his face into the mud. He rolled over onto his back and threw the tenacious girl straight up in the air, her body smacking the ground two meters to his right.

Major Ulperlip and a handful of soldiers surrounded them both as Constance and the burly native scrambled to their feet. They froze and raised their hands, staring down a dozen British rifle barrels.

"I demand to know what in the bloody hell is going on here," shouted Major Ulperlip, pushing through the line of soldiers to confront Constance and the unshaven mystery man.

•　　•　　•　　•　　•

The blasts ripped through the cemetery one after another, tearing through a section of seats occupied by dozens of New Granada natives. Sharpened splinters of wood from shattered chairs flew in the air, raining back down like a volley of arrows. A second set of explosions shattered a line of dilapidated tombstones behind Anne's empty coffin.

Smoke and dirt and debris filled the air. Shrieking mourners stampeded and trampled one another while others froze in fear. The stench of sulfur and burnt flesh filled the air and permeated noses.

Soldiers scrabbled to take position and gain control of the situation. Battlefield medics began triage; uninjured citizens melted back into the city.

Major Ulperlip left Constance and her quarry, racing back across the cemetery, zigzagging to avoid granite tombstones scattered like pick-up sticks. The burly man with the woven palm-frond hat slipped away while Constance stared at the carnage across the graveyard.

War had begun.

CHAPTER 14

Cartagena sat on the southern edge of the Caribbean with a shoreline angled towards the setting sun. Most structures stood on a piece of land resembling an island but attached to the continent by several wide strips of earth. The city wrapped itself around several saltwater bays and inlets bordered on two or three sides by land.

Sitting beside a saltwater inlet known as *Laguna de Chambacu* was a laundry service specializing in washing clothes for British dignitaries and military officers. Margaret pushed through the unlocked front door in the dead of night on her first stop after leaving the Goulden Estate. A single man sat behind the counter engrossed in a newspaper. He turned the oversized page and finished reading his story before setting the paper down on the counter.

"*Cómo?*"

"Hello. I am looking for George."

The man stared at Margaret for a minute before replying in English. "There is no one here but me, *señora*. I wash the clothes at night."

Margaret stepped forward to the counter. "Callum from the Glasgow Resistance is an old friend. He contacted Cartagena and set up a meeting with a man named George. I was told to meet him here."

"*Aye, señora.* As I said, I am alone here with all these dirty shirts. You can wait if you like; I am always happy for the company of a beautiful woman." The man gave her a wink and a wide grin.

"Thank you." Margaret flashed a sly, crooked smile at the older man. "You're a smooth talker and handsome to boot, but alas, I am a married woman."

"Please, let me get you a chair." The man disappeared into the depths of the store, returning a moment later with a simple chair made from rounded pieces of wood.

"Thank you," said Margaret. Before she could get comfortable, a dark-skinned man wearing a linen suit with a European cut entered the store. He stopped just inside the doorway.

The man behind the counter dipped his head to the newcomer, "*Buenos noches, señor.*"

The man in the linen suit nodded back. "*Buenos noches* to you. I am here to meet *Señora* Margaret Goulden."

Margaret stepped forward and stuck her hand out: "I am Margaret Goulden."

"So you are," replied the man in the white linen suit. "My name is George. *Por favor*, come with me." George led Margaret behind the counter of the laundry. He slid apart two rows of shirts hanging along the back wall, revealing a concealed doorway and a staircase leading down below the laundry.

The gentleman behind the counter removed the chair he brought out for Margaret and sat back down with his newspaper.

•　　•　　•　　•　　•

"What is your relation to Edward Goulden?"

"I already answered that question," said Margaret. She sat in a wooden chair, wrists tied behind her back. On the other side of the bare room, her personal arsenal lay spread across a table. A gigantic man wearing a pale green shirt and tan pants leaned over her.

Margaret locked eyes with her interrogator: "I understand your concerns. Edward Goulden is my husband. He works for the London bureaucracy; his family are bloody colonials." Margaret spoke without hesitation or an ounce of fear in her voice. "But my husband is committed to ending British tyranny. He works against the Empire from within."

"*Estupido*," muttered the hulking man. "That is the worst excuse I ever heard for collusion with the enemy." He turned and looked at George, standing in the corner in his clean, pressed linen suit.

George waved the back of his hand, "Move on, *mi amigo*."

The large man returned his focus to Margaret. "Callum from the Glasgow Resistance reached out to us. He asked that you be taken to meet Jose Tairona Marquez. Callum vouched for you; said he would trust you with his life."

"So, what's the question?"

"Why do you wish to meet General Marquez?"

"I have already answered that bloody question."

"*No, señora*, you have not. I asked that question already, but you have not answered it."

"That is because it is a private matter between me and the general," replied Margaret.

George stepped forward from the shadows: "Please answer the question, *señora*. We mean no disrespect; we need to verify that you are not a threat to General Marquez."

Margaret looked away from the intimidating figure standing over her. She sighed and lowered her head. "I wish to speak directly with Marquez about my sister-in-law, Anne Goulden."

"That is what we believed," said George. He walked behind Margaret and untied the leather straps binding her wrists. "We will verify your answers and make a decision regarding taking you to see Jose Marquez."

"How long will that take?" asked Margaret.

"Not long, I promise," said George, smiling. "I see your reputation is well deserved."

Margaret looked around the room. "What do you have to eat?"

George laughed, "*Café y pandebono frio.*"

•　　•　　•　　•　　•

Margaret and a small band from the Cartagena Resistance steamed up the Rio Magdalena. The wood-plank boat was short and wide, perched on the water like a duck in the slow-moving river. A thatch roof shaded most of the deck; hammocks swaying in the breeze between the roof's poles.

The river sliced through hills that rose up on both sides of the river, the jungle blanketing the visible terrain. Trees and ferns encroached on the river. Heavy branches hung over the water; thick, gnarled roots jutted out in the current. Smoke poured from the top of the boat, mingling with the mist rising from the river.

"Who's following us?" asked Margaret.

A member of the Resistance spoke without looking at her. "Two British soldiers from Cartagena." He stood up and scanned the horizon behind the boat. A sliver of steam and smoke stood out against the skyline behind them, its source hidden behind the constant twists and turns of the river.

"What do you plan to do?"

"It has already been taken care of," said the man.

"When you signaled the last lookout station on shore a kilometer back?"

"How do you know I signaled someone?"

Margaret looked at the man but did not answer the question. "What will your soldiers do?"

Now it was the soldier's turn to ignore the question. The boat chugged forward up the river, hull lurching and slowing as the propellers kicked at the water under the wavering power of the steam engine. The passengers sat in silence, watching the jungle swim past them. Ten minutes later, a series of rifle shots echoed behind them. No one turned.

•   •   •   •   •

Margaret arrived at an abandoned city high in the jungle-choked mountains days after Cartagena laid Anne's empty coffin in the ground. Margaret's guides marched her through the streets and locked inside a simple row house. Waiting within was a young woman dressed in simple canvas khakis, her long, dirty hair in a neat braid. She looked older than her seventeen years.

"Anne," screeched Margaret. She threw her arms around her sister-in-law and squeezed so hard Anne almost lost her lunch. "I came so far; I can't believe I actually found you."

"Margaret, it's so wonderful to see you," said Anne, tears welling up as she hugged Margaret. "How did you get here?"

"Edward, Constance, and I came to Cartagena. Governor Pratt called off the investigation, so we traveled here from London to find you ourselves."

"Why did they call off the investigation?"

"It's complicated. You were declared dead, though."

"Why was I declared dead?" asked Anne. "I am not dead. Who claimed to have seen me die?"

"No one claimed to have seen you die."

"Then who in their right mind would declare me dead?"

"You don't understand what's been happening. We were attacked on our flight from London, then someone broke into the garrison and blew up an airfield. The British are preparing to attack the Resistance in your name, but I doubt they know where this base is located. There was a funeral planned for you in Cartagena after I left." Margaret stopped to catch her breath after her rambling narration.

Anne stood in front of Margaret, locking eyes with the woman ten years' her elder. "Margaret, tell me who declared me dead?"

Margaret's eyes dropped to the floor. "Governor Pratt signed the death certificate. With your mother's blessing."

Anne stepped back, reeling from the news. She bumped into a kitchen chair and sat down on the peeling paint.

"My mother gave up looking for me? After two weeks and one rejected ransom. Why would she do that? Why wouldn't my mother force Pratt to either negotiate of keep searching?" Anne's eyes darted around the room without settling on anything, like she awoke and found herself in a strange place.

"I have no bloody clue," muttered Margaret.

"They treat me well here, you know," said Anne. "I assure you my journey here was as ordeal, but once I arrived, I have been treated quite well."

Margaret saw the anger cross Anne's face like storm clouds in a heavy wind. "How did you get here?"

"A gigantic mechanical jaguar swallowed me whole," replied Anne. "I lived in its hollow metal stomach for days while it ran through the jungle. I was weak from hunger and thirst and scared out of my mind. When I arrived here, a man named Francis removed me from the beast's belly and gave me something to eat and drink."

Margaret stared at her, slack jawed and unable to speak.

"They might even have returned me to Cartagena," said Anne. "Despite Pratt rejecting their demands."

"How could anyone expect the British to abandon an entire colony for the life of one person?" asked Margaret.

"What are you talking about?" asked Anne.

"That bloody ransom letter the Resistance sent. They demanded the British abandon New Granada in exchange for your life."

"That's ridiculous," said Anne. "The New Granada Resistance may have frustrated the British government for years, but no one believes the British are leaving anytime soon."

"That's what I told them," said Margaret. "Then why did the Resistance attempt to exchange you for the British abandoning the colony?"

"I was told they tried to exchange me for a prisoner being held in Cartagena," replied Anne, "but the prisoner was too valuable for Pratt to trade."

"That makes a lot more sense," said Margaret. "I suppose the other story was meant to stifle any anger over the governor's refusal. Whatever the ransom request, everyone in Cartagena believes General Marquez executed you."

"Obviously I am alive," said Anne. "After Pratt rejected the prisoner exchange, some militia leaders wanted to execute me. Others wanted to sell me off to work in a forced labor camp. General Marquez promised I would not be killed, but he said the Resistance cannot send me home without a ransom of some sort to save face.

"Until that happens, I am a prisoner. I can walk around the city as long as I take those two with me." Anne nodded towards the front window and two soldiers playing cards on a table outside the door.

"They told me I'm free to walk around, but only with an escort, same as you." Margaret sat down with a thud on one of the cots. "I came here to get you, but I came for another reason, too."

"What reason is that?" asked Anne.

"I came to stop a bloodbath. Her Majesty is sending a fleet of zeppelins powerful enough to destroy an entire city."

"They plan to destroy this city," muttered Anne.

"Aye."

"Why are they attacking one Resistance group with an entire fleet?"

"Actually, because of you," replied Margaret. "To make the colony safe and exact vengeance for your death. That's why we have to get back to Cartagena."

"If they are sending a fleet into the jungle, they must be planning to rescue me."

"The fleet's mission is not to rescue you," replied Margaret. "You were declared dead, remember."

"Why would Her Majesty's Armed Forces send an entire fleet here without attempting a rescue?"

"You don't understand," said Margaret, standing up and pacing across the room. "The fleet is not actually about revenge. They just need an excuse to invade the jungle." She turned and walked back. "The Resistance is too good at stealing bread off the government's table. The governor wants to wipe them out."

"That Pratt is a real prat," muttered Anne.

"Aye, he is that. When the zeppelins arrive, they'll bomb the city. If you and I are still here, we will die."

•   •   •   •   •

A pair of soldiers came and retrieved Margaret late that afternoon, escorting her across a city pulsating with military life. Men marched and drilled up and down narrow cobblestone streets. They passed firing ranges where soldiers shot rifles into a brick wall. Piles of course red dust lay below clusters of uneven holes and painted-on targets. Smells of gun powder and smoke struggled for control of Margaret's senses against the mildew and rot coming from abandoned buildings and the surrounding jungle.

"What is this place?" asked Margaret to her escort.

Her guard grunted but said nothing. Margaret looked in wonder at the empty shops and row houses, cobblestone roads and large, impressive buildings. Structures had a roof of either orange Spanish tile or corrugated iron rusted to a red-brown hue. Buildings wore either a redbrick façade or a sloppy, fresh coat of green paint. Places where the green paint peeled in the ever-present moisture revealed patches of hidden purple and yellow and blue plaster.

The city appeared to have slipped into a controlled state of decay. Bamboo groves filled alleys and towered over squat, one-story buildings. Trees planted in grassy parks were enormous, overgrown, and unkempt. But the main streets were in good repair and the gutters lining the roads free of debris.

Margaret's escort deposited her in front of a European-style, three-story brick building. Open parks and large buildings breaking in style with the rest of the city were everywhere. The brick building's double doors opened into a hollow space the size of a banquet hall. The fireplace on the far wall smoldered, the hot coals emitting a stale, suffocating wall of heat that hit Margaret in the face as she crossed the room.

Two dozen men stood in small groups scattered around the room, conversing in quiet voices. Half were the descendants of African slaves. A handful were Native Americans and the rest European. Bits of conversations in French and Spanish crossed the open floor to greet Margaret.

A short man in the green khaki uniform of a soldier noticed Margaret. He strode across the room, taking steps too long for his short legs and biting down on an extinguished cigar.

"Margaret Goulden of London," said the man chewing on the cigar. "Before that, Margaret Buchanan of Glasgow. You enlisted in the Glasgow Resistance when you were twelve. You had a reputation for getting hold of plans for British weapons production. Why did you join so young?"

"That's not a question I care to answer."

"Do you want us to trust you?"

"Very well," said Margaret with a sigh. "My father was a foreman in a weapons factory; he took me to visit other factories all over Glasgow. He died in an accident at work accident. We had to bury him in a pauper's grave when the government refused to pay for the funeral and burial. There isn't even a proper headstone to mark his grave."

The man chewed on his cigar, considering Margaret's response. "Later you were one of the first women to go to Oxford University. You graduated, but with poor marks. Now you are in the London Resistance, but no longer particularly active."

"You know a great deal about me," said Margaret, standing tall in front of the short man. "But who are you?"

He stroked his thick black mustache with his fingers. "You married Edward Goulden, a member of a rich colonial family from Cartagena. Edward works for the British bureaucracy in London." He stopped to consider his next words. "Although I have heard rumors about your husband. They say he helps the worldwide *Resistencia*."

"Edward is not a soldier, but he believes in national sovereignty and human rights. He uses his considerable talents with pen and paper to cause change."

The soldier smiled at Margaret's words and rubbed his pock-marked face. "I ask you again, sir," said Margaret. "Who are you?"

"You know who I am."

Margaret smirked: "You are General Jose Tairona Marquez. You are a mix of African and Indian lineage. You were born an *encomienda* on an agricultural *hacienda*, an indentured servant on a plantation. Your Spanish patron nurtured the born leader in you. He taught you to read and write before releasing you from servitude on the condition that you work towards freeing New Granada."

"Well done, *señora*. My faith in you was not misplaced."

"You worked for a decade uniting the scattered Resistance movements across the northwest corner of this continent. You joined the factions in Cartagena and Santa Marte with the remnants from the central jungles and the old Spanish capital of Bacatá." Margaret studied the general's face. "I believe that is where we are now; the abandoned city of Bacatá."

Marquez's smile grew even wider and he slapped Margaret on the back. "You are correct, *señora.* Bacatá was the center of Spanish rule on this continent, but her citizens were scattered years ago when the British came." Marquez paused for dramatic effect. "The New Granada Resistance took over the abandoned city three years ago." He turned around and started pacing the floor.

"Anne Goulden is your sister by marriage," said Marquez. "You are here because you want her released. Is that correct?"

"Aye," replied Margaret.

"I already decided to return Anne to Cartagena. She will travel next week to the coast with a caravan. Now you will go with her."

Margaret stood speechless.

"I see I have finally managed to surprise you," said General Marquez.

"Why would you release her?"

"Because she is no longer of use to us," replied Marquez in a quick, harsh tone. "We wanted to exchange Anne for a comrade held prisoner in Cartagena. Governor Pratt refused. Instead we will use Anne's return as leverage to convince your husband and his cousin to assist in liberating our comrade."

"Why would you want Edward and Constance to break someone out of jail? They're no soldiers."

"We have our reasons."

Margaret mulled over the general's words, then moved on to a new topic. "Pratt says the Resistance murdered Anne. He's sending an armada into the jungle to destroy you."

"We will handle the governor and his hot-air balloons. While you are a guest here, you may explore the city at any time, but only with an escort. *Buenos dias.*" Marquez turned his back on Margaret to ask one of his officers a question.

"General Marquez," said Margaret in a loud voice. "Do not underestimate the fleet Governor Pratt is sending for you. I have seen the new iron spires. They are sending a force that could threaten the sovereignty of Paris or Tokyo."

JOSEPH ROLLINS

A fair-skinned man standing alone in the corner of the room pushed himself off the wall with his foot. "Madame," he said in a thick French accent. "You must know that we already have this information. You were at the garrison the day our soldiers turned that buffoon Ulperlip's guns on his own spires."

General Marquez placed his hand on the Frenchman's arm. "*Por favor, mi amigo*. We should not be talking about this."

"It was just a friendly warning," said Margaret. "Do with it what you will."

•   •   •   •   •

General Marquez strolled with Francis Lefount through the narrow stone streets of Bacatá. Soldiers stopped whatever they were doing to salute the general as he passed. Marquez nodded to each of them.

Francis held a copper sphere the size of an apple in his left hand. While he walked, the Frenchman used his right hand to pull screwdrivers and pliers from the canvas pockets on his vest. His hands moved without hesitation or thought as he rebuilt the contraption.

"Are our defenses ready?" asked the general.

"*Oui*," replied Francis. "Of course."

"You are confident they can handle an assault by a full fleet?"

"*Oui, mon général*. We can defeat forty or more zeppelins, just like we discussed." Francis's hands continued to move around the gadget in his hand, pulling pieces out and slotting in new ones.

"*Bueno*," said General Marquez. "What do you make of that *mujer, mi amigo*? What do you think about her claim that this assault will be more ferocious than we expected?"

Francis sighed as he walked, eyes never leaving the devise in his hands. "*Je m'en fiche*. I doubt she could know more than us."

The two walked on in silence for several minutes. The rambling streets narrowed in places too small for a carriage to pass. Second-story window shutters of occupied buildings were open to move air through the houses.

"What of this latest plan to free Ezmeralda?" asked Francis. He finished repairs on the gadget and slipped his tools back in his pockets. With his right hand, Francis twisted the sphere counterclockwise a half turn. It came alive in his hands, buzzing and shaking. A propeller spun on top of the ball; it lifted out of Francis's hand and climbed through the air to watch the skies for intruders.

"I sent word to George to make contact, but I have not received a reply."

CHAPTER 15

Edward rose from bed the morning after Anne's funeral and proceeded with his normal routine. He washed, shaved, brushed, and dressed. Downstairs, he ate a breakfast of fried pandebono breads and fresh fruit juice.

Morning routine complete, Edward had no idea what to do with the rest of his day, so he paced the front hall between the drawing room and the kitchen. The servants avoided him at all costs, walking several minutes out of their way to complete their morning chores. Constance found him there after rising and walking downstairs for breakfast.

"How long have you been pacing the hall?"

Edward's head jerked up and he stumbled over the corner of a rug.

"I am not sure," he said. "There will be war; people will die. I haven't a clue what to do." Lowering his head, Edward resumed his processional march down the hall, spun around, and retraced his steps.

"And my wife," said Edward once he returned to Constance. "Someone will certainly kill her. Both bloody sides of this war are gunning for her."

"Margaret lives for this type of adventure," said Constance. "Tramping through unfamiliar jungles. Searching for a kidnapped compatriot. A hostile rebel group in front of her, the British war machine launching an attack from behind." Constance looked at Edward and frowned. "Are you even listening to me?"

"I am sorry," replied Edward. "My mind was elsewhere. What were you saying?"

"I said that this is the type of adventure Margaret lives for. I am sure she is fine."

"I hope you are correct," muttered Edward, "I feel so powerless. People lost their lives at the funeral and we knew something dastardly would happen."

Constance attempted to comfort her cousin, putting her hand on his shoulder before changing the subject. "Where is Aunt Lorraine?"

"My mother made it clear to me that she is furious with Margaret, and by extension, me. Therefore, she is not speaking to me." Edward scratched the back of his head and sighed. "I guess the situation is not all bad."

"All right," replied Constance. "After I eat breakfast, I propose we head into Cartagena and try to find something useful to do."

•　　•　　•　　•　　•

"Something about the town seems wrong today," said Constance, strolling through the streets of Cartagena.

"What do you mean?" asked Edward.

"The outdoor cafes and coffee shops are empty. There are no vendors selling fruit pieces on toothpicks, no impromptu public gatherings with little children running about eating strange fried meats."

"I think it's the animosity," replied Edward. He stepped over a pothole filled with water for the last three days. "I imagine the loyalties of the natives shifted after yesterday. They are in line with the colonials' call to end the New Granada Resistance."

"People resent falling in line with the governor's war mongering, but they favor the protection of the Crown now."

"Exactly," replied Edward as they passed beneath a row of pale purple houses. "On top of that is the fear."

"Every colonial is living in fear of the non-British," said Constance.

"Natives and foreigners are afraid of British reprisals as well."

They wound through the narrow city streets, gravitating towards the open marketplaces on the east side of town. The roads were remarkably empty; the pair wandered without dodging horses or taxis.

After an hour of wandering, a short man with dark hair and olive skin bumped into Edward. The stranger stumbled backward and fell in dramatic fashion over the chairs of an open-air cafe. Edward reached down to help the man to his feet.

"I am sorry, sir," said Edward, pulling the man up towards him. "Entirely my fault."

The man scrambled to his feet, brushing off his pressed, white linen pants and straightening his button-down shirt. "Edward Goulden, Constance Ventor," he said, without looking up from adjusting his clothing. Edward and Constance took a half step back.

Grasping Edward by the forearm, the mysterious stranger pulled Edward in close and whispered in his ear: "*La Resistencia de Nueva Granada* is asking for your help." The thick Spanish accent that was almost musical. "If you will listen, meet me along the road between Cartagena and the Goulden Estate, beside the avocado trees on the Lancaster Estate."

The man released Edward, locking eyes with the pale bureaucrat. "Two military spies are following you. They are behind you as we speak, in front of the coffee shop with the green sign. Pale skin, dressed poorly for colonials. If you meet me, lose them first." The stranger turned to leave but changed his mind. "I have information about Anne."

Edward's jaw fell as the man slipped away without flare. He passed by the plain-clothed soldiers without a stutter in his gait, turned left and vanished down an alley.

"If there really are soldiers following us, we should lose them," said Constance. When Edward did not reply, she grabbed her cousin's arm to get his attention.

"Fine," said Edward. "How do you propose we do that?"

Constance led Edward through an open doorway into a merchant shop, hustling past shelves stocked with bags of coffee and local pottery. The shop keeper yelled as Edward toppled a display. A dozen tiny espresso mugs, made of thicker ceramics than their delicate British counterparts, broke on the floor. Edward fumbled over an apology as

Constance dragged him past the angry vendor and shelves stacked with lightweight linens.

The cousins slipped through the rear door and into an alley only wide enough for a single person to pass. Edward and Constance turned left and walked ten paces before entering the back door of an empty cafe across the alley. The idle restaurant owners sat and watched as two Europeans hustled through their cafe, out the front door, and into the street.

"I do not see them," said Constance, her eyes sweeping the street as they walked.

"Just to be certain," said Edward, motioning across the street. They passed through another store, across the alley, and back onto the street.

"I believe we lost them," said Edward, surveying the street from a recessed doorway.

"We should meet that man," said Constance, gulping air, "and see what information he has about Anne."

"I agree," mumbled Edward, preoccupied with the possibility that someone might still be following them.

Constance led the way, walking as fast as possible without drawing attention to herself. Once they left the city streets of Cartagena, the two broke into a jog, feet plodding along the hard-packed mud road as storm clouds crept in from the ocean.

•　　•　　•　　•　　•

Edward and Constance arrived outside the Lancaster's avocado grove in under an hour. Deciding to play it safe, they slipped off the road and into the ever-encroaching jungle and crouched amongst the foliage. The damp air smelled like mildew. Fat leaves dripped warm water in their clothing, but they remained concealed, watching the road.

Constance picked at her corset and adjusted the laces on her boots. "What do you think the Resistance wants with us?"

"I have no bloody clue," replied Edward, eyes locked on the road.

Neither one said a word for ten minutes. One hour after their first meeting, the short man in the white linen suit strolled down the road and stopped directly in front of the concealed cousins.

"The fact that you are hidden makes this conversation less risky," he said in a musical Spanish accent. "My name is George." Muffled sounds of surprise came from the foliage beside the road.

"I have a message from General Jose Marquez, leader of the New Granada *Resistencia*. He wishes to ask a favor of you. But first, I have a separate message. A show of good faith.

"Anne Goulden is alive and well at *la Resistencia* camp in the jungles to the south. We will transport her back to Cartagena with the next caravan to the coast."

"My sister is alive." Edward leapt straight up from his hiding place, loose twigs and leaves stuck in his hair and clothes.

"Yes, and she will return to your family soon," said George, his tone flat. "Margaret Goulden contacted with *la Resistencia* here in Cartagena. She was taken to the camp where both General Marquez and your sister are. She is safe and will accompany your sister home."

"I told you she would be all right," muttered Constance. Edward said nothing while struggling to breathe normally.

"And now, the favor I must ask," said George. "Ezmeralda Lefount is a political prisoner held in the basement of Governor Pratt's mansion. *Señora* Lefount is an important part of our struggle for independence. General Marquez fears that our coming fight with the British fleet may fail without her."

"Because she is a Master Mason of the Holy Royal Arch," said Constance.

"*Si, señorita*," said George. "Her skills as a Freemason could save many lives in the coming days."

"Why would we free a member of the armed Resistance?" asked Edward, bringing his eyes level with George's over the wide leaves. "I sympathize with your cause, but I do not endorse violence against my countrymen. Instead I campaign for solutions rooted in negotiation and compromise. I fear freeing Ezmeralda Lefount would cost many British soldiers their lives."

George held Edward's gaze. "As you know, *señor*, members of the Holy Royal Arch take a solemn vow to use their engineering and leadership skills to improve the lives of others. If Ezmeralda takes British lives in battle, they are taken only in defense others."

The conversation paused, the words of both parties hanging in the air, mixing with the rising humidity and the hum of a thousand insects.

"Why did you kidnap my sister if you are releasing her now?" asked Edward.

"We attempted to negotiate a prisoner exchange: Anne for Ezmeralda. It failed." George stopped talking long enough to draw a short, thin cigar from his breast pocket. Striking a match he dug out of his pants pocket, the Spaniard lit the *cigarillo*, puffing to get it started. "We are releasing her as a show of good faith."

"I still do not understand why you kidnapped my sister," said Edward. "You provided Pratt with an excuse to launch an invasion and tear apart the New Granada Resistance."

"We have negotiated many prisoner exchanges in the past, *señor*. But this time was different." Blue-gray smoke curled over George's head before vanishing in the gusting winds.

"Why do you need our help to free Ezmeralda?" asked Constance, still crouched behind a pair of stunted banana trees. "The Cartagena Resistance has operatives ready and willing to attempt a jailbreak."

"You have something no member of the underground has," said George. "You have access to the inside of Governor Pratt's mansion. We would leave all planning up to you and provide whatever resources you need."

George examined the burning *cigarillo* pinched between his fingers with a critical eye as the conversation stalled once more. "I will leave you now to contemplate your decision, but I need an answer soon. Liberating Ezmeralda will save many lives. But whatever you decide, Anne and Margaret will be back in Cartagena before the end of the dry season." Thunder clouds rolled overhead in contradiction to George's words.

Emboldened with thoughts of his sister returning home, Edward stepped out of the undergrowth. "We know how devastating the coming British invasion will be. We felt the anger and fear when the bomb exploded at Anne's funeral. The New Granada Resistance is in serious trouble."

"We will do it," shouted Constance, leaping to her feet. A look of embarrassment etched across her face and she hunched her shoulders. "What I mean is that I will do it. What about you, Edward?"

Edward's newfound bravado vanished. "A few days ago, you argued that the British Empire had the right to colonize the world. How can you throw in with a militant Resistance at the drop of a hat?"

"You are right," replied Constance in a quiet voice. "I never believed Margaret's anti-British propaganda. But the blatant abuse of power by Pratt and Vickers, lying about Anne, the bombing at the funeral. They killed British citizens to justify their war."

"I plan to drag both Pratt and Vickers in front of Parliament when I return to London. I promise you they will answer for their crimes."

"But that will not stop the attack," said Constance. "Many more people will die. Breaking Ezmeralda out of prison will balance the scales a bit."

Edward turned to address, "Can you guarantee that my wife and sister will be home soon?"

"I have no proof to offer you except my word, but I give it to you now," said George. He stood in the road smoking as the humidity in the air condensed into a light rain.

"Lieutenant Vickers told us that anyone caught in the crossfire when the fleet attacks will likely die," said Edward. "If Margaret and Anne are not already on their way back to Cartagena now, I am afraid it may be too late."

"I will send a message requesting that they depart as soon as possible," said George. "*Por favor*, help us defend ourselves from the fleet. Help us defend Anne and Margaret."

Edward muttered an affirmative the others strained to hear, "It is the right thing to do."

"*Bueno.*" George clapped his hands together, *cigarillo* clenched between his teeth. "I will provide blueprints of the mansion and the location of a safe house to bring Ezmeralda to, plus two pairs of small, concealable firearms. Any other materials you require, just ask."

George removed the thin cigar from between his teeth. "We will communicate through written messages left beneath that rock there." George pointed with the back end of his *cigarillo*. "The blueprints and guns are there now."

"That's a bit presumptuous," said Constance.

"We had faith," said George.

• • • • •

"We have been down this road a half dozen times already," said Edward, his frustration seeping out between his words. "It is impossible to mount a brute force assault from the inside of Pratt's mansion that has any chance of success."

"But with the right weapons, I am certain we could do it," said Constance. Her and Edward had remained locked in a bedroom at the Goulden estate since returning home.

"You have lost sight of the objective," replied Edward.

"No, cousin, I have not," said Constance. "We are trying to free Ezmeralda Lefount."

"Without losing our lives in the process." Edward sighed and looked at the blueprints spread on the table. "Even if we successfully attack the soldiers and guards inside, Pratt will know it was us who freed Ezmeralda. He will hunt us like animals."

"Every idea we have had involves risk."

"I refuse to free a member of the Resistance just to take her place in prison," said Edward. "Besides, I believe you over-estimate our abilities. I am not Margaret. In a combat situation, most likely I will panic or freeze."

Constance sighed and looked down at her notepad of ideas. With an elaborate flourish of her pen, she drew a line through the idea on the bottom of the list.

"What about breaking in at night?" asked Edward.

"Impossible," said Constance, biting her lower lip. "They double the guards every night, expecting the Resistance to try just that. Plus, we cannot legitimately get inside the mansion at night."

"Why not?"

"Because we cannot just knock on the front door at one o'clock in the morning and ask to come inside."

"Very well," muttered Edward. "I still believe we should gain access to the mansion legitimately, then sneak down to the basement and break out Ezmeralda."

"That seems like the most obvious solution," replied Constance, rubbing her temples. "But we failed to develop that idea into a plan with any chance of success. At this point I doubt it is possible without someone spotting us. Which brings us back to the problem of brute force."

Edward stared out the window into the darkness for a long time. The household staff brought up a late supper. Edward thanked them and took the tray of soup and breads but ate nothing. The light, steady rain continued, washing away the smell of mildew in the air while feeding its growth. After an hour, Constance interrupted his wallowing.

"I think I have it," Constance said in a hushed tone. She furiously scribbled in her notebook for several minutes before standing to compare her notes against the blueprints of the mansion.

"Do not keep me in suspense," said Edward. "What's your idea?"

Constance's plan came rushing out in a wave of words. Edward closed his eyes and concentrated.

"I think you've got it," said Edward after his cousin finished. His words were slow and deliberate as he struggled to finish processing the plan.

"We will have to get a wide assortment of supplies from George," muttered Constance, tearing out a fresh page from her notebook and scribbling down items she needed.

"I will go at first light and get what you need," said Edward. He stared at his cousin for a minute before speaking. "How long will it take you to complete the engineering work required?"

"All night," replied Constance, scratching behind her ear with her pen. "And all day tomorrow."

"I will help with whatever I can," said Edward. He yawned and stood up to stretch. "Do you mind if I get some sleep?"

Constance was already filling notebook pages with complicated mathematical formulas.

•   •   •   •   •

Three days after Anne's funeral, Edward rose early and went downstairs for breakfast. He found Lorraine in the middle of her meal on the back promenade. The earth was damp and mossy, the sun burning away the fine mist hanging in the air.

"Good morning, mother," said Edward. "May I join you?"

Lorraine consented by waving her hand her son's direction without looking up at him. Edward caught the attention of the nearest servant and asked for a plate of fruit, pandebonos, and cheese.

"I meant to talk to you," said Edward after sitting down. Lorraine looked at her son but remained silent. "I have been wrapped up. No, I believe the word is consumed. Well, perhaps obsessed is a better word." Lorraine cleared her throat and Edward cut off his meandering.

"What I mean to say is that I truly believed Anne was alive. But that horrific act of terrorism at the funeral opened my eyes." Edward's voice became quiet and he struggled to continue. "My sister is gone forever. The people that planted the bomb would never let her live. I am also aware that Margaret, Constance, and I have made this situation more difficult since we arrived. Now I am uncertain if I will ever see my wife again."

Edward paused as the servant set down his breakfast and poured him a cup of tea. "I am trying to say that I am sorry. I hope you will find it in your heart to forgive me." He picked a circular pastry off his plate and tore it in half.

Lorraine keep the shock from her face. It was as if her dead husband walked up the table wearing her best corset. She snapped out of her trance a moment later and poured herself a second cup of tea.

"It demonstrates a lot of maturity on your part to come to this realization. I was beginning to wonder if you would ever show up as a reasonable young man."

"Thank you, mother," said Edward. "I was thinking that if there is one other person to whom I owe an apology, it is Governor Pratt. I would deliver the apology personally, but I do not believe I am welcome at his mansion. Would you apologize for me the next time you see him?"

"I believe it would be best if you apologized to the governor yourself. I find him to be a very understanding and compassionate man."

"As you wish," said Edward. "Then would you please contact the governor and ask when Constance and I may call upon him?"

• • • • •

Edward and Constance arrived at the governor's mansion two hours later. Sebastian, the governor's lanky footman, met them at the front door and led them upstairs and through a labyrinth of hallways. He stopped in front of the governor's office and rapped on the door.

"The governor will be with you shortly." Edward thanked the servant who turned and left, his black tails disappearing around a corner. Constance sat in a straight-backed chair across from the governor's door while Edward paced the floor.

"Are you certain?" asked Constance, staring at the governor's closed door.

"One can always count on a proper British greeting," said Edward.

"What are you talking about?"

"Pratt believes we wronged him," said Edward, sighing. "He will make us wait for at least ten minutes, even if he's not busy."

"So British hospitality is subtle condescension."

"Exactly."

"How does that work in a colony where the locals have a remarkably loose grasp of the concept of time?" said Constance.

"Not well," muttered Edward.

Constance snickered, reached up into her oversized shirt sleeve, and pulled out Professor Lecturn's four-legged spy. She smoothed the squirrel's fur with her palm before lifting the second toe on the front left paw.

"Good luck, Walden," said Constance. "Go find your target."

The squirrel clicked and whirled and came to life as Constance placed the critter on the woven rug on top of the tiled floor. The squirrel sprinted down the hallway and made a sharp left at the end, vanishing from sight.

Eleven minutes later the door to the office opened and Governor Pratt invited the cousins in his office.

• • • • •

Lecturn's invention knew where to go. It raced down corridors and around corners. It scurried downstairs, veered left, turned right, dropped down another flight of stairs. Three times the squirrel hid and waited for someone to enter or exit through a door before it could continue. It ran between the legs of a woman sweeping the clay tiles on the first floor. She swung her broom at the squirrel but came up empty.

The basement was a converted space with crumbling brick walls vaguely resembling a medieval prison. Walden arrived after a hair-raising, fourteen-minute journey through the house. The squirrel dashed past the guard station and into a narrow hall lined with iron bars. It located Ezmeralda Lefount, scampered between the bars of her cell, and sat on her feet.

Ezmeralda sat on the dirt floor leaning against the far wall of the cell. She wore a matching set of loose cotton pants and shirt. Her skin was copper despite not seeing the sun in months. Long black curls hung down to the middle of her back, greasy and matted and sultry. Ezmeralda's cell was barren. No pillow, no blanket, no thin sleeping pad, no eating utensils. The governor was wise to keep Ezmeralda in these conditions; she could pick a lock with a feather from a pillow.

With the long, slender fingers of a piano player, Ezmeralda reached down and lifted the squirrel. Holding it her palm, she turned it over and over, studying every detail.

"If I am not mistaken, you belong to my dear old friend Harold Lecturn."

Holding the critter in her left hand, Ezmeralda pushed down on the squirrel's second toe. The animal grew cold and lifeless in her hand, its jaw hinge unlatching with a click. Ezmeralda pushed the squirrel's head, rocking it back 180 degrees until the top row of teeth lined up with the bottom teeth.

A glass vial the size of Ezmeralda's pinkie peaked out of the squirrel's throat. She reached in and pinched the top with her fingernails and lifted it out. Wrapped around the vial was a piece of paper.

Dissolve lock with vial. West end of corridor. Wait for signal.

Ezmeralda held the vial up to the dingy light inside her cell. She turned it over, staring at the clear, thick liquid inside. She twisted the cap off and sniffed.

"*Dios mío*," she said, rubbing her nose and coughing into her fist. "Hydrochloric acid," said Ezmeralda. She spit on the floor and pushed the cap back in place. "Very good stuff."

Ezmeralda poked her face between the bars of her cage and looked left and right. The corridor was narrow enough for Ezmeralda to touch the stone wall opposite her cell with her fingertips.

There were no guards in sight; they were still at their station, outside the corridor and behind a steel-framed door. Ezmeralda could smell the sunlight scattering through the handful of empty cells from a hidden source somewhere outside her field of vision.

"Why not?" she muttered to herself.

She reached her hand through the bars and explored the door's iron keyhole with her fingers. Ezmeralda guided the vial to the keyhole, pressing the top edge of it against the hole. She tipped the vial, keeping her fingers clear of the acid. The cell lock hissed and crackled. A foul-smelling brown smoke seeped out of the keyhole in wisps and puffs.

Ezmeralda pulled her hands back inside the cell and stepped back, bumping into the gray bricks on the other side of the cell. She leaned against the wall and kicked the iron door as hard as she could. Her boots confiscated long ago, Ezmeralda wore only cotton stockings on her feet. Regardless, she kicked the iron bars until crimson blood soaked through her socks. The acid corroded the rusted lock from the inside out; it gave a little with each kick until a final blow sent the door flying open. A sharp metallic clang vibrated up and down the corridor as the door hit the wall and swung back on its hinges.

Ezmeralda stepped out and faced the west end of the corridor. She saw nothing except more cell doors and a gray stone wall at the end. She turned to face east, towards the heavy iron bars separating the corridor from the guard station. Despite being certain the only way out was through the guard station, Ezmeralda followed the advice of her furry savior. She trotted west down the hallway, ready for the soldiers on guard duty to burst through the metal door behind her.

Ezmeralda stopped at the end of the corridor. She looked up and gasped at the sunlight cutting through the dust floating over her head. It was an air shaft rising ten meters off the dirt floor, lined with cobblestones and punctuated with iron bars at the top.

•　　•　　•　　•　　•

Edward groveled to the governor as much as his stomach allowed. He did most of the talking, although Constance squeaked out a weak apology of her own. Governor Pratt lectured them both on loyalty and blind faith in their government, and the benevolence of his own work.

Back in the hall, Edward and Constance stuck to the script. They knew from the blueprints George provided that the governor hid audio recorders all over the estate.

"That went well," said Constance. "I am glad Governor Pratt was so amiable."

"I agree," said Edward. "If you do not mind, I would like to stroll the gardens for a short while before heading back home. Will you accompany me?"

"Yes, of course."

The pair walked outside through the rear doors of the mansion and into the manicured tropical paradise. They talked about the weather while strolling through rows of flowers and ornamental trees.

"Everything here is so different than England," said Constance.

"Yes, it really is," replied Edward. "I spent my childhood here. I suppose that is why the weather in England always seems so unbelievably cold."

That comment was the first signal: *Ready to set the first devise.*

Constance knelt to lace her boot while Edward slipped a small wooden cigar box out of his trouser pocket and handed it down to her. Constance flipped it open and examined the bird's nest of copper wires and vials of black powder. She pushed in the button on the side of an inexpensive pocket watch inside the box. The clock started ticking. She snapped the lid closed and slipped the box under the base of an ugly stone statue vaguely resembling a soldier on horseback. Edward stood tall beside her, his eyes sweeping the grounds.

Constance stood and brushed the dust off her clothes. "What do you think the weather will be in twelve days?"

The clock is ticking - twelve minutes to complete the next step of their plan.

"I think it will be sunny and warm," replied Edward.

No complications, on to the next step.

They followed a tidy flagstone path around a stone fountain and circled towards the west side of the estate. Constance halted beside a clump of ferns clustered against the wall of the mansion, again dropping to one knee to untie and retie her boot.

Edward trampled the ferns between Constance and the wall, poking beneath the shrubbery with the toe of his boot. He found an iron grate set in cobblestones on the ground, tucked up beside the building. Edward signaled Constance with a whistle and they traded places.

Constance peered between the bars and saw only darkness. She whistled and someone bounced the note back up the air shaft a moment later. Constance tied a thin rope to an iron bar and dropped the other end down the shaft. She produced a vial of hydrochloric acid and poured it on the other bars. She counted to fifty then stomped on them with the heel of her boot. Each bar cracked and disappeared into the darkness. The last thing to fall down the air shaft was a slip of paper from Constance's pocket.

"I believe we will get a rainstorm in five days," said Constance.

Five minutes until all hell breaks loose.

Her and Edward walked at a brisk clip towards the front of the manor. As they approached the driveway, a handful of soldiers turned the corner and headed towards them. Edward and Constance kept their eyes on the ground and the soldiers passed without a second glance.

• • • • •

Manfred Pratt poured himself a cup of tea from his automatic tea kettle, wiping a puddle of oil off his desk with a rag. He whistled to himself as he walked back around his desk and sat.

"Still too bloody hot," he said, slurping his tea. The governor glared across the room at his contraption and blew on his brew.

From somewhere outside an explosion tore through the mansion's gardens. It sounded like a train barreling through the first floor. Pratt's windows rattled and his heavy mahogany desk shook so violently that two pens and an ink well fell to the floor. Pratt leapt to his feet, dumping the cup of scalding tea in his lap.

"Bloody hell that's hot," he shouted. Governor Pratt goose-stepped across the office to a pitcher of cold water and poured it down his trousers. He took a couple of deep breaths before looking out his window. An immense plume of thick gray smoke rose from the center of the gardens.

The door to the governor's office burst open and an exasperated soldier fell into the room.

"There's been an explosion, guvnor."

"Of course there's been an explosion, you bloody wanker." The governor pushed the private out of his way and barreled down the hall.

Chaos greeted Governor Pratt when he stepped into the courtyard. Soldiers and household staff raced around without an apparent destination. Several deep-throated officers tried to take command of the situation, each issuing orders that contradicted the others. Smoke and ash limited the governor's visibility, stinging his nostrils and causing his eyes to water.

"What happened," shouted Pratt to a soldier crouched beside a bed of flowers with soft orange petals. When the soldier ignored Pratt's question, he hooked the soldier under his arm and dragged him to his feet.

"What happened?" the governor shouted in the soldier's face.

The young man's face was a pale, bloodless hue and greased with sweat. He babbled at the governor before scrounging enough courage to respond.

"Next to the fountain. The ground beneath the ugly horse statue exploded."

"How many casualties?" The soldier returned the governor's question with a blank stare.

"How many dead?" shouted Pratt.

"None, sir," said the soldier. The blood rushed back into his face, going from pale to pink to crimson. "The ugly horse statue is rubble, and pieces of rock damaged the big fountain. Mostly there is just a great deal amount of smoke, sir."

Governor Pratt released the soldier and stalked towards the fountain in the center of the gardens. He pushed through a line of soldiers forming a bucket brigade, dousing the burning vegetation around the fountain. The governor hit a dense wall of smoke and retreated from the fountain, coughing and rubbing eyes. He walked upwind and across the garden. Soldiers had trampled large sections of his prized flora.

After the bucket brigade finished their work and the winds carried the suffocating smoke away, Pratt approached the fountain. Large pieces of the horse statue sat in the fountain's cracked, empty pool. The stone cherub that spit water into the fountain still stood its ground, minus an arm and a leg broken off by shrapnel.

"Looks like a bloody Greek statue now," Pratt muttered to himself.

•　　•　　•　　•　　•

The crumpled scrap of paper that floated down to the basement floor instructed Ezmeralda to wait for the explosion. The talented Freemason stood two paces back from the rope her conspirators dropped, crouching like a jungle cat ready to pounce. Ezmeralda closed her eyes and focused on the rhythm of her own breath.

The explosion came from somewhere up above and rattled the stone walls in her catacomb, shaking free decades of dust. The sound bounced back and forth down the air shaft and off the walls of the narrow row of cells. Ezmeralda inhaled wisps of the airborne dust and leapt straight up and forward. She grabbed hold of the thick, knotted rope dangling in front of her and began climbing. Hand over hand, legs swinging free, Ezmeralda scrambled up the ten meters one hand at a time.

At the top of the air shaft, Ezmeralda pulled her body up onto the damp earth. She rolled over and lie on her back coughing. She stretched her hands and feet as far as she could reach, grabbing tiny fistfuls of wet fern leaves, squeezing her eyes closed under the bright sun. Ezmeralda laughed and kicked her feet in the air. She blinked up at the sun, the brightness piercing her pupils and sending color bursts into the front of her brain. Ezmeralda clamped her hand over her brow and squinted as she pulled herself to her feet. A flash of white light on the far side of the wrought iron fence caught her attention.

"Clever use of mirrors," muttered the dark-haired woman. She checked Lecturn's squirrel tucked in her waistband and examined her bloody stockings.

"*Aye, mi,*" said Ezmeralda. She put her head down and sprinted, her atrophied muscles and stiff joints barely responding. She made it across the empty lawn and dove headfirst into the shrubbery along the fence, scratching her arms on a hundred sharp twigs.

Ezmeralda poked her head up and spotted a horse and carriage waiting on the far side of the fence. The black vertical bars looked formidable; twice the height of a person and sharpened at the top like iron spears.

"*Caballos.* How very quaint." Ezmeralda found the rope she expected behind the row of shrubberies and scaled the black bars, her bloody feet collapsing underneath her when she hit the ground. A young woman appeared, hoisted her to her feet, and helped her into the carriage.

"Go, Edward," the woman cried out as Ezmeralda collapsed on the thin carriage-seat pad. The man seated on top shouted at the horse and cracked his whip, driving them forward and away from Governor Pratt's prison.

CHAPTER 16

Edward and Constance rose late the next morning and enjoyed breakfast on the sunbaked flagstone patio.

"I cannot believe the safe house we delivered Ezmeralda to is the home of British colonials," said Constance. She stirred a thick slice of white, crumbly cheese into her hot chocolate. "I have to say that the cuisine here agrees with me." She turned her face to the sun and licked her fingers.

"The safe house surprised me, too," said Edward. "Regardless, yesterday's jaunt could not have gone more smoothly."

"My only question is what do we do now?"

"Nothing," replied Edward. "We wait for Anne and Margaret to return. And we pray that few lives are lost when the British fleet engages the Resistance."

"I doubt the British have any idea where to look for the Resistance base," said Constance, sipping her cocoa. "We know Her Majesty's Forces do not know the exact location. But my gut tells me it's worse than that; they have no idea where to begin looking. Most likely their plan is to fly south and start sweeping the jungle in a search pattern."

"The jungle is thousands of square kilometers," replied Edward. "If that really is their plan, they will likely fail."

Before Constance could reply, Lorraine walked out on the brick porch, her shoes clicking on the stone patio. "Do you mind if I join you for breakfast? I am absolutely famished."

"Of course not. Please, sit."

"Thank you." Lorraine waved at a member of the kitchen staff. "I just returned from town. I had some early business with Master Johannes this morning."

Lorraine spoke broken Spanish to the young man in formal attire. When she finished, he nodded and disappeared into the kitchen.

"As I was saying, I went into Cartagena early this morning. The city is in an absolute uproar." Lorraine poured herself a glass of thick fruit juice from the pitcher on the table.

"What for?"

"Resistance terrorists bombed the governor's mansion yesterday afternoon. Word is, several soldiers were killed. They believe the entire plot was orchestrated to free a prisoner held in the basement of the mansion."

Lorraine's breakfast arrived and she began eating without acknowledging the servant who brought it.

"Several soldiers died?" asked Constance. The breakfast in her stomach turned. She glanced over to Edward; his face was a familiar shade of green.

"That's what I heard," said Lorraine, pulling apart her pandebono. "But apparently Major Ulperlip and Sergeant Vickers were prepared for just such an incident. They tracked the escaped prisoner to a safe house. A colonial home, no less. Hell has a special place for traitors such as those."

"Get on with it, mother. What happened next?"

Lorraine put her food back down on the plate and looked at her son. "Really, Edward. You have not talked to me in that tone since you were sixteen."

Edward looked down at his own plate and moved his plantains around with his fork. The crispy fried bananas were rapidly cooling. "Sorry mum."

Lorraine resumed eating and poured herself a cup of tea. "Edward used to enjoy cheese with his hot chocolate when he was a boy," she said to Constance. "He loved it so much he would not consume chocolate without cheese, nor cheese without chocolate."

Lorraine paused again then continued with her original story. "Apparently, Her Majesty's Forces are not taking the matter lightly. They arrived in large numbers and stormed the traitor's house. Killed everyone."

"They killed everyone in the house?" asked Edward, his voice almost a whisper.

"Honestly," said Lorraine, again putting down her fork to look at her son. "I would expect this sort of response from an unappreciative upstart like your wife. But after all the death these monsters inflicted on our family, I would expect you would be happy they are dead."

"Yes, mother."

"If they are dead, they cannot hurt anyone else."

"Of course," mumbled Edward.

Lorraine nibbled at the fresh slices of mango on her plate. "The rest of the city is happy about the raid. Although when I left there were dozens of natives marching through the streets towards the governor's mansion."

"Why?" asked Constance.

"To demand Her Majesty's Forces take action and exterminate these terrorists for good. The New Granada Resistance was always more militant, more destructive than the passive, propaganda-spreading Resistance on the British Isles. But anyone can see they crossed a line by murdering an innocent young woman and then bombing her funeral."

"Absolutely horrible," said Constance, pushing the food across her plate.

"It truly is, dear," replied Lorraine. "You did not see anything suspicious when you visited Governor Pratt yesterday, did you?"

"No, not a thing," said Constance.

"We made our apologies and excused ourselves," said Edward. "Rather short meeting. After that we took a carriage back here."

Lorraine shrugged and returned to her breakfast.

• • • • •

Constance nibbled at her breakfast with Aunt Lorraine for a few minutes after Edward left the table. Constance excused herself and wandered upstairs to find her cousin. She opened the door to his bedroom and froze, mouth hanging open.

"Shut the bloody door," said Edward between clenched teeth.

Ezmeralda Lefount sat in a plush Georgian chair across from the bed, her clothes and skin covered in a rich brown mixture of wet mud and dried blood. Her emerald eyes flashed vibrant green at Constance before returning to a dull hazel. Constance stepped inside the room, shut the door, and turned the key.

"What the hell is going on?" asked Constance in a hoarse whisper.

"What does it look like?" replied Edward, standing over the desk and fussing with an inadequate first aid kit.

Ezmeralda exhaled, her thick black hair shuddering with the rest of her body. "Did you hear what happened at the safe house?"

"I heard everyone was killed," said Constance.

"Not everyone," replied Ezmeralda in a crisp Spanish accent. "Some of us got away. I did not know where else to go. All the safe houses in Cartagena are compromised."

"That's why you came here? If they raided the safe house, does that mean someone followed us from the Pratt's? Do they know we helped you escape?"

"Pratt and Vickers know you helped me," said Ezmeralda. "They would arrest you, but right now they have no proof. Plus, accusing the brother of the town's martyr of treason would hurt his plans."

"How do you know all this?" asked Edward, looking up from the first aid kit.

Ezmeralda pulled Professor Lecturn's squirrel from her loose shirt sleeve. "Last night, after the raid, I had him follow Vickers." She set it on the desk. "I know this devise. A dear friend of mine built it." Ezmeralda watched Constance's face, waiting for a response.

"Professor Lecturn is my mentor at university. He sent the squirrel after me when I told him I was traveling to New Granada to search for my cousin."

"A professor now, is he," snickered Ezmeralda, before regaining her solemnity. "The fact that you have this squirrel in your possession lends you an enormous amount of credibility with *la Resistencia*. Your clever modifications speak to your engineering skills. It does not surprise me Harold put such faith in you.

"*Vamanos, Señor* Goulden. Please get on with tending my injury. You are more nervous around blood than a small child."

Edward cringed at the insult, grabbed a rag and a glass bottle of alcohol. "I need to see the wound," he said, his voice two octaves deeper than usual.

Ezmeralda shrugged off the top of her blouse to reveal her shoulder. Edward touched it with the alcohol-soaked rag; Ezmeralda yelped in pain.

"Start with a clean rag and hot water," said Ezmeralda. Edward grabbed a fresh rag and pulled a small tub of water across the desk. He gently washed off the layers of mud and blood to expose a cluster of small holes.

Ezmeralda took a deep breath as Edward finished. "Scatter gun from across the room. Friendly fire. Now get the tweezers."

Edward swallowed and stepped back. "Do you mean for me to dig into the holes? I cannot do that."

"*Dios mío*, you can, and you will," said Ezmeralda with a snap of her tongue. She looked up at Edward and sighed. "*Mi siento*. Please help me remove the little fragments. There is no doctor in town who will help."

"What do we do now?" asked Constance, staring out the second story window as Edward hunted for the tweezers.

"I will find a way to *la Resistencia* base," said Ezmeralda. "You are welcome to come with me if you like. Or you could secure passage on a commercial zeppelin bound for Britain."

"We cannot stay here," muttered Constance. Edward grunted and bent over his patient.

"No, my friend, you cannot," said Ezmeralda. "Eventually the soldiers will come for you." She flinched as Edward poked into her shoulder, pulling out a tiny metallic pebble a moment later.

"The fragments are not deep," said Edward, relief spreading across his face.

"We could return to London," said Constance.

"Pratt would be hard pressed to provide enough evidence of our involvement to get an arrest warrant for a top bureaucrat and an Oxford student living on the Isles."

"You could never come back here again," said Constance.

"I do not care," said Edward.

"You are taking a bigger risk than you think by running," said Ezmeralda.

"Doubtful," muttered Edward.

"I would not underestimate Lieutenant Vickers. I heard he had a private council with Victoria herself."

Edward continued to perform surgery on his patient in silence until Constance interrupted: "What about Governor Pratt's plan? If we leave, we may never see Margaret again."

Edward looked up from his work and stared at his cousin. "We both know it is extremely unlikely that the fleet will actually find the Resistance base."

"What plan are you talking about?" asked Ezmeralda.

Constance sighed and sat on the bed. "Walden overheard Pratt and Vickers talking about doing something brutal when they attack the Resistance base. So brutal that they needed to sway public opinion and demonize the Resistance. That is why they declared Anne dead and then bombed her funeral."

"This is a moot point," said Edward. "There is no way the British fleet will find the base."

"But what if they do?"

"Do not underestimate the fleet's technology," muttered Ezmeralda. "If they were not confidant, they could find the base they would not waste their time." She leaned forward in her chair and looked and Constance. "What are they planning to do during the attack?"

"I am not certain," said Constance. "I did not understand everything the squirrel recorded."

"May I see the rolls of paper transcribing the conversation?"

"I suppose," muttered Constance, looking away as Edward dug back into her shoulder.

• • • • •

Ezmeralda sat for a long time hunched over the desk reviewing the conversation between Pratt and Vickers. She read Constance's translation, cross-referencing with the original encoded paper rolls. When she finished, Ezmeralda pushed her chair back and stood, eyes flashing a familiar emerald green.

"We need to get to *la Resistencia* base immediately." Constance and Edward looked up from across the room.

"I believe we decided to board a commercial flight for England in two days," said Edward. "We are leaving New Granada before Pratt and Vickers come for us."

Ezmeralda blinked several times, digesting the information. "*Por favor*, I need your help. I know what Pratt and Vickers are planning for *la Resistencia*. I must get to the base and warn them to evacuate."

Edward stood at Ezmeralda's rising alarm. "What are they planning?" asked Constance in a soft voice.

"This word they keep using, *chlorine*. It is a poison gas they plan to drop from the airships. It will kill everyone on the ground. Thousands of people will have no way to defend themselves."

"I don't understand what we can do," said Edward, looking at his feet.

"I need your help to get to *la Resistencia* base. The fastest way is by airship; I know where to get one."

"Where?" asked Edward, hesitation in his voice.

"Steal one from the Cartagena garrison."

"That is absurd. Absolutely preposterous."

"I have done it before," said Ezmeralda. "But I cannot do it alone."

Edward blinked and shook his head. "No, no, we cannot. It is a suicide mission. Plus, I have no intention of getting further involved with the New Granada Resistance."

Ezmeralda sighed. "I know you are afraid, *mi amigo*. And I know this is not the fight you signed up for. But Pratt and Vickers want to kill thousands. And if they drop their chlorine poison, Margaret and Anne will die too."

•　　•　　•　　•　　•

The following afternoon, the unlikely alliance of Edward, Constance, and Ezmeralda left the Goulden estate on foot. To avoid Vickers's men, the conspirators hiked from the house and across the estate's agricultural fields. From there, they sliced through a kilometer of jungle before changing their trajectory and hiking north to the dirt road leading to Cartagena.

Once they reached town, Ezmeralda stole a small horse and carriage left unattended outside a cafe. Constance drove the buggy northeast through the city and out the other side while the others hid inside the carriage. Two kilometers from the garrison, they dismounted and sent the horse back the way they came, confident it would find its way home. They continued on foot through sparse vegetation and palm trees until they reached the shoreline.

"This is where we enter the garrison," said Ezmeralda. She dropped her knapsack in the sand and began rifling through it.

"Where? How?" said Edward, looking around, scanning the abandoned beach and palm trees bending in the wind. "This is not the garrison; I am not even sure how far away it is. You two were exceedingly stingy with the details of the plan."

Ezmeralda pulled three hollow copper tubes from her bag. Each was longer than her arm and bent to resemble a giant fishing hook.

Edward took a piece of pipe from Ezmeralda. "What are we supposed to do with these?" He turned it over in his hands, examining every detail. "They look like ordinary copper pipes. Do they explode? Do we shoot something out of them? Maybe they send out communication signals that scramble the garrison's transmissions."

"Honestly, cousin, you breathe through it." Constance took her tube and put the curved end in her mouth, pushing air in and out of the far end with deep, rhythmic breaths. "Are we going to use these to breathe while we enter the garrison through the ocean?"

"*Si*," said Ezmeralda. "We walk into the ocean until our heads are under water. Then we walk along the shore until we cross over the camp's border."

"Is this how the Resistance entered the garrison to sabotage the new iron spires last week?"

Ezmeralda began hunting for other items in her knapsack. "This is how *la Resistencia* has gotten into the Cartagena garrison for years."

Ezmeralda handed Constance and Edward an empty rubber sack. "Put your boots, guns, and anything made of leather or metal in here. Then tie it closed and strap it to your leg." Ezmeralda showed them what she meant, removing her boots and small firearms. She stuffed them in her own rubber knapsack along with a collection of small metal gadgets hidden on her person. Last, Ezmeralda untied her leather corset, revealing her thin, white cotton blouse to a blushing Edward.

Edward turned his back on the women and did as he was told, stuffing item after item into the bag before securing it to his left thigh. When he turned around, Ezmeralda handed him a length of rope.

"One end is tied to my waist, then yours, and last Constance. Just follow me through the ocean, one foot in front of the other." She tied the rope around Edward's waist, then passed the end down to Constance.

When they were ready, they trudged down to the shore, tied to each other like a chain gang. It was easy to acclimate to the warm water. The tides pulled them forward into deeper waters, the salty spray causing each of them to lick their lips before submerging.

With his head underwater, Edward started breathing through his copper pipe. It worked well so long as he focused on what he was doing and refrained from taking short, quick breaths and hyperventilating. Ezmeralda turned to her right and walked parallel to the shore. Edward felt the rope tug at his waist. He changed direction and continued to slog through the water.

They trudged through the ocean; their bright copper breathing pipes obscured by the dirty white foam blanketing the top of the water. After an eternity spent underwater, Ezmeralda turned right again and led the group out of the sea.

The sun had set and the moon rose low over the horizon as they emerged from the surf and climbed onto a desolate strip of sand. Stubby vegetation and blackened, broken palm trees littered the beach. Edward and Constance collapsed on the sand.

"Where exactly are we?" asked Constance after sitting still for several minutes.

"Garrison firing range," said Ezmeralda. "This is where the soldiers practice firing mortars."

Edward jumped to his feet, then crouched back down on his haunches, swiveling his head left and right.

"Relax," said Ezmeralda. "The range is not used at night."

Edward crumpled on ground in a heap, too tired to reply.

"We traveled a little over two kilometers in two hours," said Ezmeralda. "I want to wait until midnight before stealing the airship, so we have a couple hours to rest."

Edward fell asleep instantly, but Constance stayed awake. "Where do we go from here?" she asked.

Ezmeralda looked up from repacking her knapsack. "We sneak across the garrison to the north end. Most of the soldiers will be asleep." She walked over to the sleeping Edward and retrieved his rubber knapsack. "There will be guards on duty at the new airfield. They change shifts at some point in the night. That's when we make our move." She dumped Edward's sack at his feet and stuffed the empty rubber bag into her knapsack. "We should have a couple minutes after we lift off from the docking spire before the lookouts notice anything. Enough time to be out of sight before any ships launch in pursuit.

• • • • •

Hours after emerging on the beachhead, Constance crouched on the ground beside a fence encircling the airfield, mechanical scorpion in her hand. She glanced up at Edward's pale, sweaty face.

"Relax, cousin. It's loaded with a toxin that will knock the soldiers out, not kill them." Edward swallowed hard and looked up, scanning the terrain around the guard station. On the far side he saw dozens of black metal spires jutting up from the ground. Edward blinked several times, trying to focus his eyes on the tops of the spires and the slumbering fleet of British warships.

Constance crawled up to the shack full of guards beside the gated entrance to the airfield. She slipped the scorpion inside the door frame and waited, counting the number of bodies she heard hit the floor like a row of dominoes. Two minutes later, Constance, Ezmeralda, and Edward walked past the unconscious soldiers. They moved from ship to ship, discussing each zeppelin's strengths and shortcomings.

"*Eso es todo*," said Ezmeralda. "This is it."

Edward stared up the hundred-meter tower. He could see a giant blimp floating just above the spire's apex, anchored in place with a half dozen mooring lines. A steel-cable gangplank arched at an angle from the spire to the zeppelin.

"Do you want to know why I chose this one?"

"No, not really," replied Edward. He paused before speaking again. "How do we get up there? I don't see a lift."

Ezmeralda looked at him and smiled a wicked smile. "We climb." She pointed at a metal ladder welded to the side of the spire. "All the way to the platform on top."

Ezmeralda went first, climbing hand over hand to the platform a hundred meters in the air. Constance scaled the spire next, reaching the top in less time than it took Ezmeralda.

"Come on, old boy," Edward said to himself. "You can do this." He backed away from the base of the ladder. He broke into a run, letting out a low, guttural scream. Edward flung himself at the ladder and landed on the fourth rung. He grappled up, hand over hand, slow, steady, struggling, the iron rungs shockingly cold on his bare hands.

"Do not look up, do not look down," Edward chanted.

Without warning, two hands reached down on either side of him, hooking under his armpits and hauling him up to the platform. He looked into the clenched teeth of Ezmeralda and his cousin as they dropped him on the steel grate.

"Well done, cousin," said Constance.

Edward lifted his head and looked at the others. He smiled between gasps of air, the winds whipping and swirling this high off the ground, stealing his breath before he could properly inhale.

Ezmeralda looked at the gangplank running from the platform to a heavy metal door on the zeppelin's undercarriage. The narrow bridge was a convoluted mess of thin steel cables and crisscrossing, flexible metal grating. Ezmeralda stepped onto the grating, causing it to pitch and sway beneath her feet.

"Constance, I need you with me," she said over her shoulder.

Constance stepped out on the bridge with Ezmeralda, causing it to pitch violently beneath their combined weight. The wind whipped at them so hard it forced Constance to retreat to the tower platform.

"Wait for me to cross, then you follow," called out Ezmeralda. Constance watched her put one foot in front of the other until she reached the steel door. She turned and waved to Constance, who crossed the bridge without hesitation.

"Show off," muttered Edward as he watched his cousin bounce across the cable bridge.

Ezmeralda examined the solid steel door and the shiny metal wheel mounted to it. "The wheel opens the hatch after it is unlocked," said Ezmeralda. "How should we crack the lock?"

Constance stared at the door for a minute, then grasped the metal wheel and cranked it to the left. The door swung open, revealing a dark passageway leading into the belly of the beast.

"It's not locked," said Constance, stepping into the zeppelin's cabin.

"Show off," muttered Ezmeralda as Constance disappeared into the dark. She stepped off the gangplank and onto solid footing, turned and waved at Edward to cross.

Edward stood on the platform of the iron spire and stared across the bridge at the zeppelin. The blimp itself stretched over a hundred meters end to end. He craned his neck up but could not see the top of the giant balloon. He swiveled his head left and right, counting the separate gondolas, each with its own engine.

Edward grasped both the steel-cable handrails on each side of the gangplank, closed his eyes, and marched forward. After a dozen steps, he bumped into something solid and screeched.

"Open your eyes, you fool," said Ezmeralda. Edward opened his eyes and found himself standing in the gondola's hatch.

"Head down the passageway and wait for me at the end. I have to seal the door." Ezmeralda detached the metal clasps securing the cable bridge to the zeppelin. The gangplank swung free, dangling off the top of the iron spire. Ezmeralda leaned out and pulled the heavy hatch closed, then spun the wheel on the inside of the door.

"*Vamanos,* let's go," said Ezmeralda.

Edward followed her up and down corridors, turning corners and ascending a short ladder. The deck alternated from thin sheets of hammered steel to a black iron grating. The air was hot and stale and smelled like years of poorly ventilated tobacco smoke. They ducked through a silver, steel door frame and walked onto the bridge.

"Are we ready?" asked Ezmeralda.

Constance stood engrossed in front of a large control console. "I can release the mooring lines from here. We will float straight up, absolutely silent. God willing, the soldiers in the guard towers will not notice us."

Constance turned her attention back to her work at the pilot's console. A dozen similar consoles lined the bulkheads of the bridge with levers and dials and glass-faced gauges. Bolted to the deck in the middle of the room was the captain's chair.

"I did this once before," said Ezmeralda. "It was beautiful." She turned her attention back to Edward. "You will have to steer the ship for a few minutes. Just keep her pointed straight. Constance will show you how."

"What will you be doing?"

"There are four separate gondolas, each with its own engine and propeller. After we detach from the iron spire and float up, Constance and I have to get all four running before we can go anywhere."

"Why can't you start the engines from here?" asked Edward. "One of these buttons or levers must fire them up."

"There are no automatic engine starters on military airships," muttered Constance, focused on the work she was doing. "The risk of an explosion is too high."

"You just keep us pointed straight ahead," said Ezmeralda. "And watch the altimeter." She pointed to a gauge next to Constance. "Use the ship's radio to update us every hundred meters we climb."

Constance yanked a pair of levers down and freed the airship's anchors, sending them drifting upward. She showed her cousin how to keep the dirigible's nose straight and how to use the vessel's internal radio. Then she and Ezmeralda disappeared back into the zeppelin's bowels.

Edward watched the garrison slowly dissolve as the zeppelin drifted up through the low-lying clouds. He announced the ship's altitude every two minutes to the intercom and the empty room. A pair of engines roared to life, causing him to tumble to floor. Edward stood up and grasped the steering mechanism with both hands to hold it steady. The gondola's turbulence mellowed as the final pair of engines roared to life.

Ezmeralda and Constance reappeared on the bridge minutes later. Edward peeled his fingers off the steering column and collapsed in the captain's chair. Ezmeralda and Constance took over, pulling levers and twisting dials on different consoles like experienced aviators.

Ezmeralda turned and grinned like a Cheshire Cat. "You both did well. Now we go to Bacatá, the old Spanish capital of Santa Fé de Bogotá."

CHAPTER 17

Bacatá

One sticky September afternoon in 1751, a naval requisitions officer hitching a ride home up the Thames stepped off his ship in south London. His name was Lieutenant Fulton, and he was seeking a drink and a companion for the evening.

The lieutenant strolled down the gangplank with a skip in his step. He hummed a sailor's ballad about two ships forced to contend with French pirates while traveling to Safi. The pirates captured one ship and threw the crew overboard. When the second ship ambushed and defeated the pirates, they showed the pirates no mercy. The song was a favorite of Lieutenant Fulton.

The requisitions officer came to an abrupt halt three steps from the bottom of the gangplank and stared across the wooden-plank docks. Thirty yards away was a crowd of scruffy children. Behind them, slacking dock workers passed around a grimy bottle of cheap gin. Fulton wandered over to see what the crowd had gathered for, whistling his ballad of death on the high seas.

"What's all the happening?"

A filthy man reeking of booze and sweat looked the officer up-and-down. "Piss off, wanker."

"What? Who are you, sir?" asked Fulton, visibly taken aback.

The man ignored the officer and flagged down the bottle of gin for a swallow. Lieutenant Fulton pulled a thin black cigar from his jacket. It smelled like coal made from damp, mildewy wood. He ran the cigar under his nose and struck a match, then looked for a more accommodating member of the crowd.

"What's all this about then?" he asked a man with a congenial-looking face.

"Where you been? This is Douglas Tank's 'Mazing Mechanical Loader."

"What is an Amazing Mechanical Loader, and whom is this Douglas Tank?"

The man gave Fulton a long stare behind dull eyes. "Piss off, chuffer."

Lieutenant Fulton found a pile of thick ropes coiled up on the pier to stand on, giving him a view over the top of the rabble. What he saw caused him to fall off his perch and almost ignite a drum of kerosene with his cigar.

Douglas Tank sat behind the controls of his machine as a group of schoolchildren climbed onto the front loader. He called to the youngsters and told them to hold on tight. The crowd cheered and the kids on the machine wrapped their arms around pieces of iron. The machine belched smoke and fire, steam, and soot. It groaned and made a deep popping sound; Fulton was positive he heard a small explosion echoing from somewhere inside the contraption.

The platform welded to the front of the strange carriage crept upward. Lieutenant Fulton squinted and studied the machine, but could not find the source of power used to lift the platform. There were no people lifting it, no ropes and pulleys and livestock raising it. A loud roar came from somewhere inside a slap-dash box on iron plates bolted to the rear of the carriage. More soot and smoke poured out of a metal pipe running from the noisy box. A madman stood on the carriage, dancing as he pulled levers and twisted dials.

The children on the platform screeched and squealed and hung on for dear life, despite the loader taking a full minute to raise them a meter in the air. Fulton could see muskets mounted and facing outward all around the machine. He knew the guns would never fire. Douglas Tank hollered to the kids, then pulled and pushed more levers; the wheels of the carriage rolled forward.

The naval requisitions officer stood in awe. He imagined the loading machine-turned child's toy with working muskets mounted to it. Perhaps even a cannon. Remove that ridiculous lift on the front, lighten the load and make it move faster. Battering ram up front, wider wheels for gripping loose soil, professionally welded iron plating able to stop a musket ball shielding the entire carriage.

Douglas Tank drove his passengers twenty meters and yanked more levers. The carriage came to a stop, then turned around to face the way it came. The driver brought the children back where they started, then lowered them to the ground. A new set of kids was already scrambling up on the lift.

Lieutenant Fulton stood and watched, puffing on his cigar and waiting for the evening's entertainment to draw to a close. He forgot all about the company he hoped to find while ashore. An hour later Douglas rewarded the lieutenant's patience by announcing last ride of the day. The crowd thinned quickly after that, and the lieutenant seized his opportunity.

"Evening," said the requisitions officer.

"'Ello," replied Douglas, absorbed in the task of wrapping his machine in heavy iron chains.

"Quite a contraption you have there."

Douglas grunted a reply without looking up from his work. When he finished, he turned to leave and found the naval still standing behind him.

"What can I do for you?" asked Douglas.

"Can you tell me how it works?"

"I can, but it's complicated. People don't follow."

"Try me," said Fulton.

Douglas found the naval officer sharper than most. He understood basic mechanics and asked reasonably intelligent questions.

"It's bloody brilliant," muttered Fulton once Douglas finished. "And you did all that just to avoid lifting crates?"

"Yes."

"Well, Mr. Tank, today is your lucky day," said Fulton. "I am commissioned by His Majesty's Royal Navy to acquire new assets. I would like to purchase your loading machine."

"I think you missed the point, sir," replied Douglas.

"And what point is that?"

"If I sold it to you, I would have to go back to loading cargo by hand."

"No, you will not."

"I'm not following," replied Douglas.

"I am offering to buy your machine for fifty pounds sterling. I have the coin onboard my ship," said the lieutenant, nodding towards his vessel. "Or if you prefer, we can get a bank note on the morrow."

"That's four years' salary, sir."

"And I can offer you a position at the Royal Armory as an engineer. Pay is another fifty pounds per annum. I want you to spend all your time working on this machine of yours."

Douglas Tank stared at the naval officer for a long time before speaking. "Why are you offering me so much? I never earned anything close in my life."

"War with France is again on the horizon. I envision Tank's Amazing Machine equipped with muskets that actually fire. Storming the battlefields with armor that can deflect cannonballs. Lighter, stronger, and faster, with wheels that can cut through mud or snow. And I want to produce thousands of them."

"Do you truly believe my machine can make a difference in an actual war?" asked Douglas.

"Mr. Tank, I believe your armored vehicle could do more than make a difference. It could change history."

•   •   •   •   •

"Your Majesty, I beg you, please put down the vase. It is fifteenth century Ming dynasty. Breaking another will not solve your problems."

"Very well." Queen Victoria sighed a deep, exasperated sigh and carelessly dropped the ceramic artifact on a cushioned chair. "Why am I surrounded by such incompetent ingrates?"

"Parliament is more than compliant with your wishes. After the unpleasantness that befell the Duke of Winchester," replied Gerard, his voice trailing off.

Victoria replied in a deliberate and slow tone: "The Duke's death was an accident. The timing was merely serendipitous."

"Yes, madam. Of course it was."

Queen Victoria stared at the painting of King George III on the wall. "My grandfather was hailed as a great king. He utilized Douglas Tank's creations, first against the French, then the Spaniards and Portuguese, expanding the Empire with colonies in every corner of the world."

"King George was a great man."

"Poppycock," replied the Queen. "Granddad was crazy as a loon."

"I have heard stories about his eccentricities. Parliament was particularly nasty to him, continuously trying to usurp his power."

"He wore a dressing gown to sign the peace accords with France after squashing Bonaparte's little tantrum. He insisted on playing the French national anthem on the piano for the delegation."

"I see," said Gerard.

"Played the song quite poorly; deeply offended the French. Not that it mattered."

The Queen's attendant remained silent.

"He was more insane in victory than most who suffer defeat."

"Well, I do know that the people loved him," replied Gerard.

"My point is that he did great things for Britain despite his shortcomings. My lack of a cock is my only shortcoming, yet I fear the Empire is waning under my rule."

"The British Empire is stronger than ever, ma'am. Raw materials flow in from colonies around the world. Exported manufactured goods fetch high prices with an inexhaustible demand. Wealth pours into the Isles at a rate greater than even the Romans enjoyed."

"Again, you miss the point, and are a poor attendant at that," said Queen Victoria. With another heavy sigh she slumped in a Louis XIV sofa, draping her arm over the carved wooden armrests plated in gold.

"Please enlighten me," said the Queen's confidant. "What is the point?"

An unexpected voice from across the room startled the Queen and her attendant: "The point is that Her Majesty fears that the British Empire is little more than a house of cards." The tall, slender man took long strides across the room, his slick leather boot heels clicking on the marble floor. He wore an immaculate naval uniform, his blue bridge coat laced with gold braids and studded with polished brass buttons.

"I beg forgiveness for the interruption, Your Majesty," said the officer, bowing deeply at the waist.

"Lucius Vickers, it is good to see you." Queen Victoria nodded in acknowledgment of his bow. "If you don't mind, please explain exactly what my point is."

"Of course," said Vickers, turning to face the attendant. "Her Majesty is referring to specific Resistance groups operating in a handful of backwater colonies."

"I was led to believe that most displaced natives in the remote colonies make their way to London or Glasgow or Boston. They immigrate to one a dozen manufacturing centers and learn how to live in the modern world."

"That is partially correct," replied Vickers.

"The Resistance factions in cities such as London or Boston are little more than propaganda machines," said Gerard. "Printed pamphlets and speeches in parks; paper tigers without teeth."

"That is true as well."

"Then to what are you referring, sir?" asked Gerard.

Lieutenant Vickers smirked at the attendant and twirled his thin, black mustache. "Most natives actually stay behind and live out their insignificant little lives same as ever. However, a minority of natives always band together and form a local Resistance group, eventually tethering themselves to the worldwide movement."

"Dimwitted fools," muttered Gerard. "The Empire provides them with access to food and clean water. We build roads, bring modern medicines."

Queen Victoria grunted her agreement.

"Quite right," said Vickers. "They are ignorant dullards, destined to a life of squalor."

"Resistance groups in remote colonies are notoriously ineffectual," said Gerard. "They are weak, disorganized, poorly supplied, and tragically underfunded."

"True again, with a few notable exceptions. For example, the Resistance groups in South Africa and the Filipino islands have pushed those colonies to the brink of civil war."

"Yes, of course," said Gerard. "I did hear something about that."

"Native populations in these colonies are sympathetic to the plight of their Resistance cousins," said Vickers. "Without realizing it, these twits become the lifeblood that enables the local Resistance groups to continue. They feed and shelter them; they pass along valuable intelligence. The Resistance only survives by hiding behind the skirts of the colonial natives."

"I fear I am still missing the point," said Gerard.

"Even if we purged the more dangerous Resistance movements from the jungles and deserts, that action may jolt the natives into full revolt."

"I believe that is what you are here to discuss, lieutenant," interrupted Queen Victoria.

"Yes, madam. I have an idea involving one of the more problematic colonial Resistance movements."

"Do tell."

"I intend on burning the entire group to the ground, and I plan to do it with the support of the native population. To do so, I need an immediate transfer to New Granada. And please be aware, ma'am, we will both have to get our hands dirty on this one."

"I do not get my hands dirty, lieutenant."

"Of course, Your Majesty."

CHAPTER 18

A sharp knock echoed through Major Ulperlip's office from the outside of his door.

"Enter." The major stopped pacing and faced the door. It opened and the darkness outside spilled into the office. Lieutenant Vickers stepped into the room and closed the door behind him.

"You sent for me?" The young lieutenant sat at the conference table and put his boots up on the hardwood.

Ulperlip slapped Vickers's feet back down to the floor. The lieutenant looked at his superior officer and curled his lip in a sneer.

"I want to know what is happening out there," said the major in his most authoritarian voice. He leaned down, his face inches away from Vickers. "You are the commanding officer in charge of the new airfield. I am holding you personally responsible for losing that battleship." Spittle flew out of the major's mouth and landed on Vickers's forehead.

"I do not have time for this," replied Vickers. "Sir."

"You do not have time for this, lieutenant?" said Ulperlip, lowering his voice. "You have no time to do your job and make sure none of my bloody airships are stolen?"

Lieutenant Vickers shifted in his chair, locking eyes with the major. "Sir, who do you suppose stole that war ship?"

"How the hell should I know?"

"Ezmeralda Lefount. She is the only person in all of Cartagena capable of pulling off such a stunt."

Ulperlip stood up straight: "Just what is your point?"

Lieutenant Vickers twirled his thin mustache between his thumb and forefinger. "Ezmeralda Lefount undoubtedly hijacked that airship, most likely with the assistance of a small team. Right now, she is flying it to the Resistance base somewhere in the jungles to the south."

"Now when we locate their base, we will be forced to fight one of our own battleships," said Ulperlip. "Your incompetence will cost British lives." The major paused and stared down at his subordinate. "I will see to it that you are severely reprimanded for this failure of duty."

"You're missing the point, sir."

"And what point is that?"

Lieutenant Vickers stood and walked to the giant map of New Granada plastered to the wall behind Ulperlip's desk.

"We do not know where the Resistance base is located. Our initial plan was to spend weeks with the fleet canvasing the jungles, searching tens of thousands of square kilometers from above. Personally, I had my doubts we would ever locate the camp."

"Again, get to the bloody point," said Ulperlip. His voice was a low growl, like a dog spotting its adversary for the first time.

"My point, sir, is that when the fleet arrived, I had the foresight to equip every vessel with a tracking beacon. Right now, the stolen zeppelin is emitting a high-frequency pulse that our engineers are tracking." Vickers struck the map on the wall with the side of his fist. "The stolen zeppelin is currently thirty kilometers southwest of our position. It appears to be heading for the Magdalena River Basin."

Major Ulperlip stared blankly at the map. He tried to raise his voice, but it betrayed him and cracked instead. "Why didn't you tell me about the tracking devices?"

Vickers stepped close enough for the major to feel his warm breath. "My apologies, sir, but I was under the impression that the new airfield and the Royal Fleet were under my care."

Major Ulperlip swallowed hard. When he spoke, his voice was a whimper. "Very good, lieutenant. When will the fleet be ready to depart?"

"Sunrise. Sir."

•　•　•　•　•

Edward and Constance sat on the bridge of the HMS *Marlborough* attempting to relax in the uncomfortable metal chairs. The floor-to-ceiling windows occupied three full walls to allow officers a complete view of the battlefield. Edward and Constance sat in front of the windows an hour after dawn, soaking up the tropical sunshine. The cousins had a spectacular view; the sun lit up the jungle canopy below, chasing the cold air from the jungle floor and the zeppelin's bridge.

After they had reached the Magdalena River Basin, Ezmeralda altered their heading. Now, the river snaked through the lush jungle floor below them from its source high in the mountains to the south.

Ezmeralda slammed the steel door to the bridge open and marched into the room. "I found something interesting."

Constance looked up at her, drowsy, eyes at half-mast, "What is it?"

"Canisters of that poison chlorine gas Pratt and Vickers talked about," said Ezmeralda.

"How can we destroy them?" asked Edward.

"That was my first thought," said Ezmeralda, "but now I am not certain. I think I should study the gas once we reach Bacatá."

"We should dump it overboard," said Constance.

"I want to learn its secrets, to know how it works," said Ezmeralda.

"That way we can better defend against it."

"Makes sense," said Edward.

"No, it does not," said Constance, her voice rising. "It is a coward's weapon, capable of killing thousands of people. They drop it from above and watch innocent people die. We should jettison it from the ship immediately."

"Please, Constance," said Edward. "Settle down."

"I will not settle down. Those canisters may be used to kill many people if we do not destroy them."

Ezmeralda interrupted their exchange. "I also found a couple hundred of these." She held up an unusual contraption with leather straps, brass buckles, and a pair of glass-covered eye holes. It had two copper canisters slotted sideways below the goggles. "I do not know what they."

Constance took the contraption from Ezmeralda. "Members of Her Majesty's Department of Engineering and Advanced Design gave a lecture at Oxford some months ago on new lifesaving devices. They showed us masks like this."

Constance put the mask over her face and fumbled with the leather straps behind her head. Inside, the mask smelled like a damp fire; it was difficult to get a satisfying lung full of air. Constance continued talking, her words muffled and running together.

"We cannot understand what you are saying with that contraption strapped to your face," said Edward.

Constance removed the mask and inhaled the crisp, thin air. "Wearing the mask prevents inhaling toxic gases. The representatives from the D.E.A.D. said they would be used by fire fighters or factory workers exposed to dangerous gases."

Ezmeralda snickered: "Her Majesty's D.E.A.D. does not invent gadgets to save lives. These masks are for British soldiers when they drop chlorine gas."

Edward spoke, his voice so quiet the others barely heard him. "How will the Resistance defend itself against such a vicious attack?"

Ezmeralda stared into the mask's darkened-glass eyes. "I do not know." She looked up at the others. "You two should sleep. We will arrive at the Resistance base this afternoon." She turned on her heels and walked off the bridge, slamming the steel door shut behind her.

• • • • •

Constance wandered up and down the zeppelin's corridors, shuffling her well-worn boots along the steel grate. She found Ezmeralda sitting at a desk in the captain's quarters.

"I have been reviewing the ship's manifest," said Ezmeralda, her attention on the logbooks spread out on the desk.

"Anything unexpected?" asked Constance.

"Nothing other than the cache of chlorine gas canisters."

"I actually wanted to discuss those canisters with you," said Constance.

Ezmeralda's attention did not waver from the manifest. "According to this, they loaded the chlorine gas at Heathrow Airfield. The canisters were produced in London. Do you recognize this address?"

Constance read the sheet Ezmeralda held up for her. "Battersea, that's south of the Thames. That neighborhood is just block after block of monstrous red-brick factories."

Ezmeralda nodded and retracted the sheet. "The rest of these are standard soldier and artillery manifest items for a ship this size. It is carrying extra equipment to search the jungle for *la Resistencia*."

Constance cleared her throat and tried again. "I want to discuss dumping the canisters of chlorine gas overboard."

"I heard you the first time."

"You did not respond."

"Your statement hardly deserves a response." Ezmeralda lifted her eyes and locked them on Constance. "But if you insist on discussing the matter, make your case."

"I only wish to prevent any further loss of life," said Constance. "As long as those canisters exist, they are a threat. Sometime in the future they might fall into the hands of someone willing to use them."

"I agree," said Ezmeralda.

"Then we can dump them overboard?"

"The value of the gas as a research tool is immeasurable," replied Ezmeralda. "That's why I want it. By studying it, I might find a way to limit the gas's effectiveness. I am sure Her Majesty's Armed Forces will use it across the world very soon."

Constance was silent for a minute. "What if we limit the supply, thereby limiting its overall destructive force?"

"What do you propose?"

"You keep a single canister for study. Then we dump the rest overboard."

"No."

"Why not?"

"Because one canister is almost useless," replied Ezmeralda. "I need more samples than that."

"Ten canisters then."

"Still not enough, but I see what you are going for. What if we dump half overboard?"

"I suppose that's something," said Constance.

"Then get to work disarming the canisters so they do not pump their poison all over the jungle. We will dump them when you are done."

Constance stood by the cabin door, stalling. "Can I ask you another question?"

"I suppose."

"Why did you join the Resistance?"

"That is a complicated question," replied Ezmeralda, still engrossed in the ship's log books.

"I was recently sworn in as a Freemason Apprentice in the York Rite. I know you are a member the Scottish Rite because you oppose British colonialism."

"I am a twenty-first degree Freemason of the Scottish Rite. I have a level of mechanical expertise hard to find anywhere in the world. The Masons are an organization dedicated to improving the world by upholding a set of moral standards."

"I know that."

"Is your question how two groups of Freemasons, living by two different sets of morals, can find themselves on opposite sides of the same war?"

"Not really," said Constance. "I understand that both Rites believe they are doing what is right. One group believes in self-determination. The other believes in providing humanity with medicine and education and technology. My problem is that I am an engineer, not a philosopher. I want to know what led you to join the Scottish Rite and oppose the British Empire."

"Both sides believe they are fighting for a better world," said Ezmeralda, "but I agree with the guiding principles of the Scottish Rite. Individual freedom and national sovereignty are more important than safety and prosperity."

Constance sighed, then turned to leave. "All right then."

Ezmeralda spoke to her from behind: "You were hoping for a more clear answer."

Constance turned around, "All of my life I heard the same intangible arguments, the same faulty logic circles. In Cartagena, the descendants of African slaves have paying work and Natives have cures for diseases. But if Spain never colonized this continent, slaves and European diseases would have never been introduced."

"You think like me," said Ezmeralda. "My husband, Francis, does not see things the same way."

"I thought Francis Lefount was a member of the New Granada Resistance."

"He is," replied Ezmeralda, "but Francis is driven by his hatred for the British."

"Why does he hate the British?"

Ezmeralda put down the ship's manifests. "I was born on a hacienda in central Mexico. My parents immigrated from Spain. When the British took the colony from Spain, no British immigrated to Mexico and the colony never really integrated into the Empire. Eventually we fought for our independence and won."

"That was a long time ago."

"Not that long," said Ezmeralda, eyes flashing a vivid green. "I was a little girl when Mexico won its freedom."

"Do you fight for Resistance movements around the world because you remember living in a free and independent Mexico?"

"We only had a few years of freedom in Mexico, but we were happy," replied Ezmeralda. "We were happy because we made decisions for ourselves. Even if we made the wrong choice, it was still ours."

"What about Francis?"

"During the time Mexico was free, the landowners and the Catholic Church conspired to turn Mexico over to the French. Knowing they could not hold it for long, the French monarchy sent assessors and tax collectors to take what they could. Francis's father, Maurice, came to Mexico as an assessor with his son.

"When the British invaded, Francis and his father were fugitives trapped in Mexico. The owner of the hacienda where my family worked hid them for months. Francis was an untrained engineer, same as me. We fell in love and secretly wed.

"The British eventually found Maurice and killed him. I ran away with Francis and we joined with Mexican *Resistencia* under Benito Juarez. There was a Freemason that rode with Juarez who he taught Francis and me all he knew."

"Francis hates the British because they killed his father," said Constance.

"*Si*," replied Ezmeralda. "Francis still supports French colonialism. He believes the French moral code would ensure fair governance."

"And you do not?" asked Constance.

"No," said Ezmeralda, returning her focus to the ship's logs. "I believe colonialism in any form is flawed. It leads to corruption, which lowers everyone's quality of life."

"All I want to do is build things that help people live a better life."

"And you think you can do that working for the British Empire?"

"I do," said Constance. "As far as I can tell, this mess with you and Anne and the chlorine gas is because of Pratt and Vickers."

"Maybe," said Ezmeralda. "The problem is that there are people like those two all over the world. Power-hungry, greedy, spoiled little children."

Constance snorted. "I suppose I am waiting for mankind to grow up so I can do the work I was meant to."

"You cannot afford to wait," muttered Ezmeralda.

"Why not?"

Ezmeralda sighed and put down the ship's logs. "I spent years fighting for a *Resistencia* group in India with Harold Lecturn. I was there when he built his little squirrel spy.

"Lecturn sees something special in you or else he would not have given you one of his most favorite creations. He probably believes you are one of the best engineers of your generation. You could tip the balance of power in this war."

Constance stood in silent shock. "I do not want to fight for any side."

"You will."

•   •   •   •   •

The small crew of the HMS *Marlborough* unfurled a large, white canvas from the bottom of the airship. They watched through the broad bridge windows as the streets of Bacatá came into view, the jungle bleeding into the narrow rows of houses. The rain forest crept through the streets like a thief in the night, reclaiming a small amount of the city every year.

"Do you think they will get the message?" asked Edward, watching the ground a kilometer below the airship. The streets of the old Spanish capital were narrow and paved with stone or packed earth. City parks were still discernible; the unkempt grass was knee deep, the lush green trees brambly and heavy with old, dead wood.

"If not, Francis will shoot us down," said Ezmeralda.

"From this height? I highly doubt it," said Edward. Ezmeralda and Constance stared at Edward.

"You really are naïve," said Ezmeralda; Constance snickered.

"How do we dock?" said Edward. "Bacatá is practically ancient. I see no iron spires, and I doubt there ever were."

"That's a good question," said Constance. "Where do we park this balloon?"

Ezmeralda's eyes twinkled and flashed vivid green as she walked across the bridge to the forward steering controls. She leaned over the panel, examining the partially obscured city streets through the bridge window. She spotted her target and winked at Constance and Edward.

Ezmeralda's hands moved across the control panel, flipping switches and dropping levers. The steel girder skeleton groaned as the airship changed course and dropped altitude.

The floor seemed to fall away from the feet of the small crew, causing a pale green hue to creep over Edward's face. He clutched at a chrome control console near the bridge window, took a couple of unsteady steps, and dropped into a bolted-down chair.

Ezmeralda worked the zeppelin's controls as if she spent her whole life practicing. The zeppelin continued its dizzying descent until it reached its target altitude several minutes later.

Edward tried standing, leaning on the console in front of him for support. "Are we done? Have we arrived or did we crash and die?"

"We have arrived," replied Ezmeralda, tongue in cheek.

"What now?" asked Constance.

"The tree directly below us was modified so a zeppelin can dock to it," said Ezmeralda. "It's twenty meters below us and taller than everything else."

"Are you suggesting that we dock to a tree?" asked Edward.

"*Si.*"

"Impossible," said Edward. "As well as reckless and borderline suicidal. I absolutely insist you find another way down."

Ezmeralda walked across the bridge to the window running along the starboard bulkhead and pointed. "There are mooring rings attached to the top of the tree. I will descend to the top of the tree and anchor us in place, then Constance will lower the rope ladder to me, and I will attach it to the tree. There are ladder rungs all the way to the ground. Edward, for now I want you to stay here and monitor our position and altitude."

Constance followed Ezmeralda through the belly of the gondola to the exterior door. Beside the sealed hatch was an anchoring system with steel cables wrapped around a winch.

"I will attach this to me then step out the door," said Ezmeralda, grabbing a steel clip on the end of the fat cable. "You use the levers beside the door and lower me to the tree. It is easy, as long as the hatch is directly over the tree."

Ezmeralda found the rope ladder that worked in tandem with the anchor cable. "The ladder has a clip on the bottom rung. After I secure the anchor, attach the ladder to the cable and lower it to me. I will clip it to the tree."

Ezmeralda pulled down a harness made of leather straps and rusty brass buckles hanging on the wall. She strapped to over her corset, then clipped the anchor to the harness. A minute later she was out the door and dropping through the sky.

Ezmeralda's parking job was spot on, and she landed on top of the tree on her first try. She unclipped the cable from her harness and attached it to a steel ring bolted through the tree trunk.

Constance saw Ezmeralda's signal and clipped the bottom of the rope ladder to the cable and dropped it out the hatch. She worked the levers beside the door, lowering the ladder, the clip shimmying along the cable straight towards Ezmeralda.

After Ezmeralda secured the ladder, Constance locked the levers in place and walked back to the bridge. She powered down the zeppelin's systems before leading Edward back to the exterior door.

Edward leaned out and looked down the length of the rope ladder. "You are joking, right?"

"Completely serious. You climb down the ladder to the top of the tree."

"Absolutely no bloody way. I will vomit halfway down."

"Probably," muttered Constance.

"If I make it to the top of the tree, then what? Am I supposed to climb down the tree all the way to the ground?"

"Yes, cousin," said Constance, no longer trying to hide the annoyance in her voice. "Do you remember why we came here? Margaret and Anne are waiting down there."

"Fine," said Edward, shooting a cynical glare at his cousin. "Those two had better damn well appreciate this."

Constance strapped Edward into a safety harness attached to the anchor cable. He took a deep breath and stepped out onto the ladder.

CHAPTER 19

The tree anchoring the HMS *Marlborough* towered over the city of Bacatá, its upper branches swaying high over the buildings in the afternoon wind. A group of Resistance soldiers stood on the tree's bulging roots, watching the airship dock and the crew disembark.

Ezmeralda Lefount hit the ground first, skipping the final ladder rungs nailed to the trunk. Almost before her feet hit the ground, a tall, pale man swept her up in his arms. Ezmeralda locked her arms around his neck and they vanished into the crowd.

Edward came inching down the wooden ladder ten minutes behind Ezmeralda. The crowd gathered at the base of the tree watched him reach down with his toes to find each step. Standing on the last rung, Edward prodded the ground with his right toe. He jumped back up three steps in surprise when he felt the solid earth. The audience's laughter broke Edward out of his trance and he tried as best he could to nonchalantly finish his climb.

Edward planted both feet on the ground, drawing laughter from the crowd once more when they saw that his face matched the color of the pale avocados growing nearby. Edward took two steps towards the closest well-armed Resistance warrior and his knees buckled. He stumbled forward, one knee smacking the ground before two empathetic rebels hooked him underneath each armpit. They heaved Edward back to his feet and motioned for someone to bring him water.

A short man in the same green khaki uniform as the rest of the soldiers stepped forward. He stood close enough to Edward for the Englishman to smell the cigar smoke embedded in his clothing. General Marquez stared at Edward, stroking his coarse black beard with his thumb and forefinger. His smile seemed wider than his entire face.

"You must be Edward Goulden. I am General Jose Tairona Marquez, leader of this group of freedom fighters. I have heard very much about you." He paused, his smile somehow growing wider. "Now that we have met, I am not disappointed."

General Marquez spoke in Spanish to the two large men holding up Edward. They sat Edward down on a nearby tree stump. He tipped backward off the stump, triggering a hundred deep-throated laughs.

A minute later, a thin, young woman in a brown skirt and loose corset launched herself from the docking tree. She hit the ground hard, landing neatly on her feet. The soldiers standing closest to the tree jumped back in shock. General Marquez's eyes shot up the tree, scanning the lower limbs for any more surprises. Satisfied that the young woman was the last zeppelin passenger, Marquez grinned his trademark grin and approached the young woman.

"You must be Miss Constance Ventor." Constance stared at the soldier, suspicion and apprehension painted across her face. "*Señora* Goulden arrived a few days ago," explained the general. "She told me about you."

"Will you take me to Margaret?" asked Constance.

General Marquez straightened up to his full height; half-a-head shorter than the gangly young woman. "Margaret said you waste little time on formalities. Same as Edward, you too do not disappoint. Both Margaret and Anne will join us in another minute."

A murmur rose from the back of the throng of soldiers and drove its way to the front. Margaret pushed her way through with Anne struggling to keep up. Spotting Edward and Constance, Margaret shouldered one of General Marquez's largest bodyguards to the ground in her haste to get to her loved ones. The congregated soldiers erupted in laughter once more.

Margaret threw her arms around her husband's neck, causing Edward to fall backwards off his tree stump with Margaret on top of him.

The crowd roared with laughter as Edward struggled to get out from underneath Margaret.

Margaret straightened up and whispered something to Edward. She guided his gaze to a young woman stumbling over the bodyguard Margaret knocked down. Edward rose and helped his sister to her feet.

"Anne," he said, his voice barely more than a breath. "You are still so clumsy."

They stood in awkward silence for a moment, staring at each other. The soldiers encircled them, silent as a night at sea. Margaret slipped behind Edward and gave him a gentle push forward. Anne and Edward embraced for a long time. When they let go, the group of soldiers released a collective sigh and applauded the siblings.

"Master Goulden," said General Marquez. "We prepared living quarters for you and your family. You are free to walk anywhere in this camp, but two of my men will be with you always. I am sending you all back to Cartagena, but not for several days."

"Thank you," said Edward. "If you do not mind, we would like to retire for a while and rest." He paused, staring up through the branches of the docking tree. "In two hours, please call a council with all your officers. We need to discuss an imminent threat to your camp."

General Marquez bowed his head, smiled, and scratched his beard.

• • • • •

"I had my doubts when you were assigned second in command," said Major Ulperlip.

"Yes, sir," replied Vickers.

"Your commission was bought and paid for. You sat behind a desk in London for two years before your transfer. But it appears that you have proven yourself resourceful."

Vickers cleared his throat: "Before I was assigned my post in London, I was awarded numerous medals and accommodations for my service during the Weerstand Resistance uprising in South Africa. Before that I served as an officer on three separate campaigns to dismantle various West African Resistance groups."

"Yes, yes, of course," muttered the major. "I pulled your service records from the African campaigns. I must say, your superiors included several grizzly stories in their accounts of those campaigns. I found some to be too ghastly to consider plausible."

"I encountered many grim situations on the Dark Continent."

"Even disregarding the most far-fetched stories, your service records imply a reckless disregard for human life. I assumed your assignment to a London desk was to force you to practice restraint."

"I am certain the accounts given in my files are exaggerated," said Vickers. "I did only what had to be done."

"I am sure you did," replied the major. "Perhaps you should petition Her Majesty's high command to have the horror stories stricken from your record."

"Yes, sir," said Vickers. Major Ulperlip stared at the lieutenant for a long moment before forcing his gaze out the front windows of the zeppelin's bridge.

"What news of our prey, Midshipman Smithe?"

"They have not moved for three hours now, sir," replied a nervous communications officer seated behind a control console.

"Brilliant," said Major Ulperlip. "Where exactly are they?" He tugged a spyglass from his vest pocket and began scanning the jungle canopy.

"They appear to be holding steady over the old Spanish city of Bacatá, sir."

"That is very intriguing," said the major.

"Why is that intriguing?" asked Vickers.

The major continued his survey of the river basin: "Bacatá was the capital of the Spanish Viceroyalty. The capital was moved to Cartagena when Britain acquired New Granada a century ago. Simon Bolivar used Bacatá as his base of operations during his uprising fifty years ago. After his revolution failed and he was executed, Bacatá was again abandoned."

"I suppose you find the history of this corner of the Empire interesting," muttered Vickers.

Ulperlip lowered his spyglass. "I do not believe I understand your meaning, lieutenant."

"I apologize, sir," replied the lieutenant, "but I am only interested in the success of this mission. Not the history of colonialism in New Granada."

"I see," said the major, returning his attention to his spyglass. "Anticipating the terrain where we confront the Resistance may have significant bearing on the outcome. Dull lecture aside."

A heavy, uncomfortable silence weighed on the bridge crew, mixing easily with the humid air of the rain forest.

"Sir," said Vickers, "perhaps now is an appropriate time to discuss an issue of a more complex nature."

Ulperlip raised an eyebrow: "Go on."

"Her Majesty sent a new weapon to aid in the dismantling of the Resistance."

Ulperlip replaced the spyglass in his pocket. "I was not informed of any new weapon, lieutenant. Explain yourself."

"It's called chlorine gas. Half the fleet are carrying scores of ten-kilogram cannisters. Once dropped, they explode on impact and release the gas. I was led to believe that any person standing within fifty meters will die of asphyxiation. We have enough cannisters to blanket Bacatá and kill everyone on the ground."

"I will not have such a ghastly, cowardly weapon deployed on my watch, lieutenant," said Major Ulperlip in his most authoritarian voice.

"Yes, sir," said Vickers. His eyes narrowed above his thin mustache. "The cannisters came with orders written by the hand Queen Victoria herself. She commands we use any and all means necessary to fully dismantle the New Granada Resistance."

"Not only was I not informed of this horrendous weapon I am carrying into battle, but you failed to disclose mission orders directly from Her Majesty," roared Ulperlip, standing close enough to the lieutenant to splatter saliva on Vickers's forehead. "Why is that?"

Vickers stepped backward and wiped his face. "I am sure I do not know, sir. I assumed the chain of command made you aware of all this."

"I was not made aware," said Ulperlip. "You oversee communications with London. If you did not relay the orders, how would I have heard?"

"I am sure I do not know that either, sir," said Vickers. "You did sign the paperwork when the fleet arrived in Cartagena acknowledging receipt of the gas."

"I do not remember that."

"And whether or not you were personally informed ahead of time of Her Majesty's wishes, we do have direct orders to use the chlorine gas, if necessary, to dismantle the Resistance."

"I am not willing to order the deaths of thousands while we sit up here and watch," said the major.

"Are you saying you will intentionally violate a direct order signed by Queen Victoria?"

"We will defeat the Resistance without resorting to such brutal tactics."

"And if we fail?"

"We will not fail."

●　　●　　●　　●　　●

"This is where the war council meets," said General Marquez. He carefully stubbed out his cigar on the brick wall. "I do not like to smoke inside and breathe in the old smoke."

"What is this building?" asked Edward.

"This was the original seat of government for New Granada. After that it was the headquarters of Simon Bolivar's failed revolution." The general slid his half-smoked cigar into his shirt's breast pocket and buttoned the flap. "Come. Everyone is waiting."

The doors opened into a wide meeting hall dominating much of the first floor. Despite the smoldering coals in the fireplace, the room was cool and dark. The two dozen individuals milled about chatting in small circles.

"*Buenos días*," said General Marquez to the gathered group of officers. "Good afternoon ladies, *también*." The general gave a polite nod to Margaret and Constance, as well as Ezmeralda standing with Francis. A dozen scattered conversations in Spanish or French or Native vernaculars came to an abrupt halt.

"First, we welcome Ezmeralda Lefount back. She was greatly missed the last few months. *Muchas gracias* to Edward Goulden and Constance Ventor for their bravery bringing her back." General Marquez nodded his head towards Edward and Constance. The rest of the room stared intently at the interlopers from the Isles.

"I also have bad news. British soldiers attacked a safe house in while most of the local *Resistencia* was inside. Many brothers-in-arms died, including George."

"How did this happen?" asked a muscular man with graying hair. "The Cartagena *Resistencia* is always very cautious."

"Because of me," said Ezmeralda, her voice quiet and her eyes locked on the floor between her feet. "The governor's spies follow me after I broke out of prison. Soldiers surrounded the safe house and opened fire minutes after I got there. A few of us cut a path through the soldiers with our rifles and escaped."

"Then it must be the fault of these two," said the burly gray soldier, pointing at Edward and Margaret. "They led Governor Pratt right to our comrades."

"General Mera, *por favor*," replied General Marquez. "These two have proven their loyalty."

"They have done no such thing," said General Mera. "When I led the Santa Marte *Resistencia*, we found and executed many British informants in our ranks."

"Perhaps that is why you longer lead the Santa Marte *Resistencia*."

"Do not question me on this, Marquez," said Mera in a low, growling voice. "I know traitors when I see them."

"They are not traitors," said General Marquez. "George vouched for them himself. We knew the governor had men watching these two before Ezmeralda's escape. His spies are obviously more clever than we thought."

"I will march them outside right now and execute them," said Mera. "Who in this room is with me? Who else wants revenge for George's death?"

A small voice in the back of the room spoke up and the crowd parted around him. "We all want revenge for George's death, my friend. But killing these two is not revenge. They may be foolish, and perhaps even weak, but they are our allies. Killing them will only strengthen Pratt."

"*Gracias, mi amigo,*" said Marquez, "for those wise words. I am ending this discussion and moving on to something else." The general cleared his throat and waited; Mera said nothing.

"I called this war council to discuss the coming British invasion."

A murmur pushed forward from the back of the room: "We have talked many times about the battle plans. We know what is coming, and we know what we will do."

"What will you do?" asked Marquez.

"We will blow those British dogs out of the sky," echoed a second voice. Cries of enthusiasm met his response.

"*Si,* that we will," said General Marquez. "But first, Edward has brought us new details about the British fleet. And Ezmeralda has information about a new weapon the British are bringing. Edward, please tell this council what you know." Marquez swept the back of his hand towards the Englishman.

Edward cleared his throat; Margaret gave him a subtle push. "Yes, right, thank you," said Edward, stumbling forward. "Queen Victoria actually sent an entire fleet. Their sole mission is to wipe out the New Granada Resistance."

From the back of the room, a small voice who had not yet spoken called out: "We already know this."

Edward stammered on, "Right, well, what you do not know is that the armada coming is the Ninth Fleet, the most powerful in Her Majesty's arsenal. That makes it one of the most dangerous forces in the world." Edward's words brought silence to his indignant audience.

"Let them come," came a guttural reply. "Our defenses are strong."

"Forty-one battleships, twenty troop transports, plus another fourteen support ships carrying a lighter arsenal. Their combined firepower could turn Bacatá to rubble ten times over." Edward's words echoed off the tall brick walls, filling the empty, silent space in the room. "And with the technology available to the fleet, I doubt they will have much trouble finding you."

"I say it again," said the same unseen voice. "Let the bastards come. We will send them home crying."

"*Oui*," said a man with a thick French accent, stepping onto the center floor. "We can handle them."

"Why are you so confident? Do you not comprehend the level of firepower bearing down on us?"

"I am Francis Lefount, and I am responsible for Bacatá's defenses. I promise you that regardless of this Ninth Fleet's firepower, we will blow them out of the sky."

"Bloody arrogant," said Edward. "Governor Pratt and the Ninth Fleet were given a mandate by Queen Victoria to do whatever is necessary to wipe out the New Granada Resistance. Pratt twisted the events in Cartagena to get a similar mandate from the people. Once the fleet arrives, there will be no opportunity for surrender, no chance to disband and reform at a later date."

"We have discussed this," said General Marquez. "Governor Pratt painted the *la Resistencia* as murderers and rapists terrorizing New Granada."

"A bomb was detonated at Anne's funeral," said Constance. "Many people died. Pratt blamed the Resistance, but we believe Pratt and Vickers were actually responsible."

"The eyes of the entire British Empire are upon New Granada, demanding that your movement be dismantled and its members pay for their crimes," said Edward.

"Right now, the streets of Cartagena are filled with angry citizens," said Constance. "They are demanding the military destroy the Resistance."

The room was silent as it digested the disturbing news. A stocky soldier standing near General Marquez broke the silence. "*Dios mío.* How can anyone be so cruel and plant a bomb at a funeral?"

"Your story fits with our own intelligence," said Francis Lefount, stepping back into the conversation. "We received word that several *Résistance* movements around the world are moving to cut us out of the global network."

"I still do not understand why Pratt did such horrible things," said Margaret. "It only makes sense to me if he is setting us up for something."

"*Por que* we have lost the support of our own people," said Marquez. "A revolution without the support of the people is no revolution. We are little more than pirates now." Again, silence hung in the air, heavy from the stagnant warmth coming off the fireplace and the humidity in the air.

"If I may ask, general, what is our play here?" asked Edward.

"To defeat this armada the British are sending," said General Marquez. "Then return your sister to Cartagena where she will tell her story."

"We are not defenseless children, waiting and worrying about our father's anger," said General Mera, stepping back into the fray. The council at his back erupted in unison.

"We will not bow down to the British scum."

"We are stronger than they think we are."

"We will fight, and we will win."

General Marquez held up his hand and the voices in the crowd hushed. "You are all correct. We will fight. And we will win. But it is important to understand what our enemy can do before stepping into battle."

He turned to Francis Lefount, standing quietly in the center of the forum: "Francis, please detail our defensive firepower."

"*Oui*," said Francis. "Of course."

"This is a waste of time," said General Mera. "We have already heard the Frenchman's report."

"This counsel has heard enough of your opinions for one day, general," said Marquez. "*Por favor*, keep quiet while *Señor* Lefount updates us."

"*Merci mon ami*," said Francis. "We have a line of twelve anti-aircraft cannon surrounding the city. They sit on the jungle floor and are not easy to spot from the air. We have sixteen more guns mounted on rooftops scattered across the city."

"I did not see any large cannons on the rooftops when we docked," said Edward. "How is this possible? The anti-aircraft weapons the British use are monstrous guns several stories tall."

"You need enormous resources to build a weapon capable of bringing down a battleship," said Constance. "What you claim is impossible."

"No, *mija*, it is not," said Ezmeralda. "Before I was taken prisoner, Francis and I worked out a new design for an anti-aircraft weapon that is much smaller. It is simpler than the British designs but nearly as effective."

"I still do not understand," replied Constance. "Anti-aircraft weapons accurately fire rounds as big as a horse over a kilometer. Shrinking the cannons is not possible."

"The rounds we use are one-tenth the size of those the British use," said Ezmeralda. "Each one is hollow and packed with gun powder with a trigger on the nose. They explode on contact and destroy whatever they hit."

"They do not fire as far as British cannons," said Francis. "The guns on the jungle floor have a longer barrel. Their effective range is seven hundred meters. The cannons on the city rooftops are smaller and fire accurately up to four-hundred meters."

"That is amazing," said Margaret.

"*Oui*," said the Francis. "It is."

"Our anti-aircraft guns use hand powered mechanisms to spin the turrets and raise or lower the barrels," said Ezmeralda. "British anti-aircraft guns use an automated steam-driven system with range-finders aiming from towers."

"Our gunners have been practicing while you were away," said Francis. "Manual operations are not a weakness anymore."

"*Muy bueno, mi amor*," said Ezmeralda in a sultry voice.

Francis stepped over to his wife and swept her up in his arms. "*Mon amour*," he said, breathing heavily into his wife's ear. "I have missed you so much." He kissed her passionately, forgetting that they stood in the middle of a war council.

General Marquez cleared his throat. "Francis, *por favor*. Continue with your report." A chorus of throaty laughs echoed off the high ceiling.

"*Oui, mon général*," said Francis, breaking from his wife's embrace. Ezmeralda's skin turned scarlet beneath her black hair. "I designed another weapon to defend against an air assault. An automated flying machine that explodes when it strikes an airship."

"I did not know about that, *mi amor*," said Ezmeralda. Francis once again swept up his wife in his embrace.

"*Por favor, mi amigo*," interjected Marquez. "Save it for later. And in private." This time the audience roared with laughter. Several voices chimed in that they did not mind the show.

When the crowd regained their composure, Francis continued: "I have six depots scattered around Bacatá in the basements of buildings. Each has five automated flying machines. I just finished building the last set of machines last week. I have not yet trained any soldiers how to deploy them."

"How do they work?" asked Constance.

"Each automaton uses a steam engine and a hydrogen balloon to travel straight up. It uses atmospheric gauges to lock onto the closest heat source. It propels itself towards the heat source and explodes on contact."

"How big is the detonation?"

"Big enough to tear a hole in a zeppelin's balloon."

"What if it hits a bird?" asked Edward.

Francis stared at Edward: "Then it blows up the bird."

"How long will it take to recruit and train a group of soldiers to operate these weapons?" asked General Marquez.

"Not long," replied Francis. "A few hours, maybe a day."

"Then that is your first priority after this meeting ends."

"*Oui, mon général*," said Francis.

General Marquez shifted his focus to a small, quiet man leaning against the wall to his right, "General Fernandez."

"*Si*," replied the man.

"Please report on the fighting forces we have here in Bacatá," said Marquez.

"*Si, señor*," replied General Fernandez. "We have 4,350 soldiers here. Each one has a rifle and knows how to use it. Just over half have seen battle before. The rest are young men under twenty-five years."

"They will be battle hardened when this is over," said General Mera.

"*Si*," said Fernandez. "The British will drop bombs for a long time. Our soldiers will stay under cover in the basement shelters we have all over the city. When the British land ground troops, we will meet them on the city streets and the roads will run red with British blood."

"What of the support persons?" asked Marquez. "Those who are not soldiers."

"There are about 450 support persons in Bacatá. Mostly women who wash clothes and cook meals."

"They are good for much more than that," called out an unseen soldier. The room rumbled with laughter.

"Some are very good at what they do."

"Gentlemen, *por favor*," said General Marquez. "We need to stay focused. Continue, General Fernandez."

"*Gracias*," said Fernandez. "There are enough basement shelters to house all the noncombatants when the battle begins."

"I think we should move those people into the underground shelters now," said Francis. "Our early warning system is poor. They will only have a few minutes to find shelter once the fleet is spotted."

"I agree," said General Marquez rubbing his chin. "Are the anti-aircraft cannons currently manned?"

"No," said Francis, "we rely on the early warning system to call the soldiers to their posts."

"Send soldiers to the cannons immediately," said Marquez. "I want soldiers on those guns around the clock.

"We have one more thing to discuss. Ezmeralda found a dangerous new weapon on board the zeppelin she stole. She asked to address the council about it."

"*Gracias*," said Ezmeralda.

"*De nada, mija*," replied Marquez.

"On the stolen British battleship are hundreds of metal cannisters the size of a melon." Ezmeralda lifted a steel canister over her head. "Inside each canister is a new type of poison gas called chlorine."

"What is so special about this chlorine gas?" shouted a voice from the peanut gallery.

"If you breathe it in, you die." The room took a collective step backward away from Ezmeralda.

"If there are hundreds of those on board one battleship, there are hundreds on board all the battleships in the fleet."

"What will they do with these gas cannisters? Drop them from their airships?"

"*Si*," said Ezmeralda. "They will explode, and the gas will kill everyone on the ground."

"That is inhumane," said General Marquez. "There is no honor in killing soldiers that way."

"How do we defend ourselves?"

Sirens perched on buildings across the city pierced the air with their shrill screams. The New Granada Resistance war council dissolved without ceremony; the battle had arrived.

CHAPTER 20

The leaders of the New Granada Resistance poured out the front doors of the retired Spanish government building, squinting into the late afternoon sun, searching the skies for their assailants. Generals and officers hustled out of sight to see to their duties.

"Is the sun always shining in this bloody country?" said Margaret. She narrowed her eyes and scanned the skies for enemy airships. "A little cloud cover would be nice."

Two dozen zeppelins had breached the perimeter of Bacatá. They crept towards the heart of the city hundreds of meters in the air like a swarm of moving locusts looking for their next meal.

"General Marquez," said Edward, pushing his way in front of the others. "What should we do?"

The general studied the pale Englishman. Lit the stub of his cigar and laid a hand on Edward's shoulder. "Find the closest bomb shelter. Stay there until this is all over."

Marquez turned to address Francis and Ezmeralda. "Get to your weapons bunker; I need you to launch the drones."

"I have not heard any of our anti-aircraft cannons fire," said Francis. "Weeks of preparing and the *fils de pute* British fly right over the city."

General Marquez puffed on his cigar. "What are those explosions I hear off in the distance?"

"They are dropping bombs from the battleships," said Ezmeralda, eyes closed, concentrating on the echoes bouncing off the buildings and the vibrations in the cobblestones. "They sound like standard payload, ten kilograms, small enough to drop by hand from the belly of the airships. The explosion is big enough to tear a hole in the street three meters across."

"Where is the closest bomb shelter?" interrupted Edward.

"I do not know," replied the general. "But your wife knows where she is going."

Edward turned around and saw Margaret and Constance push through the crowd and disappear. He looked at his younger sister, standing by his side, waiting for her brother to decide what to do.

•   •   •   •   •

"Lieutenant Vickers," yelled Major Ulperlip over the heads of his bridge crew.

"Sir," answered Vickers in a dry tone.

Ulperlip spun around to look out of the large glass windows circling three sides of the bridge. "Put together a boarding party and secure the stolen HMS *Marlborough*. It's docked to a tree 300 meters west of our position." The major pointed out the window with his spyglass at a large warship bobbing in the afternoon breeze, the Union Jack insignia torn from its gondola.

"Yes, sir," replied Vickers. The lieutenant did not make a move to follow orders.

"Midshipman Johnson," barked Major Ulperlip. "Radio the fleet to target those cannons mounted on the rooftops."

"Yes, sir," replied the communications officer. "None of the cannons appear to be active."

"In a few minutes they will be." Ulperlip looked through his spyglass and surveyed the city streets. The smoke from the bombs was already filling spaces between the tall, colorful walls. Soldiers ran through the streets in a chaotic mess. From the bridge it looked a malicious child shoved a firecracker inside an anthill.

"Is there something I can do for you, lieutenant?" asked Ulperlip without turning.

"I was wondering what our battle plan is, sir," replied Vickers.

"We will follow standard procedure for Her Majesty's Navy when assaulting a hostile city from the air."

Vickers voice was flat as he recited from the officer's training manual: "Engage and eliminate airborne enemy ships. Eliminate ground-based anti-aircraft weapons. Weaken ground forces with bombs, specifically targeting any other large weaponry, ammunition stores, and troop bunkers. Once air superiority is established, land ground troops and secure the city."

"Midshipman Johnson," said Ulperlip, driving the conversation in yet another direction.

"Sir."

"Send the ships on the eastern flank towards the mass of soldiers congregating around those buildings," said the major, pointing across the city. "I want the other battleships to move parallel to us and push towards the center of the city. I wager the Resistance officers are utilizing the abandoned government buildings as command headquarters."

"Yes, sir," said Midshipman Johnson.

"Lieutenant Vickers," said Ulperlip. "Why are you still standing there? I gave you orders to retake the *Marlborough*."

"Yes, sir," said Vickers in the same droll tone.

"Is there a problem?" asked the major.

"No, sir. I was merely musing about our mandate from Queen Victoria."

"What mandate is that?"

"To dismantle the New Granada Resistance at any cost," replied Vickers.

"We are already routing the Resistance," muttered Major Ulperlip, sweeping his spyglass back and forth across the city's horizon. "We have met no opposition thus far and have established control of the skies. Already enemy soldiers lie dead in the streets. We will follow the proven procedures of Her Majesty's Royal Navy. And we will win the day."

"Very good, then, sir," said the lieutenant.

•   •   •   •   •

Shouting clusters of soldiers and exploding bombs created a convoluted din. Anne stood on her toes and stretched as far as she could towards her brother's ear.

"Where are we supposed to go?" she shouted.

Edward leaned back and shook his head, hoisting his arms to indicate that he did not know. "I will find out," he said.

Edward spotted Margaret and grabbed her arm. "Where is the bomb shelter?" he shouted.

Margaret mouthed the words: "I don't know," without trying to speak over the racket. She slipped Edward's grip and disappeared into a throng of soldiers.

Edward swiveled his head, trying to spot a bomb shelter. He spotted General Marquez doling out orders to his officers. Edward crossed the road, dodging holes where shrapnel had dislodged cobblestones. He grabbed the back of Marquez's arm and spun around the general.

Marquez used the momentum Edward provided to drop Edward with a left hook across the jaw. The Englishman hit the ground hard, landing on his backside on the shattered stone street.

"What in the bloody hell are you doing?" shouted Edward.

The general's eyes focused on the face of his assailant. He smiled ear to ear.

"*Mi siento*, I am sorry my friend." Marquez extended a hand and hauled Edward back to his feet. "Never grab a soldier from behind. Especially when bombs are falling."

Edward stood blinking at the general and rubbing his jaw. He did not bother to brush the dust off or adjust his disheveled clothing.

"Where is the closest bomb shelter?"

"*Está allá*," said Marquez, pointing down the road.

Squinting against the orange flare of the fires burning, Edward saw a row house thirty meters away with soldiers pouring in and out of the front door. Crossing back to Anne, Edward resisted grabbing her elbow to get her attention, opting instead to tap her on the shoulder.

"The bomb shelter is down there," he shouted.

A moment later a bomb exploded on the rooftop, raining down soot and rounded clay tiles. An orange blur whistled inches from Anne's head. It struck Edward above his ear and knocked him to the ground.

Anne bent over her brother, grabbed his wrist, and leaned backward. She pulled Edward halfway up before he crumpled back down in a heap. Anne stumbled and fell forward on top of her brother.

Time slowed down for Edward. The only sound in his world was a dull, high-pitched ringing. He looked to his right, then left. Soldiers and wash women rushed here and there with no clear destination. No one noticed him lying in the dust.

A trickle of blood meandered down the side of Edward's head, wrapping around his ear, mingling with sweat and soot. It reached his lips and he tasted copper, salt, and dirt. A shadow passed over his field of vision and a hot breath pushed against his face. Edward concentrated on the face of his sister leaning over him.

"Edward," said Anne, trying to yell over the chaos. "Are you all right?" He stared back up at her, jaw open and silent. "Edward, answer me. Are you all right?"

Anne's voice pierced the ringing in Edward's ears and grounded him in time and place. He shook his head no and muttered, "Yes, of course. I am fine."

Anne crouched behind her brother, hooking her arms under his shoulders. She threw her weight backward and wrenched Edward up to his feet. Anne swung to his side, draping his arm over her shoulder.

Anne paused to absorb the surrounding scene. A pair of dead bodies lie still across the street. Blood ran from their wounds into the mud and puddled in the cracks between the cobblestones. At least a dozen more people lie amongst the splintered tiles and stucco, conscious and calling for help.

"Come on, brother, we have to get to the shelter."

"Just a few more minutes, mom," said Edward.

"Oh, for Christ's sake," said Anne, her words lost beneath another explosion a block away. Fine gray dust dyed her hair like an old woman's. Anne took a step forward with Edward's arm slung over her shoulder. Instead of his feet moving, Edward's weight tipped forward and he ended up back on the ground. Anne stumbled and fell to her knees under her brother's weight.

Anne left Edward in the dust and mud and accosted the closest soldier: "Help me," she shouted. He pushed her aside and ran on to an unknown destination.

The next soldier she confronted also pushed the small woman out of his way with the back of his hand. Anne stepped back in front of the man and slapped him. The burly soldier in green khakis blinked several times and sized up his assailant. Anne repeated her plea and he agreed to help.

Slinging his rifle over his shoulder, the soldier helped Anne drag her brother back to his feet. With Edward slung between them, one arm over each of their shoulders, Anne and the soldier maneuvered him down the road and into the bomb shelter. The soldier disappeared back up the stairs of the converted basement after dropping Edward onto the packed-earth floor. Anne pressed a handkerchief to the side of her brother's head.

"Edward, how are you?" Anne asked, her voice a harsh whisper as she fought to regain control of her breath.

Edward looked up at his sister and struggled to hold her gaze: "IamalrightIthink."

●　　●　　●　　●　　●

Margaret grabbed Constance's forearm and plunged forward through the soldiers clogging the street. Margaret plowed through the teenage boys while dodging the older men. Constance dug her fingernails into Margaret's wrist, planted her feet, and pulled her friend to a stop.

"Where are we going," yelled Constance over the sounds of explosions and Resistance officers barking orders.

"To find an underground bunker before a bomb makes us a red smudge on the street."

As if on cue, an explosion detonated behind Constance and Margaret, knocking them to the floor while bricks crashed on cobblestones. The women popped back up to their feet, coughing and rubbing the dust out of their eyes.

"What do we do now?" asked Constance.

"Same as before," replied Margaret. "We need to find a bomb shelter."

"Where?"

"We just have to move; we will find one."

Constance's eyes rolled skyward, studying the cityscape and the three-story rooftops along both sides of the road. The airship that dropped the last bombs on the street hovered high overhead. More small bombs cascaded from her belly like a herd of stampeding, steel animals. A pair of battleships flanked the zeppelin on both sides.

"What do you see?" yelled Margaret.

"There are anti-aircraft guns mounted on the top of that building," replied Constance. She pointed to the roof of a bright red row house at the end of the road. "No one is firing them."

"Then we need to get there," shouted Margaret,

"Why?" asked Constance.

"That's the best way to protect everyone," replied Margaret. "If we can drive off those battleships, everyone else can get to safety."

Constance planted her feet as a bomb exploded on a nearby rooftop: "I am not firing the cannons."

Terra-cotta tiles rained down half a block behind them. Margaret looked back at Constance's silhouette; her skinny teenage frame outlined against flames burning in the front window of a house.

"This is the best way to protect our family."

"I don't want to shoot at my own people," said Constance.

"Today, those soldiers are not your people," replied Margaret. "They are the twits trying to kill you and your family." Margaret rubbed the soot out of her eyes and sighed, putting her arm around her friend's shoulder. "This is how we save lives."

Constance paused in the middle of the chaos to consider her options: "If I help you with the cannon, I do not want to be the one who pulls the trigger."

Margaret led the way, weaving through the accumulating rubble, staying clear of overhead trees and iron balconies. Constance trotted along behind.

Margaret stopped in front of the red-stucco house. "Are you positive there are guns on top of this building?"

"Yes," replied Constance.

"How do you know?"

Constance looked at Margaret with a confused expression. "How do you not know?"

Margaret rolled her eyes before barreling up the narrow staircase just inside the front door. At the top, they pushed through a wood door and emerged into the bright sunshine, the air thick with dust and smoke despite being three stories off the ground. Bolted to opposite corners of the flat rooftop were two iron cannons.

A soldier in the green khaki uniform of the New Granada Resistance stood on the gun turret closest to the top of the stairwell. Obviously poorly trained in operating the complicated cannon, he slammed home the over-sized gun bolt and wrestled with the levers. The weapon refused to respond. The women trotted over; the soldier unslung his rifle from his back and dropped the barrel flat. The women's arms shot up in the air.

"We want to help," said Margaret. "Do not fire."

The soldier spat out a short speech in Spanish, talking so fast the words rolled together into a handful of long syllables. When he finished, he turned his back on the women and returned his focus on his cannon, the gun's black-matte metal barrel stretching upward twice the height of the soldier.

Constance approached the Spaniard and his cannon with care. He ignored her, consumed with banging on the gun's turret with a ball-peen hammer. He pounded over and over, metal ringing out against hard metal, shouting at the cannon between each blow. Despite their lack of fluency in the Spanish language, Constance and Margaret recognized the string of profanities for what they were.

Constance took a deep breath and stepped onto the gun's turret. She drove levers forward and cranked dials on the gun's control console. She yanked down on the handle of the gun's manual bolt action. The soldier stopped hitting the cannon and stepped back to give Constance room to work, staring at her so intensely she became visibly uncomfortable.

Constance abruptly stopped working and looked at the soldier: "Where is the ammunition?"

"*Allá, allá,*" *he* said, pointing to a brick shed on the center of the roof.

Constance found a hundred oblong cannonballs in the shed, each one wrapped in a copper casing. She lifted one up and rested the weight on her shoulder, returned to the cannon, and plunked the round into the gun's open bolt. She slammed the handle up and locked the cannonball in the barrel. Constance spent another minute working with the soldier to spin the turret and aim the gun. When the gun roared to life, the soldier shouted in victory, despite the shot missing its target by one hundred meters.

•   •   •   •   •

Francis and Ezmeralda raced across Bacatá. They passed through the heart of the old Spanish city before navigating the twisting roads on the eastern edge of town. Occupied buildings here were sparse; the Resistance clustered their sleeping quarters and storage houses to the north and west.

The couple left the British fleet behind as they ran. The main battleship line hovered over the center of Bacatá; a handful of zeppelins broke off the main group to drop bombs over other populated areas. A second line of ships bobbed in the wind over the jungles north of the city.

Cannon fire ripped through the heavy afternoon air to the north. More anti-aircraft guns echoed the first cannon shot.

"Do you hear that?" said Francis. "Soldiers are firing anti-aircraft guns."

"How far away are they?"

Francis stood still and listened. "I can hear one cannon over the center of town and two more from the jungle floor. And a fourth gun just two or three blocks north of here."

The couple ran forward for another couple minutes. Without warning, Ezmeralda grabbed Francis's arm and dragged him to a stop.

"What is wrong?" asked the Frenchman.

Ezmeralda stood still and listened. A second later she threw her body at Francis and knocked him to the ground. An eave hanging over the street exploded, raining down red bricks and orange tiles. They coughed on the cloud of gray dust that lifted off the street.

"The British are hunting for those guns," said Ezmeralda, rolling onto her back and pointing upward. "That zeppelin swung down from the north and took out the rooftop with the cannons on it."

"*Fils de pute*," swore Francis, spitting on the ground while struggling to his feet.

"*Vamanos*," said Ezmeralda. "We have to go."

Ezmeralda ran slower and more cautious than before to avoid running blindly into falling bombs and flying shrapnel. Francis paced himself behind her. Explosions rocked the cobblestones under their feet every few steps. The air was getting thicker with the smells of sulfur and mortar dust, forcing them to pause and cough every block. They alternated vaulting over new craters and cracks in the street or stumbling to their knees and skirting the edges.

A kilometer in front of them a cannon on the jungle floor hit a supply ship hanging on the eastern flank of the armada. A string of blue and green explosions ripped across the sky as the hydrogen-filled balloon ignited in an impressive display of pyrotechnics. The sound was deafening. Francis and Ezmeralda crouched down with their hands clamped over their ears as the air pulsed and shook with rage.

"We only have a few minutes until that thing hits the ground," said Francis, yelling into Ezmeralda's ear. "We have to run. Now."

•   •   •   •   •

Anne Goulden ran down the cobblestone street, wet handkerchief clasped tightly over her mouth and nose. She reached her target and swung around to face the bewildered older woman.

"Come with me," Anne yelled into her ear. The woman responded by grasping her savior's arm. Anne led her down the street, around a corner, and through an alley crammed with debris. They emerged on another narrow road with craters in the cobblestones big enough to hide a horse. She found the row house with the underground bomb shelter and hurried the woman indoors.

Anne found her brother sitting on the floor in the corner, his back up against the brick wall. "How are you doing?"

"I will be all right," said Edward. "I still get dizzy when I stand for more than a minute."

She stroked the top of his head, "Rest, brother."

Months ago, the Resistance knocked down the walls, merging the large room with the basements of the neighboring houses. The bricks in the walls changed color and size at every intersection. At one end of the bunker were stacks of rough-hewn wooden boxes stuffed with food, water, and medical supplies.

Anne approached a group of soldiers sporting green khaki uniforms, dormant rifles slung across their backs: "I need five men to help me get the lost and wounded to safety." One soldier spoke English and translated for the rest. The group responded with laughter.

"We do not take orders from a little British girl," said the soldier.

"Normally you do not," said General Marquez, walking up behind the soldiers. They stood at attention while Marquez tore into them with a drill sergeant's tirade. Anne did not understand his words, but she understood his meaning.

General Marquez turned to Anne: "I told my men they should be ashamed. An outsider to this army acted bravely and brought our compatriots to safety while they sit here and laughed at her courage. I demoted each soldier and granted you a battlefield commission with a rank higher than theirs."

The general placed his right hand on Anne's shoulder. "Please take a group of soldiers up to the streets and retrieve every person you find. Work your way south. I will lead a second group north."

An officer standing behind General Marquez leaned over and whispered in his commander's ear.

"I do not care about the risks," shouted Marquez. "I will not sit here while our wounded are dying in the streets."

Anne muttered her thanks to the general before turning to the soldiers standing at attention.

"Move," she said in a quiet voice that was as cold and hard as steel.

"*Vamanos,*" shouted a soldier, raising his rifle over his head. The group surged forward and pushed past their new commander, a dozen bodies crowding the stairs and pushing into the streets. Anne was the last to emerge, blinking and coughing in the hazy, soot-soaked sunlight.

Anne split the men into pairs. She ordered them to carry the wounded from the gutters and dig them out of the rubble. She led the soldiers past the dead, working her way up and down the stone streets, through alleys and city parks. A fresh round of bombs fell on the soldiers as they worked. Most exploded on the rooftops; some struck the streets, shattering cobblestones and turning them into shrapnel. Blood flowed freely from fresh wounds as the soldiers labored to save every life possible.

·   ·   ·   ·   ·

"Vickers," shouted Major Ulperlip. He grabbed the copper tube at the rear of the bridge and shouted again: "Vickers." His voice bounced back and forth through a labyrinth of copper plumbing, twisting and turning past closed valves until it reached its destination.

"Sir," came the muffled reply from the brass pipe.

"Report to the bridge," said Ulperlip, lowering his tone.

The major strolled to the front window of the bridge, his black boots clicking on the steel grating. Ulperlip picked up the spyglass stashed among the dials and toggle. He swept the field glass back and forth across the burning city.

"You wanted to see me," said Vickers, appearing on the bridge behind Major Ulperlip. He stood stiff and tall with his hands clasped behind his back.

"Has the rest of the fleet reported their status?" asked Ulperlip.

"Most have, sir. So far, we have dropped approximately 350 bombs. Three hundred contain a standard payload. The rest were dropped from the HMS *Victory*, the *Vanguard*, and the *Lancaster*. They carry bombs with twice the standard gunpowder. Aerial scouts on both the *Royal Sovereign* and the *Iron Castle* estimate over ten percent of the city destroyed. Resistance soldier body count estimates between four and six hundred."

"The assault is progressing quite well," said Ulperlip. He stared out the window of his flagship, calculating the minutes until sundown. "We will continue dropping bombs throughout the night. The ground invasion will begin at dawn."

"Our spotters inform me that most Resistance soldiers are no longer on the streets, therefore our specific targets are minimal. The fires burning in the city will provide reasonable levels of visibility for our bombers throughout the night, though."

"What of the anti-aircraft cannon in the jungle surrounding the city?" asked Ulperlip. He collapsed his spyglass but kept it in his hand.

"We target them once they open fire," replied Vickers. "Unfortunately, we cannot spot them until they fire the first round. We crossed the line of cannons without knowing they were there. Since then we have taken heavy fire from behind."

"I saw the *Golden Oak* take a pounding. What is her status? I believe she is a transport ship, correct?"

"Yes, sir. The anti-aircraft weapons pierced the zeppelin's balloon in a dozen places. She is still coming down, but her rate of descent is accelerating. We expect impact in a few minutes."

"And the crew and soldiers on board?"

"More than half have abandoned ship," said Vickers. "I ordered the captain to stay onboard until every soul was safely off. God willing, he will perish in the crash." The eyes of the bridge crew swiveled to stare at Lieutenant Vickers.

"What in the hell do you mean by that, lieutenant?" snapped Major Ulperlip.

"Sir, it was Captain Berger's foolish decision that caused the *Golden Oak* to take heavy fire in the first place," said Vickers. "Before the ground cannons opened fire, he followed the line of battleships too closely in anticipation of landing troops near the city's center."

"It was a poor decision, but that does not grant you the right to condemn him."

"Captain Berger broke protocol and endangered his entire crew to capitalize on a marginal advantage. Losing him is a blessing to the fleet."

Major Ulperlip grunted, "It is my opinion that you take entirely too much pleasure watching people perish that you deem unworthy."

"Yes, sir," replied the lieutenant, his dry and drab voice.

"What other ships have taken damage besides the *Golden Oak*?"

"Four battleships sustained heavy damage, another eight report minor damages," replied Vickers. "For now, only the *Golden Oak* is lost."

Major Ulperlip turned back to watch the battle raging out the window. He picked up the spyglass and swept the terrain.

CHAPTER 21

Constance shoved another round into the empty barrel of the cannon. She grasped the bolt with both hands and rammed it home, then pulled back on the bolt lever and locked the cartridge in place.

"Ready to go," she shouted.

"The last two rounds fell short," said Margaret. "Tip the gun turret backward."

Constance grabbed an iron wheel and cranked it around three complete turns.

"That's too far," said Margaret. "The sight is lined up over the top of the zeppelin."

"*Mas*," shouted the soldier manning the second gun.

"That's where it needs to be," said Constance.

"I am telling you, it's too high now."

"Aim just over the horizon line, where the top of the balloon meets the sky," said Constance. "The issue with the cannon is range; we have to aim high."

The soldier in the second gun turret shouted again: "*Mas, mas*."

"Bloody incompetent imbecile. Get off your arse and get it yourself," yelled Margaret across the rooftop.

Margaret looked down at Constance: "What are waiting for? Lower the bloody gun."

Constance grabbed hold of the iron wheel and turned it one revolution the other way.

Margaret fine-tuned the targeting and fired the cannon. The projectile headed upward on a steep path, peaking at a height in line with the balloon before falling at an equally steep arc. It fell far short of its target, diving beneath the ship's gondola and crashing into a building several blocks away.

"Bloody stupid," muttered Constance. She kept her head down and spun the wheel, pointing the cannon up over the top of the zeppelin. She loaded another round into Margaret's gun as the soldier on the second turret yelled again.

"Go help him," said Margaret. "I can make the small adjustments from here."

Sweat dripped off Constance's brow and soaked through her corset. She knelt to tear off the bottom of her skirt.

"Smart," said Margaret.

"Just need a little room to move."

Constance stopped at the ammunition shed halfway across the rooftop. She lifted a shell up on her shoulder and carried another under her arm. She loaded one into the gun, then leaned over the soldier to line up the sight. He said a handful of sharp Spanish words before pushing Constance back off the turret.

"No," said Constance. "You are not lined up right." She grabbed a hold of the iron wheel beside the gun and began turning.

"*No mas*," yelled the soldier, kicking his boot at her.

"Yes," shouted Constance back at him. She stepped up onto the turret and leaned her face down towards his. "I load the gun and I make the adjustments," she shouted. "Your job, you stupid twit, is to adjust the targeting and pull the bloody trigger." She stood with her face inches from his, her eyes holding up his.

"*Si, señor*," muttered the soldier, looking away. "*Señora*," he said, in a voice too quiet for Constance to hear.

A shell exploded high overhead and Constance turned her face skyward. Margaret's round found its target, hitting the broadside of the forward zeppelin and exploding. The airship rocked side to side like a baby in a cradle. Crisscrossing steel reinforcement beams encased the balloon like a metal spider web; the joints and rivets groaned and cracked as the zeppelin began its death throes.

The soldier yelled in triumph and fired his own gun. His shell exploded in the air, just below the zeppelin's gondola.

"You could not wait for me to aim a bit higher, could you?" said Constance. She cranked the wheel beside the turret, not bothering to double check the targeting of the barrel. She rammed home another shell and yelled at the soldier to fire. He carefully aimed his weapon and pulled the two-handed trigger.

The shell exploded across the broadside of the battleship, dislodging a pair of steel beams and puncturing the balloon. Hydrogen gas ignited in a fantastic string of green and blue fireballs that spread from the point of impact. The battleship began losing altitude, putting on a dazzling show of colored flames for the few Resistance soldiers left to see.

• • • • •

By the time Francis and Ezmeralda reached their destination on the eastern edge of Bacatá, the battleships had moved on from that section of the city. The British troop transports were no longer visible. After a ship crashed into eastern Bacatá and reduced several city blocks to rubble, the other transports backed out of range of the cannons.

"*Aye, mi amor,*" said Ezmeralda, standing in front of a muddled mess of clay roof tiles and chunks of plaster walls. "What happened to our beautiful home?"

Francis stepped over a pile of red bricks, lifting debris and tossing it off the top of the pile. "It does not matter where we sleep, as long as we do not sleep apart."

Together they hauled away bricks and tiles and wooden beams until their bodies were tired and bruised. They paused to watch a string of explosions tear through a battleship over the center of Bacatá. Ezmeralda pulled out a length of twisted rope, burnt black at one end.

"Our hammocks," she said with a sigh.

"Now is not the time, *mon amour,*" said Francis. "We have to find the basement door."

The couple found the trap door minutes later. It was a thick plank of wood cut from the heart of a tree, laying flat on the ground to cover up the shaft leading down to the basement. Working together, Francis and Ezmeralda cleared off the square meter door. They grabbed the handles and threw their combined weight backward to hoist the door up on its end.

Francis climbed ten meters down the wooden ladder, skipping the last few rungs and landing hard on the packed dirt floor. He flipped a small lever on the wall after Ezmeralda descended. The trapdoor slammed shut and a chain of kerosene lanterns flared to life, one after another, along the room's walls.

"A minor improvement I made," explained Francis, nodding towards the lever. "Spring loaded."

The couple took advantage of their moment of solitude, pressing their bodies against one another and kissing passionately.

"In the cabinet on the far wall are four automated airship bombs," said Francis. "Next to them are hydrogen canisters to fill the balloons. Do not fill them down here; the balloons are too big to get through the door."

Ezmeralda opened the cabinet at the far end of the workshop. She took a quick inventory of the materials inside and found a pair of empty wooden crates to pack.

Each drone had a mechanical base a meter wide with a montage of brass plumbing and wiring protruding from small steel plates riveted to the body. Ezmeralda struggled to heave them off the cabinet shelf to the wood crate at her feet. She packed the hydrogen canisters on top.

"I should have built more drones," muttered Francis as he worked in the other end of the shop. "I never thought a fleet this big would attack us."

Francis handed his wife a Winchester rifle with a long, black-matte barrel, encased in an odd array of springs and pulleys. Mounted between the barrel and the scope was a tiny glass tube filled with blue liquid.

"What does this do?" asked Ezmeralda.

"Standard Winchester rifle I modified," Francis said with a mischievous smile. He rotated a dial near the shoulder butt. "Turn this, and *voila*." The gun spun to life, pulsing in Ezmeralda's hands. A thick, yellow liquid coursed through a second glass tube that crisscrossed the length of the gun.

"This is wonderful, *mi amor*," said Ezmeralda. She rested the barrel on the floor and leaned on the weapon to give her husband another kiss. "Tell me what it does?"

Francis smiled a crooked smile: "My beautiful Ezmeralda, I have missed you."

"I know," she said. "What does the gun do?"

"It operates the same as an American Winchester rifle. But I added a range booster. Adjust the distance by rotating that dial." He reached back in the cabinet and produced a copper scope that looked like a small telescope.

"This is for aiming, obviously." Francis snapped the scope into place on top of the rifle.

"And this is the ammunition." He pulled a bucket of over-sized rifle rounds from the shelf. "The bullets are standard six millimeter, but these are 88 millimeters long. I cast the lead and loaded the shells."

Ezmeralda adjusted the firearm from one arm to the other, checking the weight and balance, sighting down the scope. "What is its range?" she asked.

"Accurate to one kilometer," answered Francis. "In theory, it can take down a zeppelin. Aim for the glass windows on the ship's gondola. The Brits like to survey everything around them, ground to sky, directly from the bridge. The glass is reinforced, but these bullets will get through." Francis paused, lost in thought.

"What about targeting the hydrogen balloon?" asked Ezmeralda.

"That might work," said Francis. "But the balloons are reinforced with steel webbing. The bullet needs to puncture the balloon and ignite the leak with a spark to trigger an explosion."

The couple used a pulley to haul the wooden crates above ground before returning for the firearms, stuffing their pockets and leather satchels with ammunition. Ezmeralda returned above ground to set up the first drone in the waning daylight.

Francis turned his attention to a tall pile of cotton sheets in the corner. He pulled the white linens to the floor with one dramatic sweep of his arm, revealing an enormous jaguar built from gun-matte black steel. The monster stood three meters tall, slumbering on its hind legs. The jaguar's paws were the size of a man's head, each one housing a set of retractable silver blades. Its eyes were blood-red stained glass. Francis pulled open a pair of drawers beside the jaguar, revealing a wide assortment of tools. The master mechanic's hands moved quickly as he prepped the sleeping demon for battle.

•　　•　　•　　•　　•

Major Ulperlip and Lieutenant Vickers stood shoulder to shoulder, staring out the over-sized bridge windows. The fires burning through Bacatá lit the streets against the pitch-black jungle night. The zeppelin nearest them was on fire, filling their own bridge with the smell of smoke, earsplitting explosions, and the fear of death.

A new, deep boom of cannons to the east drew the attention of Ulperlip and Vickers. Anti-aircraft fire reaching out from the ground raked across another pair of zeppelins, every shot flashing a white explosion against the darkness.

"Captain," said Ulperlip, "adjust our flight plan. Head due east. I want to target those new ground guns."

"Yes, sir," said the captain, spinning the helm control and barking orders into a set of hollow copper tubes that disappeared into the steel mesh floor.

The major turned back towards the window and stared out, glassy eyed and lost in thought. Four battleships blanketed the center of the city with bombs. The core of the fleet was engaged with a string of anti-aircraft weapons a kilometer to the west. Other zeppelins plowed ahead, sweeping south and dropping bombs.

The zeppelin directly in front of the *Fulton* was in its final death throes. Crew members escaped the burning wreckage by parachuting the short distance to the ground. Ulperlip watched as a group of airmen landed safely in the smoldering center of the city.

The major lifted his spyglass, focusing it on the area the flight crew landed. Resistance soldiers poured out of a squat building. The airmen struggled to unhitch their parachutes and draw their sidearms before Resistance rifle fire cut them down.

"Impossible," muttered the major, breathing heavily and lowering his field glass. He lifted it again. "They must be hiding in the basements of the buildings. They are surviving our assault in underground bunkers."

"Sir, if I may offer my opinion," said Lieutenant Vickers. He stood straight and tall beside the major.

"If you must."

"The tide of battle has turned," said Vickers. "We are losing the fight for air superiority."

"It's those blasted guns," said the major. He turned away from the window and paced to the captain's chair before marching back to his second in command. "In what world are such small cannons so effective against battleships?"

"I am sure I do not know, sir," said Vickers. "But we must discuss changing our tactics to ensure victory."

"What is the latest damage report?" said Ulperlip, his voice a deep growl like a trapped dog.

"Most ships are reporting at least minor damage," said the communications officer.

"I do not want to know how much damage we sustained," interrupted the major. "I want to know how much damage we inflicted on the enemy."

"I can answer that," said Lieutenant Vickers. "We have neutralized more than half of the rooftop cannons. However, most guns firing from the jungle floor are still active. The fleet is essentially surrounded. We cannot directly engage the guns encircling the city without neglecting the rooftop cannons and taking extensive damage on that front."

"How much of the city is destroyed?"

"Close to twenty percent," said the lieutenant. "Heavy bombing destroyed much of the center of town. Major fires are burning in most sections of the city. And, of course, several blocks were destroyed when the *Peregrine* and the *Concord* crashed down."

"Is it safe to assume that at least twenty percent of the Resistance forces hiding in basements are either dead or buried beneath piles of rubble?"

Vickers did not move a muscle as he contemplated his commanding officer's question. "Perhaps, but we do not know that for a fact."

"How could they survive?"

"Actually, depending on the strength of the basement walls, they all may be alive. Any competent engineer would have built additional trapdoor exits into the streets or adjoining basements."

Silence encapsulated the bridge and its crew, while the sounds of war struggled to penetrate the glass walls.

After a minute, Ulperlip addressed his second in command: "How do you propose we our change our strategy, lieutenant?"

"Bring up a troop transport ship from the rear. Parachute a small contingent near the rooftops where the remaining anti-aircraft guns are. Then do the same for the cannons on the jungle floor."

Major Ulperlip scoffed. "Impossible; it has never been done. Every single soldier that jumps from an airship would be shot before they even reach the ground."

"The casualty rate would undoubtedly be high," said Vickers with a shrug.

"And you have no apprehension about sending those men to their demise?"

"I believe enough soldiers would survive to complete the mission. A large contingent should parachute down to ensure they are successful."

"You are offering our boys as cannon fodder," said Ulperlip.

"Better than those guns taking down another zeppelin," replied Lieutenant Vickers.

"If a transport ship flies that close to the cannons, they may be shot down."

Vickers shrugged his shoulders: "Perhaps, but in the end we will disable the cannons and the fleet can establish air superiority."

"Nonsense," said Major Ulperlip. "I have made a decision."

"Please, enlighten us," said the lieutenant in a droll tone.

"The cannons appear to have a limited range and poor targeting mechanisms. We will take the fleet higher where their weapons are less effective and continue to drop bombs."

"We are barely able to aim at the height we are at now," said Vickers. "I doubt we can disable their cannons before running out of bombs."

Ulperlip scowled and turned back towards the window. "Those are my orders, lieutenant."

•   •   •   •   •

Francis emerged from the underground shaft to the rhythmic sounds of war echoing off the buildings left standing, the ground trembling with an inconsistent consistency. Ash fell like a steady dusting of snow. Francis studied the night sky. The brunt of the British fleet had climbed to a higher altitude towards the sparse cloud cover. The closest zeppelin was a small battleship two hundred meters to the north.

Ezmeralda crouched on the ground a few meters from Francis, working to launch a drone. She rose and stepped back when Francis approached her.

"I think it is ready to launch," she said.

"*Oui*," said Francis. "She is ready."

He flipped a toggle switch on the hydrogen tank connected to the drone via a small rubber hose. A valve opened and the balloon filled with gas. In less than a minute, the balloon was a full two meters in diameter. The valve closed and Francis twisted off the rubber hose.

The Frenchman flipped a dozen more switches and dials scattered across the machine's shell. With a whirl of pent up energy the drone sprang to life, humming and clinking like a pair of wine glasses. A complicated array of mercury thermometers, air pressure gauges, and other environmental sensors extended from its casing. Handfuls of small lead weights dropped off the sides and the drone lifted into the air.

"What happens now?" asked Ezmeralda.

"It rises straight up to the height I programmed in. Then it floats about searching for one direction with a higher temperature. It flies towards the heat and homes in on the zeppelin's engines. When the devise contacts something in its path, it explodes."

"Clever," muttered Ezmeralda. "Will it ignite the hydrogen in the balloon or just cripple an engine?"

"*Je ne sais pas*," muttered Francis. "It is untested in battle."

The couple stood quietly and watched the automaton rise into the air. A short time later it was several hundred meters high and aligned with the closest battleship. A short burst of flames shot from its side and the drone drifted towards its target.

"I was wondering how you worked the propulsion," murmured Ezmeralda. "It burns a bit of hydrogen gas from the balloon to push it in the right direction. It does not generate enough heat to ignite its own balloon?"

"No," answered Francis, "at least I hope not."

"*Dios mío*," said Ezmeralda. "I swear, you are either the most brilliant man I ever met or the biggest fool."

"*Mon amour*, we shall soon see enough which it is."

"I think it is a little of both," replied Ezmeralda.

Francis and Ezmeralda watched the automated airship in captivated silence. The drone burst orange flames from its base every minute, maneuvering itself towards the zeppelin. It contacted the zeppelin's rear engine compartment and detonated, triggering a pair of smaller explosions inside the engine. Smoke poured from the compartment. The zeppelin's captain, fearing the worst, maneuvered the battleship towards the jungle to make an emergency landing. Without warning, the giant hydrogen balloon split, and a chain of explosions tore through the airship, one after another, shaking the sky itself. Francis and Ezmeralda shielded their eyes as the night sky lit up with brilliant reds and oranges and yellows.

The remnants of the zeppelin's gondola and steel girders that framed the balloon began their trek down to the jungle floor. Cabin doors all along the gondola burst open and dozens of British airmen leapt from the airship. Many had parachutes strapped to their backs; some did not.

"*Mon amour*, it seems that I am a brilliant man," said Francis.

"I will only agree that you are not a fool," replied Ezmeralda. She embraced her husband and they exchanged another long kiss as the British battleship fell from the sky.

•   •   •   •   •

Lieutenant Vickers grabbed the spyglass resting on the console between himself and Major Ulperlip. He examined the craft drifting above the tree line to the east. Small bursts of flames shot out from different points on the golden cylinder.

"The balloon is only two meters across," said Vickers. "The cylinder-shaped devise strapped underneath appears to be copper and steel with dozens of moving parts protruding from all sides. I have no idea what it is, but the last one took down a battleship."

"It's an unmanned aircraft designed to take down a zeppelin," said Ulperlip. "It appears to be aimed at the *Whitehall*. God help them."

"Impossible," replied Vickers in a breathy voice. "I happen to know that the Department of Engineering And Defense is working on a similar devise, but it is in the early stages of development. They have not even begun field testing. No black-market arms dealer could have obtained one."

Ulperlip shot a sideways glare at Vickers. "I do not know about that, and I am admittedly surprised at your level of security clearance. But you forget that this particular Resistance enlists two high-ranking Freemasons."

An idea struck the major and he turned to the ship's captain: "Signal the *Whitehall* and instruct them to fire on that object out the cabin windows with rifles."

"Yes, sir," said the captain.

A minute later a dozen cabin windows on the *Whitehall* dropped open. British airmen slung rifles outside and opened fire, their rounds bouncing off the drone's steel plated siding.

"Instruct them to aim for the balloon," bellowed Ulperlip.

The drone collided with the *Whitehall's* primary furnace before the orders could pass through the communications channels. The explosion blew a hole in the battleship's gondola, crippling the ship but failing to ignite the balloon. Ulperlip and Vickers watched in helpless horror as flaming steel girders and scorched bodies fell from the sky.

"Sir," shouted the communications officer from his post. "Two more drones just climbed above the tree line to the east."

Major Ulperlip scanned the skies, quickly setting eyes on the drones. He grabbed the speaking end of the ship's voice amplification system.

"I want to address the entire fleet," said Ulperlip.

"Aye, sir," said the communications officer, flipping switches and twisting dials.

"All hands, we have two small Resistance aircraft on the eastern edge of the city. They must be shot out of the sky with rifles. Aim for the balloon, not the metal cylinder." Moments later the major's voice bounced and bellowed throughout the entire fleet's intercom.

"Captain," said Major Ulperlip. "Set course for those drones. As we approach start carpet bombing the entire area. We need to knock out their source." He sighed and turned back towards the window.

"Belay those orders, captain," said Lieutenant Vickers. "Sir, do you think it is wise to get too close to the drones?"

"Do not question my orders," snapped Major Ulperlip. "Captain, proceed as ordered."

"That is a poor decision, sir. I believe we should send another battleship in our place."

"We do not order fellow soldiers into harm's way while we sit back and watch."

"Of course, sir," muttered Vickers. "I just do not believe it is the wisest course of action. By endangering the flagship and the lives of senior officers, you endanger the entire mission."

"Get off of my bridge," said the major between gritted teeth, pausing to enunciate every word.

"Sir," said Vickers, throwing up a half-hearted salute before sauntering out the steel hatch leading off the bridge.

●　　●　　●　　●　　●

The zeppelins had started working in groups of twos and threes, concentrating bombs on the anti-aircraft guns perched on top of buildings and hidden on the jungle floor. Bombs fell in clusters and tore through buildings, their blown-out walls and collapsed roofs exposing hollow interiors.

"Do you think the roof will collapse?" asked Margaret. Every time her cannon fired it shook the rooftop beneath her feet.

"It will hold," replied Constance, preparing to load another round. She pointed to the ammunition stacked between the two cannons. "If one of those bombs land on the shells over there, though, we are all dead."

"Why did Francis pile the ammunition up like that?" asked Margaret. "He should have realized what a hazard it would be."

"Oversight, I suppose," said Constance. She shoved another round into the gun barrel and rammed the bolt into place. "Aim high up on the balloon of the lead ship. I will tell our friend over there to do the same."

At that moment, a bomb exploded on the other side of the rooftop. Constance hit the ground hard, half diving, half falling behind Margaret's gun turret. Small bits of plaster and mortar fell and a cloud of brown and gray smoke engulfed them.

"I think they hit the other cannon," shouted Margaret, unable to hear her own voice over the ringing in her ears.

"Fire the next round," replied Constance. "I will go have a look." Body hunched down low, she weaved through the minefield of blown apart gray mortar to the second gun. The second anti-aircraft gun was intact; the bomb had torn the corner off the building's roof.

The soldier firing the cannon was slumped forward over the controls. Constance tipped him back in the gun turret's seat. Blood ran in a thick stream from a gash across his forehead. She dragged the soldier's heavy body off the turret and laid him out flat on the roof. Constance closed her eyes and said a silent prayer.

"I need someone else to fire the second gun," said Constance as she loaded Margaret's cannon. "If we each fire a gun without a second person to load and spin the turret, we will only get a round off every four minutes."

"Go find someone to fire it," said Margaret.

"Sure, I will just go down to street, grab the first soldier I find and conscript him," said Constance.

Margaret did not respond or even look at Constance, instead focusing on aiming her gun.

"Oh," muttered Constance. She sighed, headed back in the house, down the stairs and into the street. She returned to the rooftop a few minutes later, dragging a bewildered looking soldier by the wrist. Margaret was hauling another round over to her own gun.

"He speaks English," said Constance.

"That's helpful," said Margaret.

"I could not make myself understood to any other soldiers." Constance paused, biting her lower lip. "There really aren't many soldiers left on the streets. I found him two blocks over, helping a wounded soldier to safety."

Margaret grunted while she loaded her cannon. "Have him concentrate fire on the zeppelin flanking us to the west. It's wreaked damage over the center of the city all day."

Constance walked the soldier across the roof and sat him down in the gun turret's iron seat. "To aim the cannon, you adjust here and here, horizontal and vertical." Constance looked at her recruit and saw him staring at of the dead soldier lying beside the cannon.

"What happened to him?"

"He died bringing down those bloody battleships," replied Constance. "He died in the line of duty, saving the lives of his comrades."

The soldier stood tall and stiff and saluted Constance: "*Por favor*, show me how I can best serve *la Resistencia de Nuevo Granada.*"

CHAPTER 22

Major Ulperlip paced the bridge, spyglass gripped in his right hand. He could hear the crew of the *Fulton* firing rifles out a dozen windows farther down the gondola. The Resistance was now launching anti-aircraft drones from two locations on the northern and eastern edges of the city.

A midshipman entered the bridge and rushed across the steel grate floor to the major: "Sir, Corporal Dudley just had his head blown off."

"How in the hell did that happen?" bellowed Major Ulperlip.

"We aren't sure, sir. He was firing a rifle from a window at one of those drones when his head suddenly popped like a grape."

"His head popped like a grape?" asked Ulperlip, his voice slow and tired.

"Yes, sir, like a grape. If you squeeze it too hard."

Lieutenant Vickers stood up against the bridge window, the sunrise framing his narrow frame. "The enemy must have a high-powered rifle capable of firing from the ground and, to quote the young midshipman, pop a man's head like a grape."

"How do you know that?" snapped Ulperlip.

"It is the only reasonable explanation."

"Bah." Major Ulperlip turned away from the conversation and pinched the bridge of his nose. "We have not yet established air superiority. There are almost no soldiers on the streets anywhere in the city. Most of the fleet has fallen back. The rest remain engaged with the anti-aircraft weapons, but the cannons are doing considerable damage to our ships."

Lieutenant Vickers stood still in front of the window and exhaled. "What do you propose we do, sir?"

"Pull the rest of fleet out of range of all anti-aircraft fire. Then land the ground troops."

"We will not be able to provide air support for the ground soldiers," said Vickers, dragging his words out.

"The first regiments on the ground will seek out the anti-aircraft weapons," replied the major. "We outnumber them, our boys are better trained, and they are better equipped."

"Putting troops on the ground now would break protocol," said the lieutenant. "There may be large numbers of Resistance soldiers hiding in underground bunkers. Without air support, our soldiers may not prevail, placing the entire mission in jeopardy. Sir."

Major Ulperlip drew himself up to full height and let his eyes wander across the faces of the inquisitive bridge crew. "Do you have a better plan, lieutenant?"

"No, sir. As you have stated numerous times for my benefit, my role is to execute your orders."

"Very well," said Ulperlip, turning to face the bridge crew. "Midshipman Johnson, begin relaying orders to the fleet to fall back out of range of all anti-aircraft cannons and drone launch sites. Then order the troop transports to begin preparations to put soldiers on the ground."

•　　•　　•　　•　　•

"The last battleship just pulled out of range," said Constance. She dropped the heavy cannonball, cracking the roof's dirty white plaster. "What do you suppose they are up to?"

Margaret slumped forward over the trigger of the anti-aircraft gun. "They're starting the ground invasion," she said, shielding the early morning glare with the back of her hand. "Those zeppelins behind the battleships are troop transports. Each one is carrying hundreds of soldiers, plus all their gear, rifles, mortars, machine guns. Maybe even a handful of armored vehicles." Margaret paused while studying the scene from her rooftop perch. "I count fourteen transport ships."

"How do they land the troops?"

Margaret shrugged, "Depends on the situation. Those ships can maneuver low to the ground and drop a long ramp from the bottom of the gondola."

"I don't see how they can do that here," said Constance. "The jungle is too dense."

"Aye," said Margaret, pointing to a ship to the northeast. "Look there."

Dozens of harpoons shot from the underbelly of a zeppelin, anchoring steel cables into the jungle floor. Minutes later, soldiers holding metal bars clipped to the cables slid down to the ground.

Constance and Margaret watched a growing number of ships drive harpoons into the ground. From their faraway vantage point, the British ships looked like spider sacks hatching, infant arachnids propelling to the ground on silken strings. The number of soldiers sliding down the lines continued to grow. On the ground the soldiers lined up into operational units and regiments.

• • • • •

"Colonel Silcock, sir," said a young soldier, snapping to a smart salute.

The man in charge of the British ground assault looked up from the over-sized maps spread out on the table in front of him. He and his officers had set up their headquarters in a hollowed out, cavernous building near the center of Bacatá.

"Yes, private?"

"Our scouts are reporting only a minor Resistance troop presence on the city streets, sir."

"Thank you, private," said the colonel. "What of the specifics?"

"Two columns were assaulted by Resistance soldiers dropping grenades from rooftops. All enemy combatants were killed. We suffered moderate casualties."

"What else?"

"We caught three Resistance soldiers spying from hidden locations," said the private. "All are in custody and currently being interrogated."

"What of the rooftop cannons?" asked the colonel.

"Unfortunately, sir, they stopped firing before we entered the city. We are having a difficult time figuring out which buildings have the cannons on them. Everything looks quite different from down here."

Colonel Silcock turned back to his top officers, standing idly by, awaiting orders: "We need air support, but first we have to flush out the rest of those bloody guns."

"Do you think the fleet commander would send a single battleship over the city to draw their fire?"

"I doubt anyone would willingly send a lamb to slaughter like that," replied Silcock. "When we took the city, our regiments broke apart to pursue several small groups of Resistance soldiers. I need to know the precise location of all our soldiers."

"Yes, sir," replied the officer. "I will go talk with the unit commanders and track down that information." He picked his way across small piles of colorfully painted plaster, exiting out onto the street awash with sunshine.

"We should consider the notion that the majority of the Resistance forces have either been killed or fled the city," said another officer.

The colonel looked at his officer for a minute before replying. "It is too dangerous to operate under that premise for now. We must continue with preparations for battle."

"But sir," said the officer, "the number of dead Resistance soldiers in the streets is quite high. I would assume that our play to take them by surprise worked well. We have taken control of this city. And although we are actively engaging with small pockets of soldiers, there has been no major counter-offensive attempted by the enemy."

Colonel Silcock scratched underneath his chin before replying. "There may be too few Resistance soldiers left alive to mount a significant counter-offensive. However, I fear that if we let down our guard now, we may pay a steep price. And it is my decision to make."

"Then what do you propose our next move be, sir?"

"We must secure air support from the fleet. Once I know where all our soldiers are, we will organize a building-by-building search starting from the center of the city and working outward. We will look for the rooftop cannons, as well as any Resistance soldiers still in hiding."

•　　•　　•　　•　　•

"The other bunkers are waiting for us to make the first move," whispered Edward to his sister.

"I am aware," she replied.

"When the two hundred soldiers in here charge up to the streets, the rooftop scouts will signal the soldiers on the rooftops of the other bunker buildings."

"I am aware of that, too," said Anne. "The plan is not a secret. In fact, the general has gone to great lengths to make everyone aware of it."

"Seems a bit counterintuitive to have a secret attack plan and then tell everyone about it," Edward grumbled under his breath.

"Relax, brother," said Anne. "Try to take a deep breath."

Edward's face was the familiar shade of an unripe avocado. "I do not like the plan. We will probably by shot dead. And by our own countrymen, no less."

"General Marquez instructed us to stay out of the fighting."

"But you objected."

"I objected because I can be of assistance rendering first aid to the wounded," said Anne. "I must say, I was impressed when he agreed to allow me to treat British and Resistance soldiers without prejudice."

A hand clasped on top of both Edward's left shoulder and Anne's right. General Marquez stuck his head between the siblings.

"*Mis amigos*," said the general, biting down on his unlit cigar. "Are you ready?"

"General, sir," said Edward. "You know that even though I would be honored to take up arms beside you, sir, I unable to do so."

"Do not worry, *Señor* Goulden," said Marquez. "I do not expect you to fight. I only ask that you and Miss Goulden aid the wounded."

"Of course, general," said Anne.

"*Bueno.*" The general stepped aside and waved over a pair of teenagers in green khaki uniforms. "These men are too young to fight in a battle such as this. I would like to put them under your command. They can assist you with the wounded."

"As you wish," said Anne, blushing.

"*Bueno*," said Marquez, clapping his hands together. "It is time." General Marquez made his way to the front of the room and cleared his throat with a loud grunt. The room sunk into a silent trance.

"*Mis camaradas*, sons of New Granada. Today we fight to reclaim our independence from a nation that rules us from half a world away. We are fighting to live as free citizens of New Granada, rather than privileged slaves."

Marquez paused and bit back down on his cigar. He raised his rifle over his head: "*Vive la Resistencia.*"

Hundreds of soldiers, standing shoulder to shoulder in packed quarters, echoed the general's war cry.

"*Vamanos*," shouted Marquez.

The soldiers of the New Granada Resistance surged forward like an unstoppable ocean wave, flooding the streets and disbursing in every direction.

• • • • •

Colonel Silcock and his officers stood hunkered over a table in their make-shift command station. Splintered bricks held the map centered on the table, preventing it from folding over whenever a breeze pushed through the doorway. A low rumble from somewhere outside slowly grew. After a minute, the ground beneath their feet trembled. The colonel lifted a delicate copper spyglass off the table before it rolled onto the ground.

"What in the bloody hell is that?" asked Colonel Silcock.

"I haven't the foggiest, sir."

"Perhaps the fleet is bombing an anti-aircraft cannon."

An enlisted man stumbled in through the broken doors: "Colonel Silcock, sir, we are under attack."

"What are you talking about, soldier?"

"They came out of nowhere. Pouring out of a house a block south of here," said the private, pausing to hyperventilate. "Hundreds of them. Screaming and shooting. I saw a dozen of our boys shot dead."

Colonel Silcock crossed the ten meters to the doorway in a half dozen steps. Pushing aside the private, he peered out into the street. A block away, a wave of bodies in green khaki uniforms overwhelmed a handful of British soldiers. The colonel spotted a second mob pouring into the street from a building in the opposite direction. Silcock lifted the heavy wooden door off the floor and propped it up before Resistance soldiers could spot the British officer.

"Bar this door with anything you can find. I want as many men as possible up on the rooftops with rifles. And get the bloody wireless radio working."

•   •   •   •   •

General Marquez emerged into the sunshine, shielding his eyes from the sun as he tried to light his cigar. A gust of wind blew out his match, forcing the general into a narrow alley. Puffing and smiling, he returned to the cobblestone street that was now a graveyard. With him were a pair of officers from the New Granada Resistance war counsel.

"Have we heard from any other bunker commanders?"

"Three have reported in so far," said Sergeant Vasquez. "All have engaged the enemy."

"*Bueno*," said Marquez, chewing on his cigar.

"What is the next step in retaking Bacatá?"

"That depends on how the surprise attack goes," replied the general, looking to the north and another stream of soldiers charging into the street. On a rooftop over his head, a handful of British riflemen were picking off Resistance soldiers at will.

General Marquez pointed to the rooftop with his cigar. "Send soldiers into that building to clear out the British snipers."

"*Si, señor*," replied the other officer, hailing a group of enlisted men and organizing a platoon to storm the building.

Marquez turned to the south and saw his soldiers engaged in a fire fight with a large number of British soldiers. The British were intelligent enough to take cover inside the row houses on one side of the street, firing from windows and doors. Resistance soldiers rushed a pair of houses. After routing the British, they took cover themselves and fired on the British from the opposite side of the street.

"You trained your men well, *sargento*," said Marquez.

"*Gracias.*"

* * * * *

"That's it, that's the signal," said Constance. She leaned back from the rooftop's parapet and turned to Margaret. "The Resistance are attacking."

Margaret walked across the roof and leaned over the edge. Hundreds of soldiers were coming out of a building down the road. She watched for a few minutes and tried to assess the battle's progress. "We definitely have the element of surprise. Things are going well, but we need to maintain pressure and not allow the British to regroup."

Margaret turned around and saw Constance reloading the second cannon. Constance pointed the gun low across the horizon at a British battleship creeping closer, now just two kilometers to the north.

"They are trying to position themselves overhead and provide air support," said Constance.

"The cannon cannot hit a target at that distance," said Margaret.

"It doesn't matter," replied Constance. "All we need to do is fire and they will retreat."

"No," said Margaret. "We should wait until they get closer. It will only take a few minutes. We can surprise them; open up both cannons and bring the battleship down."

"No, we need to fire now," said Constance. "Otherwise the zeppelin will start dropping bombs and Resistance soldiers will die."

"It is a trade that works out to our advantage," said Margaret, her frustration rising. "To bring down an entire battleship is worth the risk."

"No," shouted Constance. "That is not how this works."

"That is exactly how this works."

"It only works that way because you decide it does," replied Constance. "If we scare them off then neither side losses people."

Margaret's voice grew quiet and difficult to hear over the screams and explosions from the ground. "We have to hold our fire. It is by far the best tactical move."

Constance balled her fists and marched up to Margaret. "If you hold your fire, I will make sure these cannons do not work when you want them to."

The Resistance soldier working the second cannon interjected. "I will fire now. It will save the lives of my brothers-in-arms."

Constance returned with him to his cannon. She loaded it while the soldier adjusted the targeting and increased the gun's range to the greatest distance possible. The cannon boomed, the explosion echoing off the walls of the narrow streets.

The shell landed on a rooftop a kilometer to the north. It splintered the eaves, sending red clay tiles and sharp spears of wood raining down on the empty street. The British zeppelin came to a stop three hundred meters beyond the cannon's range. It hung motionless in the air while the ground battle raged a dozen blocks to the south, helpless.

●　　●　　●　　●　　●

"We need to get outside the city and work our way north," said Francis, shouldering his augmented rifle. "I want to get an angle on those troop transports. They still have a thousand soldiers to put on the ground."

Ezmeralda aimed her rifle and fired into a cluster of British soldiers three blocks away. The bullets exploded on impact, inflicting injuries and sending the soldiers scattering.

"If we get out in the jungle and closer to those airships, you think we can stop some of those soldiers from reaching the ground?" asked Ezmeralda.

"*Oui*," said Francis. "I want to get behind where they are landing the soldiers. From there we can take out the mooring lines with the rifles."

"*Aye, mi amor*," said Ezmeralda in a husky voice. "You are sexy when you are plotting the downfall of an authoritarian regime."

Francis smirked. "We have to get moving; I have a stop to make on the way."

•　　•　　•　　•　　•

Edward and Anne each held a forearm of the British soldier, dragging him off the street and through the front door of an inconspicuous row house. They let go and the unconscious man slumped on the cold tile floor. Edward waited by the door while Anne talked to a Resistance soldier.

"What's wrong with him?" asked the soldier. "He looks dead."

"He took a bullet in the leg. Probably shattered the bone. But he is not dead, only unconscious."

"I do not think he will recover," replied the soldier. "We should not waste time on him."

"Apply first aid to him, same as the others," ordered Anne. "Tie off his leg with a tourniquet above the wound. Clean the bullet hole then douse it in rum. And give him a drink if he wakes up."

"I refuse to waste good rum on a dead British soldier," he said. "It is bad enough that while my brothers shoot these *pandejos*, I play nursemaid."

"Fine," said Anne, sighing. "If he wakes up, do not give him any rum. But take care of his wound, same as the others. That's an order."

The soldier stared at Anne for a minute, daring her to back down. "OK, I will," said the soldier, bowing his eyes. He turned his attention back to a pair of wounded Resistance soldiers lying at his feet.

"What has gotten into you, little sister?" said Edward once Anne rejoined him. "Staring down an armed soldier like that."

"I surprised myself many times today," said Anne, surveying the room packed with unbearable misery. "I need you to stay here and care for the wounded. I will take one of the other young men to retrieve the wounded. Your first aid skills are better than anyone else here. You will not hesitate to care for British soldiers. Plus, every one of these soldiers are quite a bit stronger than you; they can lift more than a small child."

"I see you have foregone the more subtle use of language since I left for England," said Edward. "Mother must be roiling."

Anne blinked in surprise. "You looked like you were struggling out there," she mumbled.

Edward bowed. "I apologize for my quip, dear sister. However, I would prefer to stay with you in case something should happen."

"I appreciate the sentiment, but some of these young soldiers are unable to treat even the most basic of wounds; it is a much smarter division of labor. Would you feel better if I took two armed soldiers with me?"

"I would." Edward retrieved a tourniquet and got to work treating the British soldier with a bullet in his leg.

•　　•　　•　　•　　•

Francis stood before his most fantastic creation. He and his wife were in the front room of an abandoned house a short distance from their workshop. Francis looked up at his three-meter tall jaguar, gaze lingering on the dull black metal jaws with teeth like short silver swords.

"*Mi amor, rapidomente*," said Ezmeralda. "You have to hurry; we will not last long under heavy fire." She adjusted the dials on the copper tubing running along her rifle and returned fire. Ezmeralda ducked inside the doorway and crouched low to make herself a smaller target.

"*Juste un moment*," said Francis. The Frenchman was focused like a laser, hands flying back and forth across discreet levers and knobs recessed in the jaguar's chest and legs. The top of the metallic skull was open like a giant mango split by a machete. Francis climbed up on a wooden chair and buried his surgeon's hands deep inside the beast's skull.

Ezmeralda stood up and fired another burst from the doorway, then ducked inside the room as the British returned fire. Pieces of brick and mortar burst in tiny explosions up and down the door frame.

"Francis," she yelled, "I cannot hold them off much longer." Ezmeralda hung the barrel of her rifle out the doorway and fired a pair of blind rounds.

"*Oui, oui*, almost done," muttered Francis, ignoring the life and death struggle taking place across the room. A spray of gunfire struck the wall opposite the open doorway.

"*Dios mío*," muttered Ezmeralda. "More soldiers."

She crawled away from the door and underneath a window, covered with an iron grate instead of glass. Ezmeralda lifted her head and fired another pair of shots before lying flat on her back to reload. She cursed the British outside as well as her dawdling husband. Handfuls of stucco exploded from the walls as gunfire sprayed through the doorway and window.

"Francis," she yelled, fumbling with the bullets she was loading. "Now."

Francis pushed the two halves of jaguar's skull together and flipped one final switch. The mechanical monster roared to life. The gritty, grinding, steel growl startled the soldiers outside and the gunfire paused. The jaguar crouched on all four paws like a true jungle cat, hindquarters raised, heavy tail in the air for balance. It leapt forward and was in the street before its paws touched the ground again.

A handful of soldiers emptied their rifles at the jungle cat; others ran. The brave men that held their ground were the first to die. The jaguar slashed at them with steel claws the size of butcher's knives, batting weapons away and bending the steel of the British bayonets.

"What did you program it to do?" asked Ezmeralda, sitting upright in the small house, catching her breath.

"Attack anyone wearing dark blue with a red and white sash," Francis said.

"Kill soldiers wearing a British uniform," muttered Ezmeralda. "It can recognize colors?"

"*Oui*," said Francis. "The optical units are the best I ever built."

Screams bounced off the high walls lining the narrow street, then echoed off the inside walls of the house. Neither Ezmeralda nor Francis lifted their head; neither wanted to witness the slaughter. The jaguar growled its loud, mechanical cat cry over the bodies of its victims before racing down the cobblestones in search of prey.

Ezmeralda made the sign of the cross and kissed her thumb. "The roar is a nice touch, *mi amor*. Very frightening."

CHAPTER 23

General Marquez crouched behind a pile of rubble. He whipped his rifle from his shoulder, leveled the weapon at the enemy, and squeezed the trigger. He and a dozen Resistance fighters were engaged with a large British force half a block away, caught in a stalemate, trading rifle fire from behind barriers.

A young man not yet twenty years old appeared beside the general. "General Marquez, sir," he said, panting.

"Who are you?"

"Private Mera, sir," said the soldier. "General Fernandez sent me to find you."

"*Bueno*," replied Marquez. "And what does the good general want?"

"General Fernandez wanted me to give you a status report, sir."

"Begin, *por favor*." Marquez stood up and fired a handful of shots at the entrenched British before dropping back behind the rubble to reload.

"The British have stopped landing soldiers," said the young man. "General Fernandez believes there are more on board the transport ships, but someone from our side has crippled their landing mechanisms."

"*Aye*, Lefount," shouted the general, jumping to his feet. He remembered where he was and dropped back behind the brick barricade. "*Mi siento*," said Marquez. "Please, continue."

"British soldiers overran the last rooftop cannon a short time ago. General Fernandez believes the fleet will move in now to provide air support for their ground troops."

"*Dios mío*," said Marquez. "What other information does General Fernandez have?"

"Overall, we are doing good, sir," said Private Mera. "We secured the city in the south and east; and are close to controlling the west. Fighting is most intense here, in the center of Bacatá. The British still have strength here, and in the north near their fleet.

"Good," said Marquez, pausing in thought. "I have orders for you to take back to General Fernandez."

Private Mera snapped a sharp salute: *"Señor."*

"Concentrate our forces on the center of Bacatá. From here, we will begin a coordinated push north. I wish to rout the British now, before they can coordinate air support."

"*Bueno*," replied the soldier. "Anything else?"

"*Si*, there is more," replied Marquez. Having finished reloading, he stood up and returned a volley of fire to the British.

"Relay that message to General Fernandez, then circle the city and communicate the same orders to every officer. Move through buildings and alleys. Stay out of sight and do not engage the enemy."

"*Si, general*," said the young man. He saluted before vanishing into a hollow building.

General Marquez stood again to fire, but never pulled the trigger. A mechanical jaguar twice the size of a man attacked the British from behind. In a swirl of glistening metallic, blood, and screams, twenty British soldiers were wiped from existence. A handful of soldiers tried to flee, but the killing machine ran them down.

General Marquez and his men stood and stared as the bloodthirsty cat disappeared around a corner in search of his next victim.

● ● ● ● ●

Major Ulperlip scrutinized the battle below him from the window of his command ship. Through his spyglass, he studied blocks of crumpled and burnt-out buildings. He stopped sweeping his lens through the city streets to focus on a squadron of British soldiers who pinned a rabble of Resistance soldiers in an alley.

A blur of black metal accentuated with glistening silver appeared behind the British barriers. They were all dead a minute later. Major Ulperlip watched as the mechanical jungle cat tipped its head back and roared.

"Captain," said Major Ulperlip, "coordinate a bombing raid on the northeast quadrant of the city, three blocks from the center. That bloody metal cat is still tearing our boys to shreds. I want that contraption bombed to oblivion."

"Yes, sir," replied the captain, huddling with his communications and tactical officers.

Lieutenant Vickers stepped up behind Major Ulperlip and spoke in a hushed tone: "Sir, I believe we need to discuss the next step in this battle. Our ground forces are losing and we must consider more drastic steps to ensure victory."

"Vickers," said the major, spinning around on his heels. "Do not sneak up on me like that."

"Of course, sir," replied the lieutenant.

"Now, what were you saying about losing the battle?" said the major. "The Resistance certainly have us on our heels. But as we speak, our men are regrouping and planning a new offensive. We have tentatively established air superiority over the city; the momentum will swing back in our favor."

Major Ulperlip paused his conversation with Lieutenant Vickers and turned to the ship's captain: "Coordinate a second bombing run targeting the center square of the city. Enemy soldiers continue to congregate in that region. I want the streets impassable."

Major Ulperlip turned back to Vickers. "Is there anything else, lieutenant?"

"Yes, sir, there is," answered Vickers, his voice droll and dry. "It is irresponsible for us to take any chances; we absolutely must win the day. I believe we need to deploy the chlorine gas. I do not need to emphasize the importance of this confrontation, sir. Control of the entire region rests on the outcome of this battle."

Major Ulperlip responded by emitting a slow, deep growl from the back of his throat: "You and I have already discussed the use of the poison gas. It will not happen, regardless of the circumstances. Do I make myself clear?"

"Crystal, sir," said Lieutenant Vickers, condescension in his voice. "The problem is that I have handwritten orders from Queen Victoria herself. They instruct me to completely dismantle the Resistance, and authorize me to use any means necessary to achieve that goal."

"I do not understand, lieutenant," said Major Ulperlip. "That is exactly what we are doing."

"No, sir," said Vickers. "Without deploying the chlorine gas, the best we can hope for is a victory in name only. We will, of course, declare ourselves triumphant. But the New Granada Resistance will regroup and terrorize the colony again in a year."

"That is blatantly untrue," said the major. "And I will warn you to check your tone of voice when addressing your commanding officer."

Vickers sneered: "My orders from Queen Victoria explicitly instruct me to use any means necessary, including the chlorine gas, to completely dismantle the New Granada Resistance. Sir."

Major Ulperlip stared at his second in command. "Please produce these handwritten orders from Her Majesty, lieutenant."

Lieutenant Vickers dug into a concealed breast pocket and withdrew a long, elegant envelope stamped with the broken wax seal of the Queen. He handed it to the major who pulled the letter out and read it.

"Why was I not informed of these orders before we left Cartagena?" asked Major Ulperlip.

A sneer appeared again in the corners of the lieutenant's mouth: "Her Majesty verbally instructed me to act alone and notify no one unless it became necessary to fulfill the mission."

Major Ulperlip stuffed the Queen's letter back in the envelope. He handed it to Vickers, who carefully flattened it before tucking it back in his uniform.

"We will win this fight and dismantle the Resistance using conventional means," said Ulperlip, his voice hushed and coarse.

"And if we fail?"

"That question is irrelevant," said the major. "We are on the verge of turning the tide and backing the Resistance into a corner."

"Right now we are losing," said Vickers, his voice again droll and callous. "The enemy is slaughtering our soldiers on the ground."

"We have destroyed the last anti-aircraft cannon and can now provide air support. Once we destroy that bloody metal cat, victory will be at hand."

"We have not established air superiority," replied the lieutenant. "There are still functioning cannons in the jungle. More drones are being launched. Enemy soldiers with high-powered rifles crippled two of our transport ships an hour ago. On top of all that, their metal jaguar has proven difficult to neutralize. It slaughters a unit of our men, then runs and hides in a building, only to pop up in another section of the city."

Ulperlip stood straight up, pulling himself up to his full height and puffing out his chest. "I will not drop the chlorine gas on the city."

"May I ask what your reason is for disobeying a direct order?" asked Vickers.

"Dropping a poison gas on thousands of soldiers is a grotesque, cowardly way to inflict widespread death."

"I fail to see the difference between striking down our enemies using poison gas or dropping explosives from kilometer above them."

"I do not wish to discuss this any further."

"Perhaps the only honorable means of dispatching enemies of the Crown is with broad swords in hand-to-hand combat. Then we can look each one in the eye before dispatching them."

"This conversation is over, lieutenant."

"I fail to see a distinction between killing with a gun or an explosive or poison gas. We are soldiers, charged with protecting the Crown and the Empire. We are expected to take lives when fulfilling our duty."

"I will not drop the chlorine gas on the city."

Vickers stood still, staring at Major Ulperlip for a long time. "I am sorry you feel that way, sir. And if we lose?"

"If we lose this day, the matter will be handled through the proper military chain of command at a later date. If those orders are in fact scribed by the hand of Victoria herself, I alone will face court martial."

• • • • • •

"Sir, we have to withdraw," shouted a private into Colonel Silcock's ear.

The colonel leaned out a window and emptied his rifle into the throng of Resistance soldiers on the street below him. Three enemy combatants drove their shoulders into the barricaded front door.

"Sir, we need to go. Now."

"How do you propose we do that?" asked Silcock. "Front and rear entrances are currently blocked by a mob of enemy soldiers." The colonel traded rifles with another soldier loading rounds into empty British guns. "Besides, I see the cavalry coming."

The private leaned out the window and spotted the glint of brass buttons over navy-blue uniforms; a regiment of British soldiers was two blocks away and advancing toward them. The Resistance soldiers saw the reinforcements coming too. They traded rifle fire with Silcock one more time before abandoning the British headquarters to spread out along the street. They ducked into alleys and open doorways while the larger, better-equipped British regiment marched in single file columns down the middle of the street.

The British soldiers halted, and the columns turned left and right; three rows of soldiers facing both sides of the street. An officer shouted a command and the soldiers fired a volley into windows and doors and alleyways. The Resistance returned fire, picking off soldiers standing tall in the middle of the road. The British commander called out new orders and the soldiers broke ranks to charge the guerrilla soldiers and flush them out.

Colonel Silcock took advantage of the temporary ceasefire to assess his situation. "Is this all the ammunition we have left?"

"Yes, sir."

"Our boys out there better pull this off," muttered the colonel.

"We are taking heavy losses, sir, but our boys are winning," said another soldier, watching the battle.

Colonel Silcock joined the soldier at the window just as Francis Lefount's iron jaguar appeared directly below him. It leapt from the shadows of an open doorway and cracked the street's paving stones when it landed. Its gun-black metal body, streaked with blood and oil and soot, created a sickening montage of darkness and death. The machine reared up on its hind legs and let out a gut-wrenching roar.

Colonel Silcock and his men smelled the grinding machine gears and tasted the smoke. Every soldier felt sick watching the iron jaguar do its grizzly job, slashing through the British regiment in minutes with long, steel claws.

Silcock stood up in the hollow window frame and emptied his rifle clip at the jaguar. Each round made a high-pitched ping as it bounced off the monster. The jaguar rotated its head to face Silcock in the window above and let out another deafening roar.

"I think you made it mad, sir," said the young private, eyes locked on the monster.

•   •   •   •   •

Lieutenant Vickers's face was flat and expressionless. "I am going to ask one more time, sir. Will you follow Queen Victoria's orders and drop the chlorine gas on the city?"

"I will not, lieutenant," said Ulperlip, his face inches from Vickers. "Now get off of my bridge or I will have the sergeant-at-arms lock you in the brig."

"Very well; you leave me no choice."

Lieutenant Vickers drew a concealed service revolver and fired a single shot into Major Ulperlip's stomach.

The major stood silent, both hands clasped over the wound in his belly. Thick blood that was more black than red seeped between his fingers and spread across his uniform. Major Ulperlip looked down at his stomach, then up at Lieutenant Vickers before collapsing on the floor.

Vickers stood over the major's body, smoking gun pointing out from his hip. Every crew member stared at Vickers in disbelief. The remained silent and motionless as a tomb. Most were only half aware of the confrontation that had been brewing between their commanding officers.

The ship's captain stepped forward: "Lieutenant Vickers, I have no idea what all this is about, but you are relieved of duty. Sergeant-at-arms, please escort the lieutenant to the brig."

A burly soldier stepped towards the lieutenant; Vickers raised his revolver and shot the captain between the eyes.

Vickers pulled a second revolver from a concealed holster and leveled it at the sergeant-at-arms. He began speaking, filling the cold, dead air of the bridge with a harsh whisper.

"I was personally handed orders written by Queen Victoria herself. Our mission is to wipe the New Granada Resistance from this Earth. They are terrorists and cowards of the worse kind, killing and kidnapping British citizens at will. The Queen's orders explicitly instruct us to use any means necessary to achieve this objective."

As Lieutenant Vickers spoke, his voice slowly rose. "We hold in our collective cargo bays a weapon that will ensure victory. Yet your commanding officer refused to use it. In doing so, he directly violated orders from Queen Victoria herself. That is why I shot him. I am now in command of this mission."

The lieutenant's voice was now a roar, echoing off the steel grate floor and filling every corner of the room. "Sergeant-at-arms, if you advance on me, I will shoot you as well. I will follow Her Majesty's orders to dismantle the New Granada Resistance by any means necessary."

Vickers paused, nearly foaming at the mouth. "Is there anyone here who wishes to directly disobey the handwritten orders of Queen Victoria?"

"May we see the orders, sir?" asked the first officer.

Vickers reached into his breast pocket while keeping one gun leveled, his eyes watching every twitch of the crew. Per regulations, none wore sidearms on duty except the sergeant-at-arms.

The first officer ran his fingers over the broken wax seal of Queen Victoria. Without removing the letter, he answered the lieutenant.

"I am Sub-lieutenant Jeffreys. What are your orders, sir?"

• • • • •

Constance paused and bent over, hands on her knees, exhausted. She was breathing hard, covered in soot and mud and dried blood.

"Can you get the gun to work?" asked Margaret.

"I doubt it," replied Constance. Her face was flush and her voice hoarse. "Not without my tools."

The barrel and thick iron turret of the cannon were intact, but the rush of British soldiers from the stairwell managed to fire a round into the control mechanism. Unable to gain cover, the soldiers conceded the rooftop after disabling both cannons.

Margaret walked to the edge of the building and surveyed the carnage on the streets. Bodies lie in haphazard positions: a British soldier with his feet propped up on a wall, a Resistance fighter missing his right arm and left leg.

"We need to figure out what to do," said Margaret. She watched two groups of soldiers locked in a stalemate, exchanging rifle fire at close range from behind piles of bricks and shattered mortar.

Constance hit the cannon turret with the ball hammer left behind by the soldier they first found on the rooftop. That man's body lie next to the body of his replacement.

"What the bloody hell are we supposed to do now," shouted Constance. She banged the hammer on the gun turret harder and harder with every word.

Margaret turned to face her friend. "What is wrong with you?"

Constance dropped the hammer and stepped towards Margaret: "Are you actually asking what is wrong with me right now?"

Margaret lowered her eyes and returned her gaze to the scene on the street. Air raid sirens began blasting from every zeppelin in the skies over Bacatá.

"Something is wrong," said Margaret. "The Brits are pulling out of the fight."

Constance walked over to Margaret and scanned the streets. A British soldier ignored an attacker charging with a leveled bayonet. The infantryman turned his back on the Resistance soldier and fumbled through the gear on his back. The Resistance bayonet found its home between the British soldier's vertebrate.

Constance looked up at the zeppelins blaring their air raid sirens. Cylinder-shaped canisters half the length of a rifle fell from the battleships. They blanketed the skies, filling the air with an ominous, gunmetal feel of death.

Constance gasped and covered her mouth.

"What's wrong?"

Constance pointed a shaking finger at the fresh body lying in the street. "The mask he pulled out of his gear bag before he was stabbed. It is to protect him from chlorine gas. The poison we discovered the British planned to use."

"We need to find shelter. Now."

•　　•　　•　　•　　•

General Marquez stood in front of a small cluster of his men barking orders: "Get those masks off the dead soldiers. *Vamanos, rapido.*"

Around the corner Francis Lefount's living weapon roared with a ferocity that sent chills down the spine of every soul in Bacatá's central park. Edward struggled to stay focused with the mechanical monster prowling nearby. He stripped a pair of gas masks from the hands of dead British soldiers, fastened one on himself and one on his sister.

Marquez shouted louder with the awkward contraption strapped to his own face: "Gather every mask you can, then hand them out to as many soldiers as you can."

"I do not understand what's going on?" asked Anne.

"These masks protect us from the chlorine gas," replied Edward.

"What is chlorine gas?"

Edward tilted his head straight back. He pointed at the zeppelins blanketing the city with small, metallic cylinders.

"Those canisters contain a poison gas called chlorine that kills everyone who breaths it."

"Distribute the masks to every everyone you find," shouted Marquez. "When you run out of masks, clear the streets and get everybody back into the basement shelters. Every soldier you give a mask to must help clear the streets until everyone is underground." Each soldier gathered a half dozen masks and cradled them in their arms. "*Vamanos*, we have to hurry."

The soldiers disappeared down streets leading in every direction away from the center of town. General Marquez walked up behind Edward and Anne and clapped a hand on each of their shoulders.

"*Mis amigos*," said Marquez. "You two come with me. We will work our way north."

Edward and Anne nodded and fell in, trotting behind the general and a pair of soldiers. The small group distributed their masks to the first Resistance soldiers they found. Those men joined Marquez in shepherding everyone off the streets and into the basement bunkers.

The first bombs hit the streets and released a thick, yellow-green cloud that crept low along the cobblestone streets. It filled the narrow spaces in every alley and meandered through splintered doors and hollow window frames. The British fleet continued dropping bombs, causing the gas to pile up to the two-story rooftops.

Minutes later, Anne and Edward found themselves alone, dragging a pair of coughing, wheezing, soldiers without masks towards the closest bunker.

"The shelter is only a few houses away," shouted Anne. The man hanging off Anne's shoulder went limp. His feet stopped shuffling forward and he slid to the ground.

"Get up," said Anne. She tried to pull the soldier to his feet while he clutched at his throat. Anne lost her balance and fell forward across her charge, landing on top of more dead men in green khaki uniforms. Anne lie still, unable to turn away from the dead men, their eyes bulging, hands forever locked around their own throats.

"Anne," shouted Edward, leaning down, his face beside hers. "Anne, we have to go."

He pulled his sister to her feet. She continued to stare downward at the grotesque pile of dead soldiers. Edward moved his body directly in her line of sight, blocking her view of the bodies.

"We have to get to shelter," he shouted from behind his mask. Anne shook her head, numbness creeping from her center down her arms and legs as the carnage took hold.

"Everyone on the streets not wearing a mask is already dead. We have to get to shelter or we will die." Edward threw Anne's arm over his own shoulder and stepped around his charge, lying dead beside the others. Minutes later Edward and Anne tumbled down the stairs into the nearly deserted bomb shelter.

• • • • •

Young Mr. Jeffreys, the new captain of the British flagship, looked to his new commander. "We dropped the first round of chlorine gas canisters as ordered, sir. Other ships in the fleet are visually tracking them and starting to report back."

Lieutenant Vickers peered through the spyglass at the battle raging on the city streets. He watched as British soldiers tried to disengage from a fight with the Resistance's mechanical jaguar. They wrestled with their gas masks, only to fall victim to the steel jungle cat. The monster disemboweled its prey with a swipe of its claws. From hundreds of meters overhead, Vickers saw each steel claw, long as his arm and glistening beneath black blood in the afternoon sun.

Captain Jeffreys interrupted Vickers's thoughts. "Sir, the zeppelins are reporting a high number of British soldiers dying from the gas. Our men are unable to effectively disengage from the enemy and properly secure their masks." The young man scratched at the acne scars dotting his chin.

Lieutenant Vickers lowered his spyglass, taking his time collapsing it. "My orders remain the same. Continue dropping the gas canisters from all available zeppelins. Each airship is to use exactly half of their supply before ceasing bombardment."

Jeffreys swallowed hard and nodded to the communications officer: "Relay those orders to the fleet."

Midshipman Johnson took off his headset and whispered an argument to his old academy mate.

"Just do it," whispered Jeffreys between clenched teeth. Vickers turned back to the window and raised his spyglass.

Ten more minutes dragged on and the fleet continued dropping choline canisters on the city. The battlefield below looked like a London morning when a thick fog bank rolled in off the Thames, mixing with the heavy brown industrial waste pumped into the skies.

"Sir," said Jeffreys, now biting his lower lip. "Six battleships have stopped dropping the gas. Their captains refuse to follow your orders."

Vickers stood still, pondering the problem and staring out the bridge window with the spyglass.

"Very well," said Vickers. "Do not reply or send any sort of acknowledgment to those six ships. Order six other airships whose captains are complying with my orders to drop every canister of choline gas in their holds."

"Yes, sir," replied Jeffreys. His face was pale and sweaty, but he took a deep breath and ordered Midshipman Johnson to relay the message.

CHAPTER 24

Popayán

On a sweltering, sticky South Carolina afternoon in the summer of 1801, an elderly man leaned heavily on his cane as he lumbered down the aisle. Reaching his destination, he held on to the podium with both hands and waved away his attendants. The din in the hall dropped several decibels in anticipation.

"As you know, I am a leader of the York Rite of Freemasons, Commandery of Knights Templar, Order of the Knights of Malta. Throughout my life, I have labored to achieve peace and prosperity across the world through technological innovation.

"I traveled across the Pond to voice my opposition to the formation of a new Rite of Freemasons. This so-called Scottish Rite is not condoned by the United Kingdom's Council of Freemasons."

A gentleman in a white wig seated near the speaker rose. "Master Douglas Tank," he said with a slight bow, "the commission of the Scottish Rite is not a matter of debate. The framework was agreed upon by the Freemasons of the North American Colonies months ago. Since then, it has been endorsed by Masons in a dozen sovereign nations around the world."

"Master Thomas Jefferson, I presume," replied the speaker. "I beg you, do not interrupt. I am an old man; get to the point lest my time expire behind this podium."

"Please, continue."

Douglas Tank coughed and cleared his throat: "Freemasons are foremost dedicated to enlightened thought and ethical action. My primary objection to the Scottish Rite lies in the moral code it is built upon. This code threatens the peace and prosperity of the British Empire. Establishing an order of Masons built on principles that undermine the Empire's welfare is an affront to God Himself."

"Sir, would you please clarify? Which principles you speak of?" asked Jefferson.

"Yes, of course," replied Douglas, pausing to catch his breath. "The peoples of the world fare better under the watchful eye of the British Monarchy. In conquered and colonized lands, savages living in squalor gain access to the breadth of resources at our Empire's disposal. Warring tribes make peace; people hear the word of God and have the opportunity for salvation."

"Sir, can we then conclude that you are speaking against this council's belief in the individual's right to determine their own fate?"

"Yes, Master Jefferson, I am," replied Douglas. "Although I prefer if you would not phrase it in that way. Freemasons have long advocated the paradigm that colonialism under the British Empire provides the greatest benefits to the most people."

"I regret to inform you, sir, we have searched our collective souls and discovered that the moral code justifying colonialism is flawed. Therefore, the only conclusion we can infer is that the technologies adapted by the colonies are similarly flawed."

"You are fools," said Douglas Tank, slapping the podium with a liver-spotted hand. "Self-determination is rooted in vanity. A people's best option is to cede authority to those with the expertise to rule."

"You have no right, sir, to dictate the correct form of government for any people. A people's culture, history, their very way of life necessitates one form over another."

"Bah," replied Douglas Tank, the sound getting stuck in his throat.

"It is the native citizens' prerogative to decide how to utilize natural resources," said Jefferson.

"Without enlightened central planning those resources would be squandered."

"Only the individual can determine how to pursue his own happiness."

"A meaningless platitude," replied Douglas.

"Only the individual nation can determine their own best path."

"Where did get such ridiculous ideas, sir?"

"From your own hand," said Jefferson.

"To what are you referring?"

"I heard you lecture at Oxford over twenty years ago. You told the story of leaving your home in Cumberland, walking away from your family and a life in the coal mines to move to London. You suffered through poverty and starvation to eventually build a machine that would change the world."

Douglas Tank chuckled behind the podium, wheezing like an old man: "I still give that lecture at university."

"You lecture on the freedom to make mistakes, on the impossibility of success without failure."

"And you believe these lessons apply not only to the individual, but to nations," interrupted Douglas.

"Yes, sir, I do," replied Jefferson. "It is despotism of the worse kind to rob a nation of its freedom, to block a state from making its own mistakes. Subjugated people fail to grow. They fail to meet their potential. You call colonialism benevolence, but I call it tyranny."

"You are spreading the worst kind of propaganda, sir," replied Douglas. "Feeding a starving man is benevolent. Feeding a nation is also a kindness. We are doing God's will."

An old man in a crooked wig stood up in the back. "Do you have the audacity to claim your perspective as God's will, sir?"

"Who are you, sir?" asked Douglas.

"You know who I am," said the man before sitting down.

"Bah," shouted Douglas. "You should all know better. Splitting the Freemasons along ideological lines is a fool's errand."

Thomas Jefferson turned away from Douglas Tank to address the congregation: "Today we draft a document defining the ethical bedrock of the new Scottish Rite. These documents make clear that no Mason of this new Rite will participate in England's imperialist efforts. In particular, none will develop weapons of war for the British Empire."

Rows of seated Masons stood and filled the sweaty brick hall with their angry voices. Douglas Tank bowed his head and shuffled off the podium with the help of his attendants.

• • • • •

The sun topped the mountains and forests to the east, rays piercing the thin gray haze hanging over the city. A light breeze swirled across the battlefield, quietly lifting the top layer of ash off the streets of Bacatá.

Lieutenant Vickers stood looking down from the bridge of the HMS *Fulton*. He rubbed his eyes with his fingers, dislodging the sleep and clearing his vision. He extended his spyglass and pressed it to his eye socket.

Glimpses through the haze revealed a seared and scorched battlefield. Vickers spotted the Resistance's mechanical jaguar lying in a heap of twisted steel. Oil slid down the coil lines that once lubricated the monster's joints, the black fluid smearing with the blood of the British soldiers piled underneath.

A short distance away, a cluster of British soldiers huddled in a bomb crater. A pair of rusting pipes stuck in the dry mud, tilted at an angle, aimed at the twisted remains of Francis Lefount's killing machine. The lieutenant lowered his spyglass.

"Mr. Jeffreys."

"Aye, sir."

"I have a new set of orders I wish you to transmit to the fleet," said Vickers. "I need a body count of the dead Resistance."

"Aye, sir," replied Jeffreys, turning to Midshipman Johnson. "Order the commanders on the ground to put together a body count. Wounded and dead Resistance."

"I do not believe there are any wounded Resistance soldiers left alive," said Vickers.

"Sir, there are always wounded soldiers left alive," replied Jeffreys.

"No, captain, not this time." Vickers stared hard at Jeffreys.

"I believe I understand, sir," said Jeffreys, breaking eye contact. He bent down to speak quietly with his communications officer.

After a moment, Jeffreys popped back up and barked at his charge: "Just relay the orders, sailor. I did not ask for your opinion."

Lieutenant Vickers smirked, "Jeffreys."

"Aye, sir."

"I also need a list of missing or dead British soldiers, a complete damage report from every ship, and an inventory of the equipment and materials this fight cost us."

"Aye, sir."

"I want a command station setup in the center of the city. We will leave behind three airships and one ground regiment. Standing orders remain to shoot anyone not loyal to Her Majesty on sight."

"Are we leaving already, sir?"

"Yes, we are," replied Vickers. He sighed, standing in front of the huge bridge windows. "Come here and tell me what you see."

"I see the streets of an abandoned Spanish city."

"What else?"

"I see dead soldiers from both sides. Thousands of them."

"Very good," said Vickers. "And who won this conflict that resulted in thousands dead?"

"We did, sir. I see an abundance of our men still alive, still wearing their gas masks. All the enemy soldiers are dead."

"That is correct," said Vickers. "But why would the fleet stay here when the war for New Granada is not yet complete?"

"I do not follow."

Vickers pulled out the signed letter from Queen Victoria and slapped it down on the command console. "My orders are: *any and all means necessary to dismantle the New Granada Resistance.*"

"We routed the Resistance, sir." Jeffreys waved his hand at the scene out the window below him. "There are none left alive."

"The ragtag army lying dead in the streets below was the red right hand of the New Granada Resistance. The free city of Popayán is the left. It provides food and supplies to the military, children raised there grow up to become soldiers. The militant right hand will return unless we bring the infamous White City into the British Empire."

"If you say so, sir."

CHAPTER 25

"Is it safe?" Anne stood behind General Marquez and her brother on the steps of their basement bomb shelter.

"The gas should all be gone," said Marquez. "I can smell the rain outside."

"What about the British soldiers?" asked Edward.

"I am sure they are still outside waiting for us," replied the general. "But it has been almost two days. We cannot stay down here any longer." General Marquez motioned for a dozen armed soldiers to step forward and exit the door into the street first. "The rain will provide us with a small amount of cover."

The soldiers, guns at the ready, filed up the stairs and into the muddy streets. They formed a half circle in front of the door, fanning out in all directions. Everything was quiet.

"Maybe they are gone," muttered Anne, squinting into the haze of the morning rain.

Marquez pointed up at a cigar-shaped shadow in the clouds over the south side of Bacatá: "British battleship."

The general waited until the entire contingent of forty soldiers emerged from the basement bunker. "You all know what to do. Teams of three, stick to alleys and cover the section of the city you were assigned. Get to all the bunkers, talk to any soldiers of *la Resistencia* you find. We meet in four hours in *mi encomienda* one kilometer east of the city. *Vamanos.*"

• • • • •

General Marquez surveyed the gathered soldiers. A grimy, dejected rabble caked in mud and soot with bloody tourniquets twisted around arms and abdomens.

"Is this everybody?" the general asked.

"*Si, señor,*" a messenger replied. "The streets are filled with the dead."

"*Si, yo se,*" muttered Marquez.

"We were thousands," said Francis Lefount. He stood beside Marquez and Ezmeralda. "Now we are hundreds."

Edward, Margaret, Constance, and Anne sat alone, separated from the soldiers underneath a banana tree heavy with fruit.

"What is this place?" asked Constance.

"It is an *encomienda,*" replied Edward. "A plantation once owned by a wealthy Spaniard. General Marquez said it used to be his."

Marquez's *encomienda* was as on an expansive piece of property outside the city. Abandoned years ago, the plantation's borders shrank each year as the jungle encroached from all sides. Remnants of the land's agricultural heritage were visible in the overripe mangos and avocados intermixed with the native ferns and bamboo groves.

"Marquez was an indentured servant before the British took New Granada," said Margaret.

"How do you know that?" asked Constance.

Margaret shrugged and stared through the soldiers massed in the courtyard, "Glasgow Resistance." Her eyes wandered up to the white stucco walls of the main house, the tile roof breezeway, and the gray clouds hanging over the trees.

Edward grunted and nodded towards the leaders of the Resistance. "What do you suppose they will do?"

As if waiting for Edward's introduction, General Marquez raised his voice to address his battered army: "My friends, today we are the lucky ones. We are lucky because we have another day alive in this beautiful country. We are lucky to have so many brothers-in-arms who sacrificed everything for us in battle. Most of all, we are lucky because we have a chance to take up arms and continue that same fight in the name of our fallen comrades and our country.

"The British attacked us with a terrible poison, but they were careless in their victory. Only three British airships stayed. Our scouts say most of their soldiers left with the fleet. We will watch them, we will plan an attack, and we will retake Bacatá."

The large array of soldiers managed a weak grunt of approval to their leader's call to arms.

"That is not the response I expect from soldiers of the New Granada *Resistencia*," said General Marquez. Every man lifted their eyes to meet Marquez's. "This fight is not over. We are not done until we have driven the British invaders from our homeland."

The rabble of soldiers rallied and let out a single, powerful call to arms. A slow smile crawled across General Marquez's face.

"I have given reconnaissance and preparation orders to the officers," said Marquez, waving his arm towards a group of newly promoted men. "They are good men. They follow me, and you will follow them. You will divide into regiments, then be assigned duties for today. We attack tomorrow morning, *mis amigos*, so get to work."

The officers stepped forward and began barking orders, grouping the soldiers by skill set and assigning duties. Marquez and the Lefounts walked over to the Goulden family sitting beneath the banana tree.

"Please come with me," said Marquez. Margaret stood and followed; Edward, Anne, and Constance hesitated before following the others into the main house.

Marquez led them through the rooms of the hacienda like a tour guide pointing out the things that had meaning to him. "*Mi madre* scrubbed the floors in these rooms twice a week. It would take her all day." The general picked his way over the neglected orange tile, following a trail of ants marching through the rooms.

"She was a Tairona Indian. I never knew who my father was, but I had my suspicions." General Marquez paused and opened the drawers of a desk one by one, rooting through the rotting papers and dried ink bottles. He sighed, closed them, and continued the tour.

"Years ago, a Spaniard played a critical role putting down a rebellion by Natives here in Bacatá. The viceroy gifted him this *encomienda*. His grandson was the *patrón* when I was born, and I served him until the British chased the Spaniards from New Granada." Marquez stopped again to dig through a chest of drawers in a room centered around a hardwood bedframe.

"Bah," the general said, slamming the last drawer shut and moving on to the next room.

"The *patrón* was a kind man. He taught me to read and write. He taught me about men and armies and nations. He taught me how to lead. When the British came, I left and took command of the poorly run *Resistencia* in Cartagena, then Santa Marte. I worked with other leaders to establish the free city of Popayán. To this day, it is a sanctuary for people who wish to live outside the British Empire."

General Marquez pushed through a thin wooden door and into the kitchen. It had the conveniences of a modern European kitchen, plus a pair of ovens molded from red clay and straw. He opened a drawer and laughed.

"Of course it was the cooks who left one behind." The general removed a cigar; a single tobacco leaf rolled up on itself. He lit it with a match from beside the oven and smiled. "I remember the old woman who used to smoke these."

"*Monsieur*," said Francis. "We have many preparations to make."

"*Si, si, mi amigo*," said Marquez. "I have not forgotten. But when I tell them what I wish them to do, I want them to understand who they do it for."

"Master Edward, Miss Anne," Marquez said, puffing on the tobacco leaf to make the ember burn bright. "I am sending you back to Cartagena. You will leave tonight with an armed escort. Most of the journey is very easy, you just float down the river towards the coast. Near the end you will have to cross through the jungle on foot."

"It is important to show the people of Cartagena that Anne is alive," interrupted Francis. Marquez stared at him over his cigar but kept quiet. "We need the people to see that we did not do what Governor Pratt claims."

"May I continue, *por favor*?" asked Marquez.

"*Oui*," said Francis, looking away.

"The poison gas was terrible," said Marquez. "No one should use such a weapon, even in battle."

"Tell the people of Cartagena what happened here," said Francis, interrupting again. He looked at Marquez, "I am sorry my friend, but you took so long with your story."

Marquez cleared his throat and continued. "I will send a letter to la *Resistencia* in Cartagena. They can spread the word to other Resistance groups around the world about the new British weapon."

"What about Constance and myself?" asked Margaret.

Marquez puffed on his cigar. "Francis, would you please explain?"

"*Oui*," Francis said.

"We want you to stay and help us retake Bacatá," said Ezmeralda. Francis glared at her. "Margaret, you have fought the British Empire all your life; we need every soldier we can get. And you, Constance, you are brilliant. Francis and I need help repairing the weapons, and you are the best there is."

"Absolutely not," roared Edward. "They will not stay here and risk their lives for your cause."

"Ah, I knew there was a fire in you somewhere, Master Goulden," said Marquez. "You fight for your family. I am sorry, but this decision is not yours to make."

"I will not allow it," reaffirmed Edward.

"You do not understand what is at stake," said Francis. "They may be the difference between victory and defeat."

Edward started to return fire when Constance interrupted: "If we stayed and helped retake Bacatá, when would we return home?"

"As soon as the battle is over," said Marquez in a somber voice. "Two or three days behind Edward."

"I will do it," said Margaret.

"As will I," said Constance.

Margaret turned to her speechless husband and took his hands in her own. "We are staying, my dear. I promise that we will emerge from this fight unscathed and be right behind you on the road home."

"Very well," Edward said, his voice quiet, tone subdued. "But I am afraid I will never see either of you again."

•   •   •   •   •

"Over there," said Francis Lefount, pointing out from the alley. "That building is not damaged and there is a cannon on the roof."

Francis, Ezmeralda, Constance, and three Resistance soldiers ran across the deserted street to the orange stucco building. Francis barged through the front door, then slammed it shut behind the last soldier.

"You three stay here and keep watch out the windows," Francis said to the soldiers. "Ezmeralda, Constance, come upstairs with me." Francis smirked at his wife. "If that is all right with you, *mon amour*."

"*Si, cómo no*," replied Ezmeralda, stepping towards her husband with a hungry look in her eyes.

"Would you two please stop snogging long enough for us to finish our work?" said Constance, leading the way up the stairs.

"*Aye papi*, why did we bring her along?" said Ezmeralda. "Does she not know we are madly in love and have not seen each other in months?"

"She knows. She just does not care."

The rain had eased and visibility improved, showing the shadows of three zeppelins through the low-slung rainclouds. The group scanned the streets to make sure British soldiers were not sneaking up on them.

"Make sure the cannon over there is working and prep it to fire," Francis said to Constance. He and Ezmeralda began preparing the second cannon.

"Is she as good as you say?" asked Francis.

"She the best engineer I have met in many years. She studied under Harold Lecturn in England."

"Harold Lecturn, your old mentor?"

"He teaches at university now," replied Ezmeralda. "He's too old for field work." She clamped a wrench the size of her arm onto a turret bolt and leaned her weight on it. "Trust me; Constance is good."

"I do not know, *mon amour*," said Francis, examining the instrument panel and adjusting dials.

"Do you need any help?" asked Constance, appearing next to the gun turret.

"No, I think we are fine," said Ezmeralda. "Would you please bring up the other soldiers?"

"Wait," said Francis, "what about the other cannon? Is it working?"

"Yes," said Constance, heading towards the stairs.

The Lefounts finished prepping the second gun before Constance returned. They instructed the three soldiers how to work as a team to reload the cannons, spin the turrets, aim, and fire.

"Wait inside the building until sunrise," said Ezmeralda. "You brought food and provisions; do not leave for any reason." The soldiers nodded and mumbled in understanding. "At dawn, we will attack a patrol on the north side of Bacatá, then we will blow up that building." Ezmeralda pointed to a four-story blue building several blocks away. "British soldiers will march from the south, and then the airships will come to drop bombs."

"Open fire when the airships are over that building," said Francis, pointing to the same blue building. "We will have cannons firing from eight different rooftops, plus Ezmeralda and I on another rooftop with long-range rifles. Once the zeppelins are down, rendezvous with the main army in the center of town."

"Do you understand?" Ezmeralda asked the soldiers.

"*Si, bueno.*"

$$\bullet \quad \bullet \quad \bullet \quad \bullet \quad \bullet$$

Francis and Ezmeralda stood shoulder to shoulder on a rooftop on the north end of Bacatá. They watched as the sun crested the horizon, adding a deep orange ball of light to the predawn glow. The rain and clouds burned away the previous afternoon and the morning sky was crisp and clear. The couple remained quiet, waiting, taking deep breaths of the cool air. A British patrol marched down the middle of the street below, around a corner and out of sight.

Moments later, bursts of rifle fire mixed with the shouts of battle. The acidic and sour smells of sulfur and soot drifted across Bacatá. An explosion shook the ground and the tall blue building two blocks north lit up like a torch guiding the way.

"Here they come," said Ezmeralda, gazing over the city to the south. A battleship dropped in altitude and changed course, resetting its flight path to head north.

"*Oui*," muttered Francis, watching the other two ships patrolling the skies to the west. "Come on, you bastards. Take the bait." He and Ezmeralda waited with a nervous gaze. Their plan would fail if the British did not commit all three zeppelins to the fight. After a tense three minutes, the zeppelins to the west dropped below the clouds and changed course.

"Are you ready?" asked Francis.

"Of course," said Ezmeralda. She gave her husband a soulful kiss before taking her position.

Ezmeralda unslung the rifle from her shoulder. For the fourth time in the last hour, she slid open the bolt and checked the ten-round ammunition clip. She inspected the gun from stock to barrel, verifying the gears and oil lines were ready for action. Ezmeralda lifted the rifle up and peered through the scope, scanning the long street in front of her.

"Here they come," said Francis. "I see about forty British soldiers, double-time march, coming up from the south."

Ezmeralda kept staring through her scope, waiting and watching.

"One-hundred meters away," called Francis.

Ezmeralda did not flinch.

"Ready?" asked Francis, looking through his own scope.

"*Si.*"

Francis squeezed the trigger on his augmented rifle. The ground in the middle of the regiment exploded, cobblestones blown apart, the stones raining down on the scattering British soldiers. Ezmeralda pulled her own trigger and saw a handful of soldiers fall. They fired rounds until every soldier was hiding in a building or lying dead in the street.

Ezmeralda lowered her rifle and met Francis's eyes. "*Aye, mi amor,*" she said. "I think I like this gun."

She looked across the street and saw Constance adjusting the turret for an anti-aircraft gun. Margaret sat behind the trigger, aiming the cannon. Constance finished with the gun and sprinted across the rooftop to adjust the turret for the second gun, telling the soldier how to aim his shot.

Nearby, the trio of British zeppelins converged on the burning blue building. Resistance cannons across the north side of Bacatá erupted at once in a well-coordinated volley of fire. Two airships took critical damage before their captains could turn them around. They began their requiem from the skies, plotting courses to crash outside the city while their crews prepared to abandon ship.

Two more regiments of British soldiers came up from the south, desperate to get at the anti-aircraft cannons before they lost their last battleship. Francis and Ezmeralda fired more exploding rounds, scattering the soldiers like ashes in the wind.

The third and final battleship managed to turn itself around and move away from the anti-aircraft weapons. Cannons across northern Bacatá fired round after round at the zeppelin, every single shot falling short of their mark.

"We are losing them," shouted Ezmeralda.

Ezmeralda spotted Constance working feverishly on Margaret's gun, adjusting every lever and dial on the control panel. A ball-peen hammer appeared in Constance's hand and she vanished beneath the cannon.

Constance emerged, sweat cutting clean lines through the soot covering her face. She dove to the ground, away from Margaret's gun, seconds before it fired its final round. The barrel of the gun blew apart, sending shards of black iron spraying across the rooftop. The cracked turret tipped over, Margaret vaulting off before it crushed her.

Ezmeralda's eyes wandered from the chaos across the street and up to the final battleship. The glass windows of the bridge were gone. The airship appeared to be flying with no one behind the wheel, lurching right and left and losing altitude.

"Did you see that?" said Francis, suddenly standing beside Ezmeralda.

"*Si*," muttered Ezmeralda, staring in wonder at the blown apart cannon across the street. "She got an extra two hundred meters out of that cannon."

Francis grunted: "*Oui*, but she destroyed my gun to do it."

• • • • •

General Marquez waited patiently and listened to the battle raging to the north. He felt the ground tremble when the Resistance blew up the blue building; he heard the anti-aircraft cannons crack and fire.

Hundreds of his Resistance soldiers assembled during the night without the enemy discovering them. They concealed themselves in empty buildings scattered around the heart of Bacatá. General Marquez was north of his forces, monitoring British troops during the assault on the airships. When the first column of soldiers marched past, he ordered his men to hold their positions. A second and third regiment marched past before the general received word that all three airships were crashing to the ground.

"Signal the others," Marquez yelled. His soldiers fired their rifles from the second-story windows of the row house. The general stepped into the street, armed men pouring out around him. Doors all over the center of Bacatá flew open one after another, soldiers flooding the street like a meandering row of dominoes falling.

"*Vamanos, mis amigos*," shouted Marquez, rifle raised over his head. "Fight your way forward."

The Resistance rushed forward, a wave of green uniforms and rifle fire sweeping through the city. Surprised British soldiers in the middle of breakfast charged into the streets with napkins tucked in their uniforms. Others rolled out of bed and joined the fight without time to put on their boots.

The British barely slowed the wave of furious revolutionaries. They never launched a single round from the mortar batteries in front of the government buildings. The Resistance horde overwhelmed the army in a matter of minutes.

General Marquez reconvened counsel with his officers in the old Spanish capital: "Report on the three airships."

"All three are critically damaged and heading to the ground," replied one officer.

"Where are they expected to crash down?" asked the general.

"Two are north of the city, one to the west."

"None will crash down inside Bacatá?"

"*No, señor.*"

Marquez paused and dug the stub of a cigar out of his shirt pocket. "Organize two hundred soldiers and send them north to track down the regiments that marched past us. Send another fifty soldiers to watch each zeppelin crash down and round up any survivors."

"*Si, señor.*" The officers disbursed to organize their commands and hand out orders.

•　•　•　•　•

Edward and Anne glided along the Rio Magdalena towards the coast. Dense vegetation hung over the water, obscuring the riverbanks. The heavy jungle air tempered the sibling's anxiety.

"What do you suppose is happening back there?" asked Anne.

"Well, they were planning on attacking the British at dawn this morning," said Edward.

"Yes, I know," said Anne. "But what do you suppose is actually happening right now?"

"I wish I knew."

Anne sat quietly, gazing out over the slow-moving river waters. "Do you think Margaret and Constance are all right?"

"I am sure they are fine," muttered Edward.

"How do you know?"

The gigantic soldier steering the boat's rudder stood up and bellowed: "Because *la Resistencia de Nueva Granada* won a glorious battle today."

Edward and Anne stared at the man, but remained quiet. His two compatriots, charged with getting the siblings home safely to Cartagena, raised their rifles in the air and cheered.

•　•　•　•　•

General Marquez slapped Francis Lefount on the back, "It was a glorious victory, my friend."

"*Oui,*" said the Frenchman, beaming with pride at the success of the Resistance assault.

"Francis and Ezmeralda took out forty of the soldiers after we blew up the blue building," said a young soldier reporting to his commanders.

"We took care of the rest."

"Prisoners?" asked Marquez.

"There were no prisoners, sir," said the young man. "Even the injured fired on us from the ground until we killed them."

"I never remember British soldiers fighting to the death," said Francis. "As if they are heroes."

"Heroic or scared," muttered Margaret.

"Scared of what?"

"Being taken prisoner," replied Margaret. "Afraid of what we would do to them, or frightened of what their own commanders might do later."

"What about the downed zeppelins?" asked the general.

"All three exploded on impact," said Francis. "I saw soldiers repelling down lines from two ships before they hit the ground."

"What of those soldiers? Killed, captured, or missing?"

"I do not know, sir," said a young officer. "The regiments you sent out are still in the field."

Right on cue, a Resistance regiment marched into Bacatá's center square. In the middle of the regiment was a cluster of ten British soldiers. The Resistance soldiers marched the prisoners to the middle of the grassy square and halted under a pair of tall trees. Two captives wore the leather aprons of engineers in Her Majesty's military, another pair had officer's stripes on their sleeves.

"These men bailed out of a battleship before it crashed," said a man in a green uniform to General Marquez.

"*Bueno, muy bueno,*" muttered Marquez. The general turned to another soldier: "Prepare a basement bunker to hold prisoners of war," he said. "Provide them with blankets, food, and water. Remove all weapons and communications devises." Marquez looked at the two men covered in leather, their pockets and pouches stuffed with tools and bits of hardware.

"May I?" asked Francis

"*Si,*" replied Marquez. He turned away from the prisoners to converse with his officers.

Francis and Ezmeralda stripped the mechanics of their aprons and tools and all their useful bits, leaving them in their cotton underclothes.

Without warning, Margaret stepped forward and pressed a short knife against the soft flesh of a British officer: "Where did the British fleet go?"

"Popayán," stammered the officer, his voice rising and falling and rising again as he spoke the three syllables.

"What did you say?" said General Marquez, spinning around

"Nothing," said the British officer, "I said nothing."

Marquez nodded to Margaret, who applied new pressure to the officer's gut.

"Lieutenant Vickers took the fleet to Popayán."

"Why?" asked Margaret. "What's in Popayán?"

"Popayán is a city to the southwest. It is the largest city free of British rule on the continent." Marquez studied the officer for a moment.

"Why is Vickers in charge?" said Ezmeralda. "Last I heard, Major Ulperlip was the commanding officer."

The officer remained silent, defiantly staring down Ezmeralda. Margaret slid her blade up and pressed it against his throat.

"There was mutiny," the officer said, giving up his valor. "Ulperlip was shot. Apparently, Lieutenant Vickers has direct orders from the Queen to dismantle the New Granada Resistance at any cost. When Ulperlip refused to drop the chlorine gas, Vickers seized control of the fleet."

Members of the Resistance grew quiet, each reflecting on the implications of this new information.

"How much chlorine gas was dropped on Bacatá?" asked Ezmeralda, her voice quiet and somber.

"Vickers ordered every ship in the fleet to drop exactly half their stores," said the officer, his voice hushed as he sealed his fate by aiding an enemy of the Crown.

"They plan to drop the other half on Popayán."

"And murder fifty thousand innocent people."

CHAPTER 26

"*Aye, mi amor*," said Ezmeralda, sucking in her breath. "You finished building her while I was away. *Ella es hermosa.*"

"*Merci*," said Francis. "She was a labor of love." The Frenchman stood with his feet firmly planted on the earth, hands on hips, eyes sweeping over his creation.

"It's a giant bird," said Constance, studying Francis' contraption.

"And an ugly bird at that," muttered Margaret.

"She is modeled after the Andean condor, a bird of prey larger than a man."

The mechanical bird's body was broader than a British tank. The copper and gold coloring blended seamlessly with the dark, smoky glass of the horizontal windows over the wings. Its wingspan was as wide as a Bacatá row house. A series of hydraulic pistons connected the wings to the bird's body; they folded neatly on themselves when at rest.

"It is huge," said Margaret. "Will it actually get off the ground?"

Francis snorted. "*Oui*, of course. I have flown her twice already."

"Have you flown it to Popayán?" asked Margaret.

"No."

"Where did you fly it?"

"I flew a hundred meters, turned around, and came back," replied Francis. "The second time I flew to the other side of that mountain."

Francis pointed to the east, but no one could see out of the underground chamber where the condor was stored. The room was just south of Bacatá, dug out of soft earth and covered with fallen trees.

"Is it a weapon or did you build it to transport people?" asked Constance. She stood right in front of the beast, looking up at the head of the enormous steel condor and its smoky glass eyes. From her angle, Constance could see controls and levers on the inside of the bird's metal skull.

"There are no weapons on board," said Francis.

"It looks like a fierce predator. Perhaps you should consider adding armaments," muttered Margaret.

"There is no room inside to carry bombs," said Francis. "A rifle can be fired through slits that open on the sides. But that is not her purpose."

Ezmeralda walked around the backside of the beast. She lifted a steel tail feather so thin it bent in her hands. "I see you worked hard to make it look like a condor."

"*Oui, mon amour*," replied Francis. "You know I care about that sort of thing."

"You did well," said Ezmeralda, "very realistic."

"How does it work?" asked Constance.

"It is a lot lighter that it looks," said Francis. "I designed the skeleton similar to an actual Andean condor. The steel beams are hollow and filled with a small amount of hydrogen gas. Not enough for it to float away like a zeppelin, but enough to negate the metal body's weight."

"If the hydrogen does not provide the lift, how does it fly?"

"It is like folding a sheet of paper into a shape with wings and then throwing it," said Ezmeralda, taking over the conversation. "It is so light the wings catch the air and it floats up."

"The only question that matters now is how fast she will fly us to Popayán," said General Marquez.

"She is fast enough to get eight of us to Popayán before the British fleet."

"*Bueno*," said Marquez, puffing on his cigar and staring up at the cold, steel beast.

•   •   •   •   •

"*Silencio, por favor*. Please take a seat so we can start," shouted Diego Rodriguez, head of the Popayán governing council. His fellow councilmen remained oblivious to his request and continued yelling at each other.

Diego lowered his voice, forcing his colleagues to strain to hear him. "If you would like to know the facts about the British attack, please sit. If not, please keep yelling at each other. It will give me a chance to eat my lunch."

Like the waving of a magic wand, Diego's words brought order to chaos. Thirty angry faces glared at the man behind the podium.

"My friends, there is an entire fleet of British battleships a day from our city." The room erupted once again. Diego gave up and went to find the bowl of soup he abandoned after convening the emergency meeting. He returned to find the council members calm and collected, sitting behind their tables and conversing quietly.

"Our apologies, *señor*," said a young man near the podium. "Continue, *por favor*."

"*Gracias*," said Diego, taking his place behind the podium and wiping his mouth with a cloth napkin. "Our scouts in the jungle alerted us this morning that the British are coming. The fleet may have enough firepower to break our outer defenses. The scouts also spotted troop transport ships carrying soldiers for a ground assault."

"Which direction are they coming from?" asked an old man in the back.

"From the northeast," said Diego. A murmur rippled through the council chambers. "They are coming from the direction of Bacatá; we still have heard no news from the *la Resistencia* there."

"Can we find out if this fleet attacked Bacatá?" asked the old man. Diego recognized him; he had four sons serving under General Marquez.

"We have already sent messengers into the jungle, *señor*, but it will take a long time for them to return."

"*Bueno.*"

Diego cleared his throat: "The question before this council is how we will respond to the approaching threat."

"What do you mean, *how will we respond*?" shouted a different council member. "We will fight." He paused mid-sentence, like a veteran politician waiting for a round of applause. "And they will die."

"We could stand our ground and fight," said Diego. "That is one option."

"That is our only option."

"No, it is not the only option," said Diego. "We could evacuate the city. Use the army to get the citizens out safe." A chorus of jeers echoed across the room.

"We are not afraid of the British," the council members yelled. "That is why live in Popayán and not Cartagena."

Diego sat down in a chair beside the podium to wait patiently for the group to quiet themselves. When they were calm, he rose and took his place behind the lectern. The droopy-eyed, soft-spoken man erupted from behind the podium with a fire and brimstone sermon that would make any preacher proud.

"You are the governing council of the free city of Popayán. You were each chosen by your people to represent them. Spaniards, Incas and Taironas, the grandchildren of freed slaves. Your people depend on you to make the right decisions. They depend on you to live safely as free men outside of the British Empire. The citizens of Popayán are not warriors. They are old men and children, scrub women and farmers."

Diego Rodriguez did not skip a beat, did not slow his speech as the volume of his voice jumped louder. "Do not let your vanity, your pride, or your *machismo* cloud your judgment. Our first duty is to protect the people of Popayán."

"Then you believe we should evacuate the city, *Señor* Rodriguez?" asked a more subdued member of the council.

"Yes, I do. The British are bringing a significant force against us, probably more than our defenses can repel." Diego paused and sighed. "Because we are responsible for the safety of the people, we must evacuate. The fleet will not stay forever, especially if they find the city deserted. When they leave, we can reclaim our city."

A skinny council member with a thick head of black hair stood and spoke in a calm voice. "I still believe we should we stand our ground, *señor*. We do not know that the British will leave if they find an empty city. They may use Popayán as a base of operations to hunt our people down. If we knew the invasion force could not be defeated, then we run and hide. But we do not know, and we have built so much. This is our home. We should run only if we have no other options." A dozen council members echoed his opinion.

"Very well," said Diego, "we will vote. Do we evacuate Popayán, using soldiers to move citizens into the jungle, or do we commit our resources preparing for battle?"

The thirty-member governing board voted unanimously to fight the British. The council summoned Popayán's generals.

"How many soldiers do you have at your disposal?" asked Diego.

"Eight hundred," said a general. "Another three thousand citizens participate in our emergency training program."

"We have almost four thousand soldiers available to fight?" said a council member. "We should be attacking the British, not sitting here trying to defend a single city."

"No, sir," said the general. "The three thousand are ordinary citizens who participate once a month in military training drills. They know how to fire a rifle. They can run a kilometer carrying a heavy pack. And they can follow simple orders under duress." The general paused before finishing: "But they are not soldiers."

"Very well," said the same council member. "We need you to get every soldier and citizen able to fire a rifle ready for battle."

• • • • •

"That is the most beautiful city I have ever seen," said Margaret. She stared at the window as the mechanical condor drifted over the heart of Popayán.

"Not something you typically notice," muttered Constance. Margaret glared at her.

"It is the most beautiful city in New Granada," said General Marquez. "It is the White City, named for all the white cathedrals."

Francis worked the controls of the brass bird with instinctive hands, gliding the condor down to a grass park. He manipulated a series of levers and neatly folded the condor's wings.

"Thank you for your help," Francis to Constance. "It would have been very difficult to fly this far without a third mechanic on board."

"It was exciting to work on this machine."

Francis grunted and pushed past her. He ducked to avoid hitting his head on the metal ceiling and disappeared into the belly of the beast.

"Did I say something offensive?" asked Constance.

"*Si*, but it was just offensive to Francis," replied Ezmeralda. "This is more than a machine to Francis. It is one of his children."

"Her name is *Colette*," said Francis, pushing past the women back to the front of the cabin. He pulled hard on a pair of levers and started spinning dials. A brass door, camouflaged behind a wing, opened with a hiss of hydraulics.

The gray sunshine coming through the darkened windows washed away in a brilliant white flood of light; the passengers turned their faces away. Francis leaned out of *Collete* and dropped a rope ladder to the ground.

The metal condor sat in a grassy park, complete with stone benches and manicured paths; no one sat on the benches or strolled on the paths. Surrounding the park on all sides were cathedrals. The bright afternoon sun lit up the bone-white structures, bleaching the bell towers and statues of the Virgin Mary.

"The devise that opens the door is clever, *mi amor*," said Ezmeralda.

"*Mercie*," muttered Francis. "Most engineers do not use hydraulic technologies to their potential."

Francis stepped out on the ladder and climbed down quickly. On the ground, he turned around and realized there were a dozen soldiers with rifles raised at him.

"Don't move," shouted a soldier, stepping forward.

"I would not dream of it," said Francis. He glanced to his left and right and saw more soldiers with rifles pointed at the condor.

"Hold your fire," barked a loud, authoritarian voice. "I am General Jose Tairona Marquez. I am now the senior-most officer in Popayán and your new commander."

● ● ● ● ●

A young messenger conversed privately with Diego Rodriguez when the conference room door burst open. A rabble of men and women marched in, some in blackened and bloodied military uniforms, others in equally filthy civilian clothing. The entire chamber stood to watch them march down the center aisle.

"What is the meaning of this?" shouted a council member.

"What gives you the right to barge in here?" echoed another member.

Diego stepped out from behind the podium and walked towards the haggard group. "This man has more right to be here than any of us." He opened his arms and embraced General Marquez. "It has been too long, my friend. Are you here to lead us to victory against the British fleet?"

"I wish it were that simple," said Marquez, resting his hand on Diego's shoulder. "I need to address the council."

"*Por favor*," replied Diego, sweeping his arm towards the podium.

"Members of the governing body of the free city of Popayán, I am General Jose Tairona Marquez." His voice boomed and echoed across the room, drawing reverent silence from the council. "The British sent a fleet of battle ships to attack this city. They will be here soon."

"We know," said Diego, sitting in the front of the podium. "The council voted not to evacuate the citizens. Instead we are committing every resource to defend the city."

"Then it is a good thing I arrived."

"I do not understand, *mi amigo*."

"Bacatá was attacked by this fleet several days ago," said Marquez. "Thousands died."

A murmur swept through the assembly: "What happened? Was the *la Resistencia* defeated?"

Marquez sighed again and looked down at the dark-wood podium. "*Si, la Resistencia* was defeated," he said, his voice almost too quiet to hear.

"What of the dead," shouted the man with four sons in Bacatá. "Do you know which soldiers lived and which died?"

"I am sorry, *señor*, I do not know the names of the dead. But I will learn them." Marquez locked eyes with the councilman. "We lost most of our men in the attack."

The old man slumped back in his chair. He did not rise or speak for the rest of the meeting.

"How did this happen?" asked Diego.

"The British have a new weapon," said Marquez. "*La Resistencia* battled thousands of British soldiers on the streets of Bacatá. We fought bravely for many hours. Just we were about to taste victory, the zeppelins began dropping small bombs filled with poison gas. Everyone that could not get to an underground bunker fast enough died, including many British soldiers."

"They killed their own men?"

"*Si*," replied Marquez, "the man commanding the fleet is ruthless. He will drop the poison gas on Popayán and kill women and children if we resist."

"What do we do?"

"Evacuate the city," said Marquez. "Not just the civilians, but the soldiers too. It is a hopeless battle."

The council chambers erupted in disbelief and anger. "You would have us abandon our homes and surrender?"

"*Si*," said General Marquez. "Run and hide in the jungle. Set up camps several kilometers away from the city."

"The humiliation is worse than death," shouted a voice from the back.

"No, it is not," replied Marquez. "Because if we live, we fight another day. Surrender the city to the British now. When they take their fleet and leave, attack and retake Popayán. That is what we did in Bacatá."

The congregation exploded with anger once again.

"I do not remember the governing body being like this?" muttered Marquez, stepping down to talk to Diego.

"The bickering got much worse last year."

"They do not understand. If we stay, everyone will die." Marquez shook his head with sorrow before recomposing himself and clearing his throat.

"Leaders of the free city of Popayán," shouted General Marquez, loud enough to reduce the chamber's background noise to a dull din and knock Diego out of his chair.

"You are tasked with protecting the lives of the men, women, and children of this city. If you do not vote to evacuate Popayán, I will declare this council incompetent and arrest you. Then I will evacuate the city myself." Marquez's voice echoed off the faded plaster walls and tall ceilings.

"You cannot do that," stammered an older man with a fat stomach. "It is treason."

"I speak for the people of Popayán, *señor*," said Marquez. "Failing to evacuate this city when faced with its destruction is treason."

"We will not allow it," shouted a different member from the back of the room. "I do not believe that this fleet is as powerful as you say, and I do not believe you have the power to seize control of Popayán."

"The soldiers outside that door will follow my orders, not yours," replied Marquez, growling through his teeth like a dog. Most council members slumped in their chairs, realizing the truth in Jose Marquez's words.

Diego Rodriguez stood: "We will vote on an amendment to our previous plan. All those in favor of evacuating the city?"

The council voted to follow General Marquez's plan. They left the chambers minutes later with little to say.

•   •   •   •   •

"It has not stopped raining for days."

"Brilliant, brother," said Anne, a distinct touch of annoyance in her voice.

"I am just tired of it, that's all," muttered Edward. "We have been hiking through the jungle for days and I cannot tell if we are any closer to Cartagena."

The siblings' Resistance escort was several paces in front of them, hacking through giant leaves and bamboo shoots with machetes pounded from coarse steel. A thick vine grabbed the ankles of a soldier and held on until it brought its victim to the ground. His compatriots cut him free.

"I asked the soldiers how far away we were," said Anne.

"What did they say?"

"They did not answer."

The soldier in front of Anne had a back twice as wide as the young woman's; his shoulders were broad enough to carry Anne and Edward at the same time. He came to a sudden stop and Anne marched into him, bouncing backward and running over Edward. The soldiers conversed in short, abrupt Spanish while the siblings picked themselves up out of the mud.

"We are still being followed," said a soldier.

"What?" said Edward in an alarmed voice. "By whom?"

The soldier shrugged, "British scouts maybe."

"I thought they were taken care of back on the river."

The soldier shrugged again. He slapped Edward on the back and sent the man stumbling forward. "Do not worry, *señor*. You will get to Cartagena safely." The soldiers all raised their rifles and grunted. They no longer had the energy for a wholehearted battle cry.

"Let's get going, then," said Anne. She stepped out in front of the small group, setting a quick pace and disappearing into the thicket.

CHAPTER 27

"Mr. Jeffreys."

"Sir."

"Come here."

The new captain left his post and joined Lieutenant Vickers in front of the over-sized glass windows. "Yes, sir."

Vickers kept his gaze on the horizon while Jeffreys stood still, waiting for orders.

"Are there any women on board?" asked Vickers.

"Sir? Afraid I do not understand the question."

"Sailors occasionally smuggle a woman on board for the duration of an assignment to satisfy certain needs."

"Nothing like that on board the *Fulton*, sir."

Vickers sighed, "Very well. I simply wanted to pass the time. Tell me, are all the battle preparations complete?"

"Aye, sir, everything is finished," said Jeffreys.

"How long until the fleet reaches the coordinates I gave you?"

"About eight hours, sir."

"Very good," replied Vickers. He continued to study the horizon while Captain Jeffreys stood behind him.

"Speak your mind, Mr. Jeffreys."

"We finished all the preparations you ordered, but we still have no idea how to proceed once we arrive at the city, sir."

"And your point?"

"May I ask what our plan is when we reach Popayán? What should we expect?"

"Popayán is the infamous White City built by the Spanish," replied Vickers in a bored tone. "The city has dozens of churches and cathedrals, all of them painted white. For two hundred years it was a religious mecca for pope-worshippers. Like half the cities on this God-forsaken continent, it is high in the mountains and surrounded by jungle."

"I see, sir," replied Jeffreys. "But that does not really answer my question."

"On the contrary," said Vickers, "you asked what to expect."

"I see. Perhaps I should ask what to expect when we meet the enemy."

"We will win the day, of course," said the lieutenant. "We will take control of the city and subjugate its citizens to British rule. They will undoubtedly thank us, and if they do not, their children will."

"But what is the plan of attack, sir?" asked Jeffreys.

Lieutenant Vickers sighed again. "Very well, Mr. Jeffreys, I will indulge you. But I implore you to be wiser next time I evade your question."

"Yes, sir," said Jeffreys. "Thank you, sir."

"As I stated, Popayán is a refuge for tens of thousands of people. They live outside British rule, thumbing their noses at our dear Queen Victoria."

"What a shame."

"Yes, it is." Lieutenant Vickers turned back to study the fleet out the window. "What was the name of the battleship commanded by Captain Kennett?"

"That would be the *Peregrine*, sir. A fine battleship, one of the strongest in the fleet."

"Perfect," said Vickers. "When we are a kilometer from the city, I want the *Peregrine* to take the lead. Have them move a hundred meters in front of the rest of the fleet."

"Yes, sir," replied Jeffreys, pausing for a moment. "Why?"

"The covert intelligence gathered on Popayán claims that the city is well fortified, possibly even better than what we found in Bacatá. Our spies say there are dozens of small anti-aircraft guns circling the city, plus a garrison of a thousand soldiers. I expect heavy casualties on both sides."

"I still do not understand how that relates to the *Peregrine*."

"Because, you idiot, Captain Kennett refused my orders to drop chlorine gas on Bacatá. He will either prove himself useful by punching a hole in the city's defenses or he will be cannon fodder."

Jeffreys bit his lower lip.

"What is it now?" asked Vickers in an impatient tone.

"I was just thinking that your plan is bloody brilliant, sir," said Jeffreys. "Send in the troublemakers first and let them take the heaviest fire. Shall I come up with a list of other captains who have disobeyed orders since you took command?"

Lieutenant Vickers smiled, "Please do. We will send the troublemakers over the city in a wedge formation, instructing them to drop bombs on the ground cannons. The large battleships will follow and mop up the rest of the cannons."

"What about the chlorine gas? Do you expect to use it again?"

"I did say it was a heavily defended city, did I not?"

"Yes, sir."

"And Victoria herself mandated us to dismantle the entire New Granada Resistance by any means necessary."

"That is true as well, sir."

"Then what do you think our plan of attack should be in regard to the chlorine gas?" asked Vickers.

"Once the fleet is over the city, drop the remainder of the canisters," said Jeffreys, a thin smile turned up on his lips. "No need to fight a prolonged battle like we did in Bacatá. Dropping the chlorine gas guarantees victory," he muttered, smile fading as he chewed on his lower lip.

"I agree."

●   ●   ●   ●   ●

La Catedral was the largest and most ornate of the old Spanish cathedrals, located in the heart of Popayán. The inner sanctum buried underground was exceptionally ordinary. The white plaster walls faded to a light brown, streaked with soot from wax candles burning in sconces. A pair of dusty, cracked ceramic statues sat in a corner awaiting attention. An antique candelabra cast an ominous orange glow from the middle of the room. Beneath it, a half dozen officers stood around a flimsy wooden table with General Marquez.

"By midnight everyone will be outside the city."

"*Bueno*," replied Marquez. "Where are we moving everyone?"

Another officer pointed out several positions on a map unrolled on the table. "We have temporary shelters and food reserves in nine locations outside Popayán."

"How were they set up so fast?" asked Marquez.

The officers looked at each other, "Don Rodriguez ordered the shelters built a year ago."

"That was very smart. What is to stop the British from finding them?"

"The locations are scattered in all directions. Some are camouflaged in areas where the jungle is thickest. The rest are in caves in the hills."

"*Bueno, bueno*," muttered Marquez. "Keep evacuating citizens until everyone is out, then make sure all the soldiers and officers get out."

"*Si, señor.*"

The general sighed and rubbed his eyes, "What time is it?"

"The sun set a half-hour ago, sir."

"If you will excuse me, I have things to discuss with them." Marquez nodded towards the Gouldens and Lefounts, waiting across the room with Diego Rodriguez. The officers saluted and left through the room's only door, a thick, dark slab of wood that stood out against the dirty white walls.

"What is the plan, *mon capitaine*," said Francis, squaring his legs up against the heavy table.

Marquez looked at Diego, "Someone needs to stay behind and surrender the city to the British."

"I agree," said Diego. "As head of the governing council, I volunteer."

"Why?" asked Margaret, her voice elevated.

"Why what, *señora*?" asked the general.

"Why must someone stay behind to surrender the city?"

"It is the way things are done," replied Marquez with a sigh. "If we want the British to take their fleet and leave, they need to believe we are no longer a threat."

Margaret grunted, "I don't like it."

Marquez ignored her and addressed the others. "They will take Diego back to Cartagena as a prisoner. We will coordinate a rescue later from that end."

"How will we do that if we are here?" asked Ezmeralda.

"Because we will not be here," replied Marquez.

"What part of the plan are you not telling us, *mon amie*?" said Francis.

"We will smuggle ourselves on board the British zeppelins," said Marquez. "Each one of us on a different ship. I will talk to the officers about recruiting several more soldiers to go with us. I want one person onboard each airship carrying chlorine gas."

"That seems risky," muttered Constance. "Why would we do that?"

"Once in the air, we will sabotage the poison gas canisters," said the general, looking at Francis and Ezmeralda. "I need a plan to get this done without the British finding out."

"To what end?" asked Margaret. "Even if we are successful, the factories in England will just produce more."

General Marquez pinched the bridge of his nose and rubbed his eyes. "Because every broken canister saves lives. The only way to win this war is one life at a time."

●　　●　　●　　●　　●

"Captain Kennett is reporting from the *Peregrine*, sir. The anti-aircraft cannons on the northern border of Popayán are quiet."

Lieutenant Vickers stood in silence, staring out the wide bridge windows.

"Sir, did you hear what I said?" asked Jeffreys.

"Yes, Mr. Jeffreys, I heard you," said the lieutenant, his voice dry and bored. He shuffled his feet without turning away from the bridge windows. "Why do you suppose the cannons are not firing?"

Jeffreys scratched his head. "I'm sure I do not know, sir. Either the city's defenses are abandoned, or it is some sort of trap."

"My conclusion as well," muttered Vickers. He stared out the bridge windows at the rolling hills and steep, sharp canyons. The bright green hues of the rain forest blanketed the Earth; trees stretched to the sky, layered with shorter trees below the canopy and tall ferns below the shortest trees. Trails used by animals and people crisscrossed the ground, invisible from Lieutenant Vickers's viewpoint.

Most of the fleet flanked Vickers's flagship to the left and right, while the troublesome captains crossed Popayán's threshold.

"How long until we broach the top of the hill?" asked Lieutenant Vickers.

"Minutes, sir," said Jeffreys. "That tall, white tower visible over the ridge line appears to be church bells."

"What is the status of the other turncoats?" asked the lieutenant.

Jeffreys radioed the question across the fleet. "Six more battleships now passing over the outer defenses." He paused, listening to the rest of the reply. "They are reporting all quiet from the city's defenses as well."

As the HMS *Fulton* and the rest of the fleet crested the top of the ridge, the White City spread out before entire British armada. A tight knot of brilliant white churches ornamented with spires and bell towers arched upward. Narrow roads filled the spaces between religious buildings in a haphazard pattern, accented by grassy parks with tall trees. Sprouting outward from the grove of cathedrals were layers of houses and buildings. More arbitrarily placed roads cut the city into increasingly awkward shapes.

"I want the battleships spread out in a line, then encircle the city," said Vickers, not bothering to turn around as he spoke. "All personnel need to remain at battle stations until I give the order to stand down."

"Aye, sir," said Jeffreys, as the communications officer relayed the message to the other zeppelins.

"South of downtown, just past the churches, are six iron spires. If we continue to have no armed opposition from the ground, I want this ship and the five largest troop transports to dock there in one hour."

"Aye, sir," repeated Jeffreys. "Do you want the troop transports to unload their compliments?"

Lieutenant Vickers sighed. "Yes, Mr. Jeffreys. I want the soldiers to disembark and begin sweeping the city. For all we know there are ten thousand soldiers hiding in the basements of those houses. Or perhaps they are hiding in the crypts of the churches. There are certainly enough places for an army to lie in ambush."

"Sir," said Jeffreys two minutes later. "The troop transport ships are asking for reassurance that we will not drop chlorine canisters on them once they engage whatever army is hiding down there."

"Promise them we will not drop chlorine on the city as long as the soldiers on the ground do not lose control of the situation."

"Very good, sir."

• • • • •

Lieutenant Vickers stood in the grassy park in front of *la Catedral*. Even with the benches, stone fountains, and enormous shade trees, the park was big enough to accommodate a thousand soldiers.

Despite docking only an hour prior, neat rows of canvas tents filled the park. Men disembarked using the iron spires' crude lifts, packing the camp with wool bedrolls, rickety folding chairs, and a dozen cast-iron wood stoves.

"I gave orders for these soldiers to search the city and root out the enemy," said Vickers. "Instead they appear to be setting up for a nature expedition with their children."

"The officers are setting up communications here in the city's center," said Jeffreys "They will begin dispatching patrols within a few minutes."

Vickers sat down in the shade inside his own raised canvas roof. "Is there something else you need?" Vickers asked the loitering captain.

"I was wondering why you came down here instead of staying on board the *Fulton*?"

"Because of that, Mr. Jeffreys," said Lieutenant Vickers, pointing behind Jeffreys's.

An out-of-place man with white and black flecked hair and civilian clothing wound through the camp towards Vickers. He walked with confidence, one foot in front of the other, head held high. Halfway across the square a British officer realized the man should not be there. An excessive amount of shouting followed; the man ordered to the ground with two dozen rifles aimed at his head.

Minutes later, an officer approached Lieutenant Vickers: "Sir, we have taken a prisoner who claims to be the head of the local government. He wishes to speak with you."

"Yes, yes, of course," said Vickers. "I am tired of waiting for you imbeciles to do your job properly. Bring him here at once or heads will roll."

The soldiers marched their prisoner in front of Lieutenant Vickers. "My name is Diego Rodriguez and I am the head of the Popayán government. I formally surrender the city to you."

"I see," said Lieutenant Vickers. "Where are all the soldiers and citizens of Popayán?"

"We have no soldiers here," said Diego. "The city has a civilian population of several hundred souls; they all fled yesterday to the coast."

"You are a bloody liar," shouted Jeffreys, knocking the man to the ground with the back of his hand. "Tell me the truth."

"My name," said the prisoner, rising to his feet, "is Diego Rodriguez. I am head of the Popayán government. I formally surrender the city to you."

Jeffreys raised his hand again; Diego did not flinch. Vickers laid his hand on Jeffreys's shoulder and the young man restrained himself.

"We know tens of thousands live in this city, Mr. Rodriguez," said Vickers with a touch of annoyance in his voice.

Before he could continue, the bark of the tree beside the lieutenant exploded, pelting Vickers, Jeffreys, and Diego with slivers of wood. The unmistakable crack of a rifle echoed across the camp and bounced off the cathedral walls circling the park.

A pair of soldiers grabbed Vickers by the wrists and dragged him towards the closest church. A second rifle shot rang out and one of the lieutenant's rescuers fell.

A minute later, a small contingent of soldiers dragged the lieutenant through the giant wooden doors of the *Iglesia de San Francisco*. A bullet embedded itself in the church's exterior wall, sending a shower of fine white plaster into the air just as the soldiers pushed the doors closed.

The Church of Saint Francis, although decadent, was one of the simpler houses of worship in Popayán. From the front porch the British soldiers found themselves in, a wide, open archway moved worshipers to the main part of the church. A hundred rows of dark-wood pews lined both sides of the aisle from the archway to the altar.

"Walk with me, Mr. Jeffreys," said Lieutenant Vickers.

"Aye, sir."

The lieutenant led the way down the far-left aisle between the pews and a high wall. Every ten paces they passed an alcove nestled in the wall housing a painted statue of a saint, a thin iron shelf of candles, and a kneeler. Dim light entering through a stained-glass window above each statue illuminated the dust in the air in a rainbow of colors.

"What do you see?" asked Vickers.

"The inside of a church, sir," replied Jeffreys.

"More than that."

Jeffreys paused, then answered in an uncertain tone. "Wealth?"

"More than that," said Vickers.

"What are you getting at, sir?"

"The wealth inside this building is undeniable," said Vickers, picking up a gilded candelabra and turning it over in his hands. "But the pope and his lackeys store these treasures here because it is a place of worship. People come and spend hours staring at shiny trinkets worth more than a lifetime of wages. They come here and are told how to live their lives, and they listen. This is a place of power."

"And that is a good thing."

"Power is always a good thing. Some spaghetti-slurping holy man figured out how to accumulate it over a millennium ago."

"Brilliant, sir."

"Brilliant indeed, Mr. Jeffreys. One could argue that our real mission here is to break the stranglehold this faith has on this continent's population."

"To consolidate power for the Queen," muttered Jeffreys.

A young soldier appeared in front of Vickers, saluting with one hand while clutching his rifle in the other. "Sir, we have captured the culprit who fired on you."

"Well, bring him in here so I may meet him," said Vickers.

"Her, sir," said the soldier.

"Pardon?"

"Her, sir. The rifleman is a woman."

"Just bring the culprit to me," said Vickers. "And bring in that old fool who kept trying to surrender the city to me." The young man saluted before disappearing to retrieve his quarry.

A detachment of soldiers marched Diego Rodriguez through the heavy front doors of the church. Two others dragged in a young woman. Despite having her hands bound behind her back, she kicked violently at her captives.

Lieutenant Vickers smiled a thin smile, like a jack-o'-lantern with a single slit for a mouth. "Mistress Goulden," he said with a drawl. "I told that fool Pratt your whole family would be trouble."

He wandered slowly around Margaret. "That was quite a shot you took at me. Is that the Resistance's plan? To assassinate me here in Popayán? A poor plan, reeking of desperation."

"You're a bloody murderer," said Margaret, spitting between clenched teeth as she spoke. "You killed all those people in Bacatá. I couldn't resist taking a shot at you."

"Always the hero, are we?" said Vickers. "Who else is here, waiting and watching? General Marquez? Your dear husband, Edward? Perhaps Anne is even here. It would be most helpful if you brought Anne here."

"We are your prisoners," said Diego in a fierce voice. "We demand you take us to the colonial capital of Cartagena. We will plead our case before the magistrate."

"Is that what you demand?" asked Vickers, turning towards Diego. "Mistress Goulden is an enemy combatant. She fired a rifle at a British officer." Vickers twirled his thin mustache, studying his prisoners. "During the ensuing conflict, both Margaret Goulden and Diego Rodriguez were killed."

Diego furrowed his eyebrows furrowed. "What you are talking about? That never happened."

"You bastard," shouted Margaret, lunging against here captors. "You're going to murder us."

"It is not murder, my dear, if it happens on the battlefield."

"This is a church, not a battlefield," said Margaret.

"Merely semantics," replied Vickers, turning to address a senior officer. "I want them both taken outside immediately and shot in the head."

"No, you mustn't," shouted a voice from the rafters. Another young woman peered down from the upper alcoves of the church. The soldiers craned their necks towards the voice, the white sunlight piercing through the high windows, illuminating the heavy dust hanging in the air.

"Get her," shouted Vickers. "Capture her and bring them to me."

"We are not armed," said a second voice from the rafters. "We surrender willingly."

"General Jose Tairona Marquez," said the lieutenant, sniffing the air. He wrinkled his nose as the thick dust aggravated his sinuses. "I thought I smelled a treasonous bastard when I got off my airship." General Marquez replied to Vickers hypocrisy with a flat stare.

"Do you know this man, sir?" asked Jeffreys, like a child wanting inclusion in the conversation.

"Only by reputation," replied Vickers in his dry, monotone tone. "We have never had the pleasure of meeting."

The lieutenant stepped in front of Constance. "And Constance Ventor, another of the meddling Goulden twits. By any chance are Edward and Anne here? Are they hiding in some vestibule somewhere? Perhaps Edward is disguised in clerical robes."

"We are prisoners of war, lieutenant," said General Marquez. "We stand here, unarmed, asking for a hearing with the magistrate of Cartagena."

"Pratt will just order your deaths," said Vickers, spitting out the words like a venomous snake. He stepped back in front of Marquez fast enough to cause his own men to flinch. "I believe I will save Her Majesty's fleet the trouble of hauling you back to the coast to stand trial." The lieutenant spun back around and shouted at his own soldiers. "Take them all outside and shoot them in head."

•   •   •   •   •

The soldiers crowded behind Marquez, Diego, Margaret, and Constance. They leveled their rifles and shoved the foursome forward with their gun barrels. Halfway to the carved wooden doors inlaid with iron crucifixes, Margaret dropped to the floor. She swept her feet up and over her handcuffs then popped up to a crouched position, weight on the balls of her feet.

"Margaret, no," shouted Constance. A soldier tackled the young engineer to the ground as she lunged towards her friend.

Margaret rapped a silver stud on the side of her boot with her palm. A tiny, single shot pistol the size of her finger slid out from a hidden compartment. In one fluid motion, Margaret grasped the gun, swung it up to eye level, and squeezed the trigger.

The bullet sliced through Lieutenant Vickers's temple, leaving a perfect circular entry wound. He dropped dead to the floor, unable to utter a single word.

A chorus of gunshots followed, sending round after round of echoes cracking off the towering ceilings and deep alcoves of the church. Constance screamed and sobbed from where she lay, face pressed to the ground, underneath the soldier that tackled her.

Margaret's body hit the floor beside Constance and lie still on the hard ceramic tile.

•   •   •   •   •

"Stop firing, stop firing," Marquez shouted. He stood up as tall as he could, arms up over his head, palms open.

As the soldiers' rifles emptied one by one, they stood and stared at the lifeless body of the man who hijacked their fleet, killed thousands, and led them to victory. A heavy silence settled over the confines of the church.

"What should we do?" asked a soldier in a meek voice. "Who's in charge?"

Jeffreys swallowed hard before speaking, driving the quiver from his voice. "I am, at least until we return to Cartagena. Lieutenant Vickers named me his second in command."

The soldiers looked at each other and then at Jeffreys. "All right, then, this mess is yours," one said. "What do we do now?"

"We proceed with securing the city, then return to Cartagena with the fleet," replied Jeffreys.

"No, I mean what do we do with them?" asked the soldier, nodding towards Constance, Marquez, and Diego.

"If I may speak for a moment?" interrupted General Marquez.

"All right," grumbled Jeffreys.

"I suggest you do nothing rash for the rest of the mission," said Marquez. "You have already won, and the man responsible for the coup is dead."

"Keep talking," said Jeffreys, brows furrowed as he stared hard at the Resistance general.

"Follow military procedure to the letter until you are back in Cartagena."

"You believe I should let the magistrate decide your fate," replied Jeffreys.

"Yes," said Marquez. "You will return a hero and receive a promotion."

"You are saying this so I will not execute you."

"He makes a lot of sense, sir," mumbled a soldier.

Jeffreys looked at the soldier, "You think so?"

"I think so, too, sir," said a second soldier. "We already won, and the man responsible for the coup and the chlorine gas is dead. Let's just get home without breaking any more rules."

Jeffreys sniffed and stood up a straighter. "All right, then, I order you to lock these three prisoners in the brig onboard the *Fulton*. They will accompany us back to Cartagena."

CHAPTER 28

Cartagena

"He is here, sire."

"What, what?"

"Master Tank, sire. He has arrived."

"Well, show him in," said the king. "What are you waiting for?"

The servant responded with a bow and disappeared to fetch Douglas Tank. King George III continued signing and stamping documents until Douglas entered the room. The mechanic who built an empire dwarfing Alexander of Macedon's rode in on a chair with heavy iron wheels. A small steam engine burped smoke and soot from underneath his seat while a joystick on the armrest steered the chair.

"Good afternoon, Your Majesty," said Douglas.

"Hello to you, Mr. Tank. Do you mind, I need to finish these?"

"Of course, sire." Douglas waited quietly while the king signed and stamped every page in the pile.

"What is it that I can do for you?" said the king, turning to face the elder Mr. Tank.

"I beg your pardon, sire, but you requested my presence. I received a summons two days ago."

"What, what? Yes, right, very well. I do remember requiring counsel, but the issue has been resolved."

"Very well." Douglas moved the joystick on his chair and backed away from the desk, then spun it around and started rolling back towards the door. "May I ask what the original problem that you summoned for?" he asked over his shoulder.

"The Resistance movement to the Crown that the Scottish Rite inspired is spreading," said George. "Just last month, Africans and Dutch settlers banded together and uprooted an armored vehicle division." The king paused and walked over to a window stretching ten meters floor to ceiling. He stared at the gardens beneath a floating fog bank.

"What happened?" asked Douglas, turning his chair back around to face the king.

"With what?"

"With the Afrikaner Rebellion," said Douglas.

"I ordered three divisions and a blockade on the port of Cape Town. Waited them out and retook the colony without firing a shot. The bigger problem is that those on the outskirts of the Empire continue to take up arms against us. I must do something to change the minds of the natives."

"Is that why you requested my counsel, sire?"

"I needed a long-term strategy to combat the propaganda of the Scottish Rite. Something to counter their pamphlets and speeches about self-determination and free choice."

King George III dug through a pile of loose pages on his desk. He found the pamphlet he was looking for and slapped it down in front of on Douglas. The master mechanic did not bother to pick it up; he knew what it said.

"One of them in the American colonies even wrote a book. Called it *Common Sense* or some such rubbish."

"Are the American colonies posing a problem as well?"

The king sighed, "Yes and no. North America appears to be the birthplace of these treasonous ideas. That said, the conspirators are a tiny minority within the colonial population. Many colonists on the eastern seaboard make considerable sums of money meeting the Empire's manufacturing needs. Boston is particularly rolling in wealth, and quite happy with the arrangement."

"And the rest of the American colonies? The plantations on the northern continent, the West Indies, the whole of the southern continent. What of them?"

George shrugged, "The body of the snake follows the head. Pockets of vocal dissenters, but as a whole they stay in line behind the industrialized northern cities. Regardless, as I stated earlier, your counsel on the matter is no longer required."

Douglas rolled forward and parked his chair directly in front of the king: "Why do you no longer need my counsel? I am the leading expert on the Scottish Rite threat. I have been touring the world and preaching to Freemason councils, imploring them to reject the dissenters."

"You seem very motivated to shut down this new threat."

"More than you can imagine, Your Majesty. The philosophies of the Scottish Rite undermine my life's work."

"How so?"

"The British Empire harnessed my mechanical creations to become the most powerful commonwealth the world has ever seen. The Empire has provided critical aide to countless people around the world: food to the famished, peace to war-torn nations, education to the masses.

"The Scottish Rite inspired this new Resistance movement with their propaganda. As demonstrated in South Africa, the movement is morphing from philosophical propaganda to something distinctly militaristic."

"At this point in time, the Resistance movement is undeniably global," replied King George. "They managed to network themselves in an odd, decentralized configuration. Each group fights for independence in their isolated locations without direct assistance from any other group. But they do share intelligence and resources across the globe. Worst of all, they are united in their hatred of me. Individual membership inside each local group is still quite small, which is why we must turn the tide now."

"You mentioned that you have already settled on a solution," replied Douglas, not moving his chair. "What did you decide? I have been trying to solve the Scottish Rite for years, and instead the problem continues to grow."

"It occurred to me that the philosophies of the Scottish Rite mesh well with the distorted desires of many native colonists. Yet while they dream of independent nations, they are somehow loathe to purge themselves of the wealth and resources the Empire provides."

"Unfortunately, that is too true, sire," said Douglas. "Uneducated people do not recognize all the good we do for them."

"The solution therefore is rooted in changing the fundamental attitudes within the colonies."

"Very true as well, sire. But as I said, I have worked to stem the tide of the Scottish Rite for years to no avail."

"The Scottish Rite is merely the match lighting the fuse. I plan to drown each and every powder keg."

"I am afraid I do not follow."

"We will offer more industrious British citizens incentives to transplant themselves and their families to the colonies. A fresh wave of civilian colonists, espousing the ideals of the Commonwealth, winning native hearts and minds."

"What sort of incentives are you offering?"

"Land, title, stake capital, that sort of thing. An opportunity to make a fortune establishing something like an agricultural estate or a timber consortium."

"I see," said Douglas, reversing his chair. "And you think transplanting scores of people loyal to the Crown into the colonies will change native hearts and minds?"

King George stared at Douglas for a long minute, as if trying to decide something about the elderly engineer. "As I said, we have a plan of action. Your assistance is not needed."

"Then I suppose I will just see myself out," said Douglas, turning and motoring past mahogany paneling and Persian rugs. Halfway across the room, he stopped and turned back. The king was already back at his desk, absorbed in paperwork.

"Britons mingling with native populations would certainly dilute any rebellious spirits. However, I am concerned that your plan is not enough."

King George looked up. "What, what? Why are you still here?"

"Your solution does not address a major facet of the problem."

"Bah," said the king with a heavy sigh. "You fail to impress me, sir. I advise you to find a new, more constructive way to spend your time."

"Exactly what I was thinking, sire."

"Good, then, get to it." King George returned to his paperwork.

"I want to establish a new institute. A department, funded by the Crown, recruiting young engineers from universities across the world."

"What would this department do with all these engineers."

"They would work for the Crown designing new technologies."

"Such as weapons research?"

"Of course. Plus, innovations in other fields such as transportation or communications."

"I fail to see how this relates to the Resistance movement."

"This institute will cut the head off the snake, sire," replied Douglas. "It will stop the Scottish Rite from recruiting new members by funneling talented young engineers into service for the Crown."

"Cripple the propaganda machine," said the king. "Very well. Draw up the paperwork and I will sign."

"Wonderful, sire," said Douglas. "We will change the world with His Majesty's Department of Engineering and Advanced Design." King George was no longer listening.

•   •   •   •   •

"Every day we wait, we risk the British executing our comrades before we get to Cartagena," said Francis. He ran his hand across the cold metal of his steel Andean condor.

"But we are almost ready to attack Popayán," replied a senior government council member.

"Why are the preparations taking so long?" asked Ezmeralda. "The fleet left a week ago."

"Groups of soldiers are scattered all over the jungle," replied the councilman. "We are forming ranks as fast as we can track them down. One or two more days and we will be ready."

"What is your plan?" asked Ezmeralda.

"A few soldiers will sneak into Popayán at night and recapture the anti-aircraft cannons. After they take down the three battleships the fleet left, the rest of our soldiers will invade."

"The plan sounds good," said Ezmeralda. "Similar to how we recaptured Bacatá."

"I do not understand how this affects our plan to leave for Cartagena," said Francis.

"We need your help during the attack," muttered the councilman. "We were hoping you would wait to leave until after we retake the city."

"Help to do what?"

"We have never fought a battle this size. It would be good to have experienced soldiers leading us."

"*Dios mío*," said Ezmeralda. "General Marquez could be dead before we get to him."

"*Aye, si,*" said the councilman, sighing. "If you think it is the right thing to do, then go. Tonight, when it is dark."

"Then it is decided," said Ezmeralda, eying the condor. "We leave tonight."

Francis followed his wife's gaze up the six-meter tall airship shaped like a vicious bird of prey. The folded wings, laden with gears and small hydraulic cylinders, encased the sides of the airship, obstructing most of the windows.

"God bless you in your assault on the city."

The councilman smiled and bowed his head. "*Gracias.* The people of Popayán are in your debt."

CHAPTER 29

Private Doughty rapped on Governor Pratt's office door. The young soldier hunched forward, causing his uniform to hang off his narrow shoulders.

"Yes, yes, come in."

Doughty cracked the door just enough to see the governor seated behind his desk. "Governor Pratt, sir," he said. "A Mr. Jeffreys is here to see you. He does not have an appointment." The private dropped his voice just above a whisper. "He claims to be the fleet's commanding officer."

Governor Pratt rolled his eyes. "It never ends, does it, private?"

"No sir, it does not." The young man considered his next words. "What never ends, sir?"

"Incompetent individuals wanting special accommodations from the colonial magistrate, sucking up to the Crown." Pratt sighed, "Everyone wants a piece of the proverbial pie."

The private shuffled his feet and stared at the doorknob. The governor waited, then broke the awkward silence himself.

"By all means, private. Show him in."

"Yes, sir." The private disappeared from the doorway. A moment later, a soldier not much older than Private Doughty entered Governor Pratt's office. He was thin and unshaven. Jeffreys sat across the desk from the governor without bothering to offer a handshake or wait for an invitation to sit.

Pratt looked at the young, shaggy soldier and raised an eyebrow. "I was told you are currently the commanding officer of the fleet."

"That is correct," said Jeffreys.

"How is that possible?" asked Pratt. "Major Ulperlip was the commanding officer when the fleet left Cartagena. Lieutenant Vickers was his second in command." He put his elbows up on the desk and folded his hands together.

"Lieutenant Vickers had orders signed by Queen Victoria authorizing the use of chlorine gas to exterminate the New Granada Resistance."

"Chlorine gas?" said Governor Pratt, playing dumb.

"Yes, sir," said Jeffreys, face flat. "The lieutenant informed me that you were aware of both the gas and the Queen's orders."

"I see," said the governor, sitting back in his chair. "Please, go on."

"We followed the stolen zeppelin to the old Spanish capital of Bacatá in the mountains to the south. Major Ulperlip levied an all-out attack on the Resistance stronghold, but failed to take the city. When Ulperlip refused to use the chlorine gas, Lieutenant Vickers took command."

"And Major Ulperlip just allowed the lieutenant to take charge?" said Pratt, sitting up straight.

"No, sir," said Jeffreys in a dry voice. "Vickers was forced to shoot the major."

Governor Pratt furrowed his eyebrows and sat back. "I see. I have a new automatic teapot. Would you care for a cup?"

"No, thank you."

"Ah, very well," said Pratt. "I imported it last month. Quite an ingenious contraption, actually."

The governor stood up and started making a cup of tea for himself. "If Lieutenant Vickers killed Ulperlip and took control of the fleet, why are you now in charge?"

"After Bacatá, Vickers ordered the fleet further south to the free city of Popayán. He said it was the New Granada Resistance's last stronghold."

"What happened at Popayán?"

"Everybody fled before we got there; we took the city without a fight. But Lieutenant Vickers was shot and killed."

"If there was no battle for control of the city, who shot Vickers?" asked Pratt.

"A British woman named Margaret Goulden. She was waiting for us when we landed." Jeffreys pointed at the small table behind Pratt's desk. "Your tea appears to be ready, sir."

"Bloody useless contraption," muttered Governor Pratt. He popped up out of his chair to smother the flames with a damp towel.

"If Margaret Goulden shot Lieutenant Vickers, where is she now?"

"She is dead as well, sir," replied Jeffreys.

Governor Pratt raised his eyebrows: "Are you certain?"

"She was shot a dozen times by the soldiers who witnessed her kill Vickers."

"Excellent," said the governor, pouring a cup of burnt, over-steeped tea. "Remind me again how you ended up in charge of the fleet."

"I took command after Lieutenant Vickers was killed, sir," said Jeffreys.

"If I recall correctly, there were many other officers in the Ninth Fleet that outranked you when you left Cartagena."

"That is correct. Lieutenant Vickers formally promoted me and named me his second in command after Bacatá."

"I should assume then that the lieutenant trusted you unequivocally."

"Obviously, sir."

Pratt set his tea on the desk. "But that does not answer my question regarding the fleet officers who outranked you."

"Many were lost in combat."

"Regardless, there must have been numerous experienced officers he could have named second in command," said Pratt.

"May I speak candidly, sir?"

"Please."

"Lieutenant Vickers was forced to solidify control over the fleet after he shot Major Ulperlip. The Fulton's original captain was shot when he tried to arrest Vickers. Many high-ranking officers were demoted; others were handed dangerous combat assignments."

"I suppose shaking things up a bit makes sense," replied Pratt, stirring his tea. "These officers questioned Queen Victoria's orders?"

"Yes, sir. They disputed the lieutenant's right to shoot his commanding officer, regardless of the Queen's orders."

Governor Pratt took a sip of tea and wrinkled his face at the bitter drink. "I assume you were promoted because of your loyalty."

"Yes, sir."

"Loyalty amongst officers and administrators is a rare and wonderful thing," said Pratt, reclining back in his chair. "Tell me, did you lose a lot of men dismantling the Resistance?"

"Nearly a quarter of the fleet, airships and soldiers," said Jeffreys. "Plus, six battleships and a thousand soldiers were left behind to hold Bacatá and Popayán."

"How many zeppelins returned home?"

"Fifty-three of the seventy-five that departed are currently docked at the garrison. Approximately five thousand sailors and infantrymen did not return." said Jeffreys.

"The fleet suffered heavy losses, then."

"Devastating, sir," replied Jeffreys.

"I hear you brought back prisoners," said Pratt, clearing his throat as he changed the subject.

"Three," said Jeffreys. "General Jose Tairona Marquez, leader of the Resistance militia. Head of the Popayán government, Diego Rodriguez. And a young British woman we found in Popayán, Miss Constance Ventor."

"You brought Constance Ventor back to Cartagena as a prisoner?"

"I did," said Jeffreys, "although I thought you would be more taken with the other two prisoners. Marquez and Rodriguez are ringleaders in the New Granada Resistance. Without them, the movement will certainly collapse."

"Yes, yes, they are very impressive," said Pratt. "We will have a public execution next week. Constance Ventor is a problem, however."

"Why is that?"

"I declared her dead after she disappeared with the HMS *Marlborough*. The investigators that wrote the final report surmised that Constance was kidnapped and taken hostage onboard the stolen airship. There was little doubt the Resistance executed her."

"That's not exactly correct, sir."

Governor Pratt sat quietly for a minute. "Mr. Jeffreys, would you classify Constance Ventor as an enemy combatant?"

"We took her into custody alongside General Marquez and Margaret Goulden. She was not armed, though."

"Still, in the company of those murderers, she must be a covert member of the New Granada Resistance. And we know she was involved in Ezmeralda Lefount's escape from prison." The governor stood up and walked around the desk. "We will publicly hang Marquez and Rodriguez, but I want you to privately execute Miss Ventor at the garrison."

"I do not understand why she shouldn't receive a proper trial. Most likely she would be convicted of treason."

"I would rather the events of Bacatá not be brought to light in a public trial."

"I see," replied Jeffreys.

"Will you execute Miss Ventor quietly at the garrison?"

"Of course, sir," said Jeffreys. "Assuming that I am given command of the garrison and ample authority to carry out such an order."

"I see now why Lieutenant Vickers put so much faith in you, Mr. Jeffreys."

●   ●   ●   ●   ●

"How are you doing, *mija*?"

Constance broke stride pacing the jail cell. She looked up at Diego and blinked.

"How am I doing?" she repeated. "How should I be doing?"

Diego sighed, "I suppose I already know how you are doing."

Constance stared at Diego for a minute, then resumed her march across the three-meter wide cell.

"Margaret's death was not in vain," said General Marquez in a quiet voice.

Constance stopped pacing: "How can you say that? I watched thousands die. She was my best friend; my family."

"I believe none of them died in vain," said Marquez, his voice restrained. "I have seen death and destruction all my life. Families slaughtered; friends murdered. I have to believe there is a reason."

"Have you ever found an actual reason that justifies any of their deaths?" asked Constance. "Or is this all hope and wishes?"

"Every single time," said General Marquez. "Because each time I lose someone, I make sure it was for something. In their name I help someone else, save another life, fight another day."

"*Silencio*," whispered Diego, stepping forward and putting a hand on Constance's shoulder.

"Why?" asked Constance. Diego pointed outside their cell doors.

"Bloody hell, I want to watch the wankers die too." The gruff voice was somewhere beyond their field of vision.

"Orders from the governor himself," said a second voice. "Pratt's charge of all the soldiers in Cartagena and handed operations to Jeffreys."

"Bullocks, Bradford, I already bloody-well knew that, now didn't I?" said the first voice. "Jeffreys runs the place until a new fleet commander arrives."

"And a new garrison commander," echoed the second voice. The prisoners listened to keys jingling, and the clanks of heavy metal locks and steel doors swinging on their hinges. "Anyway, they're going to hang those three tomorrow at noon."

"I'm on duty playing mutton shunter to these bloody empty cells."

"Who bloody cares?"

"Just sounds like a bloody riot, watch a hanging, that's all."

The soldier's sweat stained face appeared in front of the jail cell. He paused and looked through the bars before shoving a tray of food through the slot in the door.

"You heard that, did you?" he said with an ugly grin on his face. "Tomorrow at noon you'll be hanged in front of the whole town. Going to string you up over the ramparts for everyone to see, like the Spanish used to do pirates."

The big, square-shoulder soldier standing behind him snickered. After they left, Marquez, Constance, and Diego stared at the tray of brown, steaming food. No one said a word for a long time. No one had much of an appetite.

•   •   •   •   •

Edward and Anne approached Cartagena from the south. Rainstorms followed them for days, soaking them to the bone while providing the camouflage needed to escape the jungle.

"I still find it hard to believe," muttered Edward to himself.

"Find what hard to believe?" asked Anne.

"That we spent the last week running from a patrol airship," said Edward. "Our own country's military, hunting us."

Anne looked sideways at her brother. "Maybe it's time to move on, brother." Edward grunted but did not reply.

Anne led the small band of ragged warriors through a complicated series of animal trails and footpaths. She found the packed mud road that led past the Goulden estate, snaking between walls of trees and colorful foliage, dyed shades of gray from the darkened sky and rain.

Edward and Anne said their goodbyes to their Resistance escort in front of the black iron gates of the Goulden estate. They embraced like friends who knew each other for years.

"Where will you go?" asked Anne.

"To a safe house in Cartagena," replied a soldier.

"I thought Governor Pratt dismantled the Cartagena Resistance," said Edward.

The soldier shrugged, "Perhaps, but I am sure we can find someone willing to help an enemy of the Empire." The soldiers adjusted the rifles slung across their backs and sauntered down the road. Edward and Anne watched until the rain swallowed them.

The siblings passed through the iron gates and crossed the estate grounds, plodding past fruit trees that bloomed year-round. They padded up the front steps of the mansion and pushed open the heavy door.

Halfway up the winding tile staircase, a voice from behind stopped them. "Master Goulden, is that you?"

"Manuel," screeched Anne, suddenly unconcerned about waking the household. Ignoring the butler's shocked expression and the antique firearm he held, Anne rushed down the stairs and threw her arms around his neck. Edward stood on the stairs watching his sister. Behind him on the second-floor landing, another door open.

"Edward," said Lorraine, her shrill voice cracking. She stood at the top of the stairs, staring at her son. "I thought you were dead. Governor Pratt said you were caught up in that fiasco with that prisoner, that awful terrorist woman that escaped. I thought I would never see you again."

Edward winced at his mother's words. "I'm all right, mum."

"The governor thought perhaps you asked too many questions about poor Anne's death," said Lorraine, "and they kidnapped you as well. The governor said you were probably dead, but he did not want to sign the death certificate quite yet."

Lorraine stopped talking and looked straight through Edward. He turned to follow her gaze. Anne climbed the stairs back up to her brother, reaching out and taking his hand.

"Hello, mum," said Anne in a hoarse whisper, her eyes locked on the floor.

Lorraine gasped: "No, it cannot be true." She clutched the knob of her bedroom door and leaned her weight on it. "You are dead. We laid you to rest weeks ago. This, this must be a trick," she said, the pitch and pace of her voice climbing unsteadily. "Edward, what is the meaning of this? How can this possibly be your sister?"

"It's me, mum," said Anne, raising her head to look her mother in the eyes. She climbed the stairs and crossed the landing at a cautious pace. Standing in front of her mother, Anne stopped breathing. Lorraine reached up to embrace her daughter, then drew back and slapped the young woman across the face. Anne's eyes filled tears; she fought hard to keep them from running down her face. Edward pushed his sister aside to stand in front of his mother.

"Anne was kidnapped by the New Granada Resistance. Everything else Governor Pratt told you was a lie. The Resistance tried to ransom Anne for that woman that escaped from prison. Pratt refused. He knew Anne was alive the entire time."

"That's a shameful lie, Edward," said Lorraine, her voice hollow and far away.

"Pratt needed an excuse to wage a horrifically bloody war against the Resistance. It was a conspiracy, mother. One that most likely reaches all the way up to Queen Victoria herself."

Edward stopped talking as Lorraine raised her right hand again, this time to slap her son. Edward caught his mother's wrist and held it in the air.

"Whether or not you believe me does not change the fact that what I am saying is true," said Edward. "All of it." He calmly stared into his mother's eyes as she struggled to regain control of her wrist.

From behind, Manuel spoke in a commanding tone: "Edward, release her. Whatever has happened, she is still your mother." Edward obeyed and stepped back to his sister.

"Please, Master Edward," said Manuel. "We need to hear the entire story. We can plainly see that Anne is alive and well. Tell us how this is possible."

Edward obliged and told his story, with Anne filling in details as he went. The kidnapping and the Resistance's objective. The governor's need to justify a massacre to secure New Granada's resources. Edward omitted the part where he helped free Ezmeralda and steal the zeppelin, instead saying he and Constance suspected the truth and made their own way inland.

When he finished, Lorraine stood still, muttering to herself about lies and deception. Manuel called a lady's maid to help him walk Lorraine back to bed. The butler produced a small bottle of laudanum.

"To help her sleep," he said, handing the bottle to the maid. The decorative label glued to the colored glass advertised a product derived from the highest quality opiate seeds.

Manuel returned to Edward and Anne waiting in the upstairs hall. "Master Edward, there are some things you need to know. Tomorrow in Cartagena, Governor Pratt plans to make a big announcement."

"What kind of announcement?" asked Edward.

"I am sure he intends to tell people his version of your story. That the fleet won a glorious victory over the Resistance. New Granada is free of terrorists and Anne's death has been avenged."

"What a bloody buffoon," muttered Edward.

"There's more. The governor plans to execute two captured Resistance leaders." Manuel paused, "Your mother, she talks to everybody and hears the news first."

"Is there any news about my wife or Constance?" asked Edward.

"Not that I heard," replied Manuel. "I know that half the fleet returned two days ago after they captured the city of Popayán. There were prisoners on board."

Edward grimaced and leaned against the wall. He rubbed his red eyes with both fists.

"In the morning you can deal with all this, sir," said the butler. "Now I believe you should lie down."

Edward righted himself. "Thank you, but no. Right now, I have to think. We need a plan."

"I admire your fortitude, young master," said the butler. "But the plan appears fairly obvious to me." Edward looked at the old man and crinkled his brow.

"The answer is Anne, sir," said Manuel. "You and Anne should make a surprise appearance at the governor's speech. If your sister returns alive, people will question the governor's story. If she tells her story, people will listen."

Light flickered back into Edward's eyes. He nodded in agreement, then allowed the elderly man to lead him to his bedroom for some much-needed rest.

•　　•　　•　　•　　•

Governor Pratt stood on a stool while his servant fussed over his clothing. "This is a big day for me," said the governor. "Don't cock-up."

"Yes, sir," replied Sebastian. He tugged on a pant leg, deciding if it needed to be hemmed. "I saw the gallows being built on the old Spanish ramparts." He pulled a pair of pins from between his teeth and marked the pant leg. "Going to be a hanging, is there?"

"Remarkably perceptive," replied the governor in a droll voice.

The door popped open and Private Doughty stuck his head in the room: "Sir, I received word that all three prisoners from Popayán are ready to be transported into town." Pratt stepped off his stool, leaving the footman with a measuring tape in his hand and pins between his teeth.

"Sirwaitwhereareyougoing?" mumbled Sebastian, scooting along on his knees behind the governor.

Governor Pratt stopped in front of Doughty and stuck two fingers in the young man's chest: "Only two prisoners are to be hanged on the wall, you idiot."

"I thought we were executing all three prisoners from Popayán," replied Doughty in a small voice.

"Yes, of course," said Pratt. "But the girl is supposed to be shot by a firing squad at the garrison."

"I do not understand why, sir," said the private.

"You do not need to understand why, private," replied Pratt.

The governor walked back to the step stool: "Get back to work."

"Yes, sir."

"Sir, wouldn't it be better if the people saw the third prisoner executed?" asked Doughty.

"I am concerned that if Miss Ventor is publicly executed, the people will not understand why," Pratt replied in a heated tone. "She is a British citizen from the Isles and a blood relative of Anne Goulden." The governor lifted his arms for the Sebastian to check his sleeve length. "But she is a traitor to the Crown, caught fighting with the Resistance."

"Yes, sir," said Doughty. "If you insist, I will send word to the prisoner transport to make sure Miss Ventor stays at the garrison."

"I do insist."

"Very well," said the private, turning to leave.

"And make sure the garrison understands that Miss Ventor is to be executed by firing squad," said Pratt.

"Yes, sir," said the private. He slipped back out the door and pulled it closed behind him.

Pratt took a deep breath as the footman continued to adjust the governor's clothes, leaning in to fiddle with the governor's necktie. Pratt swatted away his hand and adjusted it himself.

"I believe you are ready to address your people, sir," said Sebastian, bowing his head and stepping back. "Have prepared some words?"

"Yes, of course," muttered Pratt, tweaking his tie one more time. "My speech writer produced something rousing for the occasion." He stepped in front of a full-length mirror to examine his attire.

"This entire set of circumstances really has turned out quite well for me," said Pratt. "The people of Cartagena will find my leadership beyond reproach. Resources will once again flow to the motherland and I will gain favor with the Queen."

Pratt stopped speaking and faced his servant: "And do you know how I have achieved all this?"

"No, sir."

"By giving the people what they want." Governor Pratt smirked, "The hard part was convincing them of what they wanted."

• • • • •

Constance sat on the floor of the small jail cell tossing pebbles through the iron bars. She jumped to her feet and pressed her face against the grate when the steel door at the end of the hall slammed shut.

"Put these on," said an unshaven British officer in a gruff voice. He tossed a set of wrist manacles through the bars.

"Why?" asked Constance.

"Because I bloody said so."

"Where did they take the other two prisoners?"

"Governor Pratt is giving a speech in a few minutes on the old Spanish seawall. Your friends will be executed as part of the festivities." The officer snorted. "An appropriate way to do away with pirates, if you ask me."

Constance said nothing, backing against the far wall of the jail cell.

"I said to put on the bloody shackles."

"Why? Where are you taking me?"

The officer sighed and looked at the enlisted men behind him. "Look, luv, this can be easy, or it can be hard. But you will be coming with us and you will be wearing those bloody shackles when you do."

"Fine," muttered Constance. She picked the iron chains up off the dirt floor and put them on. She slid them up her forearms a bit, leaving them as loose as she dared.

"That's better," said the officer.

One soldier stepped forward and unlocked the cell door. Two others grabbed hold of both her arms and walked Constance down the muggy brick hallway. Despite the sun hiding behind the clouds, Constance tried to shield her eyes with her arm when she emerged into the sun. The wind whipped her pale face and she took a deep breath, filling her lungs with fresh, salty air.

The soldiers spread out around Constance as the officer led the party through the dirt streets. They wound their way across the deserted garrison, past rows of identical brick buildings. They stopped at a hidden alcove on the outskirts of the garrison, surrounded on three sides by short bamboo walls. The fourth wall was brick and mortar.

"What is this place?" asked Constance, squinting at the brick wall and the small, blackened scars chiseled in it. "What are you going to do to me?" The soldiers remained silent and led her to the brick wall.

"Miss Constance Ventor," said the officer. "You have been found guilty of treason and espionage and declared an enemy of the British Empire. Governor Manfred Pratt, Magistrate of the British colony of Cartagena has ordered your execution."

"No," screamed Constance, falling to her knees. The officer waved to the other soldiers. They grabbed Constance under her arms and pulled her up to her feet.

"Miss Ventor, if you cannot stand in front of the wall, your arms will be shackled over your head and attached to the wall." Constance flailed her feet in the air in front of her, wiggled and struggled against the men holding her. "Miss Ventor, I will not hesitate to chain you to this wall."

Constance took two big gulps of air. "I can stand on my own," she whispered.

"Do you have anything to say for yourself?" asked the officer.

"Will it do any good?"

"There is nothing you can say that will postpone your execution," replied the officer.

"Then I have nothing to say."

The officer reached into his shirt pocket: "Would you like a cigarette?"

"I never smoked before," muttered Constance. "But why not?" The officer put a cigarette between her lips and lit it. Constance sucked in the smoke and burst into a coughing fit, bending over at the waist.

The officer waited for Constance to finish coughing. He straightened her up and picked the cigarette off the ground. "Do you still want the cigarette?"

"Yes."

"Blindfold?" he asked, producing a cotton scarf from another pocket.

"What else do you have in those pockets?" The soldier ignored the question and waited for her answer. "Bullocks, sure, I will take the blindfold." The officer tied it around her head and walked back to the firing line.

"Ready," he shouted. Five soldiers raised their rifles; Constance bit down into her cigarette.

She heard a pair of shots from somewhere far away, one on top of the other. The soldiers lined up in front of her started shouting. Constance heard the rifles fire a volley of bullets. None hit her and she bit down harder on her cigarette. She dropped to her knees, soaking her blindfold with tears. The brown tobacco juice running between her teeth made her sick to her stomach.

More gunfire erupted to her right, followed by an explosion. Another pair of rifles cracked, this time from somewhere closer. The reverberating gunfire all around deafened Constance; she saw bright spots on the inside of her blindfold. The smell of gunpowder and burnt flesh mingled with the harsh cigarette smoke wafting up through her nostrils.

The chaos ended as quickly as it started. A fist grabbed hold of the blindfold wrapped around Constance's face and yanked it off. The young woman looked up into the somber face of Ezmeralda Lefount, standing in front of her in a leather corset and men's pants. An enormous rifle adorned with copper tubes and gear-driven mechanisms hung across her back.

"*Vamanos*," said Ezmeralda. "We have to hurry."

Constance tugged at her shackles and grunted, twisting and pulling until her wrists were free.

"Clever girl," said Francis Lefount, standing nearby and watching Constance remove her shackles. He used the scope on his own high-powered rifle to sweep back and forth across the garrison streets beyond the alcove.

"The soldiers are still running around trying to figure out what happened. We have to go before they regroup."

CHAPTER 30

Spanish colonists built Cartagena's defenses during a period of history when pirates and marauders pledged loyalty to captains and kings alike, raiding the jeweled cities clustered around the Caribbean. The walls ran alongside the beach before curving inland and encircling the city. The inside of the defensive rampart had a raised stone walkway wider than the sandbar. Irregularly spaced towers augmented the wall while stairwells dropped down to a network of underground tunnels. The *Castillo San Felipe de Barajas*, a squat castle made from the same gray stones as the wall sat on a hill overlooking the harbor. No ship had fired a cannon at the Walled City since Spain handed New Granada to the British a hundred years prior.

All morning the wind whipped in from the ocean and broke against the wall. Large gusts struck the ramparts every few minutes and climbed the antique stone, ripping through the gathered spectators and forcing colonial women to chase their fancy hats through the crowd.

Governor Pratt stood in front of a thousand citizens; the gray ocean sky framed his silhouette on top of the ramparts. To his right stood gallows of heavy timber, hastily raised the previous night. Two nooses, tied from coarse rope already crusty with salt, swung in the afternoon wind. To the governor's left, a contingent of British officers stood at ease with Mr. Jeffreys in their front.

The podium built just for this speech came up to Pratt's midsection. The governor's eyes swept across the assembled mob; he adjusted the cone-shaped devise in front of him. When he cleared his throat, the sound carried through the crude network of tubes and amplified across the square.

"Three-hundred years ago, Spaniards built this wall to protect Cartagena from pirates," said Governor Pratt. His voice boomed across the ramparts, transmitted through copper tubes lining the ramparts and bouncing back off stone walls before the wind swept it away.

"Today, we will use these same walls to administer justice and purge the British Empire of pirates who murdered and plundered their way through our corner of the world. General Jose Tairona Marquez led the army of the New Granada Resistance for years as they reaped death and destruction. He and his band of fanatics are responsible for murdering Anne Goulden and planting the bomb at her funeral."

Governor Pratt paused and licked his lips. "Diego Rodriguez led the government of Popayán. He harbored dangerous fugitives while feeding General Marquez's army a steady supply of young soldiers.

"Today, these two pirates face their reckoning. Through the valiant efforts and noble sacrifices of Her Majesty's Ninth Fleet, the New Granada Resistance has been decimated.

"Our soldiers slain thousands of terrorists on the battlefields of Bacatá and Popayán. It is true that the battles were hard fought and even gruesome. When stories reach your ears about the savagery of these events, remember that it was necessary. It was necessary so these vicious killers can no longer hold our colony hostage."

Pratt rattled on into the voice amplifier for half an hour, his voice bounced back and forth off the stone walls. His pitch and tone rising and falling with the rhythm of the ocean's waves crashing behind him. The gathered crowd stayed quiet, listening to their savior, eager to put these dark days behind them.

"And now," said Pratt, his voice hoarse, "to purge the evil forces from our colony and ensure a lasting peace, we will execute the remaining leaders of the New Granada Resistance."

Governor Pratt raised his hand towards the back of the crowd. A handful of soldiers stationed on the far side of the stone-paved square lurched forward, scattering children in front of them. A path split through the middle of the crowd, like Moses parting the Red Sea. Nestled between the awkward cluster of soldiers was a pair of horses pulling a cage of crude iron bars. Chained to the floor of the cage sat Jose Marquez and Diego Rodriguez.

A child stepped out of the crowd and into the wake behind the cart, hurling a rotten banana. Freed from its trance, the rest of the crowd followed the boy's lead, shouting and spitting at the prisoners. General Marquez ducked most of the decomposing tropical fruit; Diego was not so lucky. A minute later the cage halted beneath the heavy beams of the gallows.

British soldiers unchained the two Resistance leaders and stood them beneath the nooses. An unexpected voice rang through the amplification system; a thousand heads turned towards the podium.

"*Bonjour mes amis.*" Francis's voice boomed back and forth across the gray ramparts. "Hello, my friends," he echoed in his thick French accent. "I want to introduce myself."

Francis had one arm across Governor Pratt's shoulders. His other hand was hidden behind the podium, jabbing a revolver between the governor's ribs. Francis scanned the faces in the crowd; expectant sneers and disgust stared back.

"My name is Francis Lefount. I am a master mechanic and a Freemason of some high degree or another. And, of course, what would I be without my beautiful wife, the lovely mechanic and fellow Freemason, Ezmeralda DeCampino-Lefount. *Mademoiselle*, please say hello to the crowd."

Francis waved at a stone tower behind the crowd; a rifle scope glinted from a narrow window. The gun cracked and an empty hangman's noose fell from the gallows.

"*Fantastique*," said Francis. "And my new friend, *une exceptionnelle* young woman, Miss Constance Ventor." A second rifle fired from somewhere behind the crowd. The mob gasped as the second noose dropped to the floor.

"Any soldier that moves will be shot down by my two lovely ladies," said Francis. "If anyone takes a shot at me, the governor dies."

A cluster of soldiers ignored the threat. They pushed towards the podium in a tight knot of bodies with their rifles leveled at Francis. The Frenchman dug his revolver into the governor's side.

"Back up," shouted Pratt, his voice cracking. "I said back up." The soldiers looked at each other with confused expressions but stopped advancing.

Francis whispered into the governor's ear: "If I am shot, you will die."

Francis leaned over the voice amplifier: "We are old friends, are we not, Manfred Pratt?" He gave the governor a kiss on the cheek while twisting his gun between Pratt's ribs.

"Yes, of course," said the governor, his voice carrying across the ramparts.

"Now, my friend," said Francis. "I need you to tell the soldiers to release *Général* Marquez and *Monsieur* Rodriguez."

"You know you will not escape," said Pratt in a quiet, hoarse voice.

"That is not your concern, *mon amie*." Francis patted the governor's cheek. "Now, release them."

Governor Pratt swallowed hard: "Release the prisoners."

Captain Jeffreys stepped between the cluster of soldiers and the podium. "We cannot do that, sir."

Francis pulled back the hammer on his revolver. "I said release them," screeched the governor.

"I really must protest, sir. That man would not dare shoot you. If he did, he and all his comrades would die."

"Stop stalling and release the prisoners, Mr. Jeffreys," said Pratt. "That's an order." Jeffreys sighed and signaled the soldiers guarding the prisoners.

"If you would," said Francis into the voice amplifier. "*Général* Marquez, *Monsieur* Rodriguez, please join me up here." Dumbstruck citizens parted for the Resistance leaders to make their way to the podium.

"Tell us, *s'il vous pla't*, what happened to Miss Anne Goulden. And then perhaps share with us what happened at Bacatá."

Diego Rodriguez placed his palm over the voice amplifier. "I do not think this is the best time, *señor*. We should go."

"Nonsense," replied Francis. "Tell the people what really happened. Just make it quick."

"This is foolish," said Diego.

"I will speak to the crowd," said Marquez, "but I think it is too late to change their minds." The general cleared his throat and leaned down to the voice amplifier.

"People of Cartagena, *la Resistencia de Nueva Granada* did kidnap Anne Goulden. We tried to trade her for a political prisoner. Governor Pratt refused. After that, we planned to return Miss Goulden to her home in Cartagena. We had no use for her; we are not cold-blooded murderers."

"You lie," said Pratt, spit flying from between his teeth.

"Liar," echoed a handful of voices in the crowd. "Bunch of bloody liars." The crowd shifted towards an anger mob, lobbing profanities and curses at the podium.

"It is the truth," said Marquez. "The British fleet found my army in the abandoned Spanish city of Bacatá, high in the jungles to the south. The fleet attacked, and we fought. Many soldiers on both sides died. When they could not win, the battleships dropped poison gas on the city. They murdered thousands of *Resistencia* and British soldiers in the most cowardly act I have ever seen."

The crowd responded with louder taunts and jeers. They assaulted the Resistance leaders with another barrage of rotten fruit.

"It is time to go, *mi amigo*," said Marquez, crouching behind the podium.

"I believe you are right," said Francis.

"You will never escape," said the governor, his lip turned upward in an ugly sneer.

"I fear he is right," muttered Diego. They could hear the crowd's anger growing to a fevered pitch. Jeffreys and the other soldiers vanished to find better vantage points to fire.

"What is your escape plan?" asked Marquez.

"We did not have a lot of time to work one out," said Francis. "The plan was for you to convince the crowd that we are the good guys."

Marquez and Diego stared at Francis; Pratt threw his head back and laughed.

"Do you have a backup plan?"

"Of course," said Francis. "Run."

"Is that it?" asked Marquez.

"The Andean condor is hidden a kilometer to the east along the shoreline," replied Francis. "We have to get there. Ezmeralda and Constance will provide cover fire."

"How will they get out?"

"Stop asking so many questions, *mon capitaine*."

An avocado the size of a cat hit Francis on the side of the head, sending him tumbling to the ground.

Governor Pratt dove away from his captors: "Fire," he shrieked over and over, crawling towards the mob.

Francis, Diego, and General Marquez sprinted along the top of the sea wall. Rifle rounds buzzed overhead and chipped the gray stones. Behind them the tension in the square boiled over and the crowd became a mob, foaming at the mouth like a rabid dog. As suddenly as it started, the rifles fell silent and the crowd's noise wound down to a whisper, as if the ocean winds swept away the city's anger. The shift in atmosphere unnerved the Resistance members and they stopped running.

A woman dressed in a plain, pleated dress and simple white blouse stood at the podium. Her presence served as a lightning rod, drawing in the mob's energy. She leaned forward to speak into the voice amplifier.

"My name is Anne Goulden, and I am very much alive."

"You lie," shouted someone from the crowd.

"Anne Goulden is dead."

"I saw her buried."

The man standing behind her stepped forward: "My name is Edward Goulden, and I too am alive. This is my sister, Anne. Everything Governor Pratt told you was a lie."

The mob grew restless, shouting obscenities and calling Edward and Anne liars. A woman standing near the front of the crowd climbed up beside the podium.

"She is Anne Goulden," she shouted. "I knew her for years."

"Her mom is a friend of mine," said an older colonial woman in expensive clothing. "I met Anne several times, and that is indeed her."

The crowd buzzed with anger and fear and confusion, like a wounded predator, uncertain where the hunter was.

"I am Anne Goulden, and the stories Governor Pratt told you are lies." Anne's words echoed off the stone ramparts. "The governor declared me dead to drum up support for his military operation. They attacked the New Granada Resistance with a poison gas that killed thousands of people."

Governor Pratt reappeared in front of the podium with Jeffreys and a small cluster of soldiers: "Young lady, whoever you are, I insist that you stop telling these lies at once."

Edward leaned over the voice amplifier, "Governor Pratt, with all due respect, the masquerade is over. Anne Goulden is standing here in front of all these people. If you do not let her speak, this will only get worse for you."

"Arrest them both," said the governor, spinning around to address the soldiers.

Jeffreys stepped forward to arrest Anne and Edward. A rifle cracked from the highest window of the stone silo across the square; a soldier lie wounded at the base of the podium.

A second rifle shot rang out, the bullet boring its way through the meaty part of Governor Pratt's thigh. He fell to the ground, screaming in pain and shouting obscenities. Jeffreys and his men dragged the governor sideways along the stone wall. As the soldiers pressed forward, the mob grew hostile, pelting the governor with more rotten fruit. Jeffreys led his men through the crowd, brandishing his pistol and firing it in the air. The soldiers dragged Pratt into an alley and disappeared, heading south towards the governor's mansion.

The crowd surged to the top of the city's defensive walls, the wooden podium disintegrating under a wave of angry people. Fire engulfed the roughly hewn gallows, ropes swinging in the wind as the flames brought down the entire structure.

Two dozen young British soldiers, newly battle-hardened Bacatá veterans, fired rifles in the air. The mob discarded their rotten fruit and began hurling stones and bottles. Young soldiers found themselves abandoned by their chain of command, confronted with the choice of firing on British citizens or fleeing the ramparts. The soldiers turned and ran, leaving downtown Cartagena at the mercy of the rioting citizens.

• • • • •

General Marquez surprised Anne, grabbing her arm from behind and turning her around: "We have to go," the general shouted in her ear. "*Rápidamente.*"

"This way," shouted Francis over the screams of the wrathful citizens.

He jumped off the seawall to the narrow stretch of sandy beach separating the Spanish fortifications and the Atlantic. Marquez, Diego, Edward, and Anne followed the crafty Frenchman. The party lit out as fast as they could trudge through the wet sand.

"*Dios mío,*" said Marquez. He turned around and saw the gallows topple in an inferno.

"I cannot understand how a mob can burn so many things so fast," said Francis, stopping for a moment beside Marquez to admire their handiwork. "How can they arm themselves with torches and bricks so fast?"

Marquez did not respond as he watched the scene unfold and engulf Cartagena in a full-scale riot. Sulfur from the soldier's rifles and smoke from the burning buildings mixed with the salty sea air, stinging the eyes and throats of the small band.

"What about Constance?" asked Edward, stopping to catch his breath. "And Ezmeralda?"

"They will find their out," said Francis. "*Mon amour* has survived much worse."

• • • • •

Four nights after Manfred Pratt failed to hang the Resistance leaders, the governor sat up in bed and screeched down the halls of his mansion.

"Get my bloody doctor in here."

"Yes, sir," said young Private Doughty.

Doughty reappeared with the doctor in tow ten minutes later. The physician placed a black leather handbag on the bedside table before turning his attention to his patient. The doctor's eyes were ringed with black like a raccoon.

"What seems to be the problem?"

"Deep throbbing pain in my thigh again," said the governor. "Check it for infection."

The doctor sighed a deep, exasperated sigh and pulled back the governor's blankets. He unwound the bandages and poked at the wound with a long steel pin from his black bag.

"Careful, you quack," said Pratt. He grabbed hold of his leg just above the wound, letting out a guttural whine. The doctor finished his examination and re-wrapped the bullet wound, pulling up the bed covers when he finished.

"Once again, the wound looks to be healing well," said the doctor. "Another couple of weeks and you should be back on your feet."

"Then why am I in so much pain?"

"Because you were shot. Getting shot hurts. You will continue to feel discomfort for quite a while. The pain should gradually subside over the coming weeks."

"What if I wake up dead tomorrow?" The physician turned his head and mumbled as he repacked his instruments.

"What did you say?" asked Pratt in a sharp tone.

"I can assure you that you will not wake up dead tomorrow," replied the physician.

"We will see," mumbled Pratt.

The doctor zipped his medical bag back up, "If you will excuse me, sir, there are dozens of wounded citizens awaiting care downstairs."

"Why are there dozens of wounded people in my mansion?" asked the governor.

"Many people were hurt in the riots. When you ordered me to remain here to oversee your care, I had the soldiers set up a temporary hospital on the first floor of this building." The doctor sighed again, looking at the governor's bewildered expression. "You gave your approval for the entire affair two days ago."

"I don't remember that," said Pratt. "Was I under the influence of some sort of narcotics? Perhaps I agreed after a dose of opium."

"If you do not believe me, I suggest you confer with your officers." The doctor picked up his medical bag and walked out of the room. Private Doughty poked his head in from the hallway and scanned the room before closing the door.

Unseen by anyone, a tiny mechanical scorpion scurried off the top of the bedside table and down to the floor. Its gears whirled and clicked as it curled its gunmetal tail up and over its head, one tiny piece of interlocking iron at a time.

•   •   •   •   •

"Manuel," said Lady Goulden, drawing out the word and adding a slight whine. "Do you know how long my son and niece plan to stay?"

"No, ma'am," replied Manuel, setting down the breakfast tray and tea kettle. "Would you like me to ask?"

"No, no," said Lorraine. "I just feel like a prisoner in this room."

"To my knowledge your son did not ask you to isolate yourself in your bedchamber. I wish you would return to your regular routine."

"I am afraid I no longer feel comfortable around Edward," Lorraine said, rising out of bed. "Every time we talk, he goes on and on about Margaret; he believes she died a hero. He simply does not want to hear my opinion."

"I hear Margaret's name spoken around town. Most people believe she died a hero, killing that horrible man who dropped the chlorine gas. She has brought honor to your family."

Lorraine made a disagreeable sound and walked over to the table. "Constance actually raised her voice to me yesterday. For no reason at all. That young lady simply cannot control her temper. Bit like Margaret in that way, I suppose." Lorraine sat down and poked at the fresh fruit on the tray with a spoon. "Please, sit with me while I eat."

"As you wish," replied the butler, standing beside the table with only one chair.

"I have been out of the loop; what news from around Cartagena? Other than Margaret being crowned a hero."

"The new governor arrives next week. Queen Victoria appointed him personally. I heard he has a reputation as a tough, no-nonsense man. Named Johnson, I believe. Or maybe Jackson." Manuel scratched his head. "Apparently most of the reputable governor-types refused the Cartagena position."

"Why is that?"

"All the scandal they would inherit. Besides, they are expected to keep the peace, and the native population is particularly restless at the moment."

"I see."

"Victoria found herself in a bit of hot water after the events in our corner of the world. The Queen denies all knowledge, of course, claiming a handful of corrupt local leaders were responsible. Now Resistance movements across the world are uniting behind the events that happened here."

"That's enough," said Lady Goulden, interrupting Manuel and holding up her hand. "Thank you for your candor, but that will be all."

"Yes, ma'am," replied the butler. He excused himself and left the room, winding through the upstairs hallways before descending to the kitchen.

"Good morning, Master Edward."

"Hello Manuel," replied Edward, looking up from the fried plantains he was pushing around his plate. "How are you this morning?"

"I am very well, thank you for asking," said the butler. "Sir, do you know where Miss Constance is? I went to her room to see about breakfast, but she was not there."

"Constance left to meet with Francis and Ezmeralda Lefount. She is considering joining the New Granada Resistance."

"I see," said Manuel. "I hope she stays out of harm's way; she always treated me kindly. She repaired the leaking stove flue for the kitchen staff and the grandfather clock in the sitting room."

"Constance has a kind soul, always wanting to help."

"Yes, sir."

"I suppose in the end she is a bit like Margaret."

"I am sure you are right, sir."

Edward stared at his half-eaten breakfast and pushed a plantain across his plate. "I see her everywhere; everything reminds me of her in some way."

"I lost my wife ten years ago," replied Manuel in a quiet voice.

"Does it ever get better?"

"Not really. You get used to the pain, though. Enough to eat and sleep and soldier on."

Edward pushed his plate away from him. "I am British; we soldier on. It's what we do."

"Did you know Constance might not return to university?" asked Anne, entering the kitchen. She walked over to the pantry and started rummaging for day-old pandebonos.

"Francis and Ezmeralda offered to complete her training in the field," said Edward.

"But what about Oxford?" repeated Anne. "I have dreamt about attending classes there, but I fear I may be lacking in raw talent."

Edward shrugged, "Constance believes the Lefounts are capable instructors."

"I doubt that," replied Anne, adding a grunt for emphasis. "Constance seems a very different person than I remember her."

"Constance was a very different person a few weeks ago."

"She appears to have inherited Margaret's enthusiasm for fighting British colonialism," said Anne.

"Perhaps," muttered Edward, returning his attention to his uneaten breakfast.

Anne watched her brother for a minute, then sat down on a stool beside him. "How are you doing?"

"Not well," replied Edward. "I miss Margaret more than I ever thought possible. I feel more alone in the world than when father died." Anne reached over with both arms and hugged Edward, wrapping up his shoulders and squeezing.

When she pulled away, Edward changed the subject: "Have you completed your application to Oxford?"

"Yes, brother," said Anne, rolling her eyes. "I plan to deliver it to the registrar myself."

"Are you returning to London with Master Edward?" asked Manuel.

"Yes," replied Anne.

"Do you know when?" said Manuel, dejected look on his face.

"Soon," said Edward. "Queen Victoria is anxious to prove she had nothing to do with this entire affair, so she offered me my old position in London. I am expected back at my desk in the catacombs beneath Parliament in two weeks."

Manuel turned to Anne, "Everyone here will miss you when you go."

"I will miss you, too," said the young woman, wrapping up her friend in a hug.

ABOUT THE AUTHOR

Joseph Rollins is a lover of all fiction and an avid reader. He spends much of his time viewing and creating a wide range of visual art. Joseph lives and works on a small family farm and wine vineyard in the highlands of Northern Arizona with his dog, two cats, seven chickens, wife and son.

NOTE FROM THE AUTHOR

Word-of-mouth is crucial for any author to succeed. If you enjoyed *Iron Spires Over the White City*, please leave a review online—anywhere you are able. Even if it's just a sentence or two. It would make all the difference and would be very much appreciated.

Thanks!
Joseph

Thank you so much for reading one of our
Fantasy Steampunk novels.
If you enjoyed our book, please check out our recommendation
for your next great read!

No Rest for the Wicked by Phoebe Darqueling

"...an action-packed, spectacular good time."
–Leanna Renee Hieber, award-winning author of
the *Strangely Beautiful* and *Eterna Files* series

View other Black Rose Writing titles at
www.blackrosewriting.com/books and use promo code
PRINT to receive a **20% discount** when purchasing.

CPSIA information can be obtained
at www.ICGtesting.com
Printed in the USA
BVHW081024080820
585839BV00001B/4